THE WAR AMONGST THE ANGELS

Other Avon Books by
Michael Moorcock

FABULOUS HARBORS
BLOOD: A SOUTHERN FANTASY

THE WAR AMONGST THE ANGELS

AN AUTOBIOGRAPHICAL STORY BY

MICHAEL MOORCOCK

AVON BOOKS ◆ NEW YORK

This is a work of fiction. Names, characters, places, and incidents are the product of the author's imagination or are used fictitiously. Any resemblance to actual events, locales, organizations, or persons, living or dead, is entirely coincidental and beyond the intent of either the author or the publisher.

AVON BOOKS, INC.
1350 Avenue of the Americas
New York, New York 10019

Copyright © 1996 by Michael and Linda Moorcock
Front cover illustration by Bill Binger
Inside cover author photograph by Linda Steele
Published by arrangement with the author
Visit our website at **http://www.AvonBooks.com**
ISBN: 0-380-78079-8

Library of Congress Cataloging in Publication Data:

Moorcock, Michael, 1939-
    The war amongst the angels : an autobiographical story / by Michael Moorcock.
        p.   cm.
    I. Title.
PR6063.059W29   1997   97-28609
823'.914—dc21   CIP

First Avon Books Trade Paperback Printing: December 1998
First Avon Books Hardcover Printing: December 1997

AVON TRADEMARK REG. U.S. PAT. OFF. AND IN OTHER COUNTRIES, MARCA REGISTRADA, HECHO EN U.S.A.

Printed in the U.S.A.

OPM 10 9 8 7 6 5 4 3 2 1

This book is dedicated to the memories of Harrison Ainsworth, who celebrated the English highwayman in *Rookwood*; Captain Marryat, author of *Japhet in Search of a Father*, one of the best comic picaresques of the early nineteenth century; George Meredith, author of *The Amazing Marriage*, perhaps our finest moral novel in English; and Gerald Kersh, author of *Fowler's End* and many other outstanding novels of London's lowlife. All the books mentioned are no longer published.

In particular, this book is for Jennifer Brehl and for Faren Miller. Special thanks to Caroline Oakley and, as always, Linda Moorcock.

Those who may be pleased to honor these pages with a perusal, will not be detained with a long introductory history of my birth, parentage, and education. The very title implies that, at this period of my memoirs, I was ignorant of the two first; and it will be necessary for the due developement of my narrative, that I allow them to remain in the same state of bliss: for in the perusal of a tale, as well as in the pilgrimage of life, ignorance of the future may truly be considered as the greatest source of happiness.

—CAPTAIN MARRYAT, *Japhet in Search of a Father*

I Am Born

I was born in the reign of King George VI, backstage at South London's old Brixton Empire during a lull in the Battle of Britain. My mother, Lady Eleanor Moorcock, blossoming from a retirement to which she would never return, was entertaining the troops. The pains became urgent halfway through her finale, *Home With The Milk In The Morning.* I popped out so quickly, she told me, that she was able to take the cast curtain call and accept a glass of champagne before we were given a lift home in a field-marshall's staff car to Hammersmith and our flat in Begg Mansions, Sporting Club Square.

Sporting Club Square, which lay directly between two great music-halls, the Fulham Palace and the Hammersmith Royal, had an anti-aircraft position next to the tennis courts. My mother said the ack-ack and the searchlights were blazing away for the rest of the night and it took her two large ASVs before she could get a wink, but as soon as I had been given to the wet nurse I went off like a top. She lived apart from my father, who was attached to some mysterious ministry and slept at his club when in town. He was leaving Casablanca, I believe, on that particular night.

For those times the circumstances of my birth were not re-markable. Many considered them fortunate, with four medical officers and a midwife in the audience. Two of the MOs and the midwife were killed in rocket attacks in 1945, close to the war's end, but I stayed in touch with both the others until their deaths. They regarded me with all the specific affection of uncles and by happy chance both became magistrates in later life, able to bend their principles a little when my cases came up, for I was never a lucky thief.

My parents had been separated since 1937, but preserved a peculiar loyalty and love for each other. Their rare meetings were always passionate.

My father hated to leave the family place in Yorkshire, whereas my mother pined if she was ever longer than a month away from the capital. Even through the Blitz she stuck it out. Indeed, she became a local heroine when she helped survivors climb to safety from the burning Convent of the Poor Clares behind the Square.

While I lay in the relative security of the basement shelter, the incendiary fire-storm screaming and raving outside, my mother made the nuns tea on a camp stove in her own kitchen. Peeling back the blackout curtain, they watched the blinding

incandescent torch of The Fulham Palace as she blazed into
oblivion in what seemed moments. From the Square-facing windows they saw the other mansion blocks silhouetted by the glare
from Hammersmith, where The Royal had also sustained a direct hit. The sky would not stop shouting. She sang them their
favorite old-time songs. Three sisters asked for her autograph.
They were already admirers. As Nellie Taylor she had been very
popular in the last years of the London music halls and one of
the stars of The Kilburn Hippodrome before my father took her
into marriage. After the war she became a successful character
actress.

My father is Sir Arthur Moorcock, firstly of Tower House,
Moorcock, near Dent in Wensleydale, Yorkshire and later of Far-
ring Grange, near Worthing, West Sussex. I am perhaps the only
member of the direct line not to prefer Tower House and its
endlessly changing landscapes to city life. I share the view that
I inherited more of my mother's temperament than my father's.
This was a source of some disappointment to the family but
never, it seemed, to my father who was of a phlegmatic character, with a profound sense of human individuality and liberty.
He delighted as much in my mother's qualities as he delighted
in the white hares running free over the fells in winter. "Your
mother is a wild flower," he would say to me, "and needs to
blossom where she can."

⌐〜

My childhood was enjoyed at my father's home in Wensleydale and in the ruins of London; at the Ramsden School,
near Leeds; and on regular holiday expeditions into the Lake
District, sometimes by train and sometimes by bicycle. But a
great deal of my general education came from the Gypsies.

Thanks to my father's friendships, I grew up on first-name
terms with Romanies from all over the United Kingdom and
Ireland. Every year the Hamcoxes, one of the horse-trading fami-

lies, came through and took me in an old, gaudy van, smelling of peat and camphor, to the great Gypsy gathering at Appleby. Beneath the gentle fells horses and vans filled the valley. Everywhere the men could be seen deep in conversation, occasionally exchanging substantial sums of money in rolled-up wads of notes. Traditionally, no other paper ever passed between them. They sealed bargains with a symbolic bareback ride through the river ford and a handshake. It was all the contract they'd ever need. Their fancy chrome- and brass-vans glittered and flashed even in the rain, like a vision of the mythical Silver World, said to exist behind the Cumbrian mist. The old painted wooden vans, like the one I shared with Granny Rees, were too small for most modern families. They were used to lure the *giorgios* in, to tell their fortunes for silver and lift curses off their heads for gold. Every morning and evening Granny would tell me stories of the moonbeam roads and the wanderers who roamed them. She helped clear my intellect of a hampering linearity.

My father had always made the Gypsies welcome when they arrived on his land. He let them set up their camp, providing water for them, talking horses with them. There was considerable mutual respect between our families. The Gypsies left with scarcely a broken blade of grass to tell where they had been. My father made grateful use of their wisdom and consequently had the best-kept horses in the Riding.

By a freak of geological good fortune, we were blessed with the sweetest, smoothest turf in Yorkshire. There was a time, before the fire which took so much of the heart out of my father, that Moorcock horses were highly prized by the show- and hunting-fancy and were owned all over the world.

It was the Gypsies who had saved us from the worst of the fire. They had taken to wintering in the river pasture and helped with our horses in return. Out checking his traps in the small hours, young James Lee spotted the flames in the stables and gave the alarm. Two of his brothers were badly blistered and many others of the tribe had their clothes and skin singed rescuing our terrified beasts. It had been too late to save every horse. My father's favorite mare, Thrawn Janet, was burned to death.

Though we had more than half our stock left it was the end of those golden years and my father lost interest in the stables. He stopped riding and would walk everywhere with his long, determined stride. When not fly-fishing he spent most of his time in the tower, which he had converted to a library. Gallery after gallery of books stretched up from basement to distant ceiling and only the narrowest of gangways and steps connected them.

Seated at his old library desk at the top of the tower, looking out across our beautiful Yorkshire moorland, timeless, brooding and eternally uncompromising, my father was writing a history of our family.

ᑕᕐᑐ

Like many other members of my family, I enjoyed a close familiarity with the supernatural. My mother ignored such things, but my father was prepared for what I would begin to find. Even when, in a fishing creel, I brought a score of budgerigars home from near Ribblehead Viaduct, where they had manifested themselves before my eyes as I admired a detailed vision of the busy city of Constantinople and her famous Hagia Sophia, my father merely expressed mild surprise. He contacted a pet-shop in Sedbergh and got rid of the birds there.

In the unpopulated dales, I quickly became familiar with miracles and visions and thought little of them. Occasionally there would be an interesting visitation, usually from an angel. My father counseled me to discretion. I would find it easier for myself if outside the family I didn't mention my encounters with the supernatural. The more I experienced of what he called "intratemporality," the more it would seem that time was nothing but a perpetual loop. This was an illusion, created by our own attempts to impose linearity upon what is profoundly non-linear. However, most of the family preferred to ignore the supernatural, rather than embrace it. There was a danger of becoming powerless or invisible in this world by taking too much of an interest in another. Happily, he told me, there was a tendency for the affliction to fade away as one grew older.[1]

My frequent encounters with the angelic host, my dawning understanding that it was possible to come and go in their worlds as easily as they came and went in ours, led, after my first marriage, to my taking some dangerous steps into unknown territory and choosing to play a round in the Game of Time, sentencing myself to a million years of regrets before I returned to my home only a few seconds after I had left.[2] This deterred me from continuing for a while but I had developed a lust for exploration. It was on my second expedition that I encountered Sam Oakenhurst who did not recognize me and knew nothing then of all his other lives. I sought him out because I had admired him from afar and hoped to reassure him. Also he could help me in my game.

❧

From my earliest years I had always spent some of my holidays in Mitcham, a village on the outskirts of London where my mother's family had its roots. There were strong Jewish and Gypsy family ties, though my mother and her sisters were culturally, if not physically, indistinguishable from all other South Londoners. The chief thing they had in common with their

[1] This was never to be my experience. Before I was twenty I had risked two expeditions into the Fault and met again the great Sam Oakenhurst who, for a while, became my lover, my real introduction to the company of the Chaos Engineers, those freebooters of the multiverse, whose adventures I had only read about or seen on the screen.

[2] It was before I had discovered how to experience life simultaneously on all the planes of my perception and learned to select familiar images by which, as it were, I steered. Confidence, intelligence and adaptability are, they say, the three main qualities an eternal must have, and strictly in that order. Some of us, like Turpin, elect to blind themselves to all but a little of what they can potentially experience and choose to live semi-linear lives.

Gypsy cousins was a willingness to uproot and move at a moment's notice, no matter how long they had been settled. The
chief difference was that their migrations were always within a
few miles of London's heart. They were constantly blazing fresh
trails back to the centre.

My mother, the youngest, was born during the first World War
at Stair Cottages, not far from the Common, near the old lavender fields. She and her sisters were all legendary exotic beauties
in their day. Every one made a good marriage. My grandmother
told me of Mediterranean ancestors who had come from Africa
through Spain, of noble families as old as Phoenicia. She spoke
of her husband's people, who had taken centuries to travel from
the Himalayan heartland of the world to the borders of London,
who brought Hindi and Persian and Byzantine Greek words to
add to the common tongue, together with a religion which
blended Hindu mythology with Zoroastrianism and the oldest
forms of Christianity. My grandfather was actually half Sepharde
and half Gypsy. Potent magic, as my grandmother would say
wistfully.

My grandfather had seemed wholly Gypsy. A big, dark handsome man, he had been a blacksmith until his lungs collapsed.
His sons wore colorful clothes, bright bandannas, gold earrings,
and had wonderful black, curly hair, dark eyes and white teeth.
On Saturday nights girls who my aunts told me were "not respectable" would come down to the mouth of the mews to be
picked up by those laughing, dangerous boys.

One settled tribe, the Jones, still had a camp not far from the
tram terminus, near Figges' Marsh, in an area mysteriously
known as "The Lonesome." They also lived around "The
Rocky," a small warren of stableyards and small cottages, named
for The Rocky Mountain Cafe which always attracted me with
its greasy, working class warmth. They ran the fairgrounds, too.

Since Roman times, fairs came seasonally to Mitcham. The
fairs brought the Gypsies and some of them had settled. They
had a hand in all the fairs which came through, owning most of

the big rides, the helter-skelters, the dodgems and the roller-coasters which were often winter-stored nearby. But fairs were not their only trade.

The tribe occupied both sides of an old, cobbled mews. The stables and storage were below, the living quarters above. In the security of the mews I learned to ride the sturdy, hard-headed little ponies they used for everything from pulling totting carts to giving rides to children on the Common on Saturday afternoons. They lived by scrap for large parts of the year, touting for any old iron, running junk- or breaker's-yards. They taught me their exotic language, an accumulation of all the languages of East and West. Some words are still part of the common speech of Londoners, for the theatrical profession adopted the "gay" language of an earlier outlaw caste, which in turn had borrowed heavily from Romany. It was how I understood so much of the highwayman's vernacular, which is thick with the canting tongue of several centuries. Similarly, in Soho, I absorbed Yiddish by osmosis.

Almost all that way of speaking has disappeared, reinvented by Screen People[3] into something universal and fundamentally bland.

It has been many years since I heard of a bloke going case with a mystery (a man sleeping with a woman) or a woman concluding her anecdote with "Well, in the death . . . " for "in the end." I have no East European ancestry but I will still use *schmutte* for clothing, *weisse* for a white man, *gelt* for money,

---

[3]"The mukhamirim of Cairo call them 'shades' and encounter them often. They are not above using them for their own purposes. Screen People believe their screens to be or to represent reality. Screens provide the bulk of their experience and provide them with all but certain basic functions. They communicate screen to screen, screen to screen. We are frequently therefore invisible to these people. We are safe behind their screens, behind which they falsely believe they are safe. Screens, after all, do screen. We are in danger of becoming addicted, exactly like opium addicts, to our own marvelous technologies. Opium destroyed the complex Chinese Empire. Unscreened reality will be our salvation. And it is in the name of reality itself we begin our great crusade."
—Mukal ibn 'Abla, *Green Jihad,* 1996.

dommerer or *dommy* for a lunatic, *schtook* for trouble, *schtoom* for quiet and *guntz* to mean everything. Romany words I still use, when back in London, include *cokir* for a liar, *muzzle* for luck, *beak* for a magistrate, *peckish* for hungry, *mumper* for a clever con-man, *bosh* for nonsense and *tawno* for little.

Though perpetually shifting and expanding its meanings, the language of the streets is a compendium of all the languages ever spoken in London. By the time it is recorded by professional writers it has changed, often subtly, to keep its chief function as a secret language, speaking of secret, enduring realities.

That language always returns when it's needed. Nowadays Bengali, Hindi and Urdu, sharing roots with the Gypsy tongue, have been added to Caribbean, Chinese and African. Once again the under-classes have the secret charm of their language to protect, console and ultimately empower them.[4]

∽

My aunts hated to hear that I spent so much time with the Gypsies and were always trying to improve me. They forbade me to play with my cousins. I ignored them. They attempted a different approach, inviting one of the Gypsy children to stay with me at my Aunt Pamela's. My cousins, of course, could think of nothing worse. They ignored the invitations.

My aunts decided to keep a protective eye on me and unannounced would occasionally arrive at the camp, all buttons and whalebone, to make mysterious social visits. The baffled Romanies did their best to entertain their in-laws but of course could never win my aunts' approval. Periodically, after my grandma's condition made it impossible for me to visit her, the aunts would

---

[4]"Meanwhile Screen People—consummate consumers—are content with the useless counterfeit. As with so many other things, Screen People take the style for the content and are thus eternally confused, eternally vulnerable, eternally immoral, capable only of making decisions based on their immediate appetites." —Ibid.

descend, in lace and lavender water, to gather me up and coo me off to the suburbs where my boredom led to innocent excesses so that they were always glad to return me to my mother, whom they rather admired but thought irresponsible and flighty. She was a wild flower, they said, but should never have had children.

I liked it best when my mother arrived in a chauffeur-driven Bentley to take me back to Sporting Club Square. With relief and renewed expectations I would at last step from the domestic comfort of their Yardley's into the erotic veil of her Guerlaine.

If her sisters thought her disturbing, I found my mother eternally absorbing. At home I loved to watch her blaze about the house. Sometimes I was so invisible to her that I felt like a naturalist studying some admired but alien beast, entirely astonished by its behavior. It always comforted me, however, to turn on the radio and hear her voice or see her on the screen, advertising some reassuring pie.

During my visits to Sporting Club Square I was often on my own, for she was in those years rarely out of work and had begun that famous career in commercials. I was free to explore the world at my disposal.

Once in London, I could roam from Chelsea to Notting Hill, walk into the West End, which we called "Town," or take a tram to the East End and the City. My posher relatives could be touched for half-a-bar (ten shillings) or so (they were usually glad to see the back of me, especially the ones in Parliament or Whitehall) and, the penny arcades and tupenny cinemas aside, there were a million things to do outdoors. Sporting Club Square in those days had an unrestricted rear view across ancient fields and cemeteries to the river. For me it provided all the pleasures of the country while promising the distractions of the town.

If not working, my mother was usually engaged in some parochial crisis, aiding a friend in a deception, or recruiting a friend in a deception. Only in later years, when she became radio's "Mrs. Cornelius," offering Cockney wisdom to afternoon listeners, did she settle long enough into one role to offer me any consistent attention. I continue to be fond of her. She left me alone, in an amiable sort of way, as did my father, and if I grew up to be a little eccentric, perhaps overly self-sufficient and not quite what either had hoped, they never expressed anything but interest in my well-being.

&

I would guess myself no older than seven when I decided to follow the highwayman's calling, in an age when Dick Turpin, Colonel Jack, Tom King, Claude Duval[5] and Sixteen String Jack, though separated in history by a century and a half, challenged London's scarlet thunderers with only a good horse and a couple of dragoon pistols between them and the noose, or galloped together over the twisting cobbles of Clerkenwell and Brookgate and through Surrey's rustic dust, forever in pursuit of a purse or pursued by the Runners.

At that time, my resources were limited. The opportunity of hiring in with such a gallant band was denied me for a while. I lacked both money and the authority of years.

Meanwhile, I read everything about the highwaymen, fact and fiction, ballad or novel. Fortnightly, I took *The Black Bess Li-*

---

[5]"Of this gay and chivalrous robber, his flageolet and *couranto,* his *bonnes fortunes,* his masked visitations, his gorgeous funeral, and the crowd of damsels who bewailed his loss, we have spoken at some length in our first volume; but they who desire to hear more of him will do well, if they are not already acquainted with it, to turn to a delightful essay on the subject of *Thiefs, Ancient and Modern,* in Mr. Leigh Hunt's *Indicator,* in which there is a sparkling sketch of the gallant Claude. Our only regret is that Mr. Hunt did not expatiate more upon the Highwaymen; but we trust he will repair this error in the *London Journal,* and give us a brilliant page or two on the denizens of the empire of High Toby. *A propos* of the *London Journal,* let us, even in hasty note, wish Mr. Hunt all the success in his new undertaking, which he so richly merits; and counsel all our readers who love the cordial, the kindly, the amiable, the poetical, the fanciful, and the *reasonable* in every sense, at once to become subscribers to this pleasantest of pleasant hebdomadabs. He who can turn even 'stones' to gems must possess a subtle alchemy." —Ainsworth, *Rookwood.*

brary and *Tales of the Tramways.* They were published on alter-
nate weeks. These were my favorite stories. As Lord Barbican of
the Universal Transport Company attempted to lay his infamous
grids, his straight, reassuring steel, across the planet, uttering
populist slogans about the public interest and by these means
striving to simplify a complex world to his specific profit, only
Dick Turpin and Jack Oakenhurst, the masked, devil-may-care
"Captains of the Lines," stood between him and the common
good.

Their traditional cry of "Throw down your lever!" was known
to every admiring child. Their skill at unhooking a power pulley or
mounting the outside stair of an old-fashioned "Feltham Sparker"
at full gallop was celebrated in a thousand tales and melodra-
mas. Even the great Tom Jones had played Turpin in an American photoplay to display his marvelous equestrian skills and had
led to the series *Mix of the Texas Tramway,* so popular in my
father's day.

A merrier crew never quaffed convivial ale at *The Six Jolly
Dragoons,* saved a decent young heir from scheming guardians,
or charmed a maiden to behave in her own self-interest, as that
band of eternals.

There were a dozen others who had taken to the High Toby
after being cheated of their estates or wrongfully accused of another's crime—Colonel Jack, Will Dudley, Galloping Dick Lang-
ley, Jack Sheppard, Captain Corny O'Dowd, the Irish Tory,[6] Will
Begg, who was hanged while still in holy orders, Gentleman
George Hargreaves, Captain Horatio Quelch, Colonel Langdon
"Black Gallon" Jones, the Welsh Dragoon, together with such
supernatural anti-heroes as the Phantom Horsemen of Houn-

---

[6] The word Tory, as here applied, must not be confounded with the term of party
distinction now in general use in the political world. It simply means a thief on
a grand scale, something more than a "snapper up of unconsidered trifles," or
petty, larceny rascal. We have classical authority for this—"Tory—an advocate
for absolute monarchy, also an Irish vagabond, robber, or rapparee."
—Grose's Dictionary.

slow Heath, the Night Rider of London Fields, Jack o' Lantern, Will o' th' Wisp and all.

Their wise advice to suitors was legendary. Their cool daring on the gallows with ropes around their necks was forever demonstrated. Their escapes from jail were marked by their audacity and ingenuity, as well as their athletic prowess. Their horsemanship and skills with whip, pistols and sword, and their unrelenting courtesy to women, characterized them as true outlaw heroes fighting society's hypocrisies and cruelties with laughing courage, righteous anger, and an honest wish to help the underdog. They constantly risked their glamorous lives in some altruistic cause. What better role models had a young person of my generation?

Was it, I wonder, surprising that, feeling the weight as sole direct offspring of our ancient family, I should choose the life of a Knight of the Road and, running away to London, seek immediately the gay life of the High Toby? I yearned to ride some great stallion over Hampstead Common, righting wrongs and rescuing the poor. I felt I had been born for nothing else! Thus I went to Meard Alley, Soho, where I presented myself at *The Six Jolly Dragoons* and fell in at once with none other than Captain Turpin himself. This being, of course, some while before he was due to take his famous Ride to York, which would kill Black Bess and do nothing significant to delay his own execution.

Dick Turpin was a swagger butcher from Hempstead, with a touch of Essex burr in his fashionable Cockney drawl. Entirely contrary to accounts in the sensational press, especially *The Malefactor's Register; or, New Newgate and Tyburn Calendar*, published in 1796 over a gulf of some 35 years, Turpin was as gentlemanly as he was handsome and in later life a keen dry fly fisherman who had written a monograph and political soliloquy on the subject, *The Tory Angler*.

Turpin had been a close acquaintance of Leigh Hunt, the editor and essayist and Dick's enthusiastic advocate. According to Hunt, the great highwayman boasted that he had never killed a man, lest it be in self-defense, and never insulted a woman. He had nine children by four different mistresses and had provided for each in his Will. He was a cautious accountant, for all his dash and generosity, and felt strong responsibilities towards his off-spring.

I knew his eldest son, Richard, well. He went to sea at sixteen. He was killed aboard a Norwegian whaler, crushed beneath a mountain of bone on his twenty-second birthday. After they cleared the whale's remains off him he lived long enough to thank God for his salvation.

I knew Turpin's eldest daughter best. We had a very strong friendship which lasted many trials until the last.

Mary had the true Turpin blood and a little more besides. Her mother was "Madcap" Mary Beck, the abandoned mistress of Prince Rupert, and a resourceful soul, who set up a dressmaker's in Bayswater, not a stone's throw from Tyburn, and did a roaring trade in mourning crepe, *postes restantes,* and the casual blackmail of her better off clients.

Mrs. Beck was eventually poisoned one evening at *The Six Jolly Dragoons* and died four days later in some discomfort, begging Dr. Shapiro to shoot her and get it over with. She would have done it herself if she had had the strength to reach her pistol, hidden behind the clock above the mantel. As it was she made use of her agonies to give added ferocity to the curse she put on her murderess (she was convinced she was a woman's victim) and the angry mockery with which she attacked the medical men's failure either to save her life or to deaden her pain.

It was not considered a coincidence by most of us that only a few hours after Mary Beck had gone, spitting and shrieking, to her reward, Lady Bryony Stoolbridge was suddenly smitten by a stroke and fell wide-eyed and stone dead before the mildly baffled gaze of the supine Alice, Princess Royal, half-way down the Long Walk at Kensington Gardens.

Their own grandfather, William Beck, already having met his end on the Tyburn gallows (to which all his surviving relatives were witness) a year or two earlier, my Mary and her younger brother

Thomas, were forced to fend for themselves and did so honestly, continuing their mother's business, but with a considerable loss of regular custom after the initial curiosity had died down. Soon they were tricked out of the shop by a creditor and thrown onto the street. It was at this stage that Mary made the journey to *The Six Jolly Dragoons* and put herself and her sibling on her father's ready mercy.

∽

I think it was with some relief that Dick later introduced his daughter to me. He clearly hoped for what followed. We became firm friends almost at once.

Believing himself a bad influence on Tommy, Dick arranged for Methodist relatives in Old Sweden Street, Brookgate, to raise the boy. The girl was thought firm-minded enough to resist any example the High Tobyman might offer, unless it be his preference for plain-speaking and his determined courage.

Turpin had once confided in me that, in spite of his destiny, he lived in the expectation of being extinguished at any hour. If a comet were to fall on him, for instance, he would not wish to be crushed to mincemeat feeling he had betrayed his own principles. Thus, he lived by a code stricter than any man-made law, and older, too. Indeed, the only thing it was not was *better*. It actually led to his early, somewhat pointless death, not to mention that of his wonderful mare, since he could easily have retired on his stocks and partnerships long before he rode to York. I once put this to him. He was apologetic, but every so often, he said, he felt obliged to fulfill his legend.

Tommy soon learned the ways of sinuous Old Sweden Street and nearby Leather Lane markets. He was his father's son and took pride in his risks and his skills. But he lacked his father's larger vision. When I knew Tommy he was a practiced pickpocket, mock-auctioneer, tram-steamer, general spieler and tout, selling everything from stolen silver to crack cocaine. Like all his breed, he was a loyal friend. Criminal communities celebrate

the same tribal virtues as Scottish or African clans. He was
frequently baffled by my refusal to take him up on his offer to
bash people who had upset me or steal something for me which
I had admired. It was impossible for me to reciprocate, I said.
But he expected nothing in return. As it was, Christmas and my
birthday could prove an embarrassment.

Mary, naturally, loved her father and her brother. Only occasionally did she voice the wish that they should go straight and
stop making her anxious.

Having joined that charmed band of gallants, in the usual tradition I chose a "trade name" and at first was Galloping Jim
until, in some embarrassment, I learned this was a common
term for virulent dysentery. I would thereafter be known as Captain Hawkmoon. In Yorkshire a "hawk moon" is that especially
bright full moon by which a hawk prefers to hunt.

There is no sweeter thrill than riding into the lights of a clat-
tering night express with both barkers blazing and your voice
shouting above the wind "Throw down your lever!" It was a
wonderful, if relatively brief, career. I was aware, even then, that
such splendid adventures were not granted to every soul.

∽

All this is a long way from the Brixton Empire and my mother,
who regularly gambles with her life, and until now has always won.

"Rose," she says to me, "if life isn't worth losing, it isn't
worth living. Put the highest value on your life, dear, and it
means you're always playing your best."

Mrs. Bloom, her friend, who was a colleague from the waning
years of the halls, and whom I called Aunty Boo, nods in profound agreement. "Make the most of y'self, Rosie," she elabo-
rates, "and you can afford to be generous. Nothing wrong with
giving it away when you feel like it. But you don't want to waste

it." Some people believe my mother bases her "Mrs. Cornelius" character on Aunty Boo.

∽

Needless to say, I found most of this adult advice entirely mysterious.

By the age of seventeen I had failed in more than one career and fallen in love with a Balkan speculator called Count Rudolf von Bek. I met him at Harrods. He bought my tea. I was used to dashing rogues, I suppose, and found his manner familiar. I married him and fled to the Continent in a scandalous elopement. But he proved a disappointment.

Rudy was something of an adventurer, a flier, a trained engineer and an entrepreneur, typical of the kind who flourished immediately after the War. Like so many of his colleagues, he called himself an "aeroplane salesman," but he was actually an arms dealer, an associate of the notorious Quelch, who had been mixed up in North Africa since her troubles began. Imperialism breeds nationalism and nationalism needs guns.

My life with him was not happy and his disposition proved entirely antithetical to my own. It was during my marriage to Count von Bek that I discovered my ability to enter the Second Ether almost at will (especially under stress) and walk the moonbeam roads between the worlds. To my joy, I discovered a thousand alternatives, a thousand different selves and lives. For a year my husband believed me his virtual prisoner while actually I roamed the multiverse! In the end it was a relief for him, I think, to be rid of me.[7]

---

[7]Those postwar years were golden ones for my husband and his friends. He is still alive, a lobbyist for the NRA in the US. He explains his value: As well as being the world's largest arms-exporter, the US is, after all, the world's only real domestic market for expensive, high-powered guns. Everywhere else expansion is limited and subjected to over-rigorous scrutiny or the ability of the customer to pay is in question. There is a principle at stake, something he feels worth defending and that, he points out, is pretty hard to find, these days. Where else can honest armaments makers sell their wares to the ordinary public in a genuinely competitive free market?

∽

Now I am inclined to be known again by my given names of Margaret Rose Moorcock, but the story of my translation was a long and complicated one. I still use my poor Texan cousin Michael's name for most of my fiction. Though having no love for it, I found it politic to keep my married title in private life. It put a useful distance between me and most of the world. Even before I left von Bek, Sam Oakenhurst was a great consolation to me.

I first met Sam in his mortal form during the episode I usually call *The Game of the Raped Planet*. My duty was to avenge the death of my whole race by seeking out a villain known as Paul Minct and finishing him off. A pretty straightforward mission, in essence, but full of sinuous difficulties and considerable danger. Any resolution had to involve all players in almost wholly equal positions. And there were no easy options. I was two-thirds through the scenario and completely in its grip before I realized I was part of a much more involved Game and met Sam. I required him and his arrogant friend Jack Karaquazian to help me complete my game and in turn I agreed to help them towards the resolution they sought. They are the two best players in the multiverse. Frequently they ran several games at once. You never knew which one you were in.

In London I had not seen Sam without his mask. Later, in New Orleans, I had known him as a tall, handsome African, with that refined nobility of expression you find in the Benin bas reliefs. By the third time I met him, the subtle, alien surgery of the *machinoix* had transformed him into a kind of human stick insect. But he had by no means lost his attraction. Indeed, his plight had added to his charm.

I gave him as much of myself as I could spare. I was forever agonizingly aware that he was expendable in my game. My own hand was so much better than his. All gamblers know about luck. I just had more of it. There was an inevitability to the whole thing which gave our love-making a perverse frisson I remember with little relish. But Sam seemed to enjoy it.

Sam was of a dramatic disposition and eventually took to reading only nineteenth century French, German and English Romantic poetry, so his references and signatures all reflected his enthusiasms.

In the apparent chaos of the Second Ether, where ships and people slide from one scale to another, Sam had encountered his first new "fold-zone" where it is possible to move from one scale to another. The zones' vivid greens, grays and pinks he had named *Baudelaire's Oyster*, while the great lazy waves of glimmering black and scarlet, once simply the Field of Black and Scarlet, became *Tannhäuser: The Musical*.[8] Navigators to follow his routes were forced to learn such names as *Byzantine Conversations, Ecco del' Ecco* and *The Grooming of Minerva* (he loved Wheldrake).

In the course of those expeditions I discovered a great deal concerning the structure of the multiverse and the essential simplicity of God's mighty design which allowed us to create complicated patterns for our edification and bewilderment. This knowledge, together with a good grounding in the study of superwoven carbons and so-called "buckyballs," was of particular use to me when I learned to fly.

⌒⊃

When my mother retired to one of those massive Worthing sea-front bungalows she gave me her Begg Mansions apartment. It is the nicest of all the eccentric flats designed to demonstrate the versatility of Hubert Begg, the architect of Sporting Club Square. Only in this one building, where his work-

---

[8]He had also developed a rather irritating, if sketchy, passion for Wagner.

shops and studios had also been, did he allow his late pre-Raphaelite fantasies free rein.

This was the flat to which I almost always returned after my forays into the Second Ether. By this time I had gained a reputation as a pilot but not as a guide.

I would usually arrive in the Square at dawn or at sunset, in the hope of an uninterrupted transition, for there was a protective aura of color around the place. This aura was growing weaker, however, suggesting that the protection our home had enjoyed down the years from the normal passage of time and radically changing society was about to end.

Our entire world, it seemed, was threatened by a monstrous funnel of energy capable of sucking us back into the power of the Singularity, still waiting behind its supercarbon walls, its pseudo-universe, to consume us. There were few obvious signs of this, of course, but the general unresolved conflicts within society reflected the danger.

Some of my more sophisticated friends spoke of their premonitions. They believed the entire world was about to grow deliquescent and die.

It was true, from what I knew, that at a certain stage of universal diffusion very little could be saved. The broad view suggested I take all this with a shrug, for there are so many realities in the multiverse, each only a shade apart, and the failure of one, identical in almost every detail to another, was not much to mourn; but I was attached to this one and was determined to do what I could. Moreover, I sensed this was more than the march of common entropy. I felt all the worlds, at every scale of the multiverse, were threatened.

Time, however, was running out. Clearly, we were already becoming part of the war zone.

We had attracted the attention of the Original Insect.

2

Everybody has heard of the beautiful Countess of Cressett, who was one of the lights of this country at the time when crowned heads were running over Europe, crying out, for charity's sake to be amused after their tiresome work of slaughter: and you know what a dread they have of moping

—GEORGE MEREDITH, *The Amazing Marriage*

My Schooling

Towards the end my Uncle Michael lost control of his visions and was helpless before their unending complications. In his middle years he took it into his head to raise exotic herds in Texas and bought himself a spread known as the Lost Pines Ranch, not far from the U.S. border, where he would ride night and day across the endless scrub, conversing with invisible hosts and the choir angelic. By his own cheerful admission, he had an entirely conventional vision of the Fields of Heaven. His patron, St. Michael, carrying his familiar scales and sword, occasionally visited him. He had also met, more than once, Jesus

Christ, Geronimo, Saint Mary le Dale, Saint George, Sir Francis
Drake, Mangas Coloradas, Judas Iscariot, Saint Peter, Kit Carson, Saint Patrick and, to his perpetual terror, Arioch, Duke of
Hell, whose physical and spiritual attractions were imprinted
upon his mind, perhaps his soul.

Arioch's voice, my uncle confided to me, was rarely out of his
ears. It was the sweetest music he had ever heard. In this way,
he said, he believed himself possessed. He also claimed the acquaintance of various temporal travelers whom he referred to
with great affection, as if they were very old friends. He spent
much of the rest of his time looking for the Holy Grail which
Count Ulrich von Bek had, according to legend, hidden on the
land.

∾

I remember the strange old man toying with a lighted candle,
whose wax formed tiny cliffs surrounding the flame burning
in a miniature lake of its own creation. "Myriad species, intelligent races and civilizations, perhaps universes, evolve and degenerate around the warmth of that flame. I light it, and a
glorious history begins. I extinguish it and annihilate all
sentience . . ." He did not demonstrate. His imagined power
appeared to sadden him.

His habit of allowing flames to burn down in their own time
meant that the entire house was filled with guttering candles, most
on the point of expiry. His tall, angular, poorly-co-ordinated body
would move mysteriously about the house, casting long, black
shadows everywhere. The candle-light glistened and danced on
the copper and brass of his Arts and Crafts house, one of the
few designed from American materials by Hubert Begg, a kind
of homage to his American wife. Her company, after Begg's
death, sold the plans to wealthy builders in the years before the
First War. Count Fritz von Bek, a well-known German mystical
visionary, one of my ex-husband's uncles and a distant cousin,

had commissioned the house, the only one of its kind in Texas, and lived his remaining days in that remote region, constantly threatened by nature's extremes, as well as some sixteen different deadly snakes and a similar number of scorpions and spiders, together with various larger mammals, such as cougars, given to occasional man-eating. He was fond of telling any visitors that not even the Mimbreno Apache considered the area habitable.

ᔓᓬ

The place also had vague family connections, believed by many to be the original of the Circle Squared Ranch, the setting for Warwick Begg's famous "Masked Buckaroo" series of the 1920s and 30s. There were pilgrims who still came to Lost Pines looking for signs of Shorty, Windy, Grumpy, Sarajevo, Cajun Pete, Don Lorenzo, The Breed Papoose and the rest of the boys who had, with rancher's daughter Jenny Ash, shared the Buckaroo's many adventures. If they were unfortunate enough to encounter my uncle, they received a far more intense experience than they had been expecting, since even in his madness he had little patience with what he called the sugared tranquilizer of middle-class nostalgia.

On his discovery of them, my uncle would offer these visitors recitations from Milton and Shelley. For light relief they might be given a little Swinburne, for whom he retained a loyal if unfashionable enthusiasm. Sometimes he baffled them with Browning. Those who earned his closer attention were forced to listen to his opinions of George Meredith's masterpiece, *The Amazing Marriage,* which contains a famous portrait of my grandmother, and some dry wit he had by heart.

He had a missionary's zeal for educating any native who seemed in the least curious about anything. He loved America. He felt that Americans were somehow short-changing themselves. After all his years in that country, he said, he had never encountered a people so fond of pissing in their own pond and then complaining that they had to move because the water was dirty.

My uncle shared Sam Oakenhurst's taste for Wagner and the two frequently met to discuss some favorite performance or some nuance of a story, but my uncle sought very little other company. He kept up a massive correspondence with my father, whose own circumstances were not dissimilar, though less threatened by climate or wild-life.

My father and his brother Michael had once ridden together and had founded Cairo's infamous Junior Jockey Club, where camels were raced with some panache, with even a short steeple-chase season, weather and the camel's disposition permitting. These races were noted in a number of memoirs, especially Shaw Pasha's.[9] There are members of my family living in Egypt to this day whose expertise and instincts are highly valued by local gamblers.

My father enjoyed the exchanges with his brother. Like his own, my uncle's letters were fanciful, full of eccentric reference and arcane erudition. The two had much in common, including a love of Siamese cats, especially the Oriental Shorthair, which is a Siamese of a single color, usually black, white or grey and impressively intelligent, if easily bored. They were, after the burning of our stables, the only animals, apart from fish, to hold any interest for my father.

∽

The brothers and their sister had been an inseparable though not always amicable trio. In their childhood even the Great War hardly touched them and they had known little of conventional contemporary life, somehow retaining their rather eighteenth century attitudes, which perhaps best suited their

---

[9]His memoirs contain some astonishing photographs of himself on his own camel going over fences on the JJC course.

visionary radicalism—for they were all planning to go into politics in those days. Their rhetoric proved too rich and too full of complicated reference to appeal to the ordinary voter so they failed in their efforts, though Aunt Margaret did eventually serve for some years on her local County Council where she remains a celebrity.

My aunt was always very critical of my father's "moping," after his Thrawn Janet was killed in the fire, and she remained furious with her brother Michael for "deserting the fort," as she put it, and settling in Texas. She was, however, uncritically fond of my mother and of me and I loved to be enveloped, from time to time, by her enormously irrational approval. Like my mother's sisters, she believed me neglected, but she did not blame Nellie. Nellie had a calling, she said, which was more important than any relationships and it was everyone's job to fill in for her as best they could. Aunt Margaret's maternalism was never otherwise manifested, nor was she an established patron of the arts.

She had married a man called Ackroyd. In spite of his name, he was a Londoner, a member of the family which founded Ackroyd & Sinclair, the brewers and distillers, whose Vortex Waters are still prepared at the original Uxbridge Road works. In their heyday "A&S" was the gin of choice around the Empire. Sinclair, the grandson of the founder, was a long, lugubrious, bookish fellow, with little resemblance to anyone in his family. He was rumored to be the bastard son of Lord Longford. I saw more of him than I did of the Ackroyds, who were not close and only met for board meetings.

As a child, I loved to wander around the Uxbridge Road distillery. It was the roaring engine of the A&S fortunes. I delighted in the drama of the ferocious copper vats and noisy pipes. Between the steaming glass, the gleaming pulleys and distant galleries men in stained cotton and leather aprons moved mysterious levers and tugged on cackling chains to propel one boiling mess upon another. They hurled jokes and insults across the gantries and board-walks, creating strange echoes, casting vast shadows in sunlight seething through the roof's dusty glass, their sweat mingling with all the other busy juices of the works. Those men were fond of me and had nicknames for me. I thought of them as my army of friends. They were certainly part of my schooling, as, of course, was Dick Turpin, who had made every important life decision with help from a pint of ASV, which is half-and-half gin and Vortex Water, a unique combination, not for weaker drinkers.

When I first met him, Turpin seemed reconciled to his fate. He pointed out that he was the hero of a cycle and the nature of a cycle was to go round and round. This would not be the first time he had ridden to York, he told me on that important night, and so far he had not found the experience boring. Predestination, he added with a touch of self-mockery, was a given in his line of work and you learned how to deal with it. Later he would modify this view.

Earlier, he had spoken with some sympathy of my cousin, the pirate Frenchy LaFarge, who had begun life as Peter Taylor, an advertising man from South London, and whom I had known since we were teenagers. Frenchy had never quite taken a grip of his situation as an eternal and remained perpetually astonished when the time came for him to pay his debt to society ("five minutes of pretty unpleasant throttling, if you're unlucky," says Turpin, "a few seconds if you're not"). His close resemblance to the droll French comedian Fernandel had earned him his nickname and he had continued to use it when he went to sea. Even as he came to understand his near-immortality, he remained forever upset by the idea and continued to die unreconciled. It is an odd thing to have grown up with someone of that nature and never to have realized it of them. But how much stranger when your cousin himself proves innocent of the knowledge! He might have thought and said the same things a million times before, performed identical actions and discovered identical consequences. *And he did not know it!* Then, of course, you come to wonder if you, too, are living an unconscious life, or one of many, all of which are only a whisper apart. It was some while before I learned the difference between an eternal, an immortal and a quasi-immortal, a demigod. I, like the rest of my unfortunate colleagues among the Just, am forever conscious.

I lost touch with Frenchy after he moved to the Adriatic. There have been times when I envied him his perpetual surprise.

∽

The realm of the undead or undying, as the eternally alive are erroneously called, is a rich one, requiring a strong head and a steady nerve if you are to live any kind of decent life in it. Qualities of character are important here and memory is an altogether different instrument in our time-tormented minds. Once you venture into the afterlife, as some term it, where the conventional laws of entropy do not apply, your realities are entirely dependent upon your own capacity to order and to invent, to achieve the harmony between your "law" and your "chaos" instincts, fundamental instincts raised to paramount survival skills by the *mukhamirim* who roam the roads between the worlds. A fondness for mathematics and music is a considerable help, as is any kind of developed creative gift, especially, of course, the gift of the *mukhamirim*, those gamblers trained in the religious schools of Cairo, Alexandria and Marrakech, who experienced the lost electronics of our Golden Age which they are sometimes able to reproduce by metaphysical means alone.

Though himself no *mukhamir*, having chosen the easier, if shorter, life of a demigod, Turpin let slip the bulk of this knowledge long before I made my first expedition into the Fault and met Paul Minct, who taught me much of what I learned and much of what I have since had to unlearn. That story has been told elsewhere. (My guilt can never be forgiven. My blood is the blood of the rose, as they say. My sap is the sap of the man-vine, which the people of Af, where I dwelled for a short lifetime, say is the First Sap; for in their mythology their initial buds were cultivated by a giant ape, who fed their native soil with his own blood until, utterly drained, he died. The ape is known in their language as Kong or sometimes as Don Quijon and is no doubt the echo of a common lore.[10] It always surprises me when, in our teeming and various multiverse, where so many stories are interwoven and so much diversity exists, I discover a familiar thread.)

∽

Any who know the Ramsden School, just off the A65, north of Leeds, have strong opinions about the place. Some believe it to be the best all-round education in the world, while others claim that pupils emerge from it with far too much sensibility and not enough sense. I found its peculiar brand of Christian mysticism and asceticism attractive. Ramsden's language no better described my world than did the language of the thoroughly conventional Sedbergh Grammar, which I would have given anything to attend sometimes. While helping me understand and control my inner life, the Ramsden did not, I will admit, prepare me for life outside its grounds. It was not until I was fourteen that I was introduced to some social realities by Turpin, who became my guardian and my guide through London's miseries and lures, teaching me something about compassion and how it can be satisfied.

To demonstrate the greater freedom a youth still has, Turpin dressed me up in boy's clothing and took me on a number of different tours of the city. From the world of the "swells" and "autem coves" in Mayfair and St. George's to the world of Holborn and Brookgate's "steamers" and "dips" Dick Turpin led

---

[10]I spent a girlhood exploring the vast brambles which spanned the space between planets and created a universe of roses. Some of those roads were hundreds of miles wide, if not more, larger than many earthly landmasses. And the size of the older roses was, of course, in proportion. Entire races came into being within a single bud.

me in what I know now to be exemplary excursions, illustrating
the world of O'Crook's *London Rakehell* as unromantically as it
was possible to do. Everywhere we went, he introduced me to
someone whom, if I so desired, I would be able to ask for help.
He built up a pattern of associations for me in the city and
then left me alone. He was an extraordinary personality, the
acknowledged Great Captain of the High Tobymen ("high toby"
being an old name for the main road), protected from any enemy
while he held court at Soho's *Six Jolly Dragoons*, in Meard
Alley. Even the Tram Company Runners accepted his right of
sanctuary there, and for years this custom was respected, no
matter how high the reward on his handsome, brutal head.

At the time I never appreciated the cool courage Turpin displayed by taking me out of the safety of his own small constituency. There were still almost as many hated him as loved him,
though he had seen a considerable improvement since his own
day. But "mob-madness" must always be feared by our kind, for
if we cease to become invisible in such crowds, we are frequently
attacked. The more visible we are to individuals, the more, generally speaking, they like us. But mobs grow murderous.

The advantage of becoming a legend, Turpin argued, was that
one received far more approval in that state. It offered all kinds
of social entrances which would otherwise be denied an Essex
master boucanier and rustler, no matter how successful in
Whitechapel. Baronesses boasted of his having kissed their
hands. Maidens whispered of his eyes and his smile as he accepted their pretty purses. His masked face haunted the dreams
of society women everywhere. His manly accomplishments (as
well as his figure) were admired without envy at every level,
from gutter to throne. Yet even Turpin feared mob-madness.

Captain Turpin was amused by the stories which featured him
as the hero. He read them as avidly as Buffalo Bill read his and
strove rather more successfully to live up to them. He had met
Colonel Cody several times and said that for every bumper of
ale he, Dick, tossed off, Cody could drink a bottle of A&S. Cody

was plagued by false memories, he said, unable to sort one from the other, unable to distinguish his own exploits from those of his legend. For a long time he had that trouble and his condition was wretched. A good-natured and fair man, he depended entirely upon laudanum for any rest he achieved.

I suppose it's obvious that I was in love with Turpin. But it was a schoolgirl's love and he understood it better than I did. It was a lie that I was his mistress or that my friend was a drunkard, though I saw him wilt under this century's destructive revisionism (he would bloom in a finer future). The cynical uses to which the Nazis put their national myths and heroes particularly distressed Turpin, who was a progressive democrat to the tips of his spurs and could not bear the notion of another age attaching his name to a base and cruel cause. He had no choice, of course, but for years the question tormented him.

Dick Turpin was the first to admit that Harrison Ainsworth's paean to the Knights of the Road, *Rookwood,* which spends most of its three volumes extolling the virtues of Turpin and his kind, quoting (and probably inventing) whole ballads in full, did a great deal for him. England's most famous highwayman made that sometimes impossible transition from folk tradition into literature and thus back into folk tradition in the form of adventures told in text, plays, comic strips, screens and radio.

My cousin wrote a number of Dick's adventures involving his constant conflict with the Universal Transport Company, which to a degree took the stories back to their roots. My cousin had also helped continue the memory of Robin Hood, Billy the Kid, Buckskin Annie, Strongbow the Mohawk, Karl the Viking, Buck Jones, Hereward the Wake, Sam Bass, Kit Carson, Olac the Gladiator, Tom Mix, Jet-Ace Logan, Jesse James, Sexton Begg, Wulf the Briton, Tarzan of the Apes and a dozen other stars of screen and strip, before burning himself out on twenty different serials a week, eventually having a mental breakdown in the course of which he attempted to tell each editor the entire continuing plot of each serial in case, as he suspected, he was murdered by one of his own inventions. He believed all his main characters to be living people. He had decided they were turning against him. They were unhappy, he thought, with his increasing self-parody or, as they put it, unacceptable recycling.

Returning to the family ranch, my cousin eventually recuperated and now, to his father's unspoken discomfort, is successful locally as Tex Murdoch and his Lost Pines Buckaroos, fulfilling a boyhood desire to perform as a honky-tonk country singer. He has, even his father admits, a natural yodel. Of late he has begun to specialize in old Roy Rogers and the Sons of the Pioneers songs, although I will admit he now bears a closer physical resemblance to Gabby Hayes than to Roy or any of the boys. But, of all my relatives, he is the happiest.

By the time my cousin was writing his adventures, Dick had again become closely involved with the supernatural. Scarcely a story was free of at least a ghost or two. In *Rookwood* Dick had galloped out of the Gothic and into popular reality. In his work for *The Black Bess Library*, my cousin was galloping him straight back into the Gothic again.

Dick became contemplative after his last ride. While in York he had stayed for some days with a clergyman he knew. On his return to London, by an early train, he was polite but distant. He was, he told me, considering the means by which God used us to achieve his will. He gave up drinking ASV and took to smoking marijuana in his old churchwarden. This added a humane wit to his performance, even if he was occasionally unsteady in the saddle, and for a while it was a joy to ride with him in pursuit of a prize, for there wasn't a passenger or highwayman who ever crossed that heath could match the grace of his demeanor or the quickness of his tongue.[11] Unless, though I say it myself, it were Captain Hawkmoon, who had a small reputation amongst those who regularly used the western night routes and was always very gentle with children and the ladies.

---

[11]Nor, on certain unfortunate occasions, the length of it.

My reputation for gentility in general was what saved me the
first time I was captured by the Tramway Runners. My godfather
on the bench bound me over. The second time I was caught, my
other godfather fined me and bound me over again. On the third
occasion I was due to be sentenced when it was revealed that
as a minor I could not be tried. Another form had been discovered to save me. I was put on probation in the care of my parents. Although the ultimate penalty for choosing the tobyman's
vocation is hanging, these days most people look pretty toler-
antly upon a group who are generally perceived, like the pirates,
as colorful has-beens, in the category of Morris dancers and
muffin men, and popular feeling was on my side. We were not
brutes, most of us, but eloquent thieves taking considerable
risks to earn a living. The highwayman's resistance to the Universal Transport Company, before it was taken over by the benign LCC, is still remembered by the public which sees the
"Knight of the Line" as its most effective bulwark against ruthless Big Business.

Few ever suspected I was not a youth. I was in the profession
no more than seven months, but found the experience of considerable use in later life. My career was interrupted by my falling
in love with the man I was to marry, Count von Bek. Afterwards,
when I returned to London, the life was no longer attractive and
Turpin himself very circumspect about carrying on with it. Turpin admitted it was a relief to him when, after that eventful
couple of years, I decided to go back home and take the time
necessary to get my A-levels and a decent university place.

In consequence of some few words which the Sexton let fall, in the presence of the attendants, during breakfast, more perhaps by design than accident, it was speedily rumored throughout the camp, that the redoubted Richard Turpin was for the time its inmate. This intelligence produced some such sensation as is experienced by the inhabitants of some petty town, on the sudden arrival of a prince of the blood, a commander-in-chief, or other illustrious and distinguished personage, whose fame has been vaunted abroad amongst his fellow men by Rumor, "and her thousand tongues"; and who, like our Highwayman, has rendered himself sufficiently notorious to be an object of admiration and emulation amongst his contemporaries.

—HARRISON AINSWORTH, *Rookwood*

The Dependent, Roofless Man

"I am no petitioner, sir, nor am I to be patronized! I am your nemesis, the symbol of all you would forget. I am the *result* of your prosperity. My wretchedness is necessary to preserve your security and wealth. I am your starving mother and your slaughtered calf. I am the millions who die in misery every day. I am the millions unborn who will continue to die in wretched poverty, so that you can enjoy the best the world offers. I am the unseen need, the unheard shriek, the unadmitted wound, the unacknowledged victim. I have no soul to sell. It's already in bondage to the Lords of bloody Chaos! I can be a starving freeman or a fawning slave. No other choice is permitted me. Plan your vacation in the knowledge that the worst you face when you return is bankruptcy."

Whereupon my accuser flung the pound coin back at my feet. For a moment I thought I would have to fight him. If he challenged me directly, I would have no choice.

"I am that man!" he roared. "I am that roofless man!" And his red hands clutched at the air in anger, his red mouth sought to bite the elements, whatever was responsible for so much bad luck. He was dreadfully scarred. Every limb seemed at some time to have been broken. "It is not fair! If I were you, no doubt I should be as oblivious of my good fortune. But I intend to correct that injustice. One day you'll risk everything you value to save me! Meanwhile, I am planning nothing less than the complete crushing of those who have demonstrated that they are my enemies! And if I die painfully in the attempt, so be it!" His massive body moved in its rags like the California earth. Over his head he raised his makeshift club, which also served as a crutch, and he swayed upon his single leg, an angry tree.

Standing outside Thomas Cook's Bureau-de-Change where I had hoped to cash some old travelers checks I had found, I could think of no way of placating him. I had considered the pound generous; it was my last substantial coin. I bent to retrieve my money, wondering if that club would fall on me as I did so. But when I had straightened my back he was already hopping down North Star Road, towards King Edward Buildings, his anger redirected at two grinning skins who looked over their shoulders and broke into a lumbering trot at his approach.

That was to be my first of many encounters with the Roofless Man, as he styled himself. The second time I was standing, late at night, on the platform of Earls Court station, waiting for a Fulham Palace tram, when I felt a great thump across my calves. There he was again, raging and threatening with redoubled vehemence, as if he had been pursuing me for all that intervening time. His ruined face had the vital rage of a primitive carving. Happily, he was dragged off by the pack he was drinking with and my tram came in. I saw his glaring eyes, fixed on me as if I were Satan incarnate and he an exorcising priest, before I was drawn into the safety of the tunnel. He was familiar to me. I wondered if he were some old poker partner, changed beyond recognition by booze and madness. I could not remember.

I couldn't remember a lot about those gambling days. It had been a dream. I was so under control now that I would make a donation to a charity rather than buy a raffle ticket. The high days being over and the low days only a little higher than they used to be, I was continuously tempted to go back to work. I had been one of the best. Ask anyone in the West End about Jack Karaquazian and they'll tell you the same thing. They still refer to me as Jack the Greek up there, whereas I'm actually Egyptian.

My mother was English but my father, though he had an Armenian name, traced his ancestry back to the First Dynasty. He could also trace his ancestry back to Joseph of Arimathea and told my mother she was in direct line from the holy founder of Britain, Brut the Trojan, outcast of Atlantis. He had unearthed so many family legends, with only the slimmest of connections, that our ordinary history was lost.

When I went to learn the arts of the Casino, he was ashamed of me. Then he grew proud of me again as my fame spread throughout Egypt and, eventually, throughout all Islam. Soon I was the greatest *mukhamir* on the boats carrying the secret gambling fraternities up and down the Nile. By the time I was at the height of my local glory, we had received special blessings from every respected imam in the land and were perceived as heroes in defense of Islam. My own religious beliefs were a private matter and it was no advantage to me to say anything. We were all very devout in those days, at least publicly, and the rituals of Islam are comforting to one who has few other regular disciplines. Until my father, for political reasons, converted, we had always been Armenian Orthodox.

Only when things got bad in Egypt and I decided to emigrate, taking the great wind-powered schooner all the way from Alexandria to New Orleans, did I give up any outward display of religion. And now, in London, a citizen's religion is very much their own affair and not for discussion, so I am at last at one with myself in this ancient place of mystery whose history appears to be as old as the world's.

I no longer gamble. I can't even think of starting again. I lost the love of my life to gambling and that's why I stopped. Her name was Colinda Dovero. I lost her in Mississippi, to a stupid argument in which we both thought the other was bringing bad luck to a desperate game. I never saw her again. She wrote to me. She said she loved me. She was riding, she said, a lucky streak. She told me to follow her to the Mediterranean, to the little island republic of Las Cascadas. When I got to Port Sab' she had gone. When I gave up waiting for her there, I eventually reached London, learning to breath its thick, oily atmosphere as if it were really air.

∾

To me, arriving from traveling a tired world, London seemed possessed of an almost unnatural vitality. Her factory chimneys blazed through the night and smoked constantly, evidence of the success of her industry. There was work for all. The wealth of the city was everywhere in evidence—opulent architecture and extravagant public parks—and only the wretched *giorgios* and *blancos* of the East End, those pathetic remnants of their kind, knew the desperate poverty from which our own people had emerged to take the reins of power and social responsibility.[12]

Life is a river and each of our myriad destinies a tributary which itself creates tributaries, which in turn create tributaries. That is the nature of Chaos, forever creative, forever fecund, forever unchecked, the romance of entropy. The Singularity, which represents unchallenged Law, is determined to contain it. The Singularity's purpose is to control, to check, to contain and categorize. That was the chief motivation for their first superwoven carbon experiments. These resulted in the creation of the First Ether, a quasi-universe contained within a vast, impenetrable globe. They believed it their barrier against death. It did nothing to stop the perpetually blooming scales and branches of the multiverse, which is sometimes known as the Second Ether.

Within Law's cold heartland, rationality rules. Grids, graphs and flow charts are displayed on apartment walls as signs of domestic harmony. Neatness is elevated to a sublime virtue and called Order. Individualism is abolished and the very idea has become a blasphemy.

In the multiverse, variety blossoms. Each fresh action creates new branches, virtually identical to the last. Billions of branches later, significant changes begin to emerge. And even more billions later you find yourself in a different place entirely. But to all your billions upon billions of other selves, with each fresh destiny essentially identical to the last, you are unaware of the parallels simply because they are so close. Even if you glimpse a few aspects of the multiverse not your own, you cannot tell one from the other. Very occasionally a shadow alters a fraction and you notice it or you experience a frisson of *déjà vu,* but

---

[12]I speak, of course, of the "Gypsy Nation," or the League of Travelers, which so swiftly gained ascendancy when the power began to fade. In spite of what we had endured at their hands, we bore the *blanco* and the *giorgio* no ill will, and if it were not for us, the race would doubtless have perished entirely in one of its lunatic wars, for they are a feckless, cowardly remnant—save for the occasional lunatic like the so-called Rootless Man who was, anyway, like me, of healthy mongrel stock.

such moments are relatively rare. The barriers which separate
the realms are mass and scale, not time and space.

Some of us have an instinct for scale. We can let our bodies
make those subtle substantial shifts which allow us to step easily from one realm to the next. It becomes second nature to us.
We learn not to fear the transformations. As best we can we
take charge of our own destinies and walk at will the roads
between the worlds. No matter what translations we endure, our
essential identities always remain the same. We play the same
fundamental roles. We endure the same pain.

To give understanding and hope to all we experience, we invent
meanings, complicated rituals and ceremonies. To achieve some
semblance of linearity, we play games. We create the notion of
finite time and finite space. Of *karma,* of *yin* and *yang,* of *desafio.*
We define and redefine ourselves. We invent systems. We tell stories. We live stories. To make sense of a chaotic present we invent
ourselves a past and imagine ourselves a future. We identify with
our mythologies and create mathematics to explain them, which
some call the *algebra of desire.* We believe by this means that we
can shape our destinies. If conscious of our situation, we choose
roles, loyalties, futures, duties, and many of us become *mukhami-*
rim in the great Game of Time, playing our hands, playing our
parts and taking Chaos on her own terms. In the end it is the only
remotely bearable position for a person of honor.

As *jugadors* (or *mukhamirim,* as I prefer) we gently shape ourselves to suit our environment, in opposition to the Singularity,
whose impulses are to impose simplified models upon Creation,
call that Reality and punish or exclude all that fails to conform
or agree.

The Singularity's mighty engineering success, in which they
encompassed their universe in a globe of superwoven carbon, is
proof, they tell us, of their own righteous triumph, the long-
sought-after Conquest of Entropy. Their myths and legends are
chiefly to do with their moral superiority, their victories over less
practical beings, their mechanical know-how and the successful

imposition of The Grid on irrational nature. Their epics concern their success in controlling the hideous excesses of Chaos and especially (here I have some sympathy with them) countering the irresponsible actions of the Chaos Engineers.

The Chaos Engineers are creatures who have chosen to play the Game of Time against a background of colorful instability, a reality ever in flux, barely touched by Law, where they learn to survive and thrive through self-control, mental exercise and trusting to chance. This choice is perceived as irresponsibility, passivity and negativism by the Singularity.

To the Singularity, the ever-changing scales of the Second Ether are an abomination, an insult to the Original Insect, who applied geometry and impeccable economics to the matter of its own survival and endured where all others of its race succumbed. The yearnings of the Singularity are exemplified in their revered Original Insect, a creature of cold intellect dedicated to order. Singularity mourns complexity as if it were a blight. It embraces orthodoxy as if it were a cause. It believes that uncertainty is the root of all misery.

Through its stories and self-descriptions, each side seeks at least the illusion of control over its own destinies.

∽

Raving mad, the Singularity survives by excision, by refusing the information, by denying the evidence. This forces it progressively to simpler and more brutal action. More energy is devoted to enforcing the singular view, more of their society is absorbed merely in maintaining reassuring appearances, building forts and prisons. We, on the other hand, feel our souls and minds collapsing under the weight of so much information, so much evidence, so much accumulated consciousness, so much memory. How each of us copes with this prodigious inheritance is in itself the subject of an entire school of fiction, not to mention countless academic studies.

In those days I was, as I say, retired from the Game. It did me no special good. It found me the love of my life. And it took her away. I sustained myself as best I could, working chiefly in Soho, accepting whatever opportunities arose, so long as they did not involve tables or the track.

On the day I last confronted the Roofless Man I decided to take my acquaintance, Colonel Samuel Oakenhurst, up on his proposal to join the company of which he was commander. With a cocked hat, a diamond mask, a sturdy greatcoat, a decent horse and a pair of reliable dragoon pistols, I became a mobsman and entered his story as a minor character.

The noble scion of an aristocratic family, Colonel Samuel Oakenhurst had fought well for his country, but on his return from the foreign war discovered that his father was dead and his name disgraced. He had been lured into a trap and horribly disfigured in the fire which they believed had killed him. Now his step-brother, Sir Richard Fleetwood, held the title on Colonel Oakenhurst's Yorkshire estates. Disgraced and disfigured as a result of his own hot-headedness and his step-brother's perfidy, our hero was forced to give up the woman he loved and flee, adopting the name of "Colonel Jack," earning his living from the high toby and becoming famous chiefly for his exploits along the express lines of the Great West Road.

Oakenhurst was never known to remove his mask, no matter what the occasion. He was said to have sworn that he would wear it until she, of her own volition, asked him to remove it. She, believing herself deceived and betrayed by Colonel Oakenhurst, had meanwhile married a German count, who proved to be a ruthless adventurer. When I took up with the colonel, there was still some question of whether he would ever find reconciliation with the woman he loved, or whether she would have changed so much that she could no longer reciprocate his affection.

Though a subtle wit, an impeccable ironist and a perfect gentleman, Colonel Oakenhurst was fundamentally of a melancholic disposition and he nursed little hope for a happy ending to his own misfortunes. He was, however, well-educated and of unusual intelligence, so I enjoyed his company, even when the blue devils possessed him. The "blue devils" or "blues" was what we called an attack of gloom frequently only banished by the singing of songs and the drinking of strong waters.

"Colonel Jack" was considered second only to Turpin amongst the High Mobsmen of London. As Turpin held court at *The Six Jolly Dragoons*, Oakenhurst made Mammy Bappy's Pie Shop in Covent Garden his headquarters. No great love was lost between the two famous "Knights of the Line," though there was considerable respect. As far as I know, they never worked together. There was also a hint that Turpin and Oakenhurst were rivals for the love of the same gentlewoman whose estates were in Yorkshire. It was almost demanded of those two that they have at least a dozen romantic tales attached to them at the same time. In the circles I now moved, a good Turpin story or a good Colonel Jack story was often made of some other hero's deed, until the likes of Limehouse Ben Tokaruku could sing by heart at least a hundred ballads concerning each one.

Ultimately, of course, Colonel Jack's legend only survived by becoming absorbed in Dick's and Dick's is fading now and might not last here another century, unless some kind soul revives it and tells the tale on screen of Captain Turpin's heroic deeds and his famous Ride to York. I do not envy Sam his responsibilities any more than he envies me my conscience.

I loved to hear him tell his tales of the Second Ether. He had written them all down in expensive notebooks and loaned them to me. Here I read of Pearl Peru and Billy-Bob Begg, of *The Spammer Gain* and *The Straight Arrow* and Evil Freddy Force, all creatures transformed and mutated by their exposure to the Second Ether, all playing the self-same roles, until, billions upon billions of scales away, they intersected with their counterparts playing out mundane domestic lives in unremarkable circumstances. It struck me as amusing that the extraordinary beast called Quelch, that vast and powerful Dark Angel, one of Luci-

fer's most trusted Dukes, whom his master had also made a great
Lord of Law, claimed the identity of a humble housemaster at a
minor British public school who dreamed, when he dared, of taking
to the high seas and becoming a pirate. Somewhere, I supposed,
I, too, had an angelic self even now engaging in spectacular battle
to determine the destinies of the next million centuries. Instinct
told me I must soon play against some opposite number from the
Realm of Law, but I had no intention of leaving this existence until
I was certain I should not find Colinda Dovero here.

Contrary to rumor, I was never the famous "Colonel Jack."
Sam's taking my name for his alias was what we usually call a
coincidence. There are no accidents, as such, of course in the
Second Ether, but there are unusual translations.

By all accounts crossed in love, Turpin grew tired of his
threadbare life in modern London. The fog was bad for his lungs.
His work was over, his cause won. The LCC, a public corpora-
tion, had taken over the UTC and justice was achieved. It was
his only consolation. Nothing was the same any more, he said,
and it was not worth staying—especially since his legend had
declined. By remaining on at *The Six Jolly Dragoons* and watching it turn into a tourist fiction, he was only depressing himself.
In Australia they still remembered him for what he was and he
thought he might enjoy an outback life for a while. "Here," he
said, "I feel too large for the frame, if you take my meaning."

I watched Turpin walk his horse into the bowels of the RAS
The New Zealander as the old airship grumbled at her mast in the
Croydon Aerodrome. There was little positive about his decision
and I hoped to see him back. I waved the stately liner goodbye as
she rose with all her usual girlish grace into a sky of golden blue,
turning politely against the wind and slowly positioning her nose,
her auxiliary motors buzzing like bees as they held her steady.
With a massive bellow, her four Rolls Royce "ElektroThrusters"
began to move her rapidly up to cruising speed until she could
catch her steam. Then she was rising, light as a cloud, over Croydon's mediaeval rooftops, thrusting to 200mph, white vapor boiling

like ectoplasm off her gondola, the morning sun glittering on her reflective aluminum hull so that she might have been the legendary *Spammer Gain* herself turning to shifting mercury as she slipped into the wonders of the Second Ether.

∾

As it was, Turpin wound up in a traveling show which eventually toured America. His only job was to introduce and endorse the "Ride to York" equestrian act. Tom and Buck Jones, Tim McCoy, Buffalo Bill and others had all experienced similar undignified fates at some time in their careers, but their legends overshadowed such miserable realities. There are advantages, a certain security, in being part of a cycle. The worst moments can, after all, be learned from. But there is never more than an illusion of freedom.

After a brief rise in his fortunes in Texas,[13] Turpin returned to Europe. His exploits in Spain were the subject of another entire cycle and inspired Borrow.[14] They tell of such times in the mountains when a large gang of brigands lay in ambush for Dick and his companion *Tristelune*. On a narrow, steeply descending track, impossible to retreat along, it seemed they must be overwhelmed and killed.

His observant eye catching a glint of metal, Dick determined to carry the attack while he had some small advantage of surprise. Signing silently to *Tristelune* and allowing his sabre to hang from his wrist by its thong, he drew his dragoon pistols from their scabbards, murmured a word in his mount's ear and prepared himself. Then two vigorous touches from the spurs

---

[13]Where he built himself the elaborate chalet still known as "Turpin's Castle," above the Colorado River at Port Sabatini, a frontier town which itself had been named for a Cascadian original. The place is now The Cattleman's Conference Center, whose restaurant specializes in barbeque, an irony which Turpin, who began life as a butcher and whose first crime was cattle-rustling, still appreciates.
[14]See *The Bible in Spain; Lavengro; The Romany Rye,* etc.

lifted his horse, which went off like a cannon ball. The score of
brigands were taken completely off-guard, having already anticipated their easy victory, and fell back as Dick and his companion
advanced upon them at full gallop. Seconds later, four of the
villains were shot and down and two others went to their knees
with deep sabre wounds. Then the pair were through the trap,
and riding free scarcely before their antagonists had drawn
breath.

This was the Turpin I preferred to remember. For a time he
changed his name to John Palmer and retired to the pleasant
town of Richmond, in Yorkshire, where he painted water-colors
and had a famous collection of nineteenth century three-volume
novels as well as a complete run of *Ainsworth's Magazine*. I
myself yearned for isolation in those days and dreamed of building a tranquil villa, perhaps at Las Cascadas, on a headland
looking one way toward Africa, the other toward Europe. I
wanted a sea view blown by dry desert winds allowing every
detail of water, sky and land to emerge in full contrast, the colors
so vibrant as to seem unstable, impossible to fix or to record. I
entertained a dream that Colinda and I might one day live in
such a place. But first I had to find her.

∾

Aside from a couple of unremarkable encounters with Turpin's
famous colleague, Captain Hawkmoon, my criminal endeav-
ors went without any incident worth recording. A few greedy
merchants were stopped on the Heath and robbed. An express
or two was relieved of its strong-box. There were some merry
exchanges, a couple of derailments. Nobody was killed. Those
marks we knew to be hypocrites and cheats we stripped and
sent naked back to London.

Thus, happily, the old rituals comfort us in unsettled times.

4

There is a psychologists' variation of the game of
hide-and-seek: someone conceals a small object in
a large room, and you have to find it. You do this by
linking arms with the other man and walking as it
were casually round and round with him. As you get
closer and closer to the concealed object the man
who has hidden it, by subconscious muscular con-
traction, will tend to pull you away. You concentrate
your search, therefore, where the pull-away is
strongest. In a manner of speaking, this is how you
find Fowler's End—by going northward, step by
step, into the neighbourhoods that most strongly
repel you. The compass of your revulsion may
flicker for a moment at the end of the Tottenham
Court Road, especially on a rainy March morning.
You know that to your right the Euston Road rolls
away, filthy and desolate, blasted by the sulphurous
grit that falls for ever in a poisonous shower from
the stations of Euston and St Pancras. Take this
road, and you find yourself in a hell of flop-houses,
mephitic furnished apartments, pubs, and sticky
coffee-shops. Here, turn where you like, there is an
odour of desolation, of coming and going by night.
On the left-hand side of this heartbreaking thoroughfare, the fox-holes, rat-traps, and labyrinthine
ways of Somers Town beyond which the streets run
like worm-holes in a great chase northward again to
Camden Town. But you know that if you cross the
street you will wander for ever in the no-man's-land
that lies between here and the God-forgotten pur-
lieus of Regent Square and the Gray's Inn Road . . .

—GERALD KERSH, *Fowler's End*

The Affair of the Chinese Whispers

Wearied of so much excitement and peril on the road, Dick Turpin and Colonel Jack Oakenhurst had sought for a time to lose themselves among the crowds of London town.

"Isn't it wonderful, old friend?" said Dick, as they swaggered one afternoon through the gay throng that assembled at Vauxhall. "Such a jolly crowd!"

"It is indeed," replied Jack, "though I must confess I'd rather be riding up the Hounslow tramway with a spirited horse beneath me. Still, it's good to take another look at the old Gardens."

All around them were fashionable young men and women. The richly embroidered uniforms and dresses presented a picture in themselves. At certain points bands of music were playing lively airs. Uncommon trees and shrubs, brought from abroad by hardy travelers, imparted an atmosphere that was almost foreign to the scene. Dancing, card-playing, fencing, eating and drinking were all in full swing.

"There's one fellow over there I don't like the look of," said Dick in a whisper, after a time. "He has been watching us for the last ten minutes. And I know his face from somewhere— do you?"

Colonel Jack was much too alert to turn and stare at once at the stranger. He walked forward several paces; then stopped and stooped, pretending to adjust the silver buckle on his shoe. Out

of the corner of his eye, however, he was carefully studying the
man who had so attracted Dick's attention.

"Yes," he said, walking on again, listlessly. "I know the fellow
well. He is Simon West, one of the cutest officers they have at
Brixton Hill and truly Lord Barbican's loyal eye, ear and hand.
He was pointed out to me some months ago by a friend. But
happen he's not interested in us at all and is simply here in the
course of his leisure."

They strolled on. In one booth a Gypsy woman was telling the
fortune of a pretty girl whose swain stood at her side. In another,
cakes and gingerbread were being rapidly sold.

"Just as I thought," muttered Dick. "There's another of the
tramway grabs over there, another to your right, and one passed
us but a minute since. And, Jack, I like not all the interest we
seem to be causing. More than one man has looked at me more
searchingly than seems to be justified by the ordinary clothes of
fashion that I wear."

Almost unconsciously, and without a word passing between
them, the two friends made their way without undue haste to
the principal gate of that popular place of amusement. They did
not actually reach the gate, but turned on their heels a hundred
yards from it

"As I thought," mumbled Dick. "Simon West is there before
us with two or three of his watchdogs. I can pick them out, even
at this distance. And I swear that's a company tram at the stop,
no doubt packed with grabs. We must make our exit by some
other means. It was foolish of me, as I can see now, to suggest
coming here."

"The blame is as much mine as yours," replied Jack, simply.

Still without the slightest sign of hurry they made their way
along a path that ran beside the boundary wall. Pausing, as
though listening to the band which played from a pagoda, Dick
saw that the company runner was following them at a discreet
distance.

They moved on and halted again beneath the shade of a stout

sycamore tree. About eight feet up the trunk a thick branch grew and spread itself over the wall and out into the street beyond.

Without speaking a word Dick Turpin looked up at the tree, caught the eye of Jack Oakenhurst, and winked.

The next moment both highwaymen were on the branch. Dick had leapt first, followed by Jack an instant later. Standing quite erect, they could reach a more slender branch above them. Catching this in their hands to steady them, they side-stepped along the lower limb, passed over the top of the wall, stood for a second poised above the street and looked back into Vauxhall Gardens.

The sight that met their gaze only added speed to their movements. Running down the path was Simon West, three of his satellites beside him. That they were shouting out was obvious by the way in which the ordinary visitors were flocking towards them.

"Then we *have* been spotted!" ejaculated Dick. "And no grass must grow beneath our feet this time if we're to get away."

Dropping to their knees, the two highwaymen clutched the lower branch with their hands, allowed their legs to fall into space, swung there for a moment, and then let go, alighting softly in the road.

Away up the narrow street they sped, running like hares. From behind came already the frenzied shouts of their pursuers. Every instant counted now; every inch of their start was valuable.

Suddenly, at the roadside waiting for a fare, Dick espied a hackney coach, the driver sitting sleepily on the box seat.

Snatching a couple of guineas from his pocket, the highwayman held up the glittering coins to the jarvey.

"Grabs after us for debt!" he called, sharply. "The money's yours to drive away like lightning!"

In those days it was sport rather than anything to assist a man who owed money to avoid being arrested. Moreover, two guineas was a fare not to be missed at any time.

Galvanized into sudden life, the driver whipped up his horses

magically. Even as Dick had been speaking, Colonel Jack had
flung open the door of the coach and darted headlong inside.
His companion now followed him, and the crazy vehicle went
swaying up the street at quite a good speed, narrowly missing
an oncoming "Empress of Brixton."

Peering through a little glass window at the back of the coach,
Turpin could see the mob sweeping around the tram behind
them. Every moment the racing crowd grew larger. Tram Company Runners led the multitude. The name of Dick Turpin flew
from lip to lip. At the time there was a reward of one thousand
guineas offered for the capture of the notorious knight of the
line.

Another dozen yards and the driver of the coach pulled his
horses round a sharp, right-angled corner. Never slackening
speed, the animals raced on down this other street gaining temporarily upon the pursuers.

After passing about a score of houses they reached another
corner. Swinging round, the jarvey entered this third street and
was just whipping his horses into fresh efforts when Dick thrust
his head through the window frame.

"Slow up for a moment," he called, shrilly, "just enough to
allow my friend and I to alight. After that drive on at your best
speed."

Evidently the man had done similar work before. With his foot
pressed firmly against the dash board and his body straightened
back, he eased the pair of horses. Dick and Jack shot through
the door as though they had been propelled from a bow, Oakenhurst nimbly running a pace or two and closing the portal
with a bang.

Away up the street sped the empty coach now moving more
swiftly than ever. Dick grabbed Jack by the arm and led him to
an archway that, with his usual alertness, he had perceived. The
arch gave access to a court, and the two highwaymen hid as
much as they could in a doorway, pressing themselves back
against the stone pillars.

Another moment and the mob swept by, yelling, gesticulating, armed with staves and stones. Gaining in numbers every second, the crowd pressed forward, excitedly chasing the galloping coach.

"So much for that," remarked Dick Turpin, grimly. "It wasn't a bad wheeze, and it's come off very nicely. If ever I see that jarvey again I'll give him another guinea."

"I agree with that," responded Colonel Jack. "At the same time, I think we should be taking foolish risks if we walked abroad together just now. Where singly we might escape notice, in company we are almost certain to be spotted."

"A very wise suggestion," went on Dick, taking up the conversation. "As a matter of fact, I was just thinking of the same thing. Do you, Jack, leave here first. Keep to the back streets and make your way eastwards on the south side of the river. Then, choosing your chance, cross by one of the ferries and retire to Matthew Gale's at *The Six Jolly Dragoons* in Meard Alley. I will join you there later in the day."

Without another word Jack Oakenhurst went to the archway and looked eagerly up and down the road. He could see the extreme end of the pursuing crowd melting away in the distance, but the thoroughfare was otherwise completely deserted. Returning up the court Jack took Dick's hand and gripped it warmly. The next moment he had gone speeding away, walking like a man who has urgent business to attend to.

Dick Turpin waited for about ten minutes. In order not to excite suspicion, he walked once to the extreme end of the court. Then, with a final look up and down the street, he set off boldly, following in the direction that the crowd had taken.

The highwayman was wearing the clothes he usually affected, the three-cornered hat of the period, a semi-military tunic, knee breeches and tall riding boots. At his side was buckled a sword such as was worn by gentlemen. He excited no comment as he walked briskly through the streets.

Coming after a time to the approach of Old Westminster

Bridge, Dick looked about him carefully. There was not a sign to be seen of any of the Tram Company Runners, either in uniform or civilian clothes. The highwayman knew a great many of them by sight and prided himself on his ability to detect a "grab" at first glance. Now, however, he was satisfied that the Surrey side of the bridge at all events was not under observation, paid his toll, and set out to cross.

Watching very wistfully the pedestrians who approached him in twos and threes and also the trams that came rumbling over the bridge, Dick reached the high central part without the slightest suspicion falling upon his mind. Thoroughly convinced that he had thrown his pursuers off the track, once more he drew near to the Middlesex side of the bridge with jaunty steps.

He was far more than half-way across when first he saw the company officer Simon West. The fellow was leaning carelessly over the parapet of the bridge as though watching to see that his quarry did not cross the Thames in a small boat. A little further on there were three other loiterers that the highwayman felt convinced were grabs.

In such circumstances Dick did the wisest thing possible—he turned round and was about to hurry back to the Surrey side when he caught sight of a pair of Runners walking rapidly towards him.

At that moment Turpin felt like a man who sees enemies closing in upon him on every side. To all intents and purposes he was trapped. He thought he saw the dark blue livery of a police tram emerging rapidly from the traffic, her powerful team straining like race-horses.

Glancing over the bridge, however, he saw in the water below a rowing boat. In those days the Thames was far more a highway than it is now between the City and Westminster. Boats plied then at the waterside as one finds taxi cabs on a rank at the present time.

It was the sight of the boat that gave Dick his inspiration. In a moment he had mounted to the parapet and stood there poised for just the merest fractal of time. Looking round he saw that Simon West, a heavy pistol in his hand, was racing towards him, followed distantly by three of his satellites.

Even as Dick flung his arms high into the air and took off from the parapet with a graceful header Simon West raised his pistol, cocked the hammer and loosed the ball.

The bullet flew wide, but Dick heard it ping past him as he went swishing downwards through the air. Now the water seemed to be rising up to meet him. The next moment, with a mighty splash, he had gone down into the depths.

He rose like a fish. His head was well up and his hands ready to push off. Then he struck out with strong strokes for the boat, gaining his breath rapidly.

"Grabs!" he said laconically. "After me for debt. A guinea if you land me on the Middlesex side in three minutes."

The offer of such a magnificent reward stirred the waterman to heroic efforts. Shipping his oars he gripped Dick beneath the armpits and assisted him aboard. Then, with long, regular sweeps, he drove the boat at his best speed towards the shore. In those times, it must be remembered, there was no Thames Embankment—nothing but a pebbly strand on which rushes grew in patches.

One of Dick's worst troubles was that in that perilous dive he had lost his precious three-cornered hat.

Shaking the water from him as best he could, he extracted from his breeches pocket his purse and took from it a couple of guineas, which he laid upon the thwart beside the boatman.

"There's one guinea," he said, "for putting me ashore so smartly. The other one is for your hat. Come, is it a deal?"

"You can wager it is, good sir," replied the man.

"One more thing," went on Dick, snatching the headgear from the man's cranium—"make yourself scarce. There might only be trouble for you if the grabs got hold of you after this."

Without waiting for a reply, the highwayman stood up in the little boat, balanced himself for an instant, and then took a careful step forward. Now he was in the prow of the craft. He waited patiently till the iron-bound keel grounded and then leapt overboard. A little more water would do him no harm in his present state.

Fortunately there were not many people about on the river's edge. Looking towards the bridge, however, Dick could see the company officers just leaving the approach, running their hardest. The pistol shot had made a tremendous impression on those who were passing by, and now a second mob had quickly formed to chase after the highwayman.

By his daring leap Dick Turpin had gained at least three hundred yards on his pursuers. Wading noisily ashore he looked about him. On the opposite side of the pebbly beach were houses that belonged to the nobility. They had beautiful gardens that sloped down almost to the water's brink.

Running rapidly eastward for a couple of hundred yards, Dick swung suddenly into one of those gardens, vaulting a low fence and worming his way on hands and knees through a dense evergreen hedge.

Beyond the hedge there was a pleasant lawn, now completely deserted. Dick skirted round the lawn, taking such cover as he could among the shrubs. He passed close to the front door of the house and noted that no one seemed about. Down the main drive he went, through a second garden with pretty flower-beds, until he stood at the great entrance gates that led in from Whitehall itself.

As he glanced round Dick was delighted to observe no trace of those who pursued him. They must certainly have run past the back garden by now, though it would probably not be long before they were on the trail again.

Hardly counting the risk he was taking in his present dishevelled state, Dick marched boldly into Whitehall. One or two people gazed curiously at him as he hurried across the broad thoroughfare and slipped into the narrow turning now known as

Downing Street. Here there did not appear to be a soul abroad and the highwayman gained St. James's Park.

His idea now was to make a circular course round the neighborhood of Charing Cross and so gain Drury Lane. As he passed along Birdcage Walk, however, he glanced behind him, and to his surprise, saw the advance guard of the pursuing mob thundering in pursuit.

The Birdcage Walk in Georgian times was vastly different from what it is now. Tall, gaunt old houses lined the street on the west side—houses that were both fashionable and aristocratic.

There was one of these houses, however, upon which Dick had kept his eye for some time. Its windows were curtainless and never shuttered, the glass brown with dust, soot and grime. Occasionally the highwayman had known people to live in it for a little while, but never for long. As a matter of fact the house, for some reason which Dick did not know, was reputed to be haunted, and would-be tenants were now very careful to leave it strictly alone.

Once before when pursued Dick had thought of effecting an entrance into this abode of mystery. He certainly feared no man on earth, and it was hardly likely that specters could terrify him.

Now, with the mob behind him, and nothing ahead but a long, straight avenue, the highwayman decided at all events to try his luck. He did not propose going boldly to the main front door and seeing what sort of an impression he could make upon it. Instead he turned in through a little gate in the iron railings, descended some stone steps to an areaway and approached the servants' door, which was set in an archway beneath the portico of the main entrance.

Drawing his sword, Dick inserted the blade between the door and the frame at the point where the lock should be. He levered strongly, and yet there was no sign that the obstacle would yield.

And now Dick could hear the cries of the people as they thudded along Birdcage Walk. They could hardly be more than a hundred yards away. The fact that their quarry had vanished seemed but to hasten their footsteps.

Looking upwards rather anxiously, Dick saw that over the door was a narrow glass fanlight. Reaching up with his sword he first knocked in the glass, then hacked away the broken edges from the frame, and afterwards smashed the thin woodwork that divided the glass into panels.

Another moment and he had leapt sheer from the ground, caught both hands in the framework of the fanlight and pulled himself up strongly. With his feet upon an iron knob that ornamented the middle of the door, he paused an instant, then hunched his back and worked his arms, his head, and finally his shoulders through the opening.

There was not sufficient space for him to draw up his knees and pass through the mere slit feet first. Instead, he balanced himself as well as he could, worked his body forward and then lowered his hands. Feeling about, he could discover no projection that would give him the slightest support.

There was nothing for it, therefore, but to spread out his hands so that the palms might strike the floor inside, take the weight of his body momentarily, and, at all events, break his fall.

It was in this way that Dick, by no means gracefully, gained an entrance to the house of mystery, rolling over awkwardly and noisily and then sitting up to listen for any sounds within the building.

The light itself was very bad. In the gloom, however, Dick made out a flight of stone stairs leading upwards, and quickly ascended them.

He was now in the entrance hall on a level with the front door, and the light was better, though still very dim.

Up another flight of stairs the highwayman crept, and then paused to take his bearings afresh. And, as he did so, just as he stood there uncertain for a moment how to act, he heard a dull, grating sound below that was, to say the least of it, puzzling.

Straining his ears to their utmost, he listened. There was no doubt about the matter now. Someone had just fitted a key to the lock of the front door and was in the very act of turning it to gain admittance.

(To be continued in next week's number of The Black Bess Library, Dick Turpin and the House on the Borderland, on sale everywhere.)

I think before I get too involved, I had better mark your card by telling you the strength of how I came to be a thorough layabout. It is a very dodgey thing for me to try to explain for I do not really know how it happened myself.
—FRANK NORMAN, *Stand On Me*

My Early Adventures

I first met my future husband when I was engaged to deliver a message to him one morning, to where he waited upon a field of honor. I was in my role, of course, as Captain Hawkmoon. My message was that Colonel Jack was indisposed, on account of being a guest in Newgate, and would have to meet him at another time.

At dawn, with the Vauxhall Gardens deserted save for a few horse guards exercising their animals at the Westminster end, I crossed a mist-drenched lawn to find a foreign gentleman picking about at the grass with his sword point, an expression of impatient disgust on his heavy, handsome face, as if to say "I have other opponents waiting to be killed this morning." He seemed relieved, however, when he received my message and immediately sheathed his blade. "That friend of yours, captain, is addicted to the duel. Such as he make me deuced uncomfortable, for, while honor moves me to be here, I believe the whole affair to be a conconction to satisfy your friend's appetite for sensation. You may tell him, if it pleases him, that I am in no hurry to meet him and am prepared to wait until a convenient time when I am next in England."

He spoke an old-fashioned English, very precise, sounding as some at Court still do, identifying him as a German. I had not been told the gentleman's name, but I bowed and lifted my hat, telling him that I would convey the message to my colleague and that I was obliged to him for his understanding. My tone, I think, betrayed my agreement with his analysis.

"And may I know your name, sir ?" he asked, smiling.

"The name I use in my fraternity is Captain Hawkmoon," I told him. "I'm also of Colonel Oakenhurst's persuasion, so you'll understand my reserve."

"Perfectly, captain." He put out a hand, smooth and powerful in a lavender glove, and I shook it.

"I am Prince Lobkowitz," he said.

He asked me if I rode back towards Town and I said that I did. He invited me to ride with him and I accepted, covering my face and peeling off my mask.

His costume had something of a military cut to it, reminding me of Frederick the Great's. It was bulky and unfashionable, yet he gave it a manly elegance few of the season's dandies could have achieved. He had an air of practicality which disguised his rather spiritual nature. Though a man mostly content with his own company, or that of a close friend or two, his family background had provided him with a training which made him seem far more comfortable in public life than was actually the case. He was a Deputy at that time, of course, and working very hard towards the unification of Europe, which he saw as the only way to avoid future conflicts of the kind which had brought us all so close to ruin. In that short ride, listening more to his enthusiasm than his intellect, I fell in love with him.

He is best remembered now as one of Mozart's most understanding patrons and his family still occupies the old estates. It was as a diplomat and politician, however, that he had made his name in the world. He had helped negotiate some of the longest-lasting treaties in Europe and was dedicated to creating a world without war or inequality. He had labored rather longer than most at this. He was a realist but saw no reason to stop. There were always moments, he said, when his efforts seemed not to be wasted.

We would have parted in Whitehall, but since it was the appropriate hour, he asked me if I could recommend a coffee-house nearby. I told him that Meng and Eckers had recently opened a London branch. Their coffee and laudanum was said to be the best in England.

We took the makeshift path across the craters overshadowed by Nelson's tilting monument which at that time had not been restored. The War had been won for nearly ten years, but England would never fully recover from the cost of defending herself and her allies against the Nazis. Hitler's dreams were blossoming in the nightsoil he had made of all our lives. From his ranch outside Lima he still schemed against the civilized world, but his constituency now lay only amongst the mad and insanely greedy. As Mussolini had done in the end, Hitler placed more and more of his hopes in death-rays, superbombs, space-rockets, internal combustion engines and all the other grandiose paraphernalia of schoolboy fiction.

Lobkowitz began to talk about this as we rode along. At fourteen years of age, I was no doubt naive, but my intelligence and range of reference intrigued him I suppose. Hitler had despised the voters who believed his lies, he said, and that permitted every act of barbarism which followed. They had voted for their own lack of faith, he said. They had voted for the security of

death. Democracy was a fine instrument, but in the hands of the
cowardly, the greedy, the ill-informed and the poorly educated it
could become a foul travesty of itself. Hitler had emerged from
the failures of Weimar as surely as Weimar emerged from the
failures of a Prussian autocracy which the voters believed the
Nazis would restore in a modified form. The impossibility of
recreating a past could be observed in the obscene comic opera
of the Duce's Italy or the Fuhrer's Germany, both of which re-
gimes owed more to nostalgia than to need. There was always
an element in society that misremembered the past and turned
its particular period into a Golden Age which it then worked to
resurrect. Such elements had much in common with the kind
of Communists who sacrificed all humanity to the vision of a
perfect future.

Lobkowitz believed that it was the duty of those of us who
have experienced many realities, to educate—or at least guide—
those of us who have not. This paternalistic view was attractive
to me then but I have since revised it. My respect for that humane Prince, that exemplary Odd Fellow, was never however
diminished.

On that first meeting, we enjoyed a glass or two and a pipe at
M&E's and talked until the lunch-time workers began to come
in from the nearby offices. Our costume arousing a little curiosity, if not outright suspicion, we paid our bill and went into the
back stable-yard to collect our horses.

Although I have read *Mass Psychology* and other books on
the subject, I have never understood why the eternals are so
much abhorred by crowds. Individuals usually welcome our
presence.

∽

On going our separate ways, Prince Lobkowitz again shook my
hand. "It has been a great pleasure conversing with you,
sir. I hope to have the opportunity again." From his waistcoat

pocket he produced a slip of ivory. "I stay at the Royal Overseas in St. James's when in London and a message will always reach me." He was tactful enough not to expect a card in return. In my circles one's trade was inconvenienced by the advertisement of a permanent address.

I returned to Mammy Bappy's and gave the Prince's message to one of Colonel Jack's lieutenants. Not a cove amongst those cowardly clapperdogeons had possessed the bottom to carry the message himself. Then I made haste to *The Six Jolly Dragoons*, to tell Turpin of my new friend but instead was admonished for risking capture on such an errand. Associated in fiction, those two were never great friends in real life.

Sam Oakenhurst was in Newgate on account of the villainous Captain Horatio Quelch, who had turned king's evidence to secure his own freedom. That was the first I knew of Quelch and I disliked everything I had heard about him.[15]

Perhaps the modern roller-coaster now substitutes for the sport amongst young girls of falling in and out of love at breakneck speed. Perhaps the consequences are different now. I have not felt such unthreatened pleasure since those years, for I was lucky enough not to be taken seriously by the persons to whom I declared my passion. Turpin became a father to me with the introduction of his daughter, Mary Beck. Prince Lobkowitz was the guardian of my idealism. Not until I entered the Second Ether, as a grown woman, did I make Sam Oakenhurst my lover and by that time I had experienced the bitter *Game of the Raped Planet* and barely remembered the meaning of the phrase "innocent pleasure."

I would not see Prince Lobkowitz again until I was seventeen, at a reception in Mirenburg, where my husband's family had a house. Lobkowitz would rescue me from that unfortunate situa-

---

[15]When I met him, I was immediately charmed. After a few hours in his company I fell in love with him. But that's another story, familiar enough to readers who've experienced the peculiar pleasures of the shipboard romance or enjoyed Jane Austen's late nautical novels.

tion to see me safely back to London. Rudolf von Bek would be forbidden to visit me unless he wished certain documents to be made public and his fortune to be withheld. Prince Lobkowitz also obtained the divorce settlement by which I remained the Countess von Bek and kept a small estate in Waldenstein. My husband Rudy grew increasingly dissolute, found consolation in some other poor child, supplemented his income with various shady deals, and was eventually so rejected by polite society that he became a recluse in Italy, writing reams of self-aggrandizing memoirs which no-one would publish. Even the fascists would have nothing to do with him. After the War he went to America where he works for the arms trade lobby.

When Turpin had ridden off for York for the last time, I came up behind him at a more sedate pace, taking the Great North Road as far as Derby, then branching up to Manchester and the fells beyond. These days it is no more than a few hours drive on the motorway system but Dick was doomed always to follow his old route, to fulfill his expected destiny.

From Leeds I took the night train to Hawes. Although there was an infrequent local to Dent, I had decided to ride from Hawes since I wanted to relish all the familiar sights of my childhood and savor the pleasure of my homecoming. I hated waiting for trains or trams and it was easier to ride. I had wired ahead, of course, and had a horse waiting at *The Black Bull,* whose innkeeper Mr. Greenbank was an old friend of our family and had kept the Moorcock Arms near Chapel-le-Dale. He had seen my father two days hence. Sir Arthur had come to the post office to pick up his new rod. Obstinate as usual, he had refused to ride in but had walked to Dent and caught the horse-tram. Naturally, he seemed as fit as ever.

Mr. Greenbank asked me to give Sir Arthur his very best and looked forward to seeing me next week, when I intended to bring the horse back to him. The mare was one of our own, a five-year-old chestnut called Molly Malone, and she tossed her head and she stamped her feet and acted as if she remembered me.

She had all the spirit of Sheik, her sire, and Black Bess, her mother. I considered it a nice irony that so much Moorcock blood was now chasing about on the king's highway either escaping justice or pursuing it.

❧

Rather than risk the uncertainties of the shorter route on the Pennine Way, I chose the Mossdale Road, a scar of black granite climbing up into the brazen brass of Wensleydale's autumn hills. From a pale blue sky the morning sun glistened on gorse and made the limestone flash like pewter. At such moments, the fells were a fairyland of shimmering mystery, rolling endlessly away in all directions and the steep, narrow road the only certain ground, which Molly took with determination and the caution of familiarity.

A light rain had begun to mist the hills as, just before Moorcock, I turned off on the Tower House track over Thwaite Bridge Common and began the long sinuous climb up Swifthorn Fell with an East wind starting to feel its way through the valleys and come biting up behind me like an old dog, eager to see a familiar enemy. The wind caught my cape and blew it about my head and my hat almost came off. I had forgotten how loud and aggressive that wind could be and urged Molly to quicken her pace a trifle until we reached the ragged crest.

❧

Then suddenly the wind had fallen to a thwarted murmur behind me. I dropped down into the lush green of our family land just as the sun came through the rain and cut misty furrows across our deep grass meadows, reflecting the silver streams and limestone crags that made this one of the most beautiful valleys in England. A little white woodsmoke rose from the house's tall chimneys and as I descended, saluting the waving tails of our border collies, savoring all those familiar sights and sounds, I could already sense the house's warmth. I heard the dogs barking as they caught the sound of hooves on our old flint lane. The great, eccentric house, which had been only a Norman Tower in the thirteenth century, built on the ruins of an earlier Romano-Celtic fort, was settled on the sheltered northern shore of Corum's Tarn, whose sweet waters were the source of all we valued.

Hidden from any passing eye behind the wooded drumlins of the glacial dale, surrounded by tall trees rooted in the deep, rich bottom soil, Tower House still retains an air of unsurpassed tranquillity and is almost entirely neglected by the world's upheavals and progressions. Life is added to, as my father would have it, but it is not changed. I think this was in reference to his dish which can pick up a vast number of international signals, but he might just as easily have been justifying the installation of a new kind of septic tank. The house had its own modern generators, which utilized every energy saving idea, and my father had made the place entirely self-sufficient, with stocks of solid fuel and butane regularly replenished, though he was not dependent on them. Much of this was done after 1946, when my father had some idea of surviving a nuclear war.

Rounding a spur of rock, I had a view of our valley's entire length. About half-way up, looking north, I was delighted to see that the Gypsies had made a camp on the flat meadowland beside the meandering stream which began at our tarn. Their sturdy ponies were cropping the grass and the old Romany vans, which they always took with them to Appleby, were drawn in a rough circle, their shafts to the ground and their windows open for airing. Crimson and canary yellow, sky blue and apple green, silver and gold, the vans were older than most houses and their timbers had become iron-hard.

I reined in for a moment to breathe that sweet air. I had almost forgotten how extraordinarily perfect the sight was. Yorkshire abounds in such secret beauty, hiding her comforts behind the harsh granite and treacherous limestone, the coarse grass and heather of the high fells, so that no stranger's eye has ever coveted them. Summers in Morsdale were frequently fine and hot when other parts of the country were suffering the usual climatic disappointments. And we had grown used to mild winters. These days, my father loaned his lush fields to his neighbors, the Grisedales and the Cotters, for their sheep.

It was rare for snow to settle long in Morsdale. Up on the higher fells, above the limestone terraces, which marched down the sides of our valley like a Titan's staircase, the weather could be foul and sheep would founder in ditches and gullies and quickly die. There, where Old Man Meadley still plowed with horses and shot his game with a bow and arrow, one had to have the disposition of a dumb beast to live out the winter.[16]

∽

The sun was going behind the fell as I rode down into the welcoming twilight of our ancient home. Light drifted across the dark tarn and made it glow like solid gold. The long shadows of the house stretched into the copse and disappeared into the undergrowth. I crossed the little hump-back stone bridge over the stream where ducks stood in the shallows preening themselves. I caught the evening scent of rosemary, mint and sage from our herb garden. Then I had entered the cobbled courtyard, formed by our outbuildings and stables, and dismounted at the steps of Tower House, that beloved architectural mongrel. Somehow, the tall pile of miscellaneous turrets, roofs, chimneys, buttresses, pinions, rendering, brick, stone and slate, part fortress, part manor house, part Edwardian castle, had, over the centuries, acquired a fantastic elegance of her own.

My father opened the door himself. As usual, he looked at least twenty years younger, with an alert, unmistakable Anglo-

---

[16]Come Spring, he and his dogs were indistinguishable.

Saxon head, round, blonde and ruddy. His bright blue eyes filled with tears as he stretched out his arms to welcome me.

"My dear!"

I too was close to tears as I hugged him. I could feel all my confusion and uncertainty draining away.

"Good to see you, pa," I said.

My father led me into the warmth of the house. The eccentric passages and unexpected niches were familiar to me as were all the little staircases that led only to cupboards or landings, the passages which suddenly opened onto halls and drawing rooms, the apparent cupboards which were doors to the outside. My father liked to keep Tower House dark, lit mainly by large Benson copper oil lamps which reflected the metal and glass and polished wood of his cases. I recognized with a thrill so profound it felt like desire the powerful smell of woodsmoke, coffee, books and beeswax.

∾

My father's own library, full of his particular reference, was in the tower itself. If you walked in from the basement and looked up, you might just see him in the shadows high above on a railed gantry, sitting at his library table, thumping away on his Imperial 50/60 upright typewriter, with his gramophone playing Percy Grainger at full blast. But the house's library was where we had always met for tea and sure enough there was a big iron kettle on the trivet over the fire and a toasting fork and a two-pint brown teapot. His two Siamese cats jumped down from where they lay comfortably amongst a dozen open volumes and came to greet us before strolling to the fire and positioning themselves neatly on the Turkish carpet.

My father poured me a Hine. The warmth of the old cognac added to my sense of well-being. So little was changed. The Sargents and the Whistlers and my grandfather's signed Charles Robinsons and Anne Andersons were where they always had been on the green baize walls between the tall brassbound military cases glowing in the firelight.

He settled me down in my favorite Voysey chair. "I'll get the crumpets and the tea," he said. Although only in his forties, he had a sedate, rather settled air, yet his eyes and speech were as lively as ever. He was over six feet tall, graying, with a beard which could grow to fierce proportions but was now trimmed back in a neat Imperial, showing that he had recently visited the barber in Hawes. In my honor he wore his best tweeds, a deep crimson waistcoat, gold half-hunter watch and Albert chain, a rather noisy bow-tie, and his brogues. Usually he was content with a pair of overalls, some ancient Clarke's, and an army cardigan. I knew I was honored. As a rule he would not change for anything or anyone.

"Where's Mrs. Gallibasta?" I asked. His Catalan housekeeper usually prepared the food.

"Afternoon off," he said. "Pictures in Sedbergh. *Confidential Report*. Awful rubbish. But she's a fan. Didn't think it fair to ask her not to go since we weren't exactly sure when you were coming. She'll be pleased to see you, young lady. I haven't told her anything of what happened in London or Mirenburg. Your mother seemed very distraught. You appear to have been lucky."

"As soon as mum saw me, she calmed down. She's probably forgotten all about it by now."

I told him the story of my recent adventures. He listened gravely, asking the occasional question, toasting the crumpets on a fork and handing them to me to be buttered.

"The upshot is," said my father when I had finished, "that you got into a silly situation and might have lost your life and much else. That suggests to me that I haven't taken my parental responsibilities seriously enough. Unfortunately, I'm at a loss as to what else I should do."

"Nothing, pa," I said quietly. "I didn't even find the life especially exciting. The marriage was eventful, I'll agree, but I don't think I would have died of it."

"Well," said my father, "that's a relief, at least. You have a good friend in Prince Lobkowitz. I met him a couple of times in Vienna, just after the War, in the French Zone. I was impressed. He was working against the Nazis the whole time, you know. I invited him up here to fish. Nice chap. Knows about flies."

His crumpets forgotten, he got up and began to finger a book or two in the shelves nearest him. My father hated such situations. Where my mother would by now have declaimed and wept her way through a catalog of emotions, my father cleared his throat.

"So you're not going to do it again?"

"I don't think so, pa."

"Good," he said. His step lightened as he returned to the crumpets. His hands met like enthusiastic friends and he began to whistle the *Tannhäuser* overture. His mind was once more at ease.

The crumpets were delicious. I had forgotten the pleasures of Marmite. I said nothing of my intention to enter the Second Ether as soon as I had completed my degree. Instead we talked of Turpin's adventures. My father had followed Dick's exploits in his copies of *Black Bess; or, The Knight of the Road, Colonel Jack, Will Dudley, The Blue Dwarf* and, of course, *Rookwood*, but he had known none of the highwaymen personally. He lacked, he said, the initiative. He was glad to hear that Turpin, at least, continued to live up to his legend.

"It must be very difficult for a chap like that," said my father. "These days."

∽

A little while later, dressing for dinner to acknowledge my father's own effort, I slipped into my new Dior costume. I was a girl again.

The year was 1958.

6

He seemed to learn by intuition; for though indolence and procrastination were inherent in his constitution, whenever he made an exertion he did more than any one else. In short, he is a memorable instance of what has been observed, that the boy is the man in miniature; and that the distinguishing characteristicks of each individual are the same, through the whole course of life.

—JAMES BOSWELL, *The Life of Samuel Johnson, LL.D.*

Echoing Guns:
AVEC MA SOLITUDE

Jack Karaquazian deals seven hands of poker. His skin reflects a million cultures given up to the pit long before their time; his green eyes reveal a new kind of courtesy. Coolly amiable in his black silk and white linen, his raven hair hanging straight to his shoulders, his stoic back set firmly against that howling triumph of Satan, he is content.

"You're looking better, Jack," Sam Oakenhurst takes a practiced glance at his cards. "Your old self."

"I'm feeling it, Sam," says Jack.

The chaotic shrieks and clashes behind the plate glass window
of the Terminus Café rise to cacophony, the darkness is split
by milky rays, gold and silver, ruby and emerald shards. There
are wordless voices echoing into invisible heights as the big double-decker trams begin to roll in for the night. This is where all
the night tram-men come after work to play cards and eat before
going home to their sleeping families. Reflective scarlet paint
and glowing brass, toughened glass and varnished wood worn
to deep color by a million passengers and vivid, comforting ad-
vertisements for Oxo, Guinness and *The News of the World;*
great sparking rails, lively on their overhead wires, and worn,
glinting steel tracks, looping and counter-looping, leaving and
returning, crossing and re-crossing the streets of London like
the warp and woof of some maddened weaver.

There are some who argue that London's trams were created by
the devil to punish the poor, but others know that the Universal
Transport Company, which wields so much power across the nation, is actually the name of the devil himself. UTC demands the
unswerving loyalty and moral uprightness of its employees and
ruthlessly punishes all who fail. It is a major power in the land.
Neither Jack nor Sam has ever been forced to the decision which
brought all the other players to the Terminus, to give themselves
up to Lord Barbican the great patriarch of the Company, and be
forever cared for, or endure the humiliations of endless poverty.[17]

---

[17]Immediately after the War, with so much industry in ruins and South London
in particular having sustained an especially fierce bombardment for many years,
there were few jobs available in Brixton and a job with the tram company was
considered a job for life. The Universal Transport Company, known by the nickname of "The Grand Consumer" took advantage of the bombing to clear the
ruins and lay highspeed lines. When in 1949 the trams were brought under
public ownership by the new Labour government, who also set up the London
Transport Authority to coordinate the system of trains, trams, trolley-buses and
underground railways, the Company would continue to have this attraction,
while losing its more ruthless image as the Grand Consumer.

The Company owns everything in the surrounding area except the Terminus Café. Somehow the place managed to resist their attempts to buy it and in the end they seemed to forget about it or else had decided that it functioned as a harmless morale booster for the men. It was run by an Indian, Harry Jamset Ramsadeen, who, at school in England, fell in love with a fellow pupil's sister and got her pregnant. Banished from his family estates and his young wife cast out by her father, Bunter the Pie King, they had nothing to live on but his small allowance and the property left her by her mother.

∞

Long after he had become a dedicated alcoholic and his wife Bessy had left him to open a guest house in Worthing with her brother, Ramsadeen bought the Terminus Café with the last of his resources. He and his wife had tried several unsuccessful ventures in the hotel and catering business. His dream had been to run a jazz club, hers to own a luxury hotel. This place, with one vast grimy window looking directly into the main turning shed (so the tram-men could respond to an emergency) and the other out at a busy Brixton High Road, was successful enough. He spent most of his time with the customers, joining them for an illegal game or two. The drivers and the conductors liked the café because very few inspectors ever came in. It was the one place the ordinary tram-men could use which was not under the direct authority of the Company.

There was a certain sturdy defiance about the customers who went in and out of the Terminus that made them immediately identifiable as tram-men. The drivers, affecting non-uniform scarves and three-cornered hats, their brass badges polished by constant friction, had the huge muscular forearms of their call-ing, their faces tanned by the elements, their eyes dancing with the residue of the electricity which daily passed through them, while the conductors were paler and smaller men and women, fast on their feet and able to balance on a sixpence, usually very neat in their uniforms, very precise in their games.

There was no alcohol but Harry's own flagon of Vortex Water at the Terminus Café, and that was unlicensed, but most trammen did not drink much, preferring the hot mugs of strong tea and kvas which Harry's little wizened, twittering mistress, Madam Schultz, her bleached head in a permanent state of shock, served from behind her growling engines.

Jack Karaquazian never played to win much. He was too good a gambler for that. He was toying with the notion of joining Sam Oakenhurst on the High Toby. Sam's main income came from the profession he had pursued for the past eighteen months on the Great South Circular, holding up the special express trams which ran at night with bullion shipments and secret passengers. On good horses he and his mobsmen could outride any double-decker made, even the latest streamlined T-class racers.

Sam Oakenhurst sat back in his chair and watched the last tram, a jet-black funeral monster with silver trim, coming in to prepare for an early morning run to the South London Cemetery. It shrieked on its rails, braked at the Number Three turntable, then slowly rolled against the chocks while the conductors took their long rods and, from the platform on the upper deck, disconnected the chattering live rail as the vast turntable squealed into position, readying the tram for her dawn departure.

Usually the two friends operated independently—Jack offering Colonel Oakenhurst whatever intelligence he gleaned from casual conversation during the games and letting the highwayman do what he liked with it.

Frequently, however, they received no tips of a Special and then both would play. Several of their fellow gamblers would no doubt have refused to believe that the fierce tobyman, armed with a couple of shining barkers, was the same as the quietly-spoken gentleman who played so patiently at poker and Sam took something of a delight in the knowledge, listening to anecdotes in which he featured as the chief villain and enquiring

delicately for extra details of the victim's impression of him.
Jack chided him for this habit, warning him he'd give himself
away, but Sam was careless. "These honest fellows can't put a
Night Hawk together with a cove they play cards with. Tell them
the truth and they'd be angry in its defiance. We do them no
harm, Jack."

But Jack had grown tired of the game and his puritan heart
could be appeased no longer.

ᕫᕬ

Later, in the quarters they shared over the café, Jack Karaquazian stood sleepless, naked, staring out into the sweating
darkness as if he might see at last some tangible horror which
he could confront and even hope to conquer.

"Tomorrow," he told Sam, "I'll take my stuff back to Soho.
Will you come?"

(*She had been playing the accordion on the tiny stage of the
Egyptian Coffee Rooms, her long brown fingers flicking up and
down the keys, her strong, narrow arms pumping the bellows,
her little scarlet heels tapping out the rapid beat, her hips swaying to the old tunes, the sweet tunes of celebration and sorrow.
Afterwards, she had taken a glass of gin with him at his table
and told him lies about the miracles she had seen. She was from
New Orleans, she said. She had worked for a while as a chanteuse at* The Fallen Angel *on Bourbon Street.*)

Sam Oakenhurst understood the invitation to be a courtesy.
"I think not, Jack. My luck has been running pretty badly lately
and traveling ain't likely to improve it much. Sometime I might
go over to Hounslow Heath and try a turn at the gyvie trade."

From outside came the sharp hissing of steam, a rumble and a
clatter, the flash and snap of shunted trams in the hands of the
cleaners and mechanics. The huge double-deckers could carry two
hundred passengers or several de-luxe cabins, normally used on
the cross-country lines, and they were built to last. With proper

maintenance a tram from the great Feltham works at Preston
would run for a thousand years. Their performance generally
improved with age as they seemed to become increasingly organic, one with their routes.

∼

Jack took the first Number 14 tram going north, crossing Westminster Bridge in the white dawn as the city emerged darkly
from her silence and the cold, agitated Thames slapped against
the spans. The sound made him shudder. His thin coat admitted
the cold. It was early April. A pale drizzle fell into the brooding
waters and the first river-buses began to fire up, their dirty steam
spraying against the rain, drifting across the roofs of shanties
and makeshift offices, their stacks rattling and screaming. It
would be some years before the gaudy pleasure-boats returned
and he would find employment there again, playing the tables
between Greenwich and Kew. He sat in shivering solitude at
the front of the upper deck, peering through the rain-smeared
windows, praying that the message he had had the night before
was from Colinda Dovero. He had a small carpet-bag on the floor
beside him. He wore gloves, a scarf, a three-eared cap.

The tram left the desolation of the South Bank behind and
entered the concrete canyons which had risen from the ruins on
the Vauxhall side. The great slender towers of grey, black and
shaded glass gained an impressive beauty only in the fog or on
one of those endless, sleeting days for which London is loathed
by all but her natives. Much remained of Herbert Begg's white
paint and red-brick Queen Anne fantasies of domestic mansions,
in flats, houses and shops all the way to Chelsea. They had
escaped the worst of the flying bombs and the incendiaries and
remained a comfort to Jack Karaquazian, whose mother had
grown up on the Pimlico side and had lived in Swan Street before
the War. She had since moved to Kensington Park Square, behind Whiteley's domed department store in Queensway. She

wrote romantic fiction and was unavailable for months at a
stretch.

Jack dismounted at Victoria and took a hack to Dean Street,
where he still kept a flat. The place had belonged to a popular
jazz singer who had died there mysteriously one night, perhaps
of shock, during an air raid. There were no clues. As a result,
the place was regarded superstitiously by the local whores so
Jack had taken it at a very low rent. At present, Soho was one
of the few parts of London where he felt comfortable.

In those days, when England was still trying to recover from
the War and endured an austerity economy, the world was generally colorless. It was as if the bombs had obliterated most of the
spectrum, somehow absorbing that energy as they expended
their own. What little color there was came from the theatre.
The screens were all black and white, as was much of the print.
Color was suspect. It had come too vividly and for too long from
the sky. Londoners embraced greyness like a comforting blanket.
It was as much as they could stand. Color represented levels of
drama their nerves rejected. (*He remembered the world that had
been and the world to come. He remembered the shrieking walls
of color as their ship left Biloxi behind and plunged into the
unchecked Chaos of the Fault. Now he too feared color, gave
himself up to greyness and loved to be engulfed in London's fogs,
helpless in the grip of the grey city, sipping the sweet, weary
waters of defeat and lacking the courage for further adventure.
He placed all this firmly in his future, even though the intensity
of it continuously threatened to absorb him.*)

Even the stately trams were too lively for some Londoners
while the costumes Jack and his kind preferred were, except
in certain bohemian quarters like Soho, Hampstead or Chelsea,
anathema to the public at large. His traditional clothes always
drew antagonistic comment. Dash and style, unless in uniform,
were considered impossibly vulgar qualities in 1946. Romance
was associated with the Gothic horror of the Nazi war and the
only acceptable sentimentality was a bitter-sweet sense of loss.

It would be almost twenty years before the country recovered
itself enough to explode into the 60s, singing the songs which
led it out of the ruins of the Engineering Age and into a livelier
but less certain future.

Meanwhile, Jack Karaquazian got out at Dean Street, on the
corner of Meard Alley, and took his bag into the stale air of *The
Six Jolly Dragoons,* to enjoy a quiet breakfast and see if anything
much had changed. At that time in the morning, only the pot
boy was present, reluctantly serving Jack some stale coffee and
a couple of decent croissants and remarking significantly that
the last customer had just woken up and gone home.

The place stank of sour beer and sweet, heavy ope. Jack had the
idea that he was eating someone else's breakfast. He asked after the
proprietor, Old Man Smith, that sweltering mound of swarthy, hairy
blubber who was landlord of more than the *Dragoons,* one hand always on his cricket-bat, the other deep in his filthy overalls.

"Not so bad," muttered the pot-boy, glancing furtively about
as if Jack might invoke his terrible chief.

Jack finished his breakfast and got up, placing half a crown
on the table. "I'd better pay a visit to the privy," he said casually, making a sign. The pot-boy knew this code and nodded him
towards the cellar door. Jack picked up his bag and descended.

∾

Beneath Smith's cellar floor was a staircase leading deep into
Soho's unmapped catacombs, the so-called Huguenot City
which had once sheltered thousands of refugees. If you followed
Smith's directions, you eventually came to a wooden door. With the
appropriate introductions, you were admitted. And here, in Smith's
Kitchen, the most notorious thieves' den in Europe, all London's
mobsmen, all her kings and caliphs of crime, congregated in uneasy
truce beneath sputtering naphtha, yellow gas and moody candela-
bra. There were a score of dark, labyrinthine rat-runs leading in

and out of the place but the passage from *The Six Jolly Dragoons*
was known only to a few High Mobsmen, all gamblers.

The peace of the Kitchen was rigorously enforced by Smith
and his army of tatterdemalions. "I employ scum," Smith would
explain, "because only scum is stupid enough to be trusted. I
trust 'em 'cause I can second guess 'em." He gave power to the
weak, knowing they would enforce his will all the more rigorously because of their uncertain hold on their own authority.

Smith allowed no weapons, no fighting, no raised voices, in the
Kitchen. All were welcome, to eat and plan and fence their goods,
but Smith demanded his guests behave like "lays an' gen'men,"
as he put it in English, or "Autem morts and romes" in canting
tongue, which he preferred. He had a team of ex-commandos to
back up his rules. To ease his inner self and to give a better tone
to his place he employed a small orchestra to play soothing airs.

Sometimes Smith would sit in court at his desk, at the far end
of the great main cellar, whose dimensions had never been properly charted, buying the best of the goods brought in and never
budging on the price he offered. Few cursed him for it. He was
fairer than most fences and didn't have to be.

Smith's saturnine looks, the gold rings in his ears and on his
fingers, his discreet tattoos, all marked him for a Gypsy and
explained his only indulgence, the three-piece band, fiddle, accordion and piano, which performed every evening on the little
stage beside the main bar. The fiddle player was always the
same, a tall, impeccably-groomed albino whose smoked glasses
hid dark pink eyes which stirred with a kind of permanent irony.
The rest of the musicians changed frequently and always came
to regard their leader with something close to terror. The albino
wore perfect evening dress, his silk hat and cape beside him on
a chair, and played with all the confidence and beauty of a
trained concert performer.

Jack recognized some of the tobymen who were here tonight
and were close acquaintances—Sixteen String Jack Duval, so-
called for the number of ladies' colored silk garters he wore

upon his own handsome calves—Sheppard the Escapologist, all aggressive muscle and glowering bulldog humor—Moll Turn-around, who had begun life as Michael Turner and given up the life of a pharmacist for that of a painted metaphor—Claude Duval, Jack's charming brother, whose shy pistols had won many a heart as he delicately coaxed a purse from a muff and a ring from its secret pocket—Tom King, Turpin's greatest friend, still in his grey greatcoat as he raised a manly toast to his happy doxy—and Will Dudley, the Scarlet Rider, in his hunting pink and his black leather breeches, boyish and vicious.

The Tobymen and the High Mobsmen, aristocrats of their pro-fession, greeted Jack Karaquazian as an equal. Most of them knew him as Jack the Greek, though some preferred to call him Gypsy Jack and said he was pure Romany, a refugee from Euro-pean fascism. It was politic for Jack to share a bumper or so with them, before continuing with his business here.

The band had finished by the time he shook comradely hands with his peers and there were few other customers left in Smith's. The albino was packing his fiddle away and recognized Jack as he walked up. There was a certain tension between them as if, in other circumstances, they might have embraced.

"Monsieur Zenith," said Jack, warmly enough.

"Mr. Karaquazian." The albino paused, adjusting his white cuff like a card from his black sleeve. His index finger gently stroked a silver link. "She came in two days ago. She wanted a job. I told her Clara is still with me. She said she didn't want Clara's job. She would sing. But we don't really need a singer in this place, Jack. You can understand?" After offering Jack the silver case and being refused, "Monsieur Zenith" removed a small, brown cigarette and tapped it at both ends before in-serting it between pink sensitive lips. He lit the cigarette with a modern gas Dunhill bearing a discreet monogram. He knew Jack well. They had shared a past or two together.

Zenith's skin was translucent, the color of fresh bone, and his eyes burned with the depth of cut rubies. His milk-white hair was

combed back from his handsome brow, his tapering ears gave him
an almost demonic appearance and his smile was a thing to fear
and to adore. He turned up the collar of his black car coat, preparing himself for the night. He fitted his fiddle case under his arm.

"Did she give you an address?" asked Jack, uneasily.

"A phone number." The Waldensteiner was rumored still to
own an estate near Mirenburg. He was a prince of that tiny
country, now in the fatherly hands of her Communist liberators.
He drew one of his visiting cards from his waistcoat. On the
back she had written, in her familiar careful script, *BAR 2347
AFTER SIX.*

"She was adamant I not phone before six." Zenith donned his
silk hat and, with a peculiar, wistful smile, a graceful flirt of his
cloak, left by his favored exit. "Adieu!" The iron door slammed
shut behind him.

Sometimes it was unwise to carry written messages within the
Second Ether. Only in the Realm of the Singularity could the
symbols be relied upon to travel unchanged.[18] Even now there
was no telling the number was correct.

Jack's hand trembled as he read the card, committing it to
memory. He prepared himself for disappointment. This was not
the first time his hopes had been raised.

After a moment, he picked up his bag and signaled farewell
to the invisible Smith. He left by a small, circular door under
an arch then entered the ill-lit murk of the "tubes" to make his
way across swaying wooden galleries and through noisy sewers
to the Soho Square exit.

∽

He emerged into a chilling fog which hovered around the roots
of tall, black plane trees in which crows huddled, their an-

---

[18]It was their proud boast.

cient eyes regarding the busy shoppers and workers with cold
disinterest. From Soho Square Jack entered the alley beside the
Huguenot church and slipped into Foyles' bookshop on the corner. Threading past vast tables of fiction, he stepped inside the
trembling lift cage and took it, inch by groaning inch, to the top
floor. He had decided to start with Philosophy but he had a
feeling he would eventually find what he needed in Alchemy or
Advanced Mathematics.

Anything was better, for the moment, than hanging about in
his flat. He wanted to kill as much time as possible before six
o'clock. After a while, he settled for Wittgenstein's latest, spent
a complicated time paying for it and walked rapidly round the
corner to his own flat. Dropping his bag in his door and resisting
the temptation to go in and phone, he went back to Leicester
Square, rather mournful at that hour, and then strolled over to
the drab citadels of Long Acre, her busy word factories. From
there he made slow progress through the rich air of Covent Garden's afternoon fruit and flower market to Maiden Lane, to enjoy
an early lunch at Rule's, one of the few old-fashioned restaurants which served game and still welcomed his kind. It had
been in business since Turpin had first ridden the heaths and
highways of the Home Counties.

The game-pie was perfect and a perfect claret with it. Later,
as he read *Philosophical Investigations* and sipped his Hine,
Jack half believed that Colinda Dovero might walk in just as she
had on a dozen occasions when they had agreed to meet here
and she had been late, apologizing with an affectionate, dis-
missive kiss. The book, he realized, was in reality a substitute
for her company. They had some of their most intense conversations here, over the jugged hare and the rare venison. "There's
an endless progression of cause and effect," she had said, "so
that theoretically every breath one takes becomes a moral responsibility." Hare and redcurrant jelly, with red cabbage and
roast potatoes was her favorite meal. One Spring she had made
him go with her to the house of an old lover, near Oxford, so

they could watch the hares run and box through the green corn. She loved them, Jack thought, the way a lioness is supposed to love the gazelle she brings down, purring rapturously at the moment of the kill. Alive or dead, they brought her joy.

At another time she said: "We're obliged to tell our stories and often to act them out. It is how we all survive. Language defines us; it can ennoble us or corrupt us. Language, dear Jack, determines the human condition." In those distant days he had not been convinced by her arguments, but he had loved the intensity of emotion she brought to them.

After a while, when he was the last customer, he paid his bill and made his way out of the warmly polished grain of the restaurant into the narrow gloom of Maiden Lane. The grey rain was still falling. He turned up the collar of his short black coat and took the short cut through the grass-grown rubble, on which yellow daisies and purple fireweed almost flourished, down to the Strand where he dropped in to the Little Savoy Theatre and watched the latest Pathé and Movietone newsreels, some Betty Boop cartoons and a short feature about the miracles of reconstruction. When he came back out into the Strand, the office workers were beginning to crowd onto the trams, heading for their suburbs.

It was dark. The gaslight warmed the thickening fog. It was five forty-five.

He knew a moment of panic, which he controlled. She had said after six, not at six. He could phone her in a couple of hours, perhaps. Meanwhile he could go to the pictures and kill time there. He had yet to see *The Third Man,* though its zither theme was never off the wireless.

Jack crossed the cat's-cradle of intersecting tramlines, quickening his pace until he reached Leicester Square and, darting through Newman Court, which stank as always of urine, crossed Shaftesbury Avenue and reached Dean Street just as St Ann's, Soho, was striking six. Meard Alley was passed, and *The Six Jolly Dragoons*, and then he had reached A-One Braid, the trim wholesalers, their windows full of faded ribbons, and let himself in to the door beside it. He walked up musty stairs creaking beneath the worn Axminster.

His flat was on the second floor. The other two flats were occupied by quietly-spoken older prostitutes who would always offer him a cup of tea if they weren't busy. They dressed and behaved very much like the personal assistants of executive businessmen. Without consciousness, they responded as if every word he spoke to them received their deepest sympathy and attention. "Good morning, ladies," he would say, raising his hat. "Oh, yes, dear. Oh, yes, it really is," they would assure him, as if they had just learned of his bereavement. But they were good neighbors. He tried to show them the courtesy of keeping clear of their customers, who were inclined to bolt if they saw him.

On the third step of the single flight of stairs, Jack hesitated, pulling off his gloves. He considered smoking a pipe of ope before he phoned, but he'd need a clear head if she actually answered. He had considered a thousand possibilities, but very few did not involve his disappointment. He felt for his keys in his pocket and selected the Banham. He still hesitated. He was shivering. The fog had got inside him, he thought. Still reluctant to advance, he reached into his coat and searched for Monsieur Zenith's card. He again felt panic when he could not immediately find it. Then his fingers touched the thin ivory and he drew it out. He scrutinized it. As he had guessed, the numbers were not quite the same as those he had memorized.

Swiftly Jack hurried up the remaining stairs. He sensed a date with destiny.

But observably take notice, for here is as emi-
nent an example of their subtlety as any ever the
Devil enriched their knowledge with; if you are
robbed in the eastern quarter, pursue them not
in the direct road to London with Hue and Cry,
for by some other way they are fled; but haste to
the City, and in Westminster, Holborn, the
Strand and Covent Garden search speedily, for
there they are. If northward they light on you,
then to Southwark, the Bankside, or Lambeth
they are gone; and when you find anyone, seize
all with him, for they are all companions that
are together.

—RICHARD HEAD, *The English Rogue*

Distant Thunder: Comme Moi

Only after she had answered the phone did the Egyptian realize
how terrified he was. He had dreamed of her for so long.
She was his ideal. But how much of this was imagination? He
recognized her voice, of course, but there was an unfamiliar note
in it. She had just got in from work, she said. She was out of
breath. How was he?

"Fine," he said. "And you?"

"I gather you're in London."

"The West End. Soho."

"I'm in Fulham. At least, on the border."

"Baron's Court," he said. "The phone number area."

"Well, not far. Sporting Club Square. Do you know it?"

"A short walk from Brompton Road Station." He named the nearest tube. "I had some friends lived there for a while."

"Really?" she said.

"Yes," he said. "They moved to Dorset Street."

"Do you want to meet?"

He heard a slightly impatient tone. He had a feeling she was trying to hurry him up, as if she expected someone to come in and catch her while she was talking.

"Now?"

"How about tomorrow?"

"Where?"

"You might as well come here. If you don't mind."

"You'd better give me the address."

It was in D'Yss Mansions on the north side of the Square. Number Seven.

"What's the best time?"

"Eight? We'll have a drink and eat locally. Is that all right?"

"I'm looking forward to it," he said. "You're well, I hope."

She made an indistinct response, as if distracted by something, and put the phone down. Slowly, he replaced his own instrument. He suppressed an urge to retch. There was bile in his throat. He was astonished by the intensity of his reaction. He smiled at himself. He was more alive than he had supposed.

Before the War, he had followed her from New Orleans to the independent island republic of Las Cascadas, between Spain and Morocco, in the expectation of being reunited. But when he eventually got there she had gone. Some urgent business, she had said in her note, a matter of duty. She would be back in a week.

∾

He had waited for three and a half years before going back to London in June 1939, as Spain and Italy began to draw Los Cascados into their conflicts. He stayed with his mother in Bayswater. She was afraid Hitler was going to start something. She thought he might even conquer England. In January 1940 his mother had returned to Aswan. There, she had written out the war. Her stories of hardy housewives and brave sweethearts raised the spirits and filled the imagination of thousands of war-weary readers of *Woman's Weekly* and many a lonely matron wrote to say how she could not have endured without "Micheline Arlen's" heartening tales. Thus, like the singer Gracie Fields in Capri, Jack Karaquazian's mother was able to justify her self-exile as patriotism.

Jack had done well for himself in those months immediately before and during the War. People loved to gamble and were careless of the stakes. Only as the War intensified did Jack begin to question his means of making a living. He limited his games to the Terminus and became a Civilian Volunteer. In this he was at odds with Sam Oakenhurst who was of the opinion that one's duty during wartime was principally to one's own survival.

Sam had grown cynical since his family had been cheated out of their Norbury estates, in the path of a Universal Transport Company extending its pitiless lines to the Croydon Aerodrome and beyond. Lord Barbican had boasted his express trams would soon run all the way to Brighton. He drew up plans for tunnels to take his long-haul cabin trams to France and link up with high-speed European systems.

Colonel Oakenhurst had dedicated himself to a career of profit and revenge. "Barbican would knit up the whole world with steel bonds if he could," said Sam.

Jack, dragging living, bloody bodies from the blazing rubble the Nazis had made of small people's dreams, listening to a

child's screams mingling with the shrieks of the descending
rockets, had discovered an unsuspected inner strength, a profound core of self-respect. Like many in those days who had not
considered themselves heroic, he had been astonished and quietly proud of what he had found. He continued to work throughout the War, always in the forefront of the rescuers. That was
how he had first come to Sporting Club Square, helping the nuns
out of their fiery retreat.

Like St Paul's, the Square was miraculously unscathed. Her
towers were raised against the inferno like the dreams and hopes
of the people. Never once did her anti-aircraft battery cease its
constant firing, while everything around her, including the famous Queen's Club Tennis Courts, was a roaring frenzy of incendiaries. Walls were scorched, windows were blown in, but
Sporting Club Square survived. Her turrets and domes, her
towers and buttresses, that celebration of the best idiosyncratic
English creativity, made a bizarre silhouette against the flames,
as if the capital of fairyland repelled all Hell's howling armies.

Jack had been glad when Chancellor Speer had signed the
surrender, ordering all troops to lay down their arms, saving
Germany from further destruction and allowing Poland to demand a Soviet withdrawal and preserve her independence. With
Hitler and his people already aboard the last of his Ultra-Zeppe-
lins, leading the limping remains of his aerial fleet towards the
more hospitable South, the disappointed Soviet forces had
turned their attention to the East. The newspapers predicted
that within another six weeks, the Soviet and Chinese Communist allies would be raising the red flag over Tokyo. He hoped
that would mean an end to the entire War.

∽

He had planned to return to Las Cascadas, restoring herself
after Fascist occupation, where he had been invited to help
run the Casino. That part of the Mediterranean was enjoying a

relatively quiet period and he had always preferred the climate.
The ports were wealthy again. He had heard that the arms traders had returned to their old base, the harbor of Port Sab'. This
time they were supplying most of the anti-colonial fighters up
and down the North African coast. They loved to gamble. Captain Quelch was their acknowledged leader, an audacious block-
ade-runner and a daring sailor. Quelch's old rival, Sam
Oakenhurst, who had been at one period a privateer, had suggested their present partnership.

For a second Jack entertained the notion of Colinda marrying
him and returning with him to Las Cascadas and perhaps re-
opening the Casino. Almost instantly he suppressed the fantasy.
Though impatient of self-dramatization, he believed at that moment he might die if disappointed further.

He spent the next day preparing himself, dressing in his ele
gant best, anxious that she should form a good opinion of him.
He had no trouble remembering her slender, tapering face, her
extraordinary eyes, her repertory of gestures, her expressive lips
which could never disguise her moods, the swing of her hair,
the subtle bitter-sweetness of her Mitsouki. Everything she had
worn had touched her body with almost supernatural lightness
Her movements were unstudied, rapid and graceful, and when
she was at rest, she smiled. She had revealed none of the volatile
neuroticism he had half-expected to find in someone who followed her calling.

Her self-contained tranquility, her optimistic confidence in the
future, won him to her cause. He had followed her twice into
the Mississippi cedar swamps, found color and lost her. Did she
remember anything of that? For his own part, he remembered
almost every word of their conversations, every altered note her
breath made, every movement of her hand. Memory and imagination had been for so long the twin theatres of his pain that he
had learned to ignore them whenever possible. Yet he seemed
to recall that she had once loved him for the quality of both.
Would she find him wanting? A shade?

∼

Shortly before he was due to get his taxi, Jack had an attack which took some time to control. When he had finally regained his breath and his composure, it was almost eight o'clock. He picked up the phone to dial and tell her he would be late, then he changed his mind. He was afraid someone else would answer. He preferred to enjoy a few more minutes of hope.

He hurried downstairs and flagged a taxi. The big cab cut silently across Mayfair with unusual speed, crossed the park, made an illegal turn into Kensington High Street, and was held up for a few minutes by a tram whose trolley-head had come adrift and had stopped traffic while the conductor tugged lightly on his ropes and, with his long oak pole, expertly guided the head back to the wire.

The taxi's transformers hummed impatiently. It was still not eight. Jack found a packet of M&E *Flamingo Club* in his pocket and extracted a cigarette, adjusting himself more comfortably on the long, leather seat. He took his time to light up.

Soon the taxi was moving again, making good speed through the bleak yellow brick canyons of North Star Road almost as far as Lillie Road, down into Greyhound Gardens, still in bombed ruin, right at St. Andrew's Church, completely restored and only a few beams showing signs of the fire, and then through poor old boarded up Margravine Crescent to the top end of Sporting Club Square and that sudden explosion of Art Nouveau wrought iron, the finest produced at Begg's Colchester works.

Described unkindly by cyclist-poet Philip Larkin as cast from the distracted doodles of a romantic schoolgirl, the gates of Sporting Club Square were a little more elaborate than the ironwork which Begg had made for the Tsar's never-completed Peasant's Cottage, planned as a Siberian retreat where the Romanofs could commune with nature and safely hunt.

Several residents had remarked on the rather uneasy "Russian-ness" of the square's ironwork, but Jack loved its continental sinuousness, its invitation to complexity. To him it was like a map of the multiverse, opening up further worlds to explore, describing fresh realities, all of them terrifyingly unfamiliar. For luck, he made the sign of the jackal. Then he paid off his taxi and passed through the gates.

ᚷᚩ

In those days, just after the War, the Square was at her seediest. She had housed hundreds of refugees and cared for thousands more and it was as if she had exhausted herself, had let herself go, had had no time to consider her appearance.

Of course, she was as eccentric as ever—twenty-six unique mansion blocks, mostly of red brick, each with fifteen to twenty flats, each flat different, each long-established tenant as idiosyncratic as the architecture—surrounding the tall plane trees and lawns, the tennis-courts and exotic flower-beds which no amount of smoke and ash had managed to darken and at the center of which the huge, black Duke's Elm spread her massive limbs in eternal defiance of every threat man or nature could devise. In common with many others during the raids, I had begun to identify that enduring tree with God and on more than one occasion had prayed to her as intensely as had my Anglo-Saxon ancestors.

Past the Arts and Crafts gothic and the Oriental domestic re-vival, past flourishes of flying buttress and elaborate filigree, stained glass and pink marble, minarets and spires, domes and turrets, echoes of half the cities in history, I made my way to D'Yss Mansions, whose spikey towers and brooding galleries always reminded me of a set prepared for some expressionist *Hamlet* and whose inhabitants had a reputation for lung-disease, absinthe-addiction and erotomania.

I had been disturbed to learn of her address. I hoped that she did not live there by choice.

However, as I walked up the dark marble steps towards the rank of brass bells and looked for Number Seven, I already feared that something was wrong.

∽

Years later, as a guest of Colonel Sam Oakenhurst, who was then in the service of the Egyptian Government, I remembered that moment vividly as I stared at the marble floor of the tea room's balcony and noted that it was exactly the same shade as those steps. There was a brighter slash, running like lightning through the swirl of pattern, and it was the other's twin. In her Golden Age, Aswan had flourished with quarriers and masons, many under royal patronage, their names famous throughout the Empire. Was it possible that the stone for Sporting Club Square had been quarried from the same seams as the stone for the Colossus of Ozymandius?

"This is the way the world ends," says Sam, his face turned up to a cloud, craving the moisture.

"My God, Jack, how you welcome rain when it comes! You never dream of sunlight the way you dream of rain."

He smiled sideways at me. "We had no rain at all, you know, before they flooded the valley. Now we have a little."

And so little, I thought. I longed for a New Orleans noon swamper or even a drizzling London mist.

There was no work for a gambler these days in Aswan, where one of the three greatest Islamic schools had been and where I had learned much of my trade. The hotels had all been given over to the deserving poor who, to their credit, kept them well and even retained much of their original character.

The only operating hotel dominated the heights above Aswan. The Cataract was a magnificent example of the Birmingham iron-monger's art, a Moorish-Ottoman fantasy which somehow gave the impression of solid good taste. Long and seemingly low, the vast building might have been one of Fairbanks's more ambitious sets for *The Thief of Baghdad*. The hotel was still in the hands of Cook, the famous Agent, and tolerated by the State which brought its favored visitors here to show off the advances of socialism.

We lounged in our big, wicker chairs, lazily absorbing one of the most magnificent views in the world as the Nile danced out of Nubia over smooth, grey boulders to fall noisily down the first and second cataracts to the sudden tranquility of wide water where smooth feluccas, their white sails bulging with new wind, scudded between the ruins of one dynasty and the foundations of the next.

My wife had gone to the market with Countess Rose von Bek, who was here in some official archeological role, but also to meet her lover, Sam. It had been doubly convenient for Rose that my wife and I should also be there, for it meant she could accompany us all without remark.

Sam was working on the New Dam and was unhappy with some of his instructions. He was concerned that without proper controls the Nile could become totally saturated with bilharzia, ultimately deadly to humans and animals. The British had discovered the drawbacks of their dam and the United Nations had warned of the dangers, yet with Soviet help the government was going to build the same kind again. He felt that political prestige was suddenly more important than Egypt's long-term well-being. Like almost every other civil servant who had come here, he had fallen in love with the country and was genuinely devoted to her improvement.

Though I found her, as usual, a little irritating, the Rose, with her fey beauty and her powerful intelligence had dominated the previous evening's supper. She was chiefly concerned with setting up a modern museum. The Egyptian-run ones were in terrible shape. She hoped to get funds from the Russians. East American ex-patriots, who always pouted when their patronage

was refused or modified, would not help her because she had
asked them. Only Getty and Guggenheim, those two Anglophile
eccentrics, were prepared to help, but they were hardly compati-
ble and were already making impossible conditions. The Rose
had laughed when she had told us what she was doing. "The
diplomacies of archeology. Isn't it odd how politics of this kind
has permeated almost every academic field? Yet people sacrifice
their principles in return for so little power. Surely it can't be
healthy ?"

She had asked what we thought.

"Uncertainty makes people short-sighted and greedy," I suggested. "They lose their judgment and self-esteem and become
increasingly suggestible, making ideal consumers."

I mentioned some dogs' instinct to eat when in danger, no
doubt because it might be a long time before they ate again. It
slowed them down and made them easy victims, but initially it
comforted them.

My wife had smiled at me. "We're not with you, Jack. You've
lost us."

And everybody had laughed.

"But Jack has a point," the Rose had said, putting that
strangely-colored hand on mine. "He has a point."

My wife had smiled, her silks a thousand shades of blue, as
she touched her lips to a glass of ruby port.

∾

I had loved being back in Egypt. I had looked forward to showing
my wife all the places I had enjoyed as a child. But so few
were still there. My descriptions became a litany of loss. My
memories were too vivid, I said. They imposed themselves on
this new reality.

"But your memories *are* real, Jack," she assured me. "Memory and language are all we have. It's important to cultivate
them. For us, eloquence must be a moral quality. Only through

poetry and myth can we hope to endure. We must tell our stories, Jack, to the very best of our ability. And live them out again and again. Words determine actions and so *become* actions. They become real, Jack. Look at Mussolini's rhetoric. At Hitler's. That's why we too must do what we say we will do."

She remarked on the accumulation of time in Egypt. History piled upon history, city upon city, dream upon dream. A scrapheap, she had said, of broken promises. She had grown bitter as the century ran on, yet she continued to hope. In fact I believed her to be incapable of real despair. It was not in her nature. But she had expected so much more when I first knew her.

In those pre-war days I believe she was already a close friend of Rose von Bek whom I knew slightly from my time on both the Thames and Mississippi riverboats. She had been a gambler, then, like Rose. One of the very best of the old style American-trained jugadors.

All this was a while before the disintegration of the United States into bitterly antagonistic, increasingly impoverished, warring clans and tribes, but the signs were there. Like the Romans before them, Americans had discovered that crisp new terms for orthodox ideas and sophisticated engineering skills were no substitute for social progress.

I mourned the collapse of one more failed experiment in enlightenment. America was no longer a Christian country. Though a hundred clans flew a cross on their banners Christianity had evidently been too demanding an idea. It would be a thousand years before that nation's dream was restored.

As the old empires collapsed and new ones attempted to establish themselves, the world considered itself to be unstable. I had seen what real instability was, and all I witnessed here (I thought) was the social upheaval which comes with a change in the power structure, whether it be the emergence of a particular class or the establishment of a particular interest.

But people of my background were trained not to speculate

on such lines. We were taught that society is in a permanent
state of flux. People look back to Golden Ages that were equally
unstable, but had for a while a reassuring *appearance* of cer-
tainty. It is, of course, immediately clear to us, in their future,
that their paradises no longer exist. Therefore, their certainties
were unfounded.

All the orthodox mind can do is recreate the conditions which
led to its dilemma. This gave birth to the peculiar notion, in the
early part of the 20th century, that time was cyclic! An even
cruder analogy, of course, was that time was a pendulum—that
an instrument of measurement was the thing it measured! However frequently I was exposed to them, I found such notions
deeply ignorant and fairly stupid, but they were very popular in
those days and few intellectuals disputed them.

Of course, the condition of modern America was a subject my
friends and I often discussed, since so much of our lives had
been lived there, but it was clear that only outside interference
would have any chance of clearing up the mess and it was not
in the self-interest of the Great Powers to step in. Only Britain,
no doubt with a different agenda, showed any real interest in
mounting an expedition. I knew little of the main theatres in the
former-USA. Most of my time had been spent in the South and
there was little information available about the situation there.
Only Texas remained relatively stable, having been the first State
to leave the Union.

"New Orleans is full of scalawags," Sam said, putting down
his *Al Misr* and picking up his tea-cup. "America is being
stripped of everything of value. The only order New Orleans ever
had came from the machine bosses. They had a respect for history. And now they've all gone to the Caymans."

Sam had once worked for those bosses and had more time for
them than I had. To me they were sinister individuals, chiefly
responsible for the present terrible conditions in the city.

Rather than argue with him, I turned my attention below, to
the cedars and palms on my left. They surrounded a small, flat

cobbled area set up as a snack-bar with some tables and chairs. Beyond that was the bright blue water of the Nile. In the shade, I saw the Rose and my wife at one of the tables. They were animated, laughing.

At the table next to them was a group of Nigerian businessmen in the elegant dark and light blue gellabeahs commonly favored by Alexandria's wealthy lawyers. They, too, were engaged in spirited conversation.

So far away from Cairo and Memphis, I was thoroughly enjoying the unthreatening atmosphere, the sense of tranquil isolation.

It was here that, for thousands of years, pharoahs had come, to find the pleasures currently enjoyed by their political successors. The great visionary Aton had built a university near here, far out in the desert, where scholars could work without the world intruding. The first college of applied metaphysics our race had ever known.

When Aton was ousted, said the Rose, his university was abandoned. She still believed it to be there under the sand and was hoping to persuade the present bureaucracy to let her mount an expedition to find it. She even attempted to fire us up to go with her. Her former kinsman, the *arabiste* Ulrich von Bek, was currently in the region and was going to join her. But she needed backing. I regretted that, while we were enjoying the benefits of our small Casino in Las Cascadas, we hadn't that kind of money. I had other reasons, also, for discouraging her.

The Rose insisted we must be acquainted with many rich people on our island. After all, the place was a tax-haven—and everyone knew who used her harbors during gun-running season.

I told her that taxes on Las Cascadas were not low. We had one of the most enlightened social programs in Europe and Africa. There could only be two gun-runners (privately I knew that one of them had been her lover) who might have the faintest interest in funding an archeological expedition and neither was sufficiently disinterested not to exploit any discovery to the full. She'd need clean public money, surely. What about the British?

But as usual the British were entangled in typically serpentine diplomatic knitting and the Egyptians, who had inherited the Turks' love of intrigue, would read all kinds of ambitions into some well-meaning Foreign Office representative dishing out funds for an innocent archeological dig.

She had come to believe it was the U.N. or nothing. But the U.N. was finding it difficult to raise money for ordinary peace-keeping operations on the former-US borders, and her main European backers were beginning to complain. Some thought Britain should shoulder the entire Canadian burden, though this would be seen as an act of blatant imperialism by Quebec, who still murmured uneasily of separation. The French had washed their hands of the situation. They had their own colonial problems to deal with in North Africa.

I saw what she meant about diplomacy.

At that stage I might have volunteered some information, had not my wife anticipated me and told the Rose that we were too old and settled in our ways to undertake further adventures. Who knew where such expeditions led, these days?

While I think the Rose found her old friend's interjection disloyal, she of all people must have understood with what good reason my wife had become cautious. Whatever her thoughts, the Rose affected to lose interest in the subject and remarked on the inevitable beauty of the sunset.

All this would come later. Now I stood on the marble steps of D'Yss Mansions, hesitating before Colinda's bell.

Appearing at the sessions, and seeing so many of my adversaries ready to give in their evidence against me, I concluded myself a leman; my very countenance betrayed both my thoughts of guilt and despair. In short, I received sentence of death, to be hanged at Tyburn by the neck till I was dead. I thought these sad tidings would have deprived me of my life, and so have saved the hangman the labour. All the way I went back to Newgate I fancied nothing but gibbets stood in my way, and that I saw no other trades but cordwinders.

—RICHARD HEAD, *The English Rogue*

Legends of the Badlands: Mil Noches

"You haven't changed a bit." Jack leaned back in his chair and lit another M&E. He tasted his wine. He was not surprised by its quality. She had recommended it.

"No," said Colinda Dovero, "one doesn't. Not as much as

one expects, anyway." Her smile was quick and warm as she leaned towards him. He wondered why he had assumed he was going to meet someone far less happy. Had he expected her to be grieving for him as he still grieved for her? To his alarm, and beyond his control, all his senses were coming back to life. He remembered vividly how optimistic she had been. That was why he had looked forward so much to Las Cascadas and the new life she had described for them. It did not once occur to him that she was happy now because she was with him again.

∽

She was staying in D'Yss Mansions for a few days, before her flat was ready in Garibaldi Mansions on the other side of the Square. She had rented the first thing available, she said. She apologized for her haste on the phone. She was in late and needed to tape her favorite soap opera. Also she was expecting a call about a job. She was working as a croupiere again.

The restaurant she had chosen around the corner from the Square, in Lillie Road, was run by an Italian lady, her middle-aged son and the young woman he called his girl-friend. They all loved Colinda. Mrs. Parotti came out and told her to ignore the menu, just say what she felt like eating. Julie asked what they thought of this funny weather. Peter Parotti ran his long, languid fingers through his dyed black hair and prepared to write down our orders, beaming suddenly as Colinda asked him about his next engagement. "It's Janaçek," he said. "I love Janaçek. Do you know *The Macropoulos Affair?*" He sang part-time with the E.N.O. and ran his restaurant with generous enthusiasm. Jack felt a physical pain, as if a razor cut him from neck to belly. Now he remembered how easily she made friends, what pleasure she always gave to the world around her. How uneasy this made him.

For her *hors d'oeuvre,* she ate some little raviolis. He had the potted shrimps. He had not had potted shrimps for years. They

had been a childhood favorite, a taste of empire. Every memory
was sharp, every sensation almost overwhelming, recalling a
hundred similar sensations. Only his deeply ingrained gambler's
habits allowed him to keep some self-control.

"You got my letter." She reached across the table and touched
his hand.

He shook his head. No.

"At Las Cascadas?"

"Saying you'd be back soon?" His own voice was a distant
echo.

"Oh, no. That I'd see you in London."

"I didn't get that letter, no." He recovered himself.

She frowned and then her face cleared. "I thought you
sounded odd on the phone. I wrote to say I'd see you in London
as soon as possible. I wrote to you from Paris. To Las Cascadas.
A few days after I'd left. And then the War came."

"That was eight years ago," he said.

"Was it?" This surprised her. "You know how slow time can
be here. I warned you about that, didn't I?"

He nodded.

"Something must have gone wrong with the note." She was
suddenly serious, studying his eyes.

"That's the most likely thing," he said. He knew she wasn't
lying. He looked into her wonderful, feline face. Every feature
was refined. Nothing was exaggerated. But her beauty no longer
consoled him. It almost made him anxious. "What did you say
in your note?"

"That I would meet you in London."

"Now?"

"I'd hoped to get here a little earlier. I'm sorry, Jack. It seems
we were out of synch."

For thousands and thousands of hours, thousands of days and
nights, he had thought of nothing else but her, wondering what
had become of her, whether she was dead, whether she had tired
of him, whether she was in trouble and he could not help her,

some terrible imprisonment, perhaps. Hundreds of different sce-
narios had played out their details in his tormented imagination.
He had considered suicide. He had almost lost her.

And all, it seemed, because a letter had been lost. How could
such eternities of pain merely be the result of an undelivered
letter?

"You just asked me to wait?" he asked. "Wait for you here?
In London?"

"Only if you wanted to, Jack. Of course, I'm glad you did.
How have you been?"

"Fine," he said. He had some difficulty with his breathing.
He coughed. He cleared his throat. Carefully, so that he might
light it again, he put out his M&E in the ashtray. He reached
for his glass and picked it up. He sipped some more wine.

"Lucky? Jack?"

"Lucky enough. You remember Sam Oakenhurst?"

"No," she said. "I haven't met him yet."

"We have a kind of partnership."

"You play the tables, still?"

"Not lately. And what have you been doing for the past ten
years?"

∽

S he had worked for a while, she said, as a chanteuse, at *The
Fallen Angel* in that region of Paris called Les Hivers which
lay between the Cirque D'Hiver in Boulevard du Temple and the
notorious Quai D'Hiver, the main terminus of the underground
canal system. She had half-expected Jack to join her.

Her chief motive for taking the job was to get in on a famous
game which had been playing there for as long as anyone could
remember. She had sung for a while, and was popular enough,
but it had taken her some time before she could sit at the table
and earn its respect. Thereafter, she was a popular partner. She
had an idea, she told Jack, to build them a nest-egg and take it

back to Las Cascadas. But already the island was under threat from the fascists. She did not have another plan. That was when she had written to say she would meet him in London and to be patient.

The Winter Game, as it would come to be known, had absorbed all who played it. The stakes had grown so high and the fever of the table so intense that time had passed unnoticed. When she came out of the game, she was up a few guineas but her watch had stopped, which was always a bad sign. She had come to London as soon as she could.

"I love you, Jack," she said. "All the time I was playing I wished you were with me. Sometimes I pretended you were. That's when I won most. What we could have made of that game between us!"

"Sounds good," he said. "And that's what you've been doing?"

"You can understand."

He could. He smiled. He reached for her hand, drew it towards him and kissed it. A decade of pain passed away like a breath.

It was as if they had never been parted.

And now, she assured him, they would never be parted again.

∽

"I had longed for my children's love," she said. "But I had no idea they still existed. And, if they did, there was no reason why they should love me . . ."

"I didn't know you had children," he said.

"Oh, yes," she said. "But that was a lifetime ago. People like us can't afford regrets, Jack."

They lay together in the grey silk sheets, which were the least dramatic they had been able to find in the linen cupboard at D'Yss Mansions. The whole place was furnished in black and silver, with ebony surfaces and chrome surrounds, as if resisting the original brick and plaster comforts of the *fin-de-siècle*. There was an air of arrogant mockery about the place which they both found disturbing. Perhaps the owner had made a virtue of his lack of taste. When in doubt, *reduce*.

The place was rented from a film director, she said. He had been a player for a while, but she had never met him. He was in Cannes, she thought. Making deals, apparently. "They said he was as good as some of the Italians. He shoots the same kind of films. You know, lots of bicycles and ruins and large women in wet blouses. But in London. My friend—who was the middle man—says he's Britain's great white hope. If the UK ever wants to be taken seriously in the film world, he said."

"Have you seen anything?"

"A couple, yes. Very English, you know. Lots of mannerisms and not much feeling. And Diana Dors will never be Sylvana Magnani."

"You don't do anything as an actress, these days?"

"I haven't had the chance," she said. "I have an agent. That's how I got the singing job. Now I'm a croupiere again. But so far no luck on stage, screen and radio."

"Is it what you want to do?"

"Oh, no," she said. "But there's no real gambling worth the name, is there? Not here."

"Maybe in America. Las Vegas?"

"That kind of gambling's like American religion—all distraction and no mystery. I need a little more sardonic ambiguity. A little more spirituality. A touch of irony. You know me, Jack."

"I knew you for the best gambler ever born on the Mississippi River."

"You and me, Jack," she said, and moved her soft skin against his thrilling arm. "Our southern tables were a different thing altogether. But Las Vegas is all Yankee gambling now. They have machines for it. Squadrons of Grand Turks. No ambience, Jack. No compassion. Those people have never enjoyed real defeats. They refuse to acknowledge their powerlessness. So they never address it."

He smiled. He had forgotten her Southern snobbery. As always, he found it endearing.

They made plans to leave for Las Cascadas as soon as possible. He had some savings, he said. Enough for the stake they needed.

"I'd expected to work here," she said. "I wasn't sure you'd wait."

"Until the end of time," he said.

⁂

They came to Las Cascadas on an old Catalan steamer which had taken two days to sail from Barcelona. They savored the slow approach to the island, enjoying the familiar outline rising gradually out of the heavy blue horizon, green and purple, dark yellow and red against a pastel sky.

The island was a natural fortress, sweeping upwards to a peak crowned by the Al Karin Kasbah, which had successfully resisted every invader, from Roman legionaries, Norman crusaders, Islamic holy warriors, Venetian pirates and Spanish conquistadors, Napoleon and Nelson alike, until it had finally fallen, like so much of the enduring past, to the brutal power of the Fascist Axis.

Las Cascadas had known suffering during her occupation. She had known massacre and famine, torture and terror of every kind. The Lombardians had been particularly vicious and were still unwelcome on the island. But she had steadfastly put the bitterness behind her and, under her new Governor, Don Victor Dust, had thrown herself wholeheartedly into recollecting and restoring her past happiness.

The island's fortunate position made it a popular holiday spot for those who wished to avoid the conveniences of Majorca, the Canaries or the Costa del Sol. Mass tourism had been discouraged and the majority of the new building was simply restoring what the fascists had destroyed during their wicked rule.

This preservation of the island's natural integrity was immediately evident as her great limestone cliffs, scattered with cypress, cedar and poplars, loomed over the steamer. Jack and Colinda were astonished.

"So much is still the same, Jack!"

She pointed out familiar places. As always, the clustered communities seemed to grow from the rock itself. Churches, houses and shops were perched on the very brink of the precipice, their terracotta and soft-toned plaster ripe with the sun's warmth, their vines and bougainvillea, their wisteria and delphiniums, gardenias, camellias, roses and honeysuckle pouring over rustic balconies and terraces down to the white rocks and the dark blue waters of the sea. Now, in the light of late afternoon, people looked out to the sunset, drank an aperitif and prepared to relish the evening. There was no lovelier spot in the Mediterranean than Las Cascadas, half-way between Europe and Africa.

The steamer rounded Cap' Javetos and there was the deep harbor of Port Sab' with her pink, yellow and pale green houses, striped restaurant awnings and gaudy shop-signs decorating her little cobbled quayside and quaint, green-railed promenade. At the furthest eastern corner of the harbor, the long, cream-colored *mola* had been widened a little, to make it easier to reach the circular, domed building, one of Frank Lloyd Wright's earliest and showing his Moorish influences, known as Al Mason dell' Opera, but actually the Casino. Her narrow cobbled streets winding up from the seafront, her long flights of stone stairs connecting one level with another, were dominated by the Santa Gabriel Church, the Fishermen's Union House, the *lysee* and the *casa dell ville*, all built in the ornate old Moorish style traditional on the island.

Port Sab' had once been the stronghold of the great corsair captains who had ruled this part of the Mediterranean for three centuries. Now most of the pirates were gone, or had turned to other trades. As Captain Quelch, one of the most famous, who had never been captured, was fond of remarking—steam had blown all the romance out of the profession. He had turned to gun-running, he declared, because it was more suitable work for a gentleman sailor.

He loved, he said, the solitude of sail, the silence of a great ship moving with all sheets taut before a friendly Sou'wester. When in the thirties piracy became a common pursuit of the *petite bourgeoisie* it lost both its glamour and its risks. Port Sabatini, as the British preferred to call it, was fortunate in that it did not attract this modern mechanized breed of thief. As the ferry approached the dock, Jack and Colinda saw with satisfaction that every ship in the harbor still depended for power upon the patterns of the world's winds.

No doubt the sailing captains still congregated in the little tapas bars and cantinas at the far end of the harbor, to assure each other of their moral and professional superiority over those who chose to make the air filthy with their smoke and who navigated according to wireless instructions from Liverpool, Rotterdam or Casablanca. They probably still spoke bitterly of their customers, most of whom did not care if their guns arrived on a four-masted topsail schooner or a greasy tramp whose smoke suggested she was burning human remains. Jack guessed there was still some kudos to possessing a Port Sabatini registration.

The process of docking seemed to take almost as long as the voyage and Jack grew impatient for the shore. He could see D'Armengal's Bar Oceola a few yards away and longed to sit at his favorite table, watching the business of the harbor, reading his *Al Pais* and taking a large *anis* with his afternoon bread. "I wonder how his daughter is," she said, hugging his arm as they watched the gangplank being lowered.

The dock was full of noisy little boys, people meeting their families, amiable customs officers and local couriers. The first cargo rolled in its sealed barrel down the gangplank was the mail. And then seamen in stained whites came on bouncing timber, carrying the luggage to the dock, piling trunks and suitcases on the cobblestones where grinning porters leaned on their trolleys, smoking black Arcadia reefers, ready to carry their loads to the waiting hacks or to one of the town's four hotels. Then at last the bosun signaled for the passengers to begin disembarking.

When the moment came, Jack and Colinda were almost hesitant. They had expected to be met but saw no-one they recognized. They were not sure now that everything would be as they had left it. So little had changed that Jack suspected a supernatural hand in the town's preservation. But, as they reached dry land and stood for a while getting their balance, they saw that there had in fact been quite a lot of damage. Every building, though discreetly repaired, showed some sign of the shelling received from the fascists as they fled before the imminence of the British Navy whose local commander had possessed a personal motive for liberating the island.

Commodore Sir Albert Begg had married a Cascadian and had spent most of his leisure here. It had given satisfaction to most of the parties concerned that Begg's ships had arrived in time to blow the fascist flotilla to bits and take some of the leading brutes prisoner, including the *ras* known as *Al Cangrejo*, who was publicly hanged in Milan for his crimes. Commodore Begg was now a resident, they had heard, in his wife's family home on the other side of the island. Both Colinda and Jack looked forward to renewing old friendships here.

At last, his fluttering hands clearing a way for him, smiling with a kind of benign apology as he moved straight as a die through the crowd, came the man they had expected to see. In a grey silk suit, Gaspar Luc-Major, limping on an elegant malacca cane, his long fingers writhing gracefully in the air to seize his hat and lift it, his strange, droll features alive with pleasure, his shy eyes gleaming with tears, fell forward to embrace them.

"*Mes amigos! Mes enfantas!*" It was Gaspar who had grieved most for Jack's loss, had concerned himself unsuccessfully with finding Colinda's whereabouts, who had been in love with their eternal passion, their terrifying histories, who had wanted so badly for them to be reunited. His face glowed with the fires of a profound satisfaction. "I am only just back from over there myself. My daughter had your telegram. So! You are with us for how long?"

"We're here to stay," said Jack, picking up as many bags as he could while Gaspar took the rest and led the way to his little dog-cart. "At least, we hope so. You want someone to run the Casino?"

Gaspar flung his grateful head to heaven and his long, grey hair cascaded down his silvery back. "Desperately! That's why I wrote to you. But then it wasn't possible, eh? Where's Sam Oakenhurst?"

"No longer with us," Jack said. "I'll explain everything later."

༄

"I don't think there's a soul on this island didn't suffer under the fascists," Gaspar told them as they finished their meal and relaxed in the warm evening wind blowing from Africa. "Yet we are a small enough nation to discuss what to do and come to some sort of democratic agreement. We all agreed that we must not forget the fascists and what they represented, but we must not allow them to defeat us. So we restored ourselves and here we are, as good as old, as contented as we ever were—but we are, perhaps, a little wiser, too. They might have contaminated us, by turning one against the other, as they did in some other countries. Happily, we did not allow that. Their murders, their torturings, their rapes and all their other abuses are remembered as we remember an epidemic of rabies, and we do our best to take whatever precautions are possible against a repetition. They did not contaminate us. They contaminated very few, in the end, given their efforts."

"You think our generation has seen the end of such things?" Colinda took a puff on my M&E and handed it back to me.

"I fear we'll never see the end of such things," Gaspar's graceful fingers expressed the tangled complexity of everything. "Not, at least, until we see the end of human credulity and stupidity. Not to mention that irrational capacity to hate you still see everywhere. And that dull, greedy lust for power possessed by the unimaginative and the stupid. That kind wants to rule in Auschwitz rather than serve in paradise. President McCarthy brought about America's final disintegration and was consumed by the hell he made of his country. As Mussolini discovered, cheap power is gained by creating disharmony in the body politic, but cheap power doesn't last very long. America quested for the free lunch with the same spiritual intensity knights quested for the holy grail. The search took on the character of a moral journey. It's only a fool invokes the power of the mob in a quest like that! And we still have to wait and see what Communist Asia achieves. They have preserved most of Japan's industry and, with their own, could rapidly become the greatest economic power bloc in history! These are especially unsettled times, I think."

"But not in Las Cascadas," said Colinda with a smile.

"Even in Paradise." Gaspar's eyes grew suddenly melancholy as he glanced at the neatly repaired shell hole in the wall of the nearby Damokles Hotel. "Ah," he said, almost in relief, "here's my daughter at last." He recollected something and turned to them hastily. "Please say nothing to her about any incident you may have heard mentioned. She prefers to carry on as if it had never happened."

Colinda turned enquiring eyes to Jack.

Jack shrugged.

Such work for the surgeon and midwife he
makes,/What death can compare with the jolly
town rake's?

—*The Jolly Town Rakes,*
Pills to Purge Melancholy, 1721

∽⟨━━━━━━━━━━⟩∽

The Thunder of Hooves:
Vagar sin Esperanza

My father's great consolation was his fly fishing. He studied
the art daily and practiced it whenever he had the chance.
When not inspecting some parish record, he was usually absorbed in one of Wilson's dry fly books. He corresponded with
other enthusiasts around the world and occasionally even had
fellow fishermen join him at Tower House. They were the only
other company he ever kept and after a week he was inclined to
grow testy with even the most gentlemanly visitor.

Because I enjoyed his company and loved to see him so cheer-
fully at one with himself, I frequently went with my father when
he invited me.

He had tried to teach me how to fish, but I had no aptitude for the sport, no wish to go to such elaborate lengths to coax a hook into some poor creature's throat. I loved the technique and tranquility of fishing, but I had no stomach for the end result. Usually, and because he would feel like talking to me on the way, I would go with him to whatever water he had picked and then leave him to fish in peace. If some Gypsies camped nearby I would usually pay them a visit.

I had friends amongst all the Romany tribes as well as those we called the diddecoy Gypsies, the travelers and tinkers who were so despised by old-fashioned Gypsies. The Romanies generally refused to see how much common ground they all had. They, who had suffered so much from it, were still caught up in the myth of "Blood." The younger ones were nowadays a little more understanding of the need to act in concert for mutual self-interest. The modern travelers were politically sophisticated. Many had taken to the road because they objected to the nature of the authority which sought to regulate its freedoms. They understood the power of group political action. It was the only effective weapon they had against all that threatened them. It was a weapon the American Indian had not possessed when he rode against the white-eyes with only his spear, his shield and a determination to make a brave death.

Whenever her tribe was near, I would visit my friend Mary Lee, the psychic, and she would read my fortune, sometimes for hours, until she was completely exhausted. But she would insist on continuing until she had discovered everything she could. Sometimes it was as useful to inquire about my past as my future. Such psychics help our kind navigate more easily. She had lost her family to the Nazis before they were driven out by the I.R.A. She had never been back to Ireland. Even when her tribe made their annual migration, taking the ferry to Dublin to attend the big horse fairs, she would not go with them. She stayed in Liverpool with a settled aunt who had married a vintner called Shorrock.

"I mourn my dead children," said Mary Lee. "I mourn and

mourn for what should have been. For what should have been. But, life must go on. Why are we made to grieve, Miss Rosie? What is the purpose of so much grief?"

∾

I renewed myself at home in Yorkshire, though I knew I must eventually leave again. I rode my sure-footed horse over the wild fells, through sunshine and rain and mist and snow, night and day. I revelled in the elements, in the wild sensations which brought my blood to singing life and made me thank God for allowing me to taste so much beauty.

I would often ride to a favorite spot, usually the old mine workings, where a roof still gave shelter and I could be comfortable in inclement weather. As a small child I had played tram robbers here. Now the loading platform of the mine, built above rusted rails which had once carried trucks of ore up to the refinery, was a good place to sit and look across the soft, rolling drumlins of the entire valley. On both distant sides rose sharp rock and grey, unwelcoming shale, threatening and bleak, but down here in Morsdale was sunshine and tranquility and quietly grazing sheep. Even the ruined stone workings had taken on the dignity of age. Here, at the far end of our valley, with the house out of sight and only sheep-sheds and our ancient walls as reminders of our settlement, I enjoyed a landscape which had remained essentially unchanged since the Bronze Age.

I returned to the Ramsden, finished my A-levels, got a decent place at Oxford, got a 1-2 in economic geography under Professor Harvey, learned to fence under Master Bonfiglioli, became something of an expert gamer under Doctor Oldusteim, and began an intense love affair with Prince Lobkowitz almost the moment he returned to London.

By the time I went down from Oxford, Trafalgar Square was her old self, Nelson's column stood straight again and the days of the highwaymen were done. With its take-over by the public authority,

the tram company ceased to be a predator and became an accountable civic asset. There's a great deal to be said for public ownership
of public utilities, but it has to be admitted they lose an element
of romance once they come under equitable control.

There were those, of course, who had complained bitterly
against the UTC who now complained just as bitterly about the
LTA, but most ordinary passengers still graphically remembered
the bad old days and felt little nostalgia for them. All they had
lost, after all, was the crack of a barker in the mist and a clear
command to "Throw down your lever!" quickly followed by the
clatter of the heavy brass "regulator" landing on the cobbles of
the tram-bed. Then the tobymen would swing aboard out of the
gloom, heavy figures in their cocked hats, lace and greatcoats,
leaving their big horses steaming from the gallop. Brandishing
massive dragoon pistols, another tradition of their calling, they
"passed the hat" as they put it and courteously relieved the
passengers of their purses. For most passengers the reality
lacked some of the glamour of the tales they had enjoyed in the
cheap weeklies and few mourned the passing of those audacious
rogues or their brutal enemies, the Tram Company "grabs."

∽

Those days were still alive to Prince Lobkowitz, of course. We
had shared them and he looked back to them with a certain
nostalgia of his own. "The trams are as monumentally beautiful
as always," he told me one night in bed,[19] "but they lack their
old menace. They have lost their ambiguity. They no longer represent that cruel authority, that relentless lust for power, that
evident villain we all love to blame."

"You'll admit," I murmured, "the Transport Companies were
downright evil in their greedy expansion. Lord Barbican's appetite

---

[19]Such conversations between lovers were common at that time.

was voracious and impossible to satisfy. Because of the Tram Company thousands of poor people lost homes, work and dignity. Thousands of others were exploited. And all in the name of progress!"

Lobkowitz agreed. "Oh, the blame was there, of course. And today's vital, socialist London is nothing but improvement. This is London's finest Silver Age, young woman, and you should enjoy it. Her Golden Age will be brief, when it comes, and the Iron Age will be long."

I admired the firmness of his body, the softness of his skin. I wondered how old he could be. I had never been much judge of age and nowadays scarcely knew my own.

"When you curb brute power at the top, you curb it at the bottom also." Prince Lobkowitz was an enlightened Tudor at heart. He thought that if the nobility and authorities behaved with decorum, demonstrating *charitas* and *gravitas* in their own deportment, the majority of the populace would behave accordingly. Coherence was achieved by example, he argued. "People love justice, even if they have no hope of achieving it. The angry, mindless mob is only an unignorable expression of the common distress."

He was in Britain, he told me, because at last the ideal and the actuality of her politics were closer than at any time. "It is unlikely to last," he believed. "Mortal memories are far too short."

I was in love with all his vast experience.

"The Americans called this the trickle down effect," I remember him saying as he lifted me a little by my shoulders and made himself more comfortable. "Corruption at the top leads to corruption throughout the state. They came to understand the causes of social evil all too well in the end. But those with power continued to amass it for themselves and ignore the consequences. And now, of course, it's far too late to stop the disintegration there.

"Without brutal injustice," he believed, "popular crime and criminal heroes also lose the bulk of their popular support. Without the tyranny he resisted, Pancho Villa would still be no more

than an audacious bandit. There's no Robin Hood without the
wicked Sheriff. There's no Jesse James without the swaggering
Yankee carpetbaggers. No Pretty Boy Floyd without a corrupt
Wall Street and crooked politicians.

"When just harmony flourishes throughout society, when Law
and Chaos are in true balance, such men are merely despised
thugs. All classes abhor them. Oppression never fails to produce
a crop of outlaw heroes. Old-fashioned methods get old-fashioned
results. But, of course, it is always the same when we defeat the
symbol of oppression, rather than the oppression itself."

I love to hear him talk. I fall asleep every night to the sound
of his gentle, intelligent voice.

∽

I asked Lobkowitz to come to Yorkshire with me. My father
had already invited him to Tower House to fish and seemed
unsurprised by our relationship.

I think he was relieved that I hadn't taken up with Turpin or
any of his ilk. There had been an awkward time, when I'd
brought Mary Beck, Turpin's daughter, up for the summer one
year. Mary had a wonderful holiday and fell in love with my father
and our house. But then some money was missing and Mrs. Gallibasta became suspicious. My father refused to be. Mary, of course,
was entirely innocent, but the accusation was made and, considerably upset with Mrs. Gallibasta, I left when Mary left. I wanted
her to stay with me at Sporting Club Square and continue our
holiday there, but she would not. She went back to Brookgate,
where she shared a miserable flat with her useless brother.

The money was found but Mary never would come back to
Yorkshire with me and had less and less time for me. Her father,
of course, had by then begun his travels. There were still a few
tobymen operating in the Leeds and Manchester areas in a kind
of unwitting homage to their master apologist, Harrison Ainsworth, but I had long since lost my taste for that life.

By the time I began my affair with Lobkowitz I had been through too many long games and suffered too much anguish. Sam Oakenhurst was gone—or rather he was absorbed in someone else— and I was thinking that I had had all the adventures I would ever need. I had even lost my taste for flying. I thought I might settle down to a familiar country life, marrying Lobkowitz and growing involved in the Women's Institute and the Church, helping people on a local scale rather than trying to change the multiverse.

I had learned many things in the Second Ether[20] and had grown wise in certain ways, yet the causes of social ills were almost never different and always lay in a greedy and unchristian abuse of power and authority, a failure of generosity as well as imagination. Of course, the Singularity applauded such vices as practical virtues associated with some kind of divinely-guided means to self-improvement. By giving money a moral quality, they made its accumulation seem to be the accumulation of virtue. But if money has any sort of quality of its own it is immoral. When the only value placed by society on human beings is financial, the society becomes epidemically immoral. Monetarists encouraged the old puritan idea that the more money one had, the more virtuous one was. Whereas Chaos celebrated pirates and highwaymen, the Singularity's heroes were millionaire founders of corporations.

The Chaos Engineers, those brave explorers and privateers, were secretly admired even by the Singularity, whose own near-immortals, the infamous *Iron Arrows*, were all but indistinguishable from their enemies. Illicit recordings, telling the adventures of Billy-Bob Begg, Pearl Peru, *The Spammer Gain* and her crew in their perpetual quest for Ko-O-Ko, the Lost Universe, forever folding the infinite scales of the Second Ether, were sold on a thriving black-market and Sam Oakenhurst or Corporal Pork were as well known to Singularity schoolboys as they were to the children of Chaos. Yet for all they had in common in their love of drama, Law and Chaos were divided by profound philosophical

---

[20]See *Blood: A Southern Fantasy; Fabulous Harbors; The Revenge of the Rose.*

differences concerning the very meaning of the multiverse and the nature of God. Even their experiences of the material world differed. To reconcile them required considerable patience and strength of character. Not everyone was convinced we had it in us.

"We began as a random growth, something in the moss on the face of the rock," B.B. Begg was fond of saying. "We spread like a virus and look at us now—a sentient symptom of a multiversal sickness. We are probably the most successful disease reality has ever known! There is no antidote to the proliferation of human life!"

∽

Prince Lobkowitz, like many eternals, rarely had occasion to walk the roads between the worlds. His experience was almost wholly local and he had cultivated this parochialism deliberately, but he had no intention, he said, of spending more than a few weeks of the year in Yorkshire. His duties took him frequently to Paris, Berlin, Vienna and Mirenburg. "As ever, I pursue the origins of tribalism and look for an alternative." He was a vocational diplomat. He wanted nothing less than universal understanding between all parties everywhere and a mutual commitment to common goals. He had worked for that for as long as he could remember. His was not a job, he said, for a married man.

I accused him of pursuing a calling which allowed him the luxury of few emotional commitments. He did not answer and I knew the charge to be foolish.

And I had to admit in my heart that I was not very disappointed. I had not yet retired. I was merely resting. My story was still unfolding.

When Lobkowitz had gone back to London and my father had settled into one of his long periods of study I found to my surprise that I was bored. I rode to all my old favorite places and relished the solitude, yet also found myself longing to share them with him, those secret places which I had once guarded so fiercely. I had not realized how much I would miss him. I had very little reason to stay at home. Mrs. Gallibasta made my father very comfortable.

Therefore, on the 22 May 1967, I said goodbye to my father, left several telephone numbers with Mrs. Gallibasta, and, looking back once or twice at Tower House, rode out of the valley. At *The Moorcock Inn*, I took the road for Dent Station and caught the 2.40 for Settle. From Settle I would go to Leeds and catch the express to London and my old haunts. I knew Lobkowitz was already in Berlin. I did not expect to go so far in his pursuit.

∾

London in May, with her parks, gardens and window boxes in optimistic bloom, the sunshine rewarming her Portland stone and her Buckingham brick, takes on an almost pixilated mood. The wide avenues of Park Lane and Bayswater Road are filled with dancing spots of white and pink blossom, flanked by creamy chestnut flowers, early rhododendron, cerise, violet and scarlet; profound, African green. Even in the alleys of Brookgate and Clerkenwell there's an atmosphere of jollity and renewed goodwill and the more relaxed, amiable attitude amongst Old Sweden Street's costers and barkers makes their customers forget the slights of winter.

In Soho the tables begin to reappear outside the little restaurants. The cautious Englishman slips off a layer or two of clothing and tests the air, whistling like a lark, a kind of warning to the world that he is preparing to take its pleasures again. Even the horses' hooves have a new liveliness and the cars purr like happy cats amongst the cheerful bellow of the trams.

The smell of lilac and anemones drifts amongst the electric stink of hot metal. The window boxes vibrate like living things. With buzzing transformers the cars, careless of conserving their batteries, race through the narrow streets. From every colorful awning there's the smell of roasting coffee, frying fish, hot codlings,

pies, duffs, dicks and lardy cakes, black with sultanas, all laid
out to tempt the passerby. Sandwich-board-men are hearty with
their bells. Paperboys yell mysterious headlines. Barkers call
their bargains. Mock-auctioneers gather their audiences, their
native cockney rattling like fireworks into the pale, blue air and
crowds, which a week or two earlier had snarled or grizzled, give
themselves up to the general good humor. There's a sense of
relief, as if, until now, everyone did not dare believe that Spring
would actually come round again.

I shared in this general sense of well-being when I first arrived, settling comfortably in at Sporting Club Square, which
was of course vivid with may and ornamental cherry, and enjoying the particular anonymity, a different kind of solitude,
which the city gives. I wanted to take my time before I decided
what to do next. I had no intention of looking for an academic
job. I had no vocation for journalism. I bought the newspapers
and looked through the vacancies. These proved disappointing
to me. I decided I had better try to use my old connections.

With some reluctance, I paid a visit to Smith's Kitchen. I
joined a few games. Eventually my efforts succeeded. The Duval
Brothers were opening a new gambling establishment out at Eel
Pie Island. I was invited to be their resident jugador. I accepted.

Whenever Lobkowitz returned to London he stayed with me.
I went with him to Mirenburg in the summer, and sometimes
to his place just outside Vienna.

In spite of everything, those were wonderful years. As Lobkowitz had predicted, the period between 1946 and 1978 was
to be London's Golden Age.

❧

After my brief affair with Jack Karaquazian, in which I had
vainly tried to make him a version of Sam, I finished with
the Soho tables. My singular education had scarcely prepared me
for the Swinging Sixties, let alone the Slippery Seventies, but,

knowing the Sixties to be a Golden Age, I made the most of them. And I never once had to get a respectable job. Even curiosity about the experience did not make me take work in the City.

The cultural explosion in London had attracted all kinds of wealth. There was a relaxed, cosmopolitan atmosphere which, by the late Sixties, made it possible for me legally to pursue my trade. I had soon been able to stop playing in Smith's greasy ambience. After leaving the Duval brothers and opening my own club for a number of years I was eventually bought out and became a star at the *Golden Slipper* in Shaftesbury Avenue. I completed that part of my public career at *The Fairy Cottage*, in Leicester Square, that baroque celebration of the Gay Nineties, where by dressing my part I made an easy fortune.

The games in those days were primitive compared to our modern ones. The only ingenuity involved was in finding ways to lose. I heard all the best musicians, played poker with John, George, Paul and Ringo, had a rather odd affair with Johnny Rotten and enjoyed a dense complexity of cultural life you can experience in no other city in the world. My mother found a further lease on life and was never out of the gossip columns, photographed at fashionable clubs with the successful *demi monde* known as the "Young Meteors." But when Jack went back to the Terminus, I gave up the game and looked around for another way to make my living.

Apart from gambling and driving, I was trained as a fencer. It soon became evident that if I did not wish to play for my bread, I must seek work where my sword might be of some use, and that, of course, meant leaving London. Eventually I took a commission escorting an aristocratic coffin to Mogador.

For a couple of years I worked the Mediterranean, sometimes in partnership with the notorious Quelch, who took me back to his secret island of Lost Pines—*Los Pinos*—where he spent much of his leisure time. On Lost Pines, Quelch was a popular feudal overlord. Most of his lieutenants and their families retired there. By the end of this episode I had learned the gun runners' trade and even threw myself into a play or two, which I will admit involved me in more than a little piracy.

It was during this period that I met Lobkowitz again in Las Cascadas, went back with him to Mirenburg and, having failed to persuade him to accompany me, decided eventually that I needed to restore myself in familiar surroundings.

∽

And so, once again, I found myself on horseback, laboring up the bleak slab of Swifthorn Fell in a howling October storm. I rode down into the quiet, sheltered dale with the wind no more than a memory. I saw the blue smoke of our chimneys hanging in the warm air. The Morbeck, dark with cold, racing water, poured under the stone humpback bridge, out of the tarn and down towards the distant Gypsy camp where it lost its violence in the broad reed meadows and began a more meditative progress towards the reservoirs of Lansdale and the coast.[21]

Tower House sat with a skirt of mist around her lower stones, yellow light pouring from her generous windows, my father's favorite Elgar sublime within his tower and, as I approached, the smell of Mrs. Gallibasta's "plump harries" wafting through the sharp air resurrected a thousand childhood memories. It was always at this moment that I realized how important my home was, how I could not love and relish London and the world as I did if it were not for Tower House and the unchanging security of our valley.

So many stories had begun in this place, apparently so simple and changeless, that every pebble had served its moment as narrative. Though innocent as the day the glaciers left its unyielding

---

[21]The river went underground once it left Yorkshire and emerged again in the Trough of Bowland under a different name. The Cornelius brothers had come up to visit us one year and became caving enthusiasts. It was they who had followed the river its full length and, of course, found the interesting Lonsdale tributaries which led to so many later adventures.

landscape behind, it had witnessed every infamy, every kind of courage, every possible reckless deed. Dark plots had been hatched and concluded. Whole clans had been lured here to the slaughter. Brothers had poisoned brothers or otherwise disposed of frustrating relatives. Every sod of turf had been nurtured in the lifeblood of men and beasts and every spur of rock had witnessed some long and terrible torment or been the scene of some foul betrayal. Angels and demons were frequent visitors. Sometimes they fought over us. Sometimes we fought all of them and sometimes we won. Moorcock blood had married long and urgently with the soil. The entire valley was as much a Moorcock heir as I. I felt an irrational kinship with it, as if, by some bizarre chemistry we were true siblings. I had no others. I had not considered before how I thought of our valley, as I thought of God, as an older sister. Not my mother, who continued to relish the city's pleasure, but a sister. A voice of sweeter, more patient wisdom. This revelation added to my strength in my coming trials.

It was good to find my father, unchanged as ever, still healthy and full of ideas, and spend the days and evenings with him, discussing the nature of things.

It was he who advised me to go to York and see if Turpin was over there. I said that Turpin had gone to Australia. I had seen him off aboard the zeppelin.

It could be, said my father, that it is time for you to recover yourself a little.

⌖

"What d'ye say, Meg? Feelin' jolly?" says Turpin, and slips his clever arm around the maid's yielding waist. He always had an eye for a wench who favored the gay life. I never knew him seduce anyone who had not determined their own conquest, yet I was forever uncomfortable. In my guise as Captain Hawkmoon I had to witness his sport and affect to be amused by it.

It was the 14th May 19—. Not two hours since, I had left my lodgings to come at last to *The Oddfellows Arms* in Brookgate Passage where I had intelligence of my erstwhile partner.

The Runners had broken the old truce and invaded *The Six Jolly Dragoons*. All entrances to Smith's Kitchen were watched and rumor was that Smith himself had turned King's Evidence. This was in the days when the Tram Company was expanding its lines at a ferocious rate, running ahead of the Tramway Reform Act like a devouring wolf before the hounds.

Turpin's daring exploits were threatening stock prices and there was even some talk of the company giving up the South Western routes, they had become so prone to attack. This would have meant capitulating, as Lord Barbican saw it, before the despised enemy, steam (the old London & Suburban Railway was by no means defeated).

Instead, Lord Barbican began a fresh attack. He increased the rewards. His vicious hirelings, traveling in armored trams, pursued and crushed everyone suspected of aiding the tobymen. Lord Barbican used every influence he had with press and parliament to characterize the Knights of the Tramlines as cowardly brutes. Turpin was vilified in the *Newgate Calendar* and elsewhere. At length scarcely a traveler throughout London was not somehow a potential villain and prone to harassment from the Runners. Soon the public cursed both company and mobsmen for their distress. Lord Barbican could afford to ignore their hatred. The tobymen could not. Much of Turpin's constituency had vanished. Brookgate was his last resort. For his own part, Turpin had grown a little depressed by his several defeats. He was not used to being thwarted so often and he relied upon his popularity with the public to pursue his trade. And so he turned to the gay life, by which he meant the conquest and pleasuring of any female who happened to show interest.

Soon, therefore, I began to make my own way out to the road, into Epping Forest whose wild tracts still offered cover and escape to a daring rider. There I built myself a hide and began to

ride against the old L55-G-class rattlers which still used those
night routes.

At length, of course, I induced Turpin to take a turn or two
with me, risking his life against the Runners rather than the
pox. He was soon his old self, his hard body bending in the
saddle as Black Bess took hedge and barricade with the same easy
power, his laughter and his commands roaring out of the night,
his aim as accurate as it ever was. But it was poor pickings for
the effort and the risk and we began to consider other means of
transferring Lord Barbican's own guineas to our unhealthy
accounts.

It was my idea to unite the remaining captains and carry our
attack to Lord Barbican's Hampstead mansion. Tom King,
Claude Duval, Jack Sheppard, Will Dudley and the one who
called himself The Blue Dwarf took part in the raid and a satisfying adventure it proved, netting us not only a considerable
fortune in silver and small gold but providing us with the documents which I was able to pass on to my cousin in the ministry
and so begin the work which parliament would complete. To
crown the affair, we sent certain pictures to the popular sheets
and increased their circulations mightily so we began to get our
good press back. Lord Barbican never recovered from this humil-
iation and died, broken in South Africa, three years later.

Of course, for all our renewed public esteem, Dick and I were
still hunted by the Law and we were too well known in London.
We couldn't stroll in the Vauxhall Gardens without being recognized by half-a-dozen admirers or enemies. Eventually, at my
instigation, we rode for York and from there made our way deep
into the West Riding. I believed I had persuaded Turpin to seek
immortality with me.

Then, not far from Kettlewell, after we had made a diversion
to enjoy the local ale, we ran into a party of Yorkshire Rangers
led by a Captain Simon West, who had earlier commanded a
troublesome company of Brixton Runners. He recognized us at
once. He ordered us to lay down our arms. There was a fight,

of course. I had let myself become surrounded by the constables. Their horses were pressing hard against mine and, with both pistols spent, I could not draw my sword. I heard Turpin roaring a command to let me go. Then I saw the flash of a barker and felt a sudden blow above my left hip. The ball had caught me in the side and I was badly wounded. At the sight of my blood, my assailants fell back even as, with some difficulty, I pulled my sabre free, but the effort exhausted me. I lay against my horse's neck, trying to get air.

Turpin, convinced he had killed me, called out "Hey, Tom, have I hit ye?" ("Tom" or "Jack" being the names we used to avoid identification) and when I replied to the affirmative, tried to come to my assistance. I ordered him off, saying it was too late for me. "I am dead, Jack! Save thyself!" He hesitated for a moment and then, with a shout of farewell, he rode Bess over a wall and vanished into the darkness, followed by West and his men, who believed they left me a corpse. I rested for a while in a nearby cave, then began my ride back towards home, hoping Turpin would catch up with me there and discover he had not killed me. Next morning I was within sight of Hawes when a much larger party of peace officers emerged from the mist, riding in a wide arc across the fell at my back while others advanced towards me. I was still weak from loss of blood. I could not outrun them. I could not fight them. I knew then that I had little choice but to ride rapidly towards Gowers Gap where as a girl I had found a roadway into the Second Ether. I decided I would have a better chance of survival there than at the hands of those Runners. I had a clear idea of my fate, once they discovered I was a woman. I reached Gowers Gap a few minutes ahead of them and was able to discover the road almost immediately. With some relief I left my horse behind and set foot on the moonbeam. Another second and I was safe. That was how I found myself, somewhat prematurely and rather reluctantly, involved in the war amongst the angels.

Of all the vices which disgrace our age and nation
that of duelling is one of the most ridiculous, absurd, and criminal. Ridiculous, as it is a compli-
ance with a custom that would plead fashion in
violation of the laws of our country; Absurd, as it
produces no test by which to determine on the
merits of the point in dispute; for the aggrieved is
equally liable to fall with the aggressor; and Criminal (criminal indeed in the highest degree!) as it
arises from pre-determined murder on each side.
Gentlemen talk of the dignity of honor, and the
sacredness of character, without reflecting that
there can be no honor in deliberate murder, no
purity of character in a murderer!

—*The Malefactor's Register;*
Or, New Newgate and Tyburn Calendar, 1796

Captain Billy-Bob Begg's Famous Chaos Engineers in

The Fight for the Balance

Captain Billy-Bob Begg and her Famous Chaos Engineers have
at last found Ko-O-Ko, the Lost Universe. Before they can

celebrate, they discover that the Singularity has launched an all-out attack against them, demanding nothing less than total control of the First and Second Ethers. The Great Consumer intends to devour the Cosmic Balance ensuring that it can never be in equilibrium again! We face the Death of Time, the end of all sentience. The Game will be played out on every scale, in every facet of existence. Meanwhile *The Spammer Gain* remains lost somewhere in the Second Ether, scaling down to infinity with Captain Billy-Bob (Fearless Frank Force/Sam Oakenhurst), Pearl Peru, Sterling, First Beast of the Skimlings, Professor Pop and their crews in her wake—sucked towards the point of the beginning—and beyond!!!

Chapter fourteen million and four

PAWNS OF THE INSECT

"We are used to such scales," said the Skimling impatiently. "We know the subtle shades which guide us through the fastest drops. These hot keys are without mystery. It is nothing to us. We have always roamed the roads between the worlds."

Billy-Bob apologized. She had forgotten how sensitive the First Beast could be. She felt she was wasting this pause before she again lost control of the *Now The Clouds Have Meaning*. Where was the Rose? "Then you will go with us to the *Greenheart Diamond*?"

"Of course."

Weeping, they embraced before the pale blues and creams of the Outer Halo which rimmed the shapes of those vast cosmic cathedrals known as *Karaquazian's Bend*. Massive black globes rolled overhead, purposeful towards some impossible horizon.

The Spammer Gain had called them. Beauty and terror were now inevitable. Life would become infinitely sweeter.

"Aaaahhhh," breathed the handsome First Beast, fingering his unstable scars, "our time is here again. What adventures we shall find together, eh, captain!"

And he clapped a paw of liquid silver upon the fluttering carapace of his fellow Chaos Engineer.

There was a sigh from the crew as the *Now The Clouds Have Meaning* began her first graceful slide cross-scale, her hull ticking and twitching with every shift and causing the entire complement, except Billy-Bob and the First Beast, to take to their eternity couches.

Kaprikorn Schultz, Respected Banker to the Home Boy Tong, clung to the outer folds of the ship, unsuspected by anyone but the murmuring back-brain. He was infected with a vivid form of scale-decay. It was almost impossible for him to size his limbs. But, even as parts of him became radically disproportionate, he held his place, cursing. His hatred sustained him like a stimulant and he was by now thoroughly addicted to it. He chanted a litany to himself whose meaning he had mostly forgotten, ancient codes and formulae, illegitimate descriptions of his state of being. *"Eff parentheses zed equals zed squared! Farp! Farp! You unsnessy pigbutters! Koofrudi! Hee, hee, hee! Boiling car bons! Buckyboils. Nasty buckyboils. Knitting sweaters for the stars are we! Well, they won't keep old Kappi in one of their bowls. Ner,hee,hee,ner! Slip 'em the equations, bappy-boys. We'll gollop and gollop and gollop 'em up! Glurrr. Sucksucksuck- sucksucksuck . . ."* So coarse had his signals become that it was all but impossible to detect them as having sentient origin and so his very devolvement became an element in his continuing survival.

Only Little Rupoldo, snug in the mezzanine, caught some of Schultz's monologue, but put it down to bad gravy.

Chapter fourteen million and five

"POUR MY QUILLS!"

"Pardon my French." The Countess von Bek strides aboard, greeting her old friends with familiar warmth. As she moves she trails pink and white, fine green and scarlet dust, leaving the scent of roses wherever she goes. Her skin has depths to it, shades of green and red, bone white, as if she is transparent sometimes and every vein visible, carrying her emerald blood. She has an easy swagger and is glad to be back on the bridge. She exchanges a word with every member of the crew, gives the screens her expert eye and makes a joke.

Billy-Bob Begg snorts with Frank Force's admiring laughter while Sam Oakenhurst's eyes cloud with fractal steam, and repeats the witticism to the First Beast, on whom it is lost.

"We might as well be stuck up Old Reg's arse, begging your pardon, countess," moans Corporal Pork, seeking his lost yellow mouth with his slender, myriad tendrils. He is still bleary from his bou-bou pads. "I'm not the creature I was. Forgive me. We're wasting away for lack of a guinea's worth of justice." He watches intensely, with narrowed eye, as the two comrades smooth skirts together. "Too long on the benches, marm. Too long for the boomwap. Icker. Icker. The thongs are dead. But the maladies linger on."

"Speak English, corporal!" demands the Rose. She looks to Billy-Bob for authority.

"English, corp!" confirms Billy-Bob. "Nocaboomwap! OK? Foo?"

Corporal Pork has to move his language forward. It was his only weapon. He has no other means of measurement. He cannot afford to be patient. He has no further choice. Hesitation will resolve in his death. He can hear them coming, louder and louder.

"Icker. Icker." He flaps his arms. His sharp, crazed eyes focus on me for a few seconds. Then he turns his head back to the vole he has caught. "Icker. Icker." His only choice now is the Owl. "Awoo. Awoo." It is too late for him. His vocabulary slips away and he weeps for it. Eventually, after pacing crazily about the bridge, he curls down into a corner, at Billy-Bob's feet, and sucks his belt. "Tartar," he says. "Tartartar. Chuc-chuc. Chuc-chuc."

"This will happen to more of you if you do not heed my warnings," says Billy-Bob, fondling her ruined hero. "Every definition. Every word. Every syllable. All vulnerable. All threatened. This the true reality-fold. No chuc chuc, you fellers. Chuc-chuc him feller all along dead." She puts a scintillating claw to a mouth filling with blood. "Ah, you see! Even me! Even me!"

The Rose grins at the challenge and spreads her hands above the controls. She is in her element. "Rest, redress, recoup," she says. "I have the urgency of the tables in me and this informs my power." She gasps. "Where are you? I need a number two. Hurry, hurry! Let's have a vocabulary check. Dip my blood, young 'un. We're curving in on a long one." She feels the urgency of her branches, her questing blood.

Something growls and yawns in the torn conductor boxes. The ship is falling in free fractals. Up come the yellow and black spirals, the red mouths, the lemon-colored zig-zags. The old navigation aids have put them into a spin. Their mass is rapidly destabilizing. They will be lucky to emerge alive. "*Somebody help me get out of Louisiana . . .*" happily sings the Rose, playing the light with careless grace. "*. . . Baby's in black and I'm feeling blue . . .*"

Corporal Pork sits up, hazily intelligent. His greedy eye pulses with sudden hope. "Music," he says. "Of course! We had forgotten the music!"

Little Rupoldo comes stumbling up from the back-folds with a handful of boxes.

"Hop to, young 'un!" says the Rose with an approving wink. "Give me some Hendrix and give it to me noisy!"

She strokes a knowing hand across a new, purple flank. "Don't forget to check the boxes this time. Remember what happened when you gave me Andrew Lloyd Weber."

A common shudder almost loses them the ship.

The Rose concentrates on her screens, calling back: "And have that Ives and Alkan ready for me when I need it."

The *Now The Clouds Have Meaning* pauses. A kind of palsied harmony fills her and she begins to croon. Captain Billy-Bob Begg sits back in deep satisfaction. She had been desperate, panicked. Now her judgment is confirmed. She thanks the Great Mood. Freddy Force was wrong. She had called for the Rose not a moment too soon.

Now, with a joyous, epic howl, the ship insinuated herself back under the Rose's control, looped into *The Abduction of Psyche,* stoked up on the crimson and viridian she needed and from there began to fold, scale by graceful scale, with all her past confidence.

"She knows how to treat an old girl," says Corporal Pork, easing several legs from his carapace and looking smug, as if all this had been his own idea. "We'd been too long on hold."

Sweetly powered by Havergall Brian's thrusty Gothic Symphony, the ship was soon racing to the *Greenheart Diamond,* the meeting place where all the Chaos Engineers and other privateers were congregating to debate the meaning of the Singularity's new strife and answer the call of *The Spammer Gain.*

"You are without doubt, Rose," says Captain Billy-Bob, "the greatest pilot in the multiverse. Is there nothing you cannot fly?"

Chapter fourteen million and six

POUR MA QUILLE

Four thousand ships float at stable scale against the lazy movements, gold and viridian, of *The Greenheart Diamond*. Here are all the Chaos Engineers, the Merchant Venturers, the privateers, outlaws and corsairs who, for reasons of their own, oppose and fear the Singularity.

They are met for a great conjunction, with nothing less in mind than the recreation of the First Ether, which they deem to be dying under the Singularity. They call their meeting to discuss the Conjunction of the Million Spheres when it might be possible to alter the nature of reality, to change the human condition. This is dangerous work, permitted only to the mad scientist or the creative artist, the visionary to whom the supernatural is a daily actuality. It is achieved so rarely in the great Game of Time that many doubt it can be achieved at all.

"All the tortured scales of my existence I have longed for this moment," declaims Billy-Bob Begg across the omniphone. A great psychic cheer rises from around her. "It is the opportunity every sentient being of conscience longs for. We gather here at last to journey to the center of the multiverse and change the rules of the Game of Time."

"And to do that we must follow *Spammer*," says Pearl Peru over fresh cheering. "Poor *Spammer* knows where the hub is. Only she can smell it. And only you can follow her, Rose."

Sam's eyes are still in Billy-Bob's sockets. They stare at the Rose, hopelessly in love. "I will follow you, Rose, if you will take us. You are our greatest pilot." Billy-Bob reaches out an embracing hand.

Pearl absorbs it, tenderly. "No other pilot can lead us," she agrees.

The Rose turns aside, trying to check herself. "Sam . . ." It is the only sign. Then she is in control. She is maintained by her sense of loss. And elsewhere, her husband waits for her. "I recall little but scents from my earliest months," she says. "Pine mostly and roses. I remember those trees with their roots in that soft, red earth which threatened to drown me with its smell. My mother was a wild flower. I have her blood. Pearl Peru, you honor me."

"We have reached agreement," says the First Beast. "The Rose shall lead the hunt for *The Spammer Gain*."

It is a matter of fact. Four thousand keels are at once under her command.

❧━━━━━━━━━━❧

Chapter fourteen million and seven

STALKING THE BEAR

Freddy Force, Fearless Frank's evil brother, makes a military gesture towards the screens. Old Reg has him for a renegade, he says. Disguised as his brother, he claims, he was traveling with the Chaos Engineers to discover their secrets.

"But you were betraying *someone*," says Lady Carinthia Slide, who liked to cut a fine point now and again. "You are, in fact, guilty."

"Not of disloyalty, marm."

"Perhaps even that," she muses. "But certainly of treachery. I think you should pay that price."

"What is that price?" asks grey Sung sung, licking its chops. "D—?"

"Of course not," says Mrs. Reg impatiently. "These aren't the dark ages. But it is Brussels Sprouts season." She adds a little emphasis. "*Choux de Bruxelles,*" she says with cruel relish.

Freddy Force takes her meaning. He bows his unhappy head before the justice of her decision.

He looks out of the dome at a world of steel. Ship upon shining ship raises its shaft skyward. Nothing in the First Ether is beyond their control. Everything is in order. The Grid is in place. Their marches are forever secure.

He knows more than a pang as he regrets his decision to return. He had never understood how attractive Chaos could be. He consoles himself with anticipated pain.

⌒⌒————————————⌒⌒

Chapter fourteen million and eight

COUNTING IN MILLIONS: AN IMMORTAL REMEMBERS

In spite of the alarming responsibility, I relished the chance to be flying again, using all my old skills of navigation, employing every instinct, taking the inspired risks which were my meat and drink in the Second Ether.

There was a sense of moment in our plunge through the scales of the multiverse. Time and Space have no true linearity. Carrying those who find walking tedious, our ether-ships, long-since turned almost entirely organic, move through the myriad planes of existence by following those faults, curves, *broches,* moments of self-similarity which permit intersection. Individually we see our courses winding as trails between the ever-branching planes of the multiverse. New trails must always be blazed if we wish to venture into unfamiliar planes.

Each plane is virtually identical to the next and to travel through them we must first identify them. We represent them on our instruments in terms of size. Thus we can go up-scale or down-scale and somehow cross the fields from one reality to another.[22]

Never before in known memory had so many used the same roads. We guessed that we would create at least a minor alternation in the nature of reality, just from that action alone. As I dived down the color fields, ship upon ship poured with me, like a vast school of fish. Baroque, gnarled, skittishly defined and dripping with unstable spectra, we followed the bulky, subtle intelligence that was *The Spammer Gain*, on her way to the Grey Fees where all the angels gathered to engage. Many who followed her believed she intended to commit positive suicide. Would she take us all with her? And, if so, to where? We scarcely cared. We had no patience for spiritual weather forecasts. Every soul in every ship was high on the same singular act of faith.

Once again our survival would be almost wholly dependent upon our ability to invent telling metaphor.

Pearl Peru was at my side. Captain Billy-Bob was at my side. Sam Oakenhurst was at my side. Little Rupoldo cranked up the Messiaen and my voice lifted in harmony with the sublime *ondes Marteneau,* one of the finest navigation instruments the French had ever developed.

"Ah, you are so beautiful, Rose." Pearl Peru strokes my streaming hair.

"So beautiful Rose," says Sam Oakenhurst, his eyes forbidding irony.

I chose not to regard this as a distraction. I had some options to try.

We took a curve. Our single light made little impression on the fog and the black trees on either side were like threatening giants. I knew the dangers of the South London night express

---

[22]See J. Mandelbrott III, *Making Size a Difference, The Journal of Chaos Navigation,* Vol 499, No. 11, November 172–. Also *Navigating Chaos Space, A Surfer's Manual.* Huntley & Palmer, Preston.

routes as well as anyone. I lay flat on the sloping metal roof,
ready to spring up as soon as we had gone under the Thornton
Heath Viaduct. Then I would attempt a trick I had seen done
by Tom King, Gypsy Jack and one or two of the other more
daring tobymen, but this was the first time I was doing it alone.
It was hard enough to dislodge the pole. But I meant to switch
rails, reversing the polarity and, in theory, bring the tram to a
sudden halt, rather than the gradual rolling stop we usually
achieved. The reason for this attempt was that both decks of
the tram—an up-to-date streamlined O-class—were crowded
with Runners guarding the strong box we intended to steal and
the friend we intended to rescue. A sudden stop might wind
them long enough for us to carry out the rest of our plan. Sam
Oakenhurst sat his steady horse up the line, and keeping pace
with us across the Heath rode Smith's best, recruited for this
attempt. As soon as I saw Sam I was to make what we called
the double hook-up and pray I didn't become a conductor and
make the entire vehicle live. There he was, up the line. I prepared myself.

Suddenly we were surrounded on all sides by flamingos—huge
creatures which seemed to regard our DoX as their leader. The
plane was cumbersome and I couldn't afford to make too many
fancy manouevres, but I dipped the wings a little and lost some
height, then climbed a bit—and they followed, clearly delighted
by my game.

There were German fighters spreading in on my left wing. I
didn't have any choice but slipped the Spitfire into a sideways
fall, coming under them so that, if I had the chance, I could
turn the tables. But there were too many and the mission I had
taken forbade me from unnecessary fighting. I put the wonderful
little plane's nose into the darkest clouds and hoped we didn't
bump into anything on the way home.

All I could hear now was the drone of the engines as the zep
reached for her maximum height, every inch of her shimmying
like a chorus girl until I was convinced my teeth would fall out.

The Height Coxswain looks to me but I won't give the order to level out, not yet. "Two hundred feet, Mister Oakenhurst."

Mister Oakenhurst darts a question, but obeys. Now the engines are knocking and whining, almost refusing the demanded task. The gondola threatens to come loose from the main hull. I turn to look through the semi-darkness at my crew. There isn't one not prepared to follow me to Hell if necessary, but I can tell they believe they're going to die.

The altimeters are in the danger zone. Bells are clanging everywhere, the riggers take a turn or two around their ropes, their eyes fixed on the horizon.

"Level off, Mister Oakenhurst." We're above the guns at last. I give the order to cut engines. The wind shrieks in our rigging like shellfire. I tell Mrs. Persson to break out the M&E. Those poor devils won't get any sleep otherwise. We still have a long way to fly. "Merry Christmas, chaps," I say.

"Merry Christmas, skipper." There's an atmosphere of relief on the bridge that you can taste. They would cheer me if they dared.

Now I turned the whole craft into the wind and she bent, a reed against the water, her white sails pregnant to bursting. Over the steel-blue waves and the icy breakers, I steered *The Hope Dempsey* towards the purple horizon where a royal yellow sun set to starboard and black shadows made the sea an undulating chessboard.

The air was singing in the rigging and the rain snapped against the canvas. There wasn't a sweeter schooner on the seven seas and I wished with all my soul she were mine. But she no more belonged to me than Captain Quelch, that villainous heartstealer, belonged to me and, I must admit, for a while I yearned to possess both. Now Quelch slunk somewhere behind, leading his own forces and with his own agenda. He had achieved the Singularity's rarest reward. He had been outlawed by Old Reg and denied the Eucharist of the Original Insect. He remained defiant, claiming his moral superiority against all the evidence.

His voice came over the screen: "I am prepared to take the center by force, if necessary." He believed he had the means to capture and control *The Spammer Gain!* With control of the balance, he could easily destroy Old Reg and rule Heaven and Hell and everything between. He had thrown down a challenge to Lucifer.

He was enraged that I would not help him in this enterprise. He began to display all kinds of unpleasant and demeaning aspects to his character. He accused me of petty spite against him. He mocked me for being an eternal and believing myself superior to a mere demigod like himself. I pointed out that the choice had been his. Had he not given up his soul for all this power? And had he not been warned it must inevitably corrupt him.

His fleshy features peered out from the screen, all broken vessels and unnatural bruises. "Lost my charm have I, Rose? *Lost my bloody charm!* Well, we'll see about *charm,* little missy."

I turned away, distressed by his ruin. I kept my attention upon the racing screens. My options cascaded. I made a choice. The tram lurched out of the viaduct and I was on my feet, balancing as I ran to reach my two poles up to the pulley-wire, snag them simultaneously over the runners, pull them both down in unison and snap them up together again while flinging myself flat onto the roof and hanging on to the safety bar for grim death as the whole massive machine slammed to a sudden stop and "Colonel Jack's" gentlemanly tones cut through the mist: "Throw down your lever, sir, if you please!"

Then the mobsmen had galloped out of the dark. Their heavy, greatcoated bodies, framed against the yellow light, were swarming over the insides of the tram. They were herding back the few demoralized Runners not still trying to pick themselves up, freeing Claude Duval and shooting the chains off the strong-box even as Duval helped them drag it along the aisle to the waiting gig which I now pulled up against the rear stairs, grinning like a baboon, and hardly able to contain my glee in my own skills, wanting to kiss Sam there and then on the spot.

The adventure was by no means over. Faintly now, but recognizeable, comes *Spammer's* voice.—*Ah, at last, at last I have found my fishlings. Fishlings. Sweet fishlings . . . dear, dear, fishlings . . .*

There is a legend amongst our kind which predicts the fishlings as the catalyst for a new Creation.

Behind me now comes growling Lord Quelch, Renegade Son of the Singularity, risking all to win complete control of the multiverse and despising every power except his own! He constantly attempts intrusion on my screen. "*Veni, vidi, vici,* Little Sure-shot. It's the only way to go!" He adds viciously: "*Varium et mutabile semper femina . . .*" His stench attacks our conduits. We counter with Brahms and Schumann, that uneasy duet.

—*Oh, fishlings, dear fishlings!*

We are almost at our destination. Reunited with her happy brood, *The Spammer Gain,* her joyous pulse sounding the rise and fall of dynasties, prepares for battle.

My immediate duty is done.

I give the controls into the temporary charge of Pearl Peru. "I have brief commitments elsewhere," I tell her. It is time, I've decided, to take a breather. I perform the ritual of *rubato.*

He was rarely out of her sight after their first
meeting, and the ridiculous excuse she gave to
her husband's family was, she feared he would
be kidnapped and made a Cossack of! And young
Lord Cressett, her husband, began to grumble
concerning her intimacy with a man old enough
to be her grandfather. As if the age were the in-
jury! He seemed to think it so, and vowed he
would shoot the old depredator dead, if he found
him in the grounds of Cressett: "like vermin,"
he said, and it was considered that he had the
right, and no jury would have convicted him. You
know what those days were.

He had his opportunity one moonlight night,
not far from the castle, and peppered Kirby with
shot from a fowling piece at, some say, five
paces' distance, if not point-blank.

But Kirby had a maxim, *Steady shakes them*,
and he acted on it to receive his enemy's fire—
and the young lord's hand shook, and the Old
Buccaneer stood out of the smoke not much injured, except in the coat-collar, with a pistol
cocked in his hand, and he said:—

"Many would take that for a declaration of
war, but I know it's only your lordship's
diplomacy . . ."

—GEORGE MEREDITH, *The Amazing Marriage*

The Rovers' Return

eanwhile, back at the ranch, my Uncle Michael had become obsessed with his conviction that Annie Oakley was Jewish. Her father, Jacob Moses, and her mother, Susan Wise, were Quakers, but the face that peered so steadily at us above her gunsights was unmistakably Mediterranean. That, at least, was my uncle's view.

He had written to various surviving members of her family, asking them for more details of her parents, but so far he had received no replies. This confirmed his belief. He told me he had been approached to take part in a White Anglo Saxon Protestant plot against Jews, Catholics and people of color. His evidence for this was an invitation from a local minister to join the Baptist Church. And everyone knew, he said, that joining the Baptists was also a direct entrance into the Ku Klux Klan.

Suspecting his High Church prejudices, I asked him where his information came from and he said from ex-Baptists and many academics throughout the South. I wasn't familiar with the suggestion, I said. He told me that it was not a suggestion. The Klan had been responsible for killing both Kennedys and many other major public figures.

It has always been my opinion that conspiracy theories are merely a diversion, allowing us to avoid any responsibility as individuals for the kind of society we help create.

I must admit that my chief curiosity about America was why the country smelled so strongly of vanilla. It was the predominant smell, wherever one stepped off the ship. It could not only be ice-cream. It permeated the entire nation, although occasionally challenged by cinnamon. It had taken me some years to identify the smell, because, of course, there are several pungent elements which make up any national odor. In France it is still Gitanes and Gauloises. In Italy, dependent on the region, it is usually tomato paste. Garlic, olive oil and street fumes, of course, are other important ingredients in a characteristic odor. Country areas usually smell pretty much the same, depending on local land uses. English cities smell mainly of fried fish, beer and disinfectant.

Joined by Prince Lobkowitz, who had been ordered to rest, I had traveled to Texas as soon as I learned my father had placed Tower House under the care of Mrs. Gallibasta and sailed from Liverpool, bound for Galveston.

Because of the peculiar supernatural circumstances surrounding the advent of the infamous "Biloxi Fault," which presently only threatened to materialize in our plane but which was already giving off disruptive waves through the entire field, my father had asked to stay with his brother for an indefinite period. At that time, Dick Turpin also had his lodge nearby and with the usual prescience of our kind had invested well in oil. My poor cousin Michael was still in London, struggling to establish himself as a boys' story writer and determined to return to Texas in triumph. He had little taste for real or imagined violence which can be a drawback for a man of his ambitions. While he only dreamed of earning his living as a honky-tonk singer, he had yet to find his niche in Girls Crystal and School Friend, where he would become a legend in Fleet Street for his ability to insert lewd innuendo (totally beyond his readership) into every story he wrote. He argued that the family name lent itself to such exercises.

Another visitor to my uncle's ranch at that time was Tex Brady (who had some notoriety as the original of The Masked Buckaroo). The Westerner had just ridden in from the Arizona territory where, he said, he had seen five separate conferences of angels atop the great range of red buttes known as the Devil's Battlements which marked the boundaries of the Navajo Empire.

"They were a pretty good size, sir," he confided to my father, who was most familiar with such things, "an' every one of 'em wearin' some kind of shell or armor, like they were covered in barnacles. I guessed they were armed to the teeth. Most had wings, but not all. An' some of those hombres were wounded or just plain tuckered out. It was like they were regroupin' after a battle, same as the Apache. And always at sunset. How is that, sir?" Carefully he dusted his chaps.

My father reiterated his understanding of supernatural visitation and how they were accompanied by discrepancies in those myriad time waves which made up the quasi-infinite—the multiversal Time Field.[23] A random intersection of one plane with another, he believed, was the cause of the effect. This disruption was sometimes caused by an especially intrusive form of travel used by the followers of The Singularity.

This explained, of course, how we perceived all kinds of other supernatural phenomena. His proposals had made my father a leading figure in the world of applied metaphysics. He was even now considering the Norman Bean chair at the University of Texas. Bean, of course, had seen his first angels in Arizona and Texas and had believed them to be Martian "Tharks." Visionary experience flourished in the local conditions and my father would never be short of study subjects. The entire literature of the South West, and especially Texas, was characteristically visionary and loaded with vibrant metaphor, from its raw pulp writers like Robert E. Howard and Jim Thompson to sophisticated fabulists like McMurtry, McArthy, Spencer or Waldrop. So profoundly unsettled was the territory, my father argued, that mankind was not here a clear victor as in so many other parts of the world. This allowed a greater parity between Man and

---

[23]Such sudden intersection of the planes, which allowed a visitation to occur, led, he believed, to a spacial-temporal adjustment which always resulted in the appearance of sunsets or sunrises. More accurately, witnesses experienced a slight repositioning of the planetary system in conjunction with the visitation, thus causing their perceptions to alter minimally to adjust for the shift.

Nature which in turn allowed a greater range and intensity of visionary experience. "Couple that with the settlement of so many Scotch and Irish, not to mention Teutons and Apache, with their notorious penchant for exaggerated romanticism and hysterical metaphysics—and bingo you create the Wild West and all it offers us!" Shamans, he said, were still respected and trusted for their wisdom and good advice in the surrounding communities. Most poor people used them instead of doctors.

"That," I argued, "is on account of this country's appalling healthcare situation, is it not? They can't afford anything else!"

"Ma'am, are you sayin' these witch-doctors make bad medicine?" asked Tex with a frown, shifting his guns uneasily in their holsters.

We all reassured him we meant the opposite. I was merely seizing the chance, as usual, to score a perhaps inappropriate moral point, as was my nature. I have learned to tolerate this vice in myself rather more readily than have my friends and family. It was at this point in the conversation that I left to walk over to the stables and collect myself, so I am unable to report the rest of it. Sometimes I am shocked and depressed when unwelcome aspects of my character are revealed to me and it takes me time to adjust. I know that this means some people think me moody, but I am not always able to control my responses in this respect. I am a solitary creature by nature, but I value the approval of my intimates.

When I returned, they had arranged themselves around the big fireplace which was burning sweet mesquite and cedar. Turpin, for all the world a local rancher in his tan-colored Western suit and string tie, was extolling the virtues of the local ales which, he swore, beat some of the best in England. He seemed very happy in those days and I was never sure why he packed up and left suddenly for London, where he remained, careless of his own disintegration. They say there was a woman involved, a wife even, but he never spoke of one.

In those happier days, Lobkowitz still enjoyed a little leisure and was more than content to be in Texas in the last days of winter. Our relationship only improved. My father and my uncle were in their element, their experience and their logic at one as they raced like happy hawks into the upper regions of what another would deem abstraction but what was to them, as it was to most of us there, urgent reality. Tex Brady was a pleasant man whose friendly innocence was refreshing amongst so much unworldly wisdom and I flirted with him more than was fair.

They were discussing an expedition they planned to make the next morning, before sunrise. They meant to ride twenty miles over towards De Quincey and see if there were any angels gathering on those flat limestone crags. They insisted I go with them. It was useless to tell them that I was here to relax. They were excited and reliving some of the enthusiasms of youth. Even Lobkowitz had been drawn into the game.

I put the best face I could on it and told them I would be ready in the sheds before sun-up. Like many of the big Texan landowners, my uncle had established private tram-lines across his property. Powered by his own hydro-electric generators, the cars were supplied by the famous Philadelphia Street Car Co. and ran all over his range, enabling him to reach difficult areas with his horses still fresh. There were those who said the little sparking single-deckers had ruined the Texas landscape, but others were of the opinion that this particular Texas landscape could only be improved.

∾

The tram took us to the region of scrub-covered hills known as Karaquazian's Bend. There had once been a river here, but it had dried up long ago. We got our mounts out of the horse-box and began walking them up the other side of the shallow valley, keeping as low as possible. We were well-protected against the surrounding rough sage, mesquite and cactus by our heavy chaps and riding coats.

Because of the swiftness of tram travel we had begun our approach before dawn so that if there were any angels on top of the buttes we should sight them long before they saw us.[24] My father was in the lead, as the most experienced of the party, and Tex brought up the rear. He was content to let the experts lead the expedition. All he hoped for was another sight of an angelic conference.

Suddenly my father paused, cocking his head to one side, then turning towards a sound only he had heard. Whereupon, grinning like an ape, a familiar buckskin clad figure rose from the brush and cautioned us all to silence. It was our old friend Colonel W.F.Cody, the famous Buffalo Bill, dressed in his plainsman's finery. With one fringed and beaded gauntlet he pointed towards a certain cliff on the horizon.

And there they were!

∿

I counted eleven of them, but there could have been more. The sun flashed on their quills and carapaces, on their elaborate weapons and armor. They seemed to be only a scale or two up from our own. They were probably bigger than Colonel Cody (the tallest of our party) by a head and shoulders, but it was not easy to tell their exact size. They were clearly resting and communicating amongst themselves. From where I was, I could not distinguish which tribe they belonged to, whether to Law, Chaos or one of their many cadet branches. They frequently adopted blazons and badges, but from our perspective they could be meaningless or confusingly asymmetrical. Those subtle differences, over which they were prepared to die, were frequently lost on the observer. We were downwind of them and even from here could smell their earthy, brute stink.

My father and Colonel Cody went ahead carefully, leaving their horses with us. There was a chance the angels would turn on

---

[24] It is not always possible to make the right connections.

us and if they did we each had a good, heavy-loaded repeating Sharps in our saddle scabbard and were every one of us expert shots. I put my gloved hand around the glossy leather of my pommel and prepared to mount in an instant if I had to. I had perhaps the most direct experience of the creatures and knew how volatile they could become, but it was not appropriate to air my knowledge at that time.

The horses tethered, we bent low and followed the famous Scout and my father up the rise until all of us were lying full-length observing the heavenly conference.

We could now hear a distant murmur, as of thunder, punctuated with high shrieks and growls, squeals and bellows, which was how we usually perceived the conversations of angels. The air directly above the peak was characteristically still, but all around it roiled the familiar shimmering spectrum denoting a rupture in the scales. Crystalline pinks and golds, shimmying brass and copper, eruptions of scarlet and crimson, deep gashes of blues and yellows, all surrounded by the bruised greens and reds typical of this kind of manifestation. One or two of the angels looked vaguely familiar to me, but the pixilated air made it hard to focus on them.

"That's pretty much exactly what I saw in the Arizona territory," murmured Tex, crawling up beside me. "D'you reckon they're hostiles, ma'am?"

I told him I didn't think they were interested in us at all.

"Then why are they here?" the young buckaroo wanted to know.

"Because, Mr. Brady, there is War in Heaven," I said, "and all we are seeing is a glimpse of it."

"Is that so! What are they fightin' for?"

"The fate of the multiverse."

"An' whose side are we on?"

"That depends on your temperament, Mr. Brady."

"Whether you go for the good hombres or the bad?"

"How you define those things."

My father glanced back and glared us into silence. He had his telescope out and offered it to Colonel Cody who used it to scan the surrounding country. In the dawn gloom the limestone crags stood dramatically against the grey-green scrub and the pale blue of the horizon. Now, as the sun put its crown over the horizon, sudden broad, glaring rays burned the landscape into unrelenting contrasts. Every gnarled branch and twisting succulent was defined in violent contradiction, shadows were deepened to vibrant black and every stone was suddenly alive.

Then, without warning, there came a massive *CRACK!* as if the entire Earth had split asunder. I fell back, blinded by a wash of bloody light, got to my feet and ran towards my horse and my Sharps. I heard my uncle yelling something and Tex Brady's shouting in reply. Then a hot wind almost blew me off my feet as I reached my saddle and flung myself into it. I was up, the nervous horse under my control, and looking around for the source of danger. Without my being conscious of it, the Sharps had come into my hand and I had already put a shell into the breech.

I could now see again. The limestone crag was melting like mercury, forming a wide, pewter-colored poisoned lake all around it. The lake was spreading towards us but not at a dangerous rate. Colonel Cody stood up now, his rifle in the crook of his arm, shielding his eyes, while my father, next to him, continued to peer through the telescope as if he had not noticed the interruption. I saw glittering, dark shapes in the sky, circling and flapping like dragons, until with an almost discreet *gulp*, they had vanished. The horizon was calm, like any ordinary morning, and only the quicksilver lake, which they had made of the crag, marked their visit.

My father had taken all this for granted. He passed the telescope to Colonel Cody, pointing towards the South East. "What do you make of these fellows, Colonel?"

Buffalo Bill accepted the glass. He needed only a few moments to decide. As he lowered the instrument I reached to take it, to see for myself.

"Comancheros would be my guess, Sir Arthur," offered the famous scout.

"Mine, too," agreed my father.

I could see them now. A band of fifteen or twenty riders, dressed in a miscellany of clothing borrowed—or probably stolen—from almost every culture which occupied this territory. They were filthy, ragged, and carried scalp-pouches at their belts, as well as a scalp-pole, to which was attached a rather sparse bag of mixed hair, predominantly infants'. These Comancheros had not done well for some time and would no doubt be pleased to see us. It was unusual for them to risk coming so close to a tram-line.

Turpin brought his great black mare up beside my palomino. I lent him the glass. "Uncouth looking ruffians," he said. "Can we take 'em ?"

"Easily," I said, "though we could get injured in the process. We could board the tram and be back at the ranch before they were half-way to us."

"Do that by all means, anyone who wants to," said my uncle, overhearing me, "but I'm inclined to stay and find out why they're on my range."

Naturally, we all decided to remain and sat our horses patiently, sipping a sturdy but subtle St Emilion '89 and munching on the smoked salmon sandwiches and Stilton Prince Lobkowitz had fetched up from the tram's coldbox.

I was not surprised, when I next looked through the telescope, to recognize the man who led the renegades. Indeed, it was almost as if he had been left behind when the others fled, for this was a substantial player in the Game of Time, none other than my old adversary and lover Captain Horace Quelch. Even now he was grinning to himself and sliding sensitive fingers over his dirty stubble as if aware that I was looking at him. I lowered the glass. I wished that I had shown more strength of mind on the previous day and refused to go on this expedition.

Quelch, though dressed better than his ruffians, was no cleaner. He wore a crumpled European suit, over which were crossed ammunition bandoliers, and on his head was a stained panama. There was a bit of cigar in his mouth, as usual, but it looked as if a rat had been chewing on it. His linen trousers were pushed into high, Mexican riding boots, so incongruous on him they could only have been pulled off a dead man. He used an English saddle and rode with an alertness denied his men, who were clearly weary. Their condition did not make them any less likely to attack us. Indeed, their judgment was probably so bad and their tempers so frayed they were all the more of a threat to us. I hoped Quelch was able to keep them under control.

Turpin had reached down into his saddle-bag and pulled out a brace of flintlocks, which he always felt comfortable with. He claimed he was more accurate with his "poppers" than the latest revolvers and he had certainly demonstrated this claim in the past. Seeing him slipping the guns down into his deep pockets, under his chaps, I imagined him back on Thornton Heath again, with his cocked hat on his head and a jaunty set to his shoulders. Indeed, he did seem to take on some of his old air as he prepared to meet the shambling tribe of desperadoes who were now so close I could almost feel their sweating heat. There wasn't a rag on their bodies which had not been torn from some victim. They had the primitive predatory instincts of wolverines and, given the choice, would always heap the maximum cruelties on any living soul they caught. These were so scrawny and wretched I suspected they had been eating their own numbers. It seemed to me they looked at us not as human beings, or even as antagonists, but as meat.

Captain Quelch draws up what's left of a good cattle pony and salutes the men, tips his hat to me. "How do, gents? Rose."

Behind him, his foul army comes to an undisciplined halt.

"You are on my land, Captain Quelch," says my uncle sternly. "You are trespassing."

"It seems to have come under your control, sir, since I was last here. I beg your pardon. I thought this prairie was the property of the devil himself."

The group of us sat our horses unspeaking as he arranged himself, wiping his face with the shreds of a Liberty's silk.

"Be that as it may, sir," says my uncle, "you are still trespassing. What's your purpose here?"

"Purpose?" Quelch snorts. "Purpose, sir? Why, you see us as you find us—we are wandering, sir. We are simple Gypsies. We are lost. We have suffered a number of set-backs on the trail."

"But managed to take a few small scalps, I see," said Tex Brady, unable to keep the loathing from his voice.

"We found the pole along the way, sir. Gaspar, there, took a fancy to it." He indicated the man who lounged in his saddle, his arm curved around the scalp-pole, his sunken eyes glaring steadily out of his mottled skin. "I warned him he would give a poor impression." His tone was admonishing as he turned his attention back to us. "We are a detachment of Major Brunner's men, sir. Would you have any news of the Major by any chance?"

My father, watching the comancheros carefully, slipped his telescope into its case so as to leave both hands free. Prince Lobkowitz lit a cigarette, studying the gang with cool candor. On his saddle was a holstered Mauser machine pistol.

Captain Quelch seemed surprised by our evident wariness and disgust. He took a look back over both shoulders as if seeing his followers for what they were for the first time. "Strange how a man's own story slips away from him, ain't it?" He chewed meditatively once or twice on his cigar and darted an innocent, questioning glance in my direction, as if I had the answer.

He caught sight of the tram-lines behind me and raised an eyebrow. "The electric tram has conquered the world while I've been away. I gather that's where the money is, these days. Transport and Communications . . . Electrics . . ."

Nobody replied to him and at length my uncle said again, "What is your business on my land, captain?"

"Just passing through, sir. We were on our way to San Antonio where I have a little money waiting. And then I planned to take the train East. If you could lend us fresh horses and a few provisions, I'll ensure you're paid back the moment I reach the city."

My uncle pointed westward, to a peak that was just visible on the horizon.

"That is where my land ends, sir. Beyond it is the United States of America. My property is protected by the very latest systems. I would be obliged if you and your party could be at that border and making progress into the U.S.A. by this time tomorrow. Otherwise, sir, we shall have no choice but to regard your presence as aggressive."

"*Aggressive*, sir? Poor old Captain Quelch and his starveling band *aggressive*? You do us too much credit, sir."

Only I knew Quelch for what he truly was. While his followers could be dealt with fairly quickly, he would give us far more trouble if he decided to fight.

Yet, with a shrug, he turned from us, motioning those vicious skeletons towards the western horizon. "You are an uncharitable man, sir. My apologies. I had taken you for a Briton."

"You took me right, sir. I made no such mistake in your case."

My uncle could not have scored a more telling thrust. Quelch, who had taught the virtues of the Anglo-Saxon empire, winced. I saw his hand move towards one of his pistols, but he had lost the heart for battle. Slowly his men began to follow him, looking back at us as if cheated of their game.

We sat our horses, watching them until they had disappeared below a distant rise, and then we took the tram home.

I determined that I would not join any further expeditions to look for angelic manifestations. The presence of Quelch here had alarmed me too much. If I did not rest, I thought, I would be unable to deal with my coming responsibilities.

Our horses made comfortable in their boxes, we were glad of the tram. I fitted the lever, screwing it tight into the control-lock as I flipped to power.

Just before I started up I heard my uncle saying to Buffalo Bill: "You knew Miss Oakley well, I take it. I wonder, did she ever speak to you of any Eastern European or possibly Levantine ancestry?"

When I was mounted on my steed,
I thought myself a man indeed;
With pistol cock'd, and glittering sword,
"Stand and deliver!" was the word;
Which makes me now lament and say,
Pity the fall of Claude Du Val!
Well-a-day! Well-a-day!
— *The Lament of Claude Du Val*

DISTANT HOOFBEATS:
La Valse de Deux Familles

Monetarism was now obsessing Buffalo Bill who had, of course, lost millions in the course of his career. He was a man of his word and preferred to behave as if others were men of theirs. He said those were the values which had won the West. Sadly, that age, in which genocide was the chief instrument of government policy, had existed only in fiction, but it was a myth insistently endorsed by Cody and the millions of readers influenced by Colonel Prentiss Ingraham's unsurpassed accounts of his adventures in the pages of *Wild West Weekly*, as if by this insistence their better world could be made actual.

"I find myself in a time," said Cody, "when money is no longer an instrument of measurement but is considered to be the thing it measures. This is genuine superstition, a form of cargo-cultism. The scale has become confused with what it weighs. Monetarists believe they can control the future. Communists believed the same thing. They cannot. In their persistent delusions, their irresponsible attempts to exercise their power over the abstract, they create monumental disasters and we are always the victims. Why do we let these lunatics into power? What a compulsion we must have towards self-destruction! We persist in giving up our civic power to madmen!"

He reminded us when, not so long ago, we had seemed to be electing sane, rather decent people to represent us. He had been in London after the War, in time to witness the achievements of the great reforming Labour government, one of the most popular parliaments the country has ever known. For a time, idealism and reality seemed closer to harmony than ever before.

"Now," said Tex, "it can only get worse. There is big-scale yankification going on. Those carpetbaggers want to run the whole world. They think they have a handle on it. We used to laugh at 'em. Now we're going along with 'em. We're even talkin' and thinkin' like 'em. It took the bastards a hundred years but they finally broke the South."

"Well, they ain't broke the West, yet," said Bill Cody.

"Don't bet on it, colonel," said the tall buckaroo.

❧

Prince Lobkowitz was fascinated by the famous Scout. He asked him how he had come to be in the area. Cody said that he had been out here for some time. He had drifted down from the Great Plains. He had wanted to return to the wide open spaces, where he could be at one with himself. He felt, he said, immortality slipping away from him. He had succumbed to a common melancholy amongst his kind.

Turpin reminded him of the good old days, when he and his friends, including Sitting Bull and Miss Oakley, would visit us at *The Six Jolly Dragoons*.

"You were filling Earls Court to capacity. Everyone came to see you. It was a field-day for the dips, I'll tell you. The stuff that passed through Smith's hands, just from Earls Court, is still being talked about in the Kitchen. It was American a lot of it and people were curious. Thousands of pounds worth, even at Smith's prices!" That was how Turpin measured fame, but it did not console Cody.

"They said I was exploiting Bull," he said. "Believe me, I wanted to show people what real Indians were like and how they lived, and Bull got to meet the ladies he liked. Our show was educational. At any rate, that's how we started out. I didn't want it to die. I wanted people to remember it. The horses and the shooting was just the icing on the cake, to make the public take an interest. Also, I'll admit, we enjoyed showing off now and again. Bull joined for the women. He loved women. And they loved him. Bull was a cosmopolitan by nature. That's why he couldn't stand it up there in Canada. Bull wasn't any kind of noble savage. He never saw himself like that. I never knew a more down-to-earth realist. Everyone took his advice. It was just a shame he was on the losing side. But we respected our defeated enemies. We weren't responsible for what our government did."

"Miss Oakley always spoke well of you, sir," murmured my uncle, before I could reply, and this meant something to Cody, who smiled his thanks. "I was fonder of Missie than I was of anyone," he said.

With an effort of self-control I changed the subject and again asked him how he had come to be where we found him.

The fine old plainsman, with his silky white hair and goatee, his noble, weather-beaten features, still held himself with all his natural dignity as he sat in the big armchair before the fire, a glass of Ackroyd's in his hand. He said he had been in Oklahoma when he had found angel spoor but had not then known what it was. He had followed it and found several branches. Eventually he had met up with Wild Bill Hickock, on the same mission, who had told him what he was stalking. He and Wild Bill had ridden together for a while ("though Hickock's lost his taste for adventure and was only interested in getting some spoor he could sell back East"). He had been watching that particular brood since the previous day.

"But those aren't the only ones you've seen, eh?" asked Lobkowitz. "How do you stalk them, colonel?"

"You pick up the scent first, of course." Cody's voice became more animated. "That's unmistakeable. Then you start to see little shifts of color in the air, in the sky. Then maybe you'll see a shaft of rainbow light and suddenly it's sunset. You hear them—those ear-splitting howls and groans which seem to be their language but make you want to throw up—almost always on the top of a hill or a mountain—maybe a couple. Occasionally you'll see just one. Mostly, though, it's small groups of seven or eight. Usually they leave color behind, but it's what the miners used to call 'fairy color' and it's good for nothing. I've only once had an angel attack me and I guessed him to be crazy, some kind of rogue. I let him have it with my big Henry and stopped him in his tracks. There's a lot to be said, in times like this, for a good old fashioned buffalo gun."

"You killed him?"

"I don't believe it's possible for us to kill them, prince," said Cody seriously. "But I made him change his mind about eating me."

"And what did he look like ?"

"Same as the big fellows we saw today. All crusted over like a desert toad, like barnacled crabs, with the shifting, vivid color. I have a feeling that this was a young one. He didn't act like he knew what he was doing. You can't read much of an expression in those weird fly eyes so many of them have. A kind of mottled, fishy face—big eyes and lips. And a silver crest—maybe a badge?—and—well, the other things we don't generally mention in mixed company."

∽

I said nothing, of course. I remembered the first angels I had seen, as a little girl, amongst the gentle hills of Morsdale. Those had not been at all warlike and had seemed very respectable to me.

I had left the path which leads away south of Corum's Tarn and gone down into a little secret spot only I and my father knew about. He had the sense, of course, to leave the place alone. As I began to drink my flask of Tizer and eat a fishpaste sandwich, I looked up. An entire choir of them were directly overhead, spiralling into heaven, rank upon rank, the lowest and broadest ranks hovering some fifteen feet above my head. Their faces shone like polished pewter and brass and their folded wings were rustling ivory. They were engaged in some kind of dance. The dance was, I think, a way of communicating between themselves. A few of them showed a casual interest in me. I caught snatches of sound. They had seen me watching them and seemed to approve. Together with unconditional love, their dark eyes contained everything I had ever wished to learn. I sat in the heather, my tender back against a limestone spur, my little pink feet dangling in the bright ripple of water below me, and watched them for a lifetime.

I witnessed at least three similar visitations every week throughout 1952 and 1953. It did not occur to me then that it was as easy for me to pass into their sphere as it was for them to pass into ours. Eventually, of course, and against all my father's warnings, I put my first tentative foot into the Second Ether and found myself on a moonbeam road. During the so-called *Game of the Raped Planet* I had a million years to regret that step. But now I am glad I took it.

Immortality is not easily earned, nor kept. We 'eternals' are doomed to perpetual vigilance and an uneasy relationship with time, yet I have no yearning towards death as popular myth suggests. My life is lived to the fullest and in moderation. Prince Lobkowitz taught me much about the pleasures of self-restraint and the ecstacy which comes when standing silent and still, alone amongst the elements, or from taking a different, subtler kind of path to one's desired destination. While one learns, one lusts for immortality. And so one continues to learn.

My mother had much the same attitude in her own life. Her curiosity was so closely associated with her sexual desire that she could not satisfy one without gratifying the other. This naturally led to the vast and varied list of lovers she had enjoyed, but gave her a certain reputation for flightiness, which I do not believe was earned.

I had stayed with her after both my god-fathers had contacted her and warned her of my wildness and I had escaped justice for the third time, on account of my youth. I had given my word that I would remain in Sporting Club Square until I returned to Yorkshire and indeed I was quite ready to know a familiar, domestic life again. Although I had enjoyed my escapades on the High Toby and had learned a few skills which would serve me in later life, I was not temperamentally suited to the work.

My mother seemed unusually welcoming and wanted me to reassure her that my challenge to the Law would not be repeated. I told her it would not be repeated in that manner, at least.[25]

During the afternoons, I would go into the square when very few people were there. Quite often I would come upon a small manifestation. On other days I would watch the huge jackdaws, which had nested here since the Celtic farmer plowed his first

---

[25]By 1983, the re-privatization of the transport company had put many of us in the position where we felt we had to do something to resist. After the transport workers' strikes failed in their object, some of the dismissed tram-men joined the tobymen and there was a brief revival of our old glory. In the end, however, the majority of us began to look for political solutions to the situation and succeeded at least in checking the excesses of the monetarist revolution poor Bill Cody had decried.

furrow for the farm that became Foulsham. The birds had a
complicated social life and, once they were sure of me, lost any
self-consciousness. I grew fascinated with them, much as another would watch a soap opera, and followed their careers with
concerned interest.

∽

Sometimes my mother, in all her painted, bewigged glory,
would come with me and we would enjoy the jackdaws together. She did not want to experience any visions, however.
She was firm on the matter. She had no interest in developing
her psychic gifts. She had chosen her path in 1942, she said,
after I was born. She had never looked back and she had never
once regretted anything.

"I remember," said my mother, "when we thought we'd pretty
much laid the groundwork for Utopia. Everyone was talking
about the 'problem of leisure' and the coming universal equality.
It seemed almost inevitable. And within the context of that inevitability, people began to act as if Utopia were already here, and
someone else was keeping it all for themselves. Their desire for
tranquil security was translated into a hatred of all which might
be denying them their share of paradise. Injustice breeds injustice, dear. Inequality makes criminals. That's the trouble with
telling people they've never had it so good. They wonder where
their share is. I'm voting Liberal again, dear, though it does
no good."

My mother had twice been persuaded by the Liberal Party to
stand as their parliamentary candidate for the area. I still have
one of their rather ill-conceived posters which attempted to capi-
talize on everything and created only confusion—LADY ELEA-
NOR TAYLOR (BBC's "Mrs. Cornelius") SAYS VARIETY IS
THE SPICE OF LIFE. VOTE LIBERAL, reads one black and
orange dayglo pronouncement.

Even when a few of her old records were aired and her fan

club put on a revival at The Players, Charing Cross, she never came better than a close second, first to the Labour candidate and then to the Tory.

She had expected to be asked to stand again, in the coming election, but had decided she was probably not the most viable candidate. Nonetheless she remained faithful to the party of Lloyd George and would still do a full turn for the odd benefit. I believe she was approached to stand again, but it was a matter of courtesy. She understood that.

As she grew older, and continued into her thirty-fifth season of "Mrs. Cornelius," she seemed to grow wiser. All her virtues came to the fore, while the volatile and somewhat careless nature of her earlier years faded into memory.

I learned to enjoy her company increasingly as she saw death "leaning on the next lamppost down the road" as she put it. The notion of dying did not distress her at all. She was not sure, she said, there was much more fun to squeeze out of life's sponge and she was ready for what she called "the gentle translation from sentience to untroubled spirit." She knew exactly when she intended to die. "It will be the day they tell me I need incontinence knickers, dear."

Meanwhile, she didn't plan to waste her life and while I stayed with her we would go to Portland Square to record her regular "Mrs. Cornelius" episodes in the morning, have a light lunch at Fortnum's, then perhaps go shopping in Bond Street until around four, have tea at Liberty's and then see a play or a film. We would take a taxi home and I would make us a snack for supper. It was our favorite way of spending time together. Sometimes, if the day was nice, we would walk in one of the parks. London has a way of letting you go at your own pace and finding zones of quiet in the middle of all that noisy commerce. It is almost always possible to find somewhere to rest in London.

My mother insisted it was the only city in the world worth growing old in, in spite of the horrible air. London was made for the elderly, she thought, and was kinder than most cities in that respect. She was never very clear about what she meant, but she was certainly content. She hated leaving London. It made her shiver to think about it, she said. London was her life. She was convinced that the moment she set foot in the suburbs fate (in the shape of some avenging warrior goddess bursting out of Old Lud's Hill) would strike her down. Given her vast range of superstitions, her second-sight and her rich experience, I did not argue with her and always respected her wishes in the matter of thrown salt, touched wood or dropped metal.[26]

When she was feeling particularly sentimental about Nature, usually in the warmest weather and on the quietest days, when London's noise often drops to a murmur and bees and butter-flies swarm everywhere, she liked to make what she called an "expedition to the river." This meant packing a small picnic hamper and leaving Sporting Club Square by the back way, through what used to be the nunnery's tradesman's door. We passed through St. Swithold's churchyard, full of lilac and elder, into a landscape of rural harmony. Neatly tilled patches of land were like a model for harmonious life in a Tudor tapestry. The thatched almshouses were freshly whitewashed and creosoted.

---

[26]Because of the usual variations, it is not always easy for some of us to keep track of the "timestreams" (which of course only exist in the imagination). When we follow those streams (or "go linear" as some prefer to say) we have to be careful. In those circumstances, a wrong word can make a great deal of difference to one's fate. It is wise to respect all formalities and beliefs at least until one understands their function. Languages and rituals do not develop at random. Superstitions, however, sometimes do. Baseless superstitions (those developed from theories of race, for instance) are not always immediately distinguishable from some with a solid foundation in fact. Thus, the consequences of walking under a ladder were not necessarily as grave as the result, say, of parliament's passing an apparently sensible transport bill. In the end, as Prince Lobkowitz was fond of saying, all we had was our capacity to love and our penchant for creativity to help us steer a stable course, and the only really workable social systems we created were based on that understanding. He himself worked to produce at least a temporary stability wherever he went. For a while after his passing a region would know peace and sanity. In Europe they would say that "the rune staff has touched us," a reference to his old family legend, part of which George Meredith used in *Farina: A Legend of Cologne.* There are also subtle references to that family's oriental history in *The Shaving of Shagpat,* which George Eliot admired so much and which functioned for a while, of course, as a famous move in the Game of Time.

The old graveyard's yew trees, willows and dreaming monuments crowded together, a press of centuries. There were a few distant spires visible above the massive oaks and elms lining the Thames all the way to Chiswick Bridge, perhaps the finest of Norman Shaw's civic designs. You could see the terracotta towers once you reached the Bishop's Park whose lawns stretched down to the water's edge, where a few anglers, their hooks masked amongst the drifting blossoms of the surface, pitted their wits against the cunning London salmon, claimed to be the sweetest table fish in Britain and the hardest to deceive.

"Why on earth should anyone demand more of the world than this?" my mother said one high summer afternoon. She wore white lawn trimmed with *broderie anglaise* and a wide gainsborough shaded her face. She touched her legendary lips to a piece of Texas chevre, which my uncle had sent over for her birthday. She said it was the best in the world and I was inclined to agree. She drank her own little bottle of Krug and I enjoyed my Smith-Lafitte rouge. The city still valued peace, after the cacophony of War, and everything closed on a Wednesday or a Thursday afternoon. On those days, the clang of an invisible tramcar, far away on the bridge, was no more than a reminder of the luxury of rest.

We would eventually come to our favorite destination and push open the little ironbound wooden door which led into the Tudor herb garden. A few rustic picnic tables and benches had been placed on the grass and the warm, red bricks seemed to glow with the light of all their centuries and smell of every sweet-scented herb that had ever come to life here. Rosemary and thyme and basil and sage, lavender and witchbalm all added to the air's heady wealth, enough to send us both to sleep, dreaming of some Elizabethan Arcadia.

My mother was always happy after our outings and came to desire them more and more. Even in winter, sometimes, she would go a little way through St Swithold's churchyard, wrapped in her old fox, and sit on a bench for a while. Typically, she

struck up a lively acquaintance with the vicar, a man in his
nineties who seemed to see himself as the custodian of civiliza-
tion, the last outpost of enlightenment as the dark ages fell
across England. He did not, he said, expect this little corner of
old London to be here much longer. Some privateer or other had
already bought the Chelsea Physick Garden. We thought him
wildly pessimistic. The Reverend Cole wrote poetry which was
well-thought-of in literary circles. He had won awards. He was
a great admirer of my mother. He also knew another resident,
Edwin Begg, the famous Clapham Antichrist, a recluse I was to
meet much later and in odd circumstances.

My mother spoke from time to time of buying a small dog,
but decided in the end that it would be too much of an emotional
responsibility. Then she was given, by Noel Coward, an oriental
short-hair kitten, which adored her and would happily accompany her on her walks. The distances she preferred were ideal
for both of them. When the cat complained that it was tired, she
would pick it up and drape it around her shoulders like a stole.
The cat would begin purring loudly and remain happily relaxed
while she walked back to Sporting Club Square. It would also
go with her when, as they grew older, she ventured only into
the square or the churchyard.

When Dick Turpin, another enthusiast for the breed, came to
visit us, he and my mother would sometimes talk nothing but
cats. Turpin liked to accompany us to the river, since fly fishing
was still the pastime which relaxed him most. He would wade
out a little way in his great boots, his cocked hat on the back
of his head, his greatcoat on the bank beside his creel. His linen
glittering against the water he would make one of his careful,
delicate casts.

Dick always got on well with my mother, though if they were
ever lovers I never had a hint of it. She flirted with him, naturally, and he would flirt back, discharging at her all his elaborate,
eighteenth century flattering ironies and making her laugh like

a child. He recalled, she said, the old rogues of her childhood, the last vestige of those easier, Regency manners.

Though she had chosen not to become one herself, my mother loved "eternals." She felt sympathetic to them. Possibly my best memories were of kindly Turpin as he was then. I can see him leaning on one weathered, muscular arm, his booted toes pointed towards the water, munching a cucumber sandwich and sipping tea from a thermos cup while he told my mother impossible stories of trams which had leapt chasms and horses which had followed them.

In the winter, Prince Lobkowitz, with his long grey hair tied in the old-fashioned style, would occasionally stay at the Square, and Turpin, too, would visit. Then it would be a good, coal fire, a trivet for the kettle and a toasting fork for the crumpets, with all of us clustered around like puppies, our closeness and warmth making us profoundly comfortable in contrast to the cold outside.

Jack Karaquazian, who always carried an indefinable loneliness with him in those days, also got into the habit of dropping in on my mother and myself and generally seemed more cheerful on departure than arrival. His own mother had an apartment near us which Jack borrowed from time to time. He had some of that tormented, self-involved air women often take for attractive femininity in a man.

My mother guessed Jack to be an alcoholic still in love with drink. It could be that he had an addict's nature and could never be free of some obsession. I know now, of course, that he had denied himself the Game. And Jack Karaquazian was the best and most famous jugador on four continents. The Game was his life. He must have known extraordinary pain. And he had not then, I believe, discovered that he had been separated from Colinda Dovero far longer than necessary, because of a misdelivered letter.

Since I learned his story, I have rarely committed anything I value to paper. In my world, too many ructions are caused, directly or indirectly, by notes which do not arrive or are seen by the wrong eyes. These days answerphones, fax machines and e-mail complicate and hasten this process of degeneration.

"Gypsy Jack's" best friend was Sam Oakenhurst but these were the days before Jack decided to blame me for Sam's martyrdom. Jack thought we were too much the same, he said. That, for me, was sufficient insult. Curiosity, it seems to me, figures far larger in sustaining relationships than romance and generally lasts much longer. I had none about Jack.

I met Edwin Begg, who had also been a minister of religion, in peculiar circumstances. For a while I found it impossible to return to Sporting Club Square for any significant amount of time. I was told by someone that this is called the "Morphail Effect" and has to do with nature's refusal to have her fundamental design tampered with, her attempt to avoid a threatened paradox. Usually the Square is my most useful coordinate. During the period I mention, however, I had either failed to make the right connection or take the right path. Or something was deliberately stopping me from going home.

Whatever the reason, the Square was frequently denied me. Only through Begg could I get in at all, but generally he wanted me to take him into the multiverse, to see the moonbeam roads. He proved a good amateur traveler and I never had to regret my decision. He did, however, get me pregnant and insisted on marrying us. With Edwin's death, it became easier for me to return. I have puzzled over that.

∾

Lobkowitz and I left Texas on November 5th, 1964, five days before the State again seceded from the Union. It signaled the beginning of the end. The war amongst the angels was manifesting itself more and more in our ordinary lives. By declaring herself neutral, Texas hoped she could negotiate with the victors. Someone, she said, had to want her beef.

Any old how the game commenced, with four
geezers playing, Phil and Spar being two of them
and the other two were a couple of rubes that I
had never seen before, the rest of us stood
around the table punting to a book at eleven to
four, that is except for me, because of the usual
reason. Another thing about Phil was that he
was a born gambler. I have seen him, when he
has got a good hand at rummy, have a side bet
with the bookie for his guntz, which might be
anything at all.

—FRANK NORMAN, *Stand on Me*

Hotel Victoria

"This is going off like a fire in an ammunition factory," said
Prince Lobkowitz to me over his morning *Al Pais*. I
poured him some coffee. Through the stateroom window I
looked out at easy blue water. A couple of yachts sailed in our
shadow as it moved across the water. Their passengers waved
as we flew by, high above. We were on our way from Mirenburg,
having changed at Barcelona for the last stage of our journey to

Las Cascadas. We had taken the midnight zeppelin and expected to arrive at what the Moors still called Port Sab'al-khar[27] by noon. My husband was referring to the diplomatic mess created by the nationalist's restoration of the Wäldenstein monarchy and the reverberations which would now sound throughout the Balkans.

For the moment, he had done all he could and had learned to discourage regrets. He turned the page and began to read the arts news.

For the past three years we had been trying to persuade governments and politicians to make progressive decisions. The childish folly and self-serving greed exhibited by so many of the grown men involved had sickened me and depressed him. The usual rituals and war-dances were being performed now and it seemed to me that until the people of the region pulled themselves together and put all their myriad superstitions behind them there was no hope for the voice of reason.

As so often happened in a crisis, the voice of reason was the first thing to be silenced with a ferocity only the demonically possessed can muster. It was clear to me that the War, which had seemed so far away, was coming closer and involving us more directly.

I was, of course, ready with my own strategies and knew my duty, but I was determined to enjoy this Silver Age until it was finally destroyed, once and for all. My father had returned to England and was looking for a house on the South Coast. My mother had been persuaded to leave London after the disaster there and admitted that she was not sad to go.[28] This world was

---

[27]This is the Arab name from which the present name of the port derives. It is still given in Arabic at the aerodrome and elsewhere, but generally the town is signposted in the Latin alphabet and frequently referred to by its British title of Port Sabatini (honoring the famous pirate, who retired here). This is not to be confused with the town of Port Sab near Guadalajara or the small town in Texas, claimed to be the first European settlement in the state.

[28]Thereafter, however, she would continue to complain about her exile, even though there wasn't a neighbor in ten miles of her who was not her fan. She could have packed the Worthing Pavilion every night and revelled in the knowledge. It gave her career another ten years, at least, and she eventually returned to London.

clearly on the brink of disintegration and I would mourn its passing if the worst happened. For the immediate future, however, I had no one to consider but Lobkowitz and myself.

I must admit that I was not always comfortable around Mr. Karaquazian, who was known for his ability to hold an irrational grudge and was used to women he could control, but I looked forward to seeing Colinda Dovero. It had been she, initially, who had brought Jack here and there was no doubting their mutual love. I knew his pride. He would respect me for her sake. I rather hoped that he would behave a little less coolly towards me now that he had settled.

We had last met all together in Aswan, when I was seeing Sam Oakenhurst. There had been some talk of an expedition. I had been enthusiastic but Jack had been reluctant. What he would have done on his own account he would not do if I appeared to be leading. His machismo sometimes astonished me. Yet at least he was a complete old-fashioned gentleman, who would die to defend his honor, a woman or a child. He could always be trusted. I knew he remained my greatest ally, my only equal.

Jack had held to his grudge against me as if it were a principle.

Jack knew Sam was not dead, but had been translated in the course of my last end-game. Sam had volunteered. Jack thought I had maneuvered him into an inescapable position. Since Sam opted to join his soul to Billy-Bob Begg in the Second Ether, Sam's story was now Billy-Bob Begg's and their story in turn had united with Pearl Peru's to create what was virtually a new epic. Jack would not be convinced that this was all Sam had ever wanted. Even though Sam had participated in the process, Jack was prepared to believe that I was the arch-manipulator and that my motives could well be sinister. I think he felt jealous of us, too. There is a self-involved streak to Jack which he attempts to control but is always evident.

*S*am Oakenhurst had his own irritating quirks of character. He and I had stayed in Paris that last summer before the War, in a little flat we were renting off Boulevard du Temple, a few streets behind the Cirque D'Hiver and in that ancient but not especially wholesome district known as Les Hivers, which was either a reference to the circus's winter quarters or a corruption of the old French *Hiv-eau!*, called out as the boatmen hauled on the big ropes drawing the barges up to the warehouses along the northern border where, for a stretch, six busy canals emerged from Paris's complex underground waterway system into the light.

I was always an early riser, unlike Sam, and I would often get up in the morning and go down to the waterfront to one of the rivermen's cafes, *Le Terminale,* where the coffee was particularly good and the croissants were hearty. Not once did I ever experience anything but impeccable courtesy from the bargees who used the place. I even enjoyed the smells from the canals, the faint green mist which rose from the surface slime at dawn reminding me, for some reason, of childhood mornings in Yorkshire. I could not believe that the anglers, who always lined the opposite bank, ever caught anything they would want to eat.

Because I was there so often I made casual aquaintances amongst the other regular customers, many of whom played chess, dominoes or cards all day. There was an old Jewish lady, Madame Stone, who had been widowed by the last War and yet radiated a sweet optimism which I found attractive. I always looked forward to seeing her bright little features, never less than perfectly made up, across the table from me. Sometimes, I admit, I sought her out for my own consolation.

Madame Stone's particular friend was a middle-aged bookseller with a rather amiable, pale reptilian face, who lived in the same building as madame, across the courtyard. His name was Monsieur Vermuth and his shop was up near the Place de la Republique. It specialized in late nineteenth century bohemia, especially Montmartre and Montparnasse. It was full of dusty

Willette pierrots and Steinlein cats, faded pastel bindings and posters for forgotten cabarets. I visited him once or twice there.

Monsieur Vermuth seemed to have no interest in his stock— he looked on it with a kind of melancholy distaste as if it represented the folly of his youth. "The stuff has become so popular, these days," he would murmur in mild self-reproach.

His real enthusiasm was for the English writer and politician Benjamin D'Israeli, who had been one of the great reforming imperialist prime ministers in the nineteenth century and had persuaded Queen Victoria to let him buy the Suez Canal. Vermuth seemed a kind-hearted man and if I mentioned an obscure author I enjoyed or spoke of a book I had been unable to find, he would usually bring me what I was looking for the next day or leave it with Esmeralda behind the bar. He was naturally reclusive but he cared for books, especially those which fashion ignored, and loved to distribute them. He always wore the same wide-brimmed trilby hat, a black overcoat, a blue shirt, red and black bow tie, a burgundy waistcoat with dark green corduroy trousers. The overcoat's pockets were invariably full of books and catalogs. He never removed it in my presence. It was his briefcase, he said. He carried everything in it and it left his hands free. Also, he was never likely to leave it on a bus or in a restaurant.

After he had presented me with his latest find Monsieur Vermuth would look at me with expectant, lizard innocence, then drop his eyes in an expression of satisfaction when I voiced my pleasure. Madame Stone told me that he had given so much away that sometimes he was hard-pressed to find the rent for his shop. Sardonically, he called himself *Le Ressusciter*.

—*Mon experience de la vie domestique est tres limitée,* he offered, by way of explanation, as if he understood his enthusiasm to be a weakness.

When I brought the books home Sam was never pleased for me. He would make slighting remarks about Monsieur Vermuth's motives and would suggest that I watch out for seedy

old booksellers, everyone knew they were perverts. I would either tell him sharply to stop or would ignore him, but it depressed me when Sam acted childishly. On two occasions he got
up at the same time as I did and insisted we go down to the
docks together. It was not, of course, the same experience. On
one morning I introduced him to Madame Stone and on the
other to Monsieur Vermuth. Once he had met them he seemed
impatient to leave.

On the first morning I went with Sam when he wanted to go.
On the second morning, I stayed. This meant, of course, that
Sam was in a poor mood for the rest of the day. He was convinced I would sooner or later betray him. I forgave him much
of this because of his understandable insecurities, his peculiar
destiny, but I did not realize he had confided these fears to Jack.

Sam was always better when he was allowed to play a hand
or two somewhere. I encouraged him to go with me at night to
the same area, near the canal junction, where a local casino, *La
Fixe Profonde,* attracted some major gamblers. He was reluctant
at first, grumbling about playing with amateurs, but he soon
learned how good these Gitanes were and began to enjoy the
games, falling in with the great patriarch of Les Hivers, Jacques
Le Bec, and thereby winning the approval of the ruling clan.
Within a fortnight, Sam Oakenhurst was admitted to La Rondo,
the Gypsy fortress hidden deep in the tangle of canals, and could
have called on the entire able-bodied population of Les Hivers
in any venture to which Papa Jacques gave the nod.

Sam's other great pleasure was the cinema. At that time in
Paris it was possible to see every kind of film, new and old. He
developed, for a while, an interest in silent Chinese erotic films
of the 1930s and would drag me along to everything he could
find to watch. I grew quickly bored, even rather uncomfortable,
and luckily his craze did not last as long as his obsession with
the screen heroes and heroines of the Second Ether, especially
Pearl Peru. He remembered them, he said, from his childhood.
I thought this must be a false memory, but he denied it.

Sam became addicted to the screens.

I tired of arguing with him. I was ready to be by myself again. It was no great hardship to me to let him go on his own. I found the things he enjoyed either boring or horrible. The stories were repetitive and I could not tell which character was which, but Sam knew them all and could quote whole scenes in French, Spanish or English. He also read the fan magazines. Something infantile in him, he said, was satisfied by all this. I believed there were other less wholesome explanations.

While, as I say, I was rather glad to have more time to myself Sam was not content to let me pursue my own quiet pleasures. Almost immediately, he began to show signs of jealousy, as if my visits to Monsieur Vermuth's shop or my explorations of the underground canals with the friendly rivermen were something less than innocent. When I pointed out that I was occupying my time with other things because I had no interest in screen adventures, he grew baffled and wounded and stormed off to the theatre. Later, he would often apologize.

In these circumstances I was walking in the Luxembourg Gardens one morning, wading, for some reason, through a silt of history and psychic reference, when I failed to recognize Prince Lobkowitz. I heard my name called, but did not respond. His was not the only voice speaking my name at that moment.

"Madame! Contesse! My dear Rose!" If he had not insisted, I would have continued on, attempting to shed the "dust" of memory which clung all around me. All of us know that terrible sensation, of suddenly experiencing dozens of events at exactly the same time and failing to regain control of one's perceptions, of collapsing under a weight of realities. He made a particular sound, which I recognized. It was a life-line. I managed to turn and recognize him. Almost immediately my ghosts dispersed. It was not the first time I had experienced that famous "*runestab-ruhren,*" the so-called runestaff-touch. Now, rather than the steady murmur of the ages, I heard ordinary bird-song, the calls of children and parents, the rumble of pneumatic wheels. There he stood, raising his wonderful hat, a tall, manly figure in a great black coat, his long white hair tied with a black linen bow, his white cuffs and collar relieving the black of his jacket and trousers. His fine, ascetic features were full of friendship for me; he smiled a little and advanced his hand, as you might calm a wild creature. "My dear Rose!"

"I was in a daydream," I said, "I'm sorry. Prince. How pleasant." I shook the hand with a firmness which seemed to reassure him. He fell in beside me and we continued to walk towards the Boulevard St-Michel. It was one of those pretty grey-green Paris days, warm and misty, which almost inevitably lead you down to the Seine.

∽

Lobkowitz had some time to spare and so did I. We wandered, exchanging reminiscences, asking after old friends, until we came to one of my favorite little cafes on the Quai Voltaire, the Cafe de Sade, named in more innocent days. We had some coffee and pastries until it grew dark and I realized Sam would be on his way home. I telephoned. He was not back. I told Lobkowitz I would see him again the next day, if he liked.

"In the same place?" he suggested with a smile. He kissed my hand. He said that it had been a wonderful afternoon and he looked forward to tomorrow.

Sam did not, on that occasion, come back until almost nine. He had watched a particular episode through twice, he said, because he could not believe the implications of it. Apparently it involved Pearl Peru. His name, he was sure, was mentioned. Unfortunately the print he had seen was in Vietnamese. He was going to see if he could find out what the English or French version was called. I began to tell him I had seen Lobkowitz, but he kept referring to the screen drama he had seen. Eventually he went to an all-night house in St-Denis, where he hoped to find a man who could help him.

Everyone is going mad, I thought casually.

Next morning I had my breakfast with Madame Stone and her daughter, who was visiting from Poland. She said things were very good in Poland these days. "But there is too much crime," she said. "Like the last century—on the roads—bandits."

They stopped trams, she said, and robbed them. They stopped cars and drove away in them. The police were bribed. The authorities responded only to crimes involving murder. It was anarchy in some districts.

"But otherwise," she said, "things are very good."

What I perceived as signs of social disintegration, she perceived as the price of progress.

～

Lobkowitz and I soon got into a long conversation over the woman from Poland. This time I had no particular sense that I should return home early, so I agreed to have a light supper with my friend at Lipp's brasserie, which had been a favorite spot of ours in the Boulevard St-Germain.

As someone who worked to create what he saw as "zones of tranquility" in the general flux of the multiverse, Lobkowitz was dismayed by the breakdown of the established forces of law. I suggested the outlaw gangs might be the first stage in a fresh development towards a stabler social state. Could we be witnessing a particularly aggressive class-struggle?

In this respect I saw the Polish woman's point of view. Just as many Russians had earlier believed they endured a necessary "stage in history" in their progress towards Communist perfection, now they believed they endured "an inevitable development" in their progress towards the ideal free market capitalist democracy. Sometimes it seemed to me Slavs pursued fatalism the way Americans pursued the free lunch—driven by an almost identical intensity of vision.

Lipp's was never less than excellent and that evening was

especially pleasant when Colonel Lipp himself recognized us from before the War. He was full of nostalgia for an age when, he believed, he had attracted a better quality of customer. "These days," he said, "it's all tourists." He had recommended that we not start with the goose liver or the mussels. Both were too coarse for his taste. He had shrugged an apology, making a small, contemptuous gesture with his fingers towards a large party of Prussians behind him.

∾

When I returned, Sam was sitting at the dining room table reading one of his pulp magazines. He seemed in good temper and I asked him if he had managed to track down the photoplay he was looking for. Not yet, he said. I made a joke about his trekking off across the world in search of his screen self. He laughed and stood up. He suggested we eat at the little restaurant below us. I told him I had already had supper. He asked with whom and I told him Lobkowitz.

He began to speak in that unpleasant, hortatory whine he used when he felt angry and betrayed. I could not reason with him. I left.

I was in considerable confusion. I loved Sam and knew that I was faithful to him, but I had allowed his obsession with the screen to give me the freedom of movement which was so dear to me. There had been no clear agreement. No discussion. At the same time, I had to admit he had been a disappointment to me with his juvenile obsessions, his going to any lengths to watch his screens, ignoring my requests to talk and so on. I hardly felt I was to blame for what was happening to our relationship.

At the apartment Sam had gone out again, no doubt in search of fresh entertainment. I packed my bag and went over to L'Odeon and a little backstreet pension I stayed in when on my own. I knew in my heart I did not mean to leave Sam, then. But

I did need breathing space. I phoned Lobkowitz and told him where I was but made it clear that I wished to have some time alone.

∽

I don't know how Sam found Lobkowitz. I know he went to Lipp's, looking for me there and someone told him where to go. Lobkowitz's address was public knowledge. I think he watched the place for a while. Sam never did discover the name of my hotel, but he did call on Lobkowitz in his town house on the Avenue Burne Hogarth and leave his card. On the back of the card Sam had written:

I believe there is an outstanding matter of honor between us.

And named a time and place.

With the result that he was arrested in possession of a pair of firearms in the Tuilleries at 5 a.m. the next morning and Prince Lobkowitz took the Munich express, on his way back to Mirenburg, leaving me to perform the usual formalities and get Sam released in my custody.

I realized that it was Sam's old-fashioned temper that most attracted me to him.

Thereafter, our relationship was much improved. Sam even sent Lobkowitz an apologetic note and received some piece of graceful wit in return. Lobkowitz remained wary of Sam, however, for the rest of his career. We went back to New Orleans for a while and then Sam fell in with the machinoix and I lost him once more. He was addicted, I decided, to addiction itself.

Only later would I meet Lobkowitz, in the circumstances I have described, and agree, after some hesitation and some incidents in between, to marry him. A time comes in one's life, as my mother used to say, when a peer is a pearl beyond price. I had accompanied him on several satisfactory diplomatic adventures and into this welcome semi-retirement. There was nowhere more subtly civilized than Las Cascadas, which had mixed the blood of the world to make its enduring stock.

To own property on Las Cascadas, if you are a foreigner, you must be prepared to pay a high tax. It is no cheaper to live here than in London. There is, however, considerably greater social justice and therefore social stability. We had made our investment two years earlier and had bought the baroque Villa Harper, built by a retired Scottish diplomat, who stayed only briefly before marrying a local widow and moving to her estate, selling the villa to the Duchess of Crete, the last representative of the ancient Dukes of Crete. That family of noble alchemists had finally died out with the last Duchess and local superstition decided the villa was cursed. The place had been a ruin, but we had restored it and could now walk safely around our old marble terraces, with views across our gardens, our cedars and poplars, blue water and some of the most beautiful coastline in the world.

The Villa Harper was about a mile above Port Sabatini on the western point of the bay. It was reached from town by a winding single track road which could be traveled best by a horse-drawn gig. Although only twenty minutes from the port, the villa had an air of timeless security and I looked forward to arriving there to find young Mrs. Gallibasta awaiting us with the rest of her able and cheerful staff.

It was always a great pleasure to arrive on the island by air. Because the zeppelin had to travel the length of Las Cascadas in order to approach the aerodrome, you could see all the island's extraordinary features. She was virtually a continent in miniature, with spectacular mountains, rivers and lakes, forested valleys, rich lowlands and vine-covered terraces. She was famous for her white beaches, gorgeous cliffs and bays but there was far more to her than that. Her architecture described the passage of every culture which ever made a mark on the Mediterranean; her history was a record of every noble deed, every possible infamy.

We saw the slender turrets of the Villa Harper briefly from one

of the forward ports as we took our seats for the final descent to
the old Valderrama mooring fields. As usual with zeppelin flight,
there was very little sense of motion and it was not until we felt
the familiar shudder as the nose-cone connected with the mast's
massive winch that I knew we were anchored. Then, gradually,
we began to descend. I saw the ground come up and I unbuck-
led, taking a deep breath of the warm air blowing through the
open window. At last, with a kind of sigh, we were aground and
we prepared to disembark.

As we moved along the main deck to the embarkation lounge,
Lobkowitz spoke of cognac and his slippers and pointed out
familiar features of the aerodrome. I was glad to see him so free
of care.

He was still chatting amiably as we followed our porter down
the gangplank and I heard a voice I recognized.

I looked back and was shocked by his grinning eyes. Black
Burma cheroot in the corner of his mouth, a naval cap on his
head, wearing a civilian linen suit and waving a malacca cane at
the three men bearing his luggage behind us, came Captain
Quelch, swearing in Latin and calling to me. On his arm was a
tiny oriental, got up in fetishistic silk and heavily painted. This
creature held a leash at which strained two tall Afghan hounds.
I could smell his concubine and the dogs' breath from ten feet
away.

"Rose! Countess! My dear, dear Rose!" cried Quelch in apparent delight. "We are all turning up at the same time it seems."

He lowered his heavy lids to regard his companion. He stroked
the creature's head with absent-minded affection. It turned ador-
ing eyes up to him and opened a red, hungry mouth as if to
be fed.

"What can it mean, I wonder, this gathering of the clans?"

"Yes. *'All for One and One for All'* is romantic. Good enough for the Three Musketeers," said Cruikback. "Work it out in its statistical correlation, and what have you got?" He was at a loss for words, so he cantered off in another direction. "The code of the racketeer is what you have there, one thing. And while the code of share and share alike is a *bloody* good thing to cut your milk teeth on, Laverock, the end result is what we call—"

"Fascism and the corporate state?" I said.

"Communism," said Copper Baldwin.

"What we call *Anarchy*!" cried Cruikback, clapping us both on the shoulder. "I'm glad you agree."

—GERALD KERSH, *Fowler's End*

Blues du Saoulard

"Bugger bloody Dresden," said Dick Turpin, lighting his luxurious churchwarden, "they shouldn't have voted for Hitler, then, should they? They went for the easy option and look where it got them. Whining bunch of bad losers, sir! I mean, we didn't march into Czechoslovakia and Poland or slaughter ten or twenty million assorted *untermenschen,* did we? There are very few inconsequential actions in a genocidal World War. Eh, Jack?"

But I refused to be drawn into the argument. I glanced back towards Colinda. I envied my wife her company at that moment.

"I'm simply saying I felt guilty," said Sir Sexton Begg, raising a mild eyebrow. Because of an Intelligence mix-up, he had found himself taking part in the punitive Dresden raids and been shot down. "Especially when those old women were so kind to me. They weren't saying it was my fault. They showed a charity I'm not sure I was capable of. And I'd bombed their city into ashes. After several days it was still burning around me. I'm not talking about blame or right or wrong, I'm talking about my action as a human being and what I did to other human beings. That was wrong, Captain Turpin. I'd have to think about it, if asked to do it again."

"Well, well, sir," said Turpin, lost in his own angry reminiscence, "we can now all stay at home and press buttons if we feel like performing a mass murder or two. We're living in dark and dangerous days, sir."

Turpin tended to be defensive in the presence of Sir Sexton, whom he continued to see as a better class of Brixton Hill Runner. He was also upset about the privatization of the tramways, after so many years of peace and stability. Talk of computerization had put him into a depression. He was used to pitting his wits, he said, against people, not pixels.

"Pixies ?" said Sir Arthur Moorcock, giving him an odd look and getting a wounded glare in return. "Not in this neck of the woods."

At Sporting Club Square, we were all taking a winter's tea. The dark green velvet cloth was on the oak table and the brass service caught the crimson light of the coals as Sir Arthur, with the same concentration with which he teased a cunning fish, carefully toasted the crumpets to perfection and laid them on the plates which Lady Eleanor, his actress ex-wife, took from the big copper Benson warmer. Even the faint smell of paraffin from the warmer's burner added to that general air of coziness which, unlike the others, I found vaguely threatening. Rose von Bek came back from the curtains she had just drawn. "It could still snow," she said. She turned to where Colinda was setting out the butter, the honey, the Marmite, the curds and preserves. "A few flakes, perhaps."

Her mother got up to turn on the wireless. "Vaughan Williams," she said, "that's nice. Or Percy Grainger, is it?" She glanced slyly at her ex-husband who smiled to himself, doubtless at some private joke between them, and slipped another crumpet onto his prongs.

I was glad to see Turpin again. After Captain Oakenhurst, Turpin had been the one I admired most amongst the Smith's Kitchen scampsmen. Like me, he had done some traveling since we last met. He had toured, he said, most of the English-speaking world and was rather glad to be home. He was of the opinion that London fog, regularly inhaled, caused the lungs to clean themselves out. London was the healthiest spot in the world, he said, all things taken together.

Personally, I considered this a brave interpretation of his unhappy circumstances. It would have been cruel of any of us to remind him of his shrinking constituency. He was such an amiable fellow, with a good reputation for square-dealing amongst his fellow Knights of the Toby, we did our best to bolster his good-spirits. On that particular evening, he was unusually cheerful. He had one of his children with him, a blonde woman in her thirties with a coarse, pretty face and challenging eyes who seemed glad to see Rose, yet was plainly uneasy. I think there had been some sort of childhood friendship between the girls until class got in the way, as it so often does in civilized society, especially if race is also involved.

This was a pity, given Turpin's own equitable nature, which had been remarked upon by his victims, as well as all those who had ridden with him. While rarely announcing the fact, Turpin really had robbed the rich and given much of his profits to the poor. Many of his contributions had been directly political. Of all the London tobymen, Turpin had made the best transition to political activist, and that was why he had so many supporters in the city. Judges, belted earls and corrupt officials had been Turpin's main prey, together with greedy merchants and their stooges.

I had no penchant for politics, myself, though I believed it my duty to protect the weak. Turpin found my principles old-fashioned and impractical, I think. But socialism—democratic, Christian or pacifist—has never appealed to me, perhaps because of my background. I believe in strong leadership, in setting a good example and living according to one's best ideals, but I also believe in respecting another's views and I rarely found myself in any seri ous differences with Turpin. If all his political fellows were like him, I might well have joined his party.

I wanted to ask him if he kept his home on Las Cascadas but he got into some serious fishing conversation with Sir Arthur and all I heard from him next were a thousand words for water. Then they went from bream and dace and tench to salmon and trout, even pike. I have never had the need to do something while seeking solitude and gave up angling when I kept catching fish. It is a distracting business, I find, trying to contemplate a new move in the Game of Time while having to dig out the right blade on the Swiss Army knife in order to finesse the hook from a fish's mouth as painlessly and with as little damage as possible.

To those who make a spiritual exercise of the sport, it is all, of course, of a piece—the casting, the catching and even the consuming. We all find ways of refining and explaining our brute impulses, of bringing rules and justice to a predatory world. With me it used to be the duel. Then it was the tables. For a while it was the High Toby. Now occasionally I play the Game of Time.

Colinda liked these Sporting Club Square gatherings better than I did. I have always been a man of action and after a while I become bored with the telling and hearing of stories, no matter how curious or exemplary. I am a restless soul, I suppose. The High Tables were all the life I ever needed for half my career, until I met Colinda when the drowsy air was so thick even the mosquitoes could not fly and the accordion sounded, slow and weary, somewhere on the lower deck, and she sang *"O, pierrot, ma pierrot bleu. Adieu!"*

And I was lost forever.

∾

The English are addicted to their eating rituals. Irrespective of circumstance, they perform them all over the world. It has not been unusual for me to be invited to piping hot scones and Assam in the height of a Cairo heat-wave or to find myself commenting on the flavor of a treacle tart while a tropical tornado threatens to rip off the roof.

The Rose was particularly partial to these ceremonies and somewhat insistent on pursuing them. The woman had considerable manipulative powers, but they had very little effect on me. Clearly this tea-taking and crumpet-toasting was how she provided herself with familiar securities. I was also impressed by the way she controlled both her father and her mother. They almost performed for her. She was what my mother called a witch. In other words, she had the power to alter reality, if only for a short while.

Colinda insisted that I was over-harsh in my judgment, but I had seen how she had used Sam, how she had maneuvered me.

"She preys on our weaknesses," I said.

"For what purpose?" Colinda needed to know.

I said that the purpose did not matter. But that wasn't Colinda's view. She thought me narrow, but I could not change my understanding of something until my experience changed. My alliance with the Rose, however, was never in question as she would discover in Las Cascadas later.

I believe I was never entirely at ease in London. It was not my native city in the sense that it was Turpin's, the Rose's or, even more, the Beggs', and no matter how long I lived there or how much of its deep world I came to know, I would always be something of a stranger. Increasingly, I grew glad to leave.

"Well," said the Rose as we prepared to go home that evening, "two or three months and we'll be seeing you again, eh?"

That was the first I heard of their deciding to take up residency on the island. It rather colored the rest of my visit.

∾

Thankfully Colinda was also finding a few weeks out of the year in London to be more than enough for her. We no longer traveled as much. We returned when possible to New Orleans and Cairo. Mostly, however, we enjoyed the slower pace of life in Las Cascadas, with her visiting orchestras, operatic and theatrical companies and her own high standard of local entertainment. Our interest in the casino gave us as much money as we needed. We had a house above the harbor where I could watch the fishing boats in the morning. I still liked to get up at dawn and sit on my balcony, enjoying the port as it came to life. We sometimes spoke of getting a place further away from town, but neither of us really wanted to be divorced from the ordinary life around us. The occasional stink of fish or the noise of winches and shouting men before sunrise was the price one paid for living in the real world.

When Prince Lobkowitz bought the massive Villa Harper on the headland and began to renovate it, there was no doubt of his serious intention to retire to Las Cascadas. Colinda was delighted because it would mean her friend would live nearby. The Countess von Bek had improved herself, even more successfully than her mother. She was now the owner of a name as old as Europe. For myself, I could only promise to be civil to the new princess.

I had no great belief in Lobkowitz's altruism. I thought he interfered too readily in the world's affairs. His reputation as a disinterested peacemaker was hugely inflated. I liked him well enough, though his worldly good humor frequently grated on me. That weary, ironic tolerance affected by Central Europeans is too often a means for their pretending to principles they are never called upon to make concrete. We embraced different kinds of fatalism, I suppose.

My guess was that we would tolerate one another for a while and then gradually drift apart. The Lobkowitzes would find friends with the same social interests. They were already on good terms with the Governor, whom we rarely saw these days. I said nothing of this to Colinda, but waited to witness the inevitable unfolding of my prediction.

Common politeness demanded we meet them at the aerodrome. Prince Lobkowitz was in his usual amiable humor, but the Rose seemed shaken. As we walked towards the calash, she mentioned seeing Captain Quelch disembarking from the same ship. Almost as soon as she had begun to describe their exchange, she stopped, pointing towards the tram stand. "There he goes. Look."

Quelch was, indeed, lounging beside the sign for the little tram which carried passengers to and from the port with stops at convenient points for the hotels. His oriental hermaphrodite held a pair of Afghans on short leashes and glared towards us with hungry interest. The other passengers stood away from them, studying their newspapers and praying they would not take the same route.

Standing head and shoulders above the rest of them, Quelch saw me, glanced away, then raised his hat. "The usual confusion, eh, Rose?" he called, making a sympathetic face. "The usual confusion!" His voice sounded thin in that warm air. *"Tantaene animis caelestibus irne?"*

"What's he saying?" asked Colinda.

"*Sub rosa,*" said the Rose with a comradely wink. When she looked at me, her expression changed. She shrugged.

I went forward and took her hand. "Like old times," I said.

"Or even better," she said, "if we work at it a little."

I found myself agreeing to the pact. I bowed and kissed her pretty knuckles.

∾

That night we all had dinner with Christian and Jorges Vacarescu in the private room above the main floor of their restaurant. There was carre d'ascension, roast suckling pig, bouef brazilien, melon cabbage, peridor potatoes and Salad Al-Raschid, all the subtle specialties of the island, drawn from the kitchens of the world and cooked by the best French-Catalan chef, Albert Llull, who had been made a knight in Sweden.[29]

The Vacarescus had lived in Port Sab' for at least three centuries. Their name was apparently Hungarian and dated back to an early expedition to the island which had a number of legends attached to it but few historical records. There were Vacarescus married into every family on Las Cascadas, buried in every graveyard, and any family likeness was absorbed into the general, slightly gnomish features of the natives, most of whom never grew much above five and a half feet.

The people had the Spanish habit of adding name to name There was many a Vacarescu-Harper-D'Armengal-Alfaid-Vicos who thought nothing of marrying a partner with the surname of Vicos-Alfaid-D'Armengal-Harper-Vacarescu. They might even have the same first names, as was the case with Christian, whose name was actually Christian-Marya and who was married

---

[29]King Gustav hoped to keep him in Stockholm by this means. The strategy did not work on Llull. It was not so much the suicidal winters that made him leave, he said, but the desperate summers. The entire nation was seasonally schizophrenic and insanely overorganized.

to Marya-Christian. This practice, some anthropologists argued, was what gave our tiny nation its extraordinary coherence and allowed it to tolerate foreigners so readily, absorbing them casually into the common stock.

In the years of Las Cascadas's greatest power, as the hub of a pirate empire, so many peoples of every continent mixed freely and married, Korean to Jew, Icelander to Indian, exiled Madagascan master to former Caucasian slave, that the island had never been able to develop a class system based on race and had transformed readily into the present social democracy. There were, of course, classes, but no system to sustain them. Nonetheless the Governor and the various politicians, actors, writers and other artists who lived here, formed a kind of elite into which Colinda and I were automatically included because of our background.

I had always preferred the card table to the dining table and felt easier holding a laconic conversation with a full house rather than a lobster fork in my hand. I found the island's upper crust decent enough and many of them had seen serious action in the War, but their small-talk irritated me and my own friends were, like the Vacarescus, people of ordinary rather than extraordinary experience, who had somehow survived.

In the case of the brothers their most intense experience had, of course, been the Occupation and their involvement with the Resistance. Yet, on principle, the moment the foreign soldiers were routed, the brothers made any Lombardian not directly connected with the occupation as welcome as anyone. I knew that I would not have been so forgiving. As a further example of their principle, they had been known to throw out native islanders, French, Germans, Britons and Americans who behaved "*alla fascisti,*" as they said. Some Cascadians said the brothers were motivated only by a desire to make money, but their War record and their general egalitarianism showed the Vacarescus guiltless of even that uncomplicated ambition.

I felt that we had a fairly decent balance. Both the Rose and her husband got on well with the brothers. I was rather impressed by the Rose's behaviour. I had the feeling, naturally, that she was trying to impress me. That meant that she wanted something from me. With mild curiosity, I awaited her next play.

The Vacarescus had heard that Quelch was back.

"But without his schooner," said Jorges, making that sly smile of his under his massive nose. "Could he be on such hard times?"

"The ship's been seen in Porto Andratx and Casablanca." His brother had all Jorges' features, only in moderation, and he was handsome. "Francisco told me. He saw it himself. New paint. Shipshape as usual. So who owns her now? Did the Count buy her?"

"It's always interesting when Quelch comes back to the islands." Jorges leaned sideways in his chair and stared across the silver blue bay. Everything shone with the same magical color. "He's quite a hero in Las Cascadas, you know. He and his kind knew never to offend the locals. They endowed schools, creches, family crisis centers, tram services to remote areas. Quelch was particularly big on libraries and higher education. They paid no taxes, of course, but what the people judge to be their right from a government, they understand to be largesse from an individual. Yet, who's to say those schools and centers would exist, if government bureaucracy were responsible for them? They would probably still be at the planning stage."

The Rose spoke of the English tobymen and the Texan outlaws, who had also understood the importance of pleasing the ordinary people. "The popular thief is as dependent upon his public as the actor or the novelist. His fate, in the end, is entirely in their hands. He is, in this respect, an altogether nobler creature than the politician, who is never so accountable."

The Varecescus were adamant, however, that private charity was no substitute for public rights.

"Captain Quelch lives off his fellows," said Christian. "He is a predatory beast and has no business in civilized company."

"Not his view at all, I gather," said Prince Lobkowitz, who seemed very tired. He lifted his head a difficult inch. "He thinks we are all predatory beasts, but disguise it better than he. By that logic, he's baffled if he's ostracized. He thinks we're hypocrites."

"But what's he doing back at Las Cascadas?" asked Colinda. "Is there something going on?"

"Perhaps he's here for the Conference," said the Rose sardonically.

Lobkowitz had been a prominent publicist for the international peace conference which would take place next month at the special center on the other side of the island. He had spoken of urgent issues and a need to see the broader picture. I wondered how many decent people down the centuries had like him talked so earnestly, with such astute judgment, as they slid helplessly into the Pit.

"He could be here as some kind of lobbyist," I suggested.

"For whom?" said the prince.

I did not know.

"A repentant arms trader, maybe," said Colinda. "Retooling for plowshares."

"Quelch himself has a vested interest in tension. A world at peace is the last thing he desires." The Rose accepted the wine I poured.

"So you think he could be here to sabotage it?" said Jorges.

"It could be a coincidence," I said.

"I've learned, Jack," said the Rose, "that every move Captain Quelch makes is calculated to the last detail. That doesn't, however, mean that he's here because of the Conference itself, but for what he might gain from it. Maybe he wants to meet someone, or be seen with someone. His motives are frequently extremely obscure. But there are usually several. I'm uneasy about this . . ."

At that moment there was a noise in the narrow street between the restaurant and the promenade. We looked down over the balcony and saw that Horace Quelch, himself, his oiled catamite and his two jittery dogs, had joined in heated debate with four Germans in Bavarian hats and lederhosen who had apparently taken exception to Quelch's slighting remarks. Quelch was in some kind of naval uniform, which rather threw the Germans, who stood open-mouthed as he continued to comment on the largeness of their bottoms and the meatiness of their thighs. The Germans, with some dignity, began to move away, only to be stopped by the Afghans and the panting boy.

Quelch continued to hector them as they looked around helplessly for the policeman who, with his familiar instinct for avoiding trouble, had just turned to go up towards the main square.

Then, with his little entourage behind him, Quelch saluted, adjusted his cap and with rather pompous dignity stepped out of our sight into the restaurant below.

I was amused by the whole incident. To me, Quelch was merely a buffoon, an old character past his prime. My friends' response seemed melodramatic, strangely self-important. I began to change the subject.

"He seems confident enough," said Lobkowitz, thoughtfully to his wife. "How much harm could he do us?"

"Quiet a bit," she murmured.

I was determined.

"How was this season's opera in Mirenburg?" I asked.

They looked at me in astonishment.

At this time Turpin was watching at a small distance; and riding towards the spot, King cried out "Shoot him, or we are taken": on which Turpin fired, and shot his companion, who called out "Dick, you have killed me"; which the other hearing, rode off at full speed. King lived a week after this affair, and gave information that Turpin might be found at a house near Hackney-Marsh; and on enquiry it was discovered that Turpin had been there on the night that he rode off, lamenting that he had killed King, who was the most faithful associate he had ever had in his life.

For a considerable time did Turpin skulk about the forest, having been deprived of his retreat in the cave since he shot the servant of Mr. Thompson. On the examination of this cave there were found two shirts, two pairs of stockings, a piece of ham, and part of a bottle of wine. Some vain attempts were made to take this notorious offender into custody; and among the rest the huntsman of a gentleman in the neighbourhood went in search of him with bloodhounds. Turpin perceiving them, got into a tree, under which the hounds passed, to his inexpressible terror, so that he determined to make a retreat into Yorkshire.

—*The Malefactor's Register;*
or, The New Newgate and Tyburn Calendar

Plaisir d'Amour

During the Peace Conference, we saw little of the Rose and her husband. The thing went off with all the usual resounding speeches and ambitious plans for a new world order; the moral high ground was established, villains were castigated, the men of violence were named, goals were set and lines were drawn and the famously good went back to their various struggles. For me, such conferences were always a bad omen. They suggested that the situation was desperate and that the chips, such as they were, were down for the last time. Even Lobkowitz privately admitted to me that all he was playing for was time in the hope that some new factor might improve the situation. Originally he had hoped to put everything on a higher level, offering the perspective which one gains from playing the Game of Time.

The media, of course, had linked all this with the increase in angelic manifestation reported world-wide.

On the day the conference had begun, an entire war-party of some twenty or thirty angels, one of whom might have been, from the clearest description I read, Lucifer himself,[30] appeared

---

[30]It was actually Lucifer, whose own constituency had diminished in a heavenly war where the issues and the loyalties were no longer clear, attempting to contact Ulrich von Bek, who had retired to Aswan in Egypt and was a close friend of my mother. On that occasion, Lucifer was unsuccessful. The whole story is reported in detail in *Barbican Begg; or, The Consumer's Tragedy* by Warwick Colvin Moorcock. The best contemporary report is in *The Times* for Tuesday, May 25th, 1996, whose reporter quotes Jose Felice D'Alegmany as saying the "captain of the angels" had a face of glorious beauty but eyes which sucked the heat from your body. Those students of the Grail legend will also know that Lucifer's bargain with God depended upon the Prince of the Morning finding a cure for the world's pain. The War in Heaven had, however, long since ceased

over the water in the little bay of Porto Poye, on the western
side of the island. There was the accompanying stink, the agitated air, the vivid, unsteady color. There were no photographs
of them, of course, but every newspaper, in every language, carried drawings. The screens were crammed with animated render-
ings, most of them as crude as the magazines Sam Oakenhurst
was so fond of reading whenever he could find them.

It was impossible to recognize individuals from the drawings.
They had some of the quality of old representations of exotic animals done by an artist from another's description—giraffes with
the bodies of horses, elephants which resembled oxen with trunks
and tusks—and generally made what was beautiful seem disproportionate and grotesque. The colors were too violent, the carapaces
too angular, the eyes apparently blind, the wings awkwardly placed.
There were still many who were prepared to offer their views on
the phenomenon. It was a clear example of mass hallucination, the
invention of hysterical crowds seeking some kind of anchor. There
were even some theorists who believed that human yearning had
brought the angels into existence on the spot.

In Texas both the Rose's uncle and Buffalo Bill (whom her uncle
by now resembled) became famous for their expertise at finding
angels. They had led several well-publicized expeditions into the
borderlands. The publicity was a welcome boost to Bill's career
and if he could have corralled a few of the evil-smelling supernatu-
rals no doubt he would have taken another magnificent show on
the road. I had a strong dislike of the creatures myself and had no
doubt that our race would be considerably better off without them.
They had probably come into existence long ago at our demand,
to help resolve the perpetual war which goes on within every individual human soul between what we once chose to name Good

---

to be between God and the Devil. Now it was between a myriad different interests, each increasingly losing sight of its original goals in a series of pointlessly
cynical alliances and compromises made hopelessly for unworthy prizes. "The
celestial rot was well set in," as "Mrs. Cornelius" told her radio audience later.
Many believed that God had disengaged himself from the fight.

and Evil or, more accurately, Law and Chaos. Certainly their origins were human. Few experienced players of the Game of Time see any evidence for the theory that we are corrupted versions of the angels. There is no question that, for all their power and mystery, they have less subtle minds than ours. It could be, of course, that the closer one goes to the source of the multiverse, the further one leaves complexity behind. It is, after all, only our imagination which continues to create and complicate a multiverse which is fundamentally as divinely simple as the godhead itself. It is the means of our creativity as well as our inspiration. It is also the means of our corruption and despair.

Like the Rose, I have long-since ceased to play the Game of Time for any spurious sentimental or altruistic reasons. I play because I love the Game, just as she does. It could be argued that we are, in fact, the ones who sustain the struggle, though we see ourselves as conciliators. Creatures like ourselves, in whom mysterious contradictions rage, lust for the Game, for any activity which will produce that sense of inner resolution, if only for a while. That is why so many of us are travelers or engaged upon quests.

Most of us still believe that when we achieve that inner balance we also contribute to the stability of our surroundings. Lobkowitz was the first to admit that the men and women of peace who came to the conference were all individuals of the highest ideals and noblest motives, but could not change human nature. Only the human will could do that. And that is our Game. And the stakes we risk are our eternal souls.[31]

There are those whose interests are threatened by any hint of a cessation in the struggle. Such forces identify with Law, Chaos and a thousand variations of their causes. I believe the so-called Chaos Engineers as well as the Singularity would fade into nonexistence once their function was lost. Because of their vested interest, they are always unreliable allies.

---

[31]"The Lords and Ladies of Paradox, Born of Entropy and Born to Defeat It," as The Rev. W.E. Barclay wrote in that strange, self-published account of 1831, *Angelic Manifestations in England, France and the Netherlands*, which got him defrocked.

∾

Far steadier was Dick Turpin, who had successfully hung on to his determinedly mortal soul through thick and thin. Much invigorated, he was once again making headlines in the London press. There was considerable speculation as to his "real" identity, since it had been assumed for some time that Turpin had died on the gallows. He had begun a fresh round of daring assaults against the newly privatized transport companies, extending himself to include inter-city expresses, underground railways and the new LCC1 supertrams, the last to be built in public ownership and even more magnificent than the old A-class Felthams.

Sir Sexton Begg[32] was also in the papers. I read that he had been brought out of retirement to help in the case of the Fellini (or Bastable) Chalice, which had disappeared from Sir John Soane's Museum in Lincoln's Inn. A group of Christian fundamentalists had claimed the crime but the actual thief was thought to be a mysterious Middle European nobleman, an albino who used the pseudonym "Monsieur Zenith" and had been a thorn in Scotland Yard's side for some years. Begg, it was said, had followed his quarry into the Western Sahara and had last been seen buying camels in Th'amouent.

The story which drew my attention, however, I read in a day-old copy of the *Telegraph*. It said that a body, thought to be that of Colonel Oakenhurst, had been found in Egypt. The authorities had yet to announce the circumstances leading to the discovery. There had always been a mystery surrounding Sam's disappearance. The paper hinted at a journey into "angel country," but I knew he had never come back from an ill-conceived expedition with the Rose, looking for the site of Q'fa, the legendary university city of Aton, that inhumanly beautiful androgyne who perished trying to enlighten

---

[32]As "Sexton Blake," his adventures were known to every schoolboy in the British Empire, but Begg was embarrassed by this popular fame and made every effort to disassociate himself from the adventures recorded in *The Sexton Blake Library, The Union Jack, Detective Weekly* and elsewhere.

Egypt. According to the Rose, they were overwhelmed by a large party of unfriendly Zanussi. She escaped but Sam did not. I had never heard of Zanussi making that part of the desert their territory. Those famous law-makers never attack strangers without considerable reason. I do not believe the Rose killed Sam Oakenhurst, but I suspect she abandoned him in the desert, maybe leaving him for dead and saving herself. She said nothing of finding the lost city.

I knew that she took her breakfast fairly regularly down at the *Patisserie Alfaid* on the waterfront and I went there the next morning, with my paper. I sat at one of the back tables, under the awning. It was a busy time. Balancing their big, overburdened silver trays, the waiters, in their long white aprons and black shirts, moved rapidly amongst the tables, taking orders which were sometimes conveyed by the flick of an eye, the lifting of a finger. The sea was busy with little whitecaps and the gaudy fishing boats bounced in their moorings. The catch had long-since been landed, but its smell remained as the burly women in seaboots and overalls drove off the gulls, swilling the pavement of guts and bones and calling to one another in those raucous voices which had been developed to carry sound over long distances or strike an erring husband to stone.

When the Rose finally arrived, I signaled to her and, perhaps a little reluctantly, she wove a course through the seated crowds to join me. I wondered if she had heard the story, but it did not appear so. Her attention was still on Quelch.

Had I heard, she wondered. Quelch's schooner, *The Hope Dempsey*, had arrived a couple of nights ago, in the harbor, and Quelch had gone aboard. The next morning, the schooner had vanished.

"Quelch has left the island," she said. She ordered her *cofee-al-lata* and a croissant. "I wonder if it's significant."

"Where did he go?" I asked her.

"North Africa, I gather. Back to Casablanca, perhaps. Or even Mogador. We still don't know why he was here."

"Waiting for his ship?" I suggested, mildly.

She took this as a joke. "That's it, of course."

I let her eat her pastry and drink her coffee before I told her what I had read. "The Egyptians have Sam's remains," I said.

"His body?" she asked.

I thought it an odd response.

"I gather they don't mean his mummy," I said.

She made some kind of apology and then shook her head, frowning. "What sort of condition was it in?"

"Does it matter?" I handed her the *Telegraph*, folded over to the picture of Sam and the story. "They found a satchel, I gather, with some documents."

Of course she betrayed no emotion to me as she took the paper and read it, but I believe her skin changed color for a hint of a second. "This says nothing." She put the *Telegraph* on the table. "They've merely announced finding a body near to what could be Sam's document case. It doesn't mean it's Sam."

"You mean Sam's not dead."

"I never said he was dead."

"You told me he'd been murdered by Zanussi tribesmen."

"I said that we had been attacked and separated. Sam never came back."

"That was the last you saw of him?"

She became a little distant. "I believe I've been through all this with you before, Jack."

"This story revived my curiosity," I said.

"It's too vague," she complained. "It raises all sorts of questions. We just don't know."

"You know what happened, though."

"Of course I do. We were separated. I never saw what finally happened to Sam."

"And it was the Zanussi."

"Oh," she said, "no. That was a mistake. They were Gora, I gather."

Suddenly the whole story made sense. Those outlaws were capable of anything.

"You should have told me that earlier," I said.

She was innocently surprised. "Why?"

"Did you find Aton's university?"

"No. The sand covered it thousands of years ago. It's down there somewhere, but only a freak of the sand dunes will bring it back. Frankly, Jack, I'm not even sure it exists."

"It exists," I said. "I was educated there."

∽

Jack Karaquazian sits at his game, wagering the highest psychic stakes from a position conventionally known as the Dead King's Chair. His stoic back is against the whirling patterns of Chaos ceaselessly forming and reforming. His fellow gamblers know him as Al-Q'areen. All these jugadors have the abstracted, dedicated ascetic appearance of a strict order. The Egyptian smiles on them, a kindly jackal.

The Rose leans out of the baffling light into the shadows where he sees her face at last. "You're looking better, Jack," she says, "your old self."

"I'm feeling it, Rose," he says. He believes he should have known her by her style, he has played her so often. Had her strategy achieved this unseemly draw? It had her mark on it. He could do nothing but admire her audacity.

"Your arrogance and mine, Jack," she says, laughing quietly into his face, "are what serve us best and will soon need to serve us again, I think."

It was her last card and it charmed him, of course. He was won over to her cause, if not to her character. He found himself agreeing to meet her in Sporting Club Square in the Autumn of '97. She would give him the exact date and time later.

∽

I had sometimes wondered if Jack Karaquazian, in common with certain other members of his trade, was a chronic liar. He

made few claims for himself, but the ones he made were large.
It was the mark of his game.

It scarcely mattered in this case if he played or not. I think
there was truth in what he was telling me.

"You attended Aton's university?" I had not expected such a
surprise during breakfast. "How many centuries ago?"

"Just before the War. As far as I know students still currently
attend," he told me. "Aton merely founded our order. The place
is well known to mukhamirim of a certain class."

I ignored any inference. "Then why didn't Sam and I see it?"

"Its entrances are underground. They have been for two millennia. They sit astride the planes. There is only one guide to
take you to Madrasah-al-Aton; a small grey Oriental cat who
walks casually between the worlds. He is Niphar, son of Bast.
You must follow him if you wish to find the living Madrasah,
rather than its shadow."

"You followed the cat?" I asked.

"Oh, yes. Daily. Sometimes, it seemed, for years. It is a discipline in itself."

"Which life was this, Jack?" I slipped one of his M&Es from
the pack on the table. Automatically, he lit it for me.

"Who knows?" he said. He picked up his glass of anis. I
heard the ice creak against the yellow liquid. He looked over the
light heads of the German tourists and the English settlers, the
dark Cascadians, out past the fishing boats to the harbor's steep
cliffs, their clustered houses and churches and shops defying
gravity. "It doesn't do for the likes of us to separate one existence from another, does it, Rose? *Going Linear* is the only game
you play that's guaranteed to drive you crazy. The only game
you can't win. If you could, there would be no hope at all."

"We know the question," I said. "We know the answer, too,
probably. But we don't know what's in between. We don't know
how to make it coherent . . ."

"It *is* coherent," said Jack Karaquazian contemptuously. "It
is we who defy coherence, Rose. By our very insistence on lin-

earity. And therein lies our failure to understand. Is that not damnation?"

Jack was always of a theological disposition. I refused his tempting abstractions.

"Well, I'm a simple soul," I said. "I prefer to think that one thing and everything are the same and that I am the multiverse in miniature, no more and no less."

"Perhaps," he said. He got up, leaving the paper for me. He still stared towards the horizon. "I'll be seeing you very soon, no doubt."

"No doubt, Jack. *B'slama.*"

He responded with a brief comradely gesture which surprised me.

I watched him pick his way carefully through the crowd and walk rapidly up the corniche, towards the red and black awning of Hernando's Bar.

A couple of minutes later, Lobkowitz joined me. He was normally not down in town at this time, but had had an early appointment at the bank. I was glad to have another large coffee with him. I told him that I had seen Jack. I showed him the newspaper. I described what Jack had told me.

Lobkowitz seemed less skeptical. "I have heard of such a university, but I thought it was somewhere in Mauritania, in the Far Atlas. Maybe there's more than one. They teach that the Game is only a symbol of inner conflicts, that the real game is played against oneself. They have a motto. They say that when we wrestle with a moral problem the angels war within us—the angels of death and the angels of life who are perpetually seeking reconciliation. That reconciliation is impossible while they are in conflict. Any resolution can only come from within and can only be arrived at through experience, intelligence and imagination."

"But you believe the war is endless."

"I believe we can achieve moments of peace and that's all I work for."

"I want more than that," I said.

"It is one of the reasons I love you so much," he said.

A little later we watched as Jack Karaquazian raised his sail and made his way out over the angry water as if pursued.

∽

Jack Karaquazian was not the only old acquaintance I saw that day. Just as Lobkowitz was going through his usual laborious process of working out the tip and I was looking in my purse to see if I had any spare drachim, I heard an extraordinary scream—as if everyone in the port had called out at once.

I looked up and there, wading out of the harbor and somehow avoiding doing damage to the rocking boats or the parked calashes whose horses were going crazy, was a gigantic, nightmare figure. Its flesh was coruscating crystal, flashing with a million colors. Its head and shoulders trailed brilliant clouds of etherdust. Its eyes flickered through a thousand optical options until it could focus accurately on the crowd, some of whom were throwing up or otherwise relieving themselves and most of whom were unable to move.

Even Lobkowitz gagged at the stench as the angel stepped carefully ashore and moved towards the *Patisserie Alfaid*. But I recognized the figure and saw its beauty, understood its voice. Then everyone else, including Lobkowitz, began to cover their ears and back away as it uttered a cacophony of moans and whines and thunderous groans, of piercing shrieks and disgusting grunts, but I heard the melody of it and I smiled.

"I greet the Merchant Venturer, Pearl Peru," I said in our common tongue. "How did you pass so far between the scales?"

∽

The Merchant Venturer, Pearl Peru, lowers a benign head, her eyes searching through countless spectra to find her comrade, the great pilot, Rose von Bek. "Ah, sweet Rose, succulent

flower, so long! We fly at *Greenheart Diamond*. We are to be
united with *Spammer*. It is time to return, Rose, and take the
controls of the *Now The Clouds Have Meaning*, to which I have
blended all—all, Rose! I have been absorbed by her, together
with my ship *The Smollettsphere*. Now we have the strength to
defeat the Singularity. You found *Spammer* for us, Rose. You
must join the final fight! We are in unusual danger."

"You sought me here?"

"No. I seek my other half. He too is needed for the battle. I
am here to be united with Jack Karaquazian, since he has been
unable to find us." Pearl smiled and her tenderness embraced
the multiverse. Few had ever loved with the patience and pleasure of Pearl Peru. She looked benignly upon the mortals scattering away from the muttering jewelled lizards that were her
feet and called to her retreating audience a reassurance which
set them to retching all over again or becoming helpless in
pseudo-epileptic seizures. I cautioned her to silence until the
last pink, panicking tourists had heaved their elephantine bodies
in their vast shorts and culottes up the Gallibasta Steps and
hurriedly turned the corner into the churchyard.

I told her that I thought Jack was on the way to the mainland
and she fumed with disappointment. Massive crystals smashed
from her eyes to the pavement. "But I cannot wait, Rose. You
must come back with me. To where *Spammer* anchors."

"I promised to return," I said. "But I must tell you that I
have other pressing engagements to fulfill and they cannot all
be combined."

"You will be serving the cause of Chaos," Pearl reminded me
piously. "We are about to be consumed by the Original Insect."

I knew Pearl's tendency to exaggerate. I refused her panic.
Like Jack Karaquazian I was learning how to control my own
destiny and serve first our common human cause.

"I will decide shortly," I told the angel.

I turned to kiss my courageous husband. His startled eyes
demanded reassurance.

And as Dick and his band rode off on their journey to London to meet Tom King, they left behind two more staunch friends who had cause
to bless the name of Dick Turpin, righter of injustices, helper of those in need and the scourge
of the Evil-Doer . . .

In early eighteenth century England, the living
legend of Dick Turpin spread to the far corners
of the land. To rogues, thieves and vagabonds,
it brought the chill of fear. Yet to many honest
people the King of Highwaymen was known as
a true friend.

—Dick Turpin, *Thriller Picture Library*, 1957

The Call of the Canyon

Two horsemen were approaching a mining camp in a spur of the
Rocky Mountains, and were riding at a leisurely pace, as
though their trail had been a long one, and they were glad to have
a resting-place.

The two men are known the wide world over, their daring
deeds having been told in history and romance, for they an-

swered on the Wild West border to the names of Wild Bill Hickock and Buffalo Bill Cody.

Their trail led them along the banks of a small stream winding down a narrow valley, upon either side of which rose a bold and rugged mountain range.

Suddenly two sharp reports rang out in quick succession, fired from a distance, and the two horsemen drew rein and swung their rifles around for use, while their keen eyes searched ahead.

That they were in a dangerous locality they well knew, and though no whizzing bullets had followed the reports to show that they had been the targets at which those who fired the shots had aimed it was necessary to be upon their guard.

"We were not their game, I guess, Bill, because no man could fire so wild as that," remarked Buffalo Bill, composedly.

"No; but yonder is where the shots came from. Fully half a mile away," and Wild Bill pointed up the mountainside further down the valley, where two little white clouds of smoke were floating away from a rocky spur almost hidden in pines.

"There is a cabin there, too. But what were they shooting at?" And Cody had already levelled a powerful field-glass he had swung to his belt at the spot indicated by his comrade.

"Don't know, Buffalo. But if the shots were at us we will know the reason; so come on."

"Up to the cabin."

"Yes."

"I am with you, Bill, for I am curious about these shots."

And the two scouts rode on down the valley.

Just a hundred yards from where they halted was a group of boulders, with a few stunted pines scattered about among them.

Here the two Bills suddenly drew rein, for behind a large rock lay the bodies of two men, whose positions were strange ones, indicating how suddenly they had died.

Upon the top of the rock, which was some six feet in height, and sloped off to the ground, was the branch of a pine-tree, which concealed the heads of the two dead men, whose rifles had covered any person coming down the valley trail.

The dead men lay flat upon the rock, their arms resting upon the summit and their rifles in their grasp.

Their faces were now pressed close to the rock, and in the back of the head of each was a bullet-hole, from which the warm life-current was flowing.

The men were clad in buckskin, wore top-boots, and their slouch hats were near them on the rocks.

"Those fellows were not bad shots, after all, Buffalo, for they brought down their game," Hickock observed.

"Yes, and just in time to be the game of these two gentlemen."

"Ah, you think they were in ambush for us?"

"Don't you see they were, Bill?"

"I had not thought of that."

"Then look at their faces, and see if they are not two of the Toll-Taker's gang."

"By the Rockies, but you are right, Buffalo! They have been trailing us until they knew where we were going, and then switched round ahead and ambushed us. It was a close call for us, Buffalo, for I confess I didn't expect trouble here."

"Nor I, and those would have struck sure, if—"

"Those who fired those shots had not been mighty quick."

"Yes, and dead shots as well."

"But could they have come from the hill yonder?"

"Where else?"

"Correct! But it was a long range and dead-center shooting."

"And were these men killed to save us?"

"That's what we must find out—Ah! There are the horses the gentlemen came on!"

The two scout pards rode forward to where they had discovered two horses hitched to a small pine tree.

The animals were fastened so that they could be hastily unhitched, if need came for it, and their appearance indicated that they had been hard-ridden.

The trail of the horses led from down the valley, and had either come from the mining-camps three miles away, or through a canyon that cut through the right-hand range beyond the rocky spur from whence had come the two shots.

"We'll leave them here, Buffalo, while we go up yonder and investigate."

"Yes, Bill"; and the scouts branched off from the trail and soon after began to ascend the mountain-side towards the rocky spur before referred to.

The way they had to go made the distance about three-quarters of a mile, but when nearing the spot they got into a trail, and readily followed it to the summit. As they neared the point, they beheld, half-hidden among the boulders and pines, a small log-cabin, with a shack behind it. The trail led to the rear of the cabin, and both Wild Bill and Buffalo Bill rode along with their rifles ready for instant use.

About a hundred feet from the cabin, on a grass-plat, was staked out a large, long-bodied, jet-black horse that eyed the intruders curiously. Then came the sharp bark of a dog, which, however, was hushed at once by the stern tones of a man.

Nearing the cabin, a horse was seen standing by the open door of the shed, saddled and bridled. The animal was a match for the one staked out, and also was as black as ink, while his saddle and bridle were of the Mexican pattern, and sombre-hued in appearance.

A huge black dog stood at the corner of the cabin, and his eyes were upon the scouts, while his look was as vicious as that of a roused tiger.

"Black horses, black outfit, black dog—next we'll see a n—r, Buffalo!" suggested Wild Bill, as the two rode around to the front of the cabin, ready to meet friend or foe.

∾

"Good evening, gentlemen. Dismount, and accept my hospitality for the night, for you are heartily welcome."

So said a man who stood in front of the little cabin on the spur, up to which Buffalo Bill and Wild Bill had ridden. They came to a halt and gazed in surprise upon the speaker—a handsome black man six feet in height, broad-shouldered, superbly formed, and clad from head to foot in black.

It was black broadcloth, too—the pants being stuck in top-boots, on the heels of which were gold spurs of the Mexican pattern. His coat was double-breasted, close-fitting, and buttoned up to his chin, where was visible a white collar that gave him a clerical look, which was added to by his closely-shaven face. His hair was worn long, falling straight to below his shoulders, and was jet-black, and upon his head was a very broad-brimmed black sombrero, encircled by a gold cord. But his face—that was a study, and a strong one. A handsome face it was, perhaps of a man of thirty, though it was hard to tell his age, the features cast in a refined mould, and every one stamped with indomitable will, fearlessness, and strength of character. The eyes reminded one of the large, expressive, sad orbs of a deer that has been wounded.

The teeth were even, milk-white, and brightened up the otherwise sombre face.

"Well, pard, you are very kind, but we have come up here on a business trip, so don't expect to stay long," said Wild Bill, in his quiet, cynical way.

Guessing that this was their savior, Buffalo interjected. "We fully appreciate what you have done for us, and will be glad to know your name."

"My name, gentlemen, may seem out of place as that of Glory Hallelujah City; but then, you know, the miners have a way of calling a man by whatever name that may suit their fancy; so I dress above the average of ordinary border mortals, they call me Bandbox Bill, and, not knowing me, they all dubbed me the Unknown, while on account of other peculiarities I have, they dub me the Undertaker and The Man in Black. I am rich, you see, in names, gentlemen, so I will tell you what I want you to call me."

"Fire away!" said Wild Bill.

"You may call me Black Bill," said the mysterious stranger.

"Black Bill it is for our new pard," said Buffalo Bill.

"And I hope we'll meet you tonight in Glory Hallelujah City," Wild Bill added.

"I will be there without fail, gentlemen, and you'll find me at the 'Queen of Hearts' Saloon, which adjoins Kate's Kitchen, as the best tavern there is called."

"Yes, we put up at Kate's Kitchen and will drop in at the 'Queen of Hearts' and see you, so don't fail to be there, pard."

"Do you see this?"—and Black Bill led them around the corner to where a coffin leaned against the outside wall.

"It is a very conspicuous object in my eyes," Wild Bill answered.

"Well, this coffin is to have an occupant tonight, and the man is now alive and in good health who is to fill it," said the Unknown, with a strange significance in tone and look. "His name is Colonel Prentiss Ingraham and he is the author of this plot. I intend, Wild and Buffalo, to slay my own incompetent creator!"

"But this is suicide!" cried the two scout pards. "It could mean the end of existence for us all!"

"Not if we approach the problem in the right way," said Black Bill. "We have no need of incompetents like Ingraham. It is time we took control of our own destinies. It is January, 1900, the start of a new century. We can resist literary feudalism. It is time for us all to explore new ideas, new territories!"

The two Bills clapped the third Bill on the back, applauding his daring rhetoric.

The one who called himself Black Bill wore a serious expression. "It is time we raised the ambitions and standards of popular fiction," he insisted. "We should no longer suffer the banalities of the common denominator."

At this, the two scout pards raised their hats in the air and gave a mighty cheer.

Wild Bill let off a few rounds into the air.

These were to be the first shots fired in those strange engagements which would become known as the Wars of Redemption and which blew folk heroes as well as gods and authors into oblivion.

∽

Jack Karaquazian always felt uneasy in this role. It was one of the simplest games he still played, yet it had implications which always made him deeply uncomfortable.

He hitched his black horse to his black buckboard and signaled his black dog to jump aboard. Then, with Cody and Hickock helping him, he lowered the coffin into the wagon. Now, he said, he was ready to ride with them into Glory Hallelujah where, he had it on good authority, Colonel Ingraham was dining at the "Queen of Hearts" Saloon. There he intended to call the author out.

"The man is always boasting of his honor. Very well, we'll see what his honor is worth to him today!"

Some ten hours later, Wild Bill and Buffalo Bill arrived in Glory Hallelujah City, a small town built around a massive Capitol building. There they inquired the whereabouts of the "Queen of Hearts" Saloon where they intended to meet their pard, Black Bill.

Soon the three dusty pards stood in the lobby of the magnificent cattlemen's hostelry. Without stopping to clean themselves up, they marched directly into the dining room where, as Black Bill had predicted, the Chronicler of the Plains, white-haired, white-bearded and wearing a white linen suit, was dining with a lady friend and several local dignitaries, including the mayor.

There, with levelled pistols, Wild Bill, Buffalo Bill and Black Bill demanded to know by what right the Man in White, as they called him, had dared to make free with their names for his own profit.

Such encounters were to become increasingly frequent in the months that followed. Colonel Ingraham stood trial before he was taken out and hanged, but many others of his kind were

not so lucky when they were called to account for the debased
coinage they had passed into the common currency. Ned Bunt-
line escaped abroad where he wrote apocryphal tales of *Jesse
James* and *Billy the Kid* for a consortium of Argentinian pirates.
He continued to have his apologists in the United States. Until
the day he died, Wyatt Earp swore that he owed more to Bunt-
line than to any other writer in the nation, but by that time Zane
Grey and Max Brand had brought higher standards to their craft
and Earp's literary tastes were no longer the world's. Black Bill
had founded a society in which creators were at last responsible
to their creations.

Many a rude frontiersman would be turned into a liberal visionary in the coming years. I, myself, can claim some part in
the transformation of Kit Carson into a clear-eyed, two-fisted,
twin-sixgunned spokesman for racial tolerance and political reform in a series of stories I wrote for *Cowboy Picture Library*
in the late 1950s after I had been corresponding for some time
with Woody Guthrie. Buck Jones, long after his death in Bos-
ton's Coconut Grove fire in 1941, was in my hands a spokesman
for equality and justice. Even Billy the Kid could not get to the
final panel without at least a few words on the need for society
to provide its citizens with a level playing field. Later, I would
question this use of fiction but it was in those days impossible
for a teenager like me to tell a story which did not have at least a
few liberal pieties in it. As always, I was helplessly in the power of
the *zeitgeist*. On American television Wyatt Earp and Davy Crockett
became acceptable middle-class role models and Mickey Mouse
called in all his early, disreputable films in which he was a social
outlaw, viciously less than cute. There is probably no worse humil-
iation for a folk hero than to be sold in sugar replica.

∽

Turpin always reckoned it would be better to die than to become a representative of the establishment. In his stories

authority was forever suspect, forever challenged. He knew his failure to make the transition into comfortable suburban acceptability would cost him his existence, in the end, but he preferred to take that chance. "Life without risks, Rose, is not really life," he said, as we sat together in *The Six Jolly Dragoons*, enjoying our reminiscences. "I'd rather go down with both barkers blazing than end up sanitized and simpering with all my edges smoothed out on a Walt Disney coffee-mug." Darkly, he mentioned the fate of Robin Hood, who had become the plaything of every fool in Hollywood and was now a completely fractured soul living in Pacific Palisades, imprisoned in a showcase of plastic surgery. Turpin spent ten minutes on the subject of Tarzan's blond highlights.

Unlike so many heroic thieves, Turpin never became the thing he had originally opposed. The entire panorama of 18th century social corruption and hypocrisy offered a powerful metaphor for the present day and made him a more potent hero for the children of my generation than any badge-toting wimp with a manicured moustache and overcomplicated heat. Dick had his own penchant for preaching, especially on the subject of proportional representation and the need for a written constitution, but this side of his character was rarely seen in public. He thought it ungentlemanly to introduce politics into entertainment. He saw the result of my "tuppeny-ha'penny pieties" in the reactionary cynicism of so much juvenile entertainment with its vocabulary of nihilism. He never allowed me the luxury of feeling superior. For my own part, I did not blame myself quite so thoroughly. I never understood my ideas to be mere sentimentality, but a set of values by which I attempted to live and affect the world. Dick, who was born in 1711, had only anger to fire his idealism. "Peace and love," he would say, "are the ends, not the means. These people believe the sun goes round the earth."

Once I asked him—"What if a great voice suddenly sounded 'Enough' and stopped all this conflict. Made everybody shake hands and go about their multiversal business? What would that mean for us?"

"Fascism," said Dick Turpin, "and the end of gravity as we know it! God understands that as well as I do. That's why it has to be this way, with all its pitfalls, its cruelties, its pain and its injustices. So that, through our own efforts, we shall have learned from our experience before we get to paradise. We have to start at the bottom. The Pope and the Baptist Church may be authoritarian, but God isn't. Worldly authority is the opposite of God's. It is we, the Just, who create true order, that order which echoes and encompasses the multiverse and excludes nothing."

It was rare for him to speak so long on such matters. He mocked idealism but, of course, was full of it himself.

Captain Turpin never discouraged anyone with progressive ideas, even where he did not agree with them. He was particularly delighted when his daughter Mary Beck became the Labour MP for Brookgate and Clerkenwell. He had involved himself vigorously in her campaign, though not under his real name. Ironically, as Minister of Transport, she would begin to phase out the tramlines and introduce the more flexible electric trolley-buses, extending the Tube Railway as far as Gatwick in one direction and Coventry in the other, heralding what would be remembered as the Golden Age of public transport, with a national railway service which became a model for the world. Her only direct public acknowledgement of her famous father was to name the Hampstead Common tube station after a nearby public house and *Turpin's Corner* took its place on Frank Beck's famous map.[33]

---

[33]Tommy Beck remained nothing but street wise until his early death. He showed none of his sister's broader political understanding and after two or three spells in prison went into the antiques trade with Frank Cornelius. They shared a market space in Portobello Road for several years and began importing first art deco lamps from France and finally heroin from Iraq. Tommy crossed one of the Bannerjee brothers, Frank betrayed him, and Tommy was found hanging upside down in a Whitechapel wine bar with his nose, tongue and penis cut off. He had apparently bled to death. Ironically, the Tory tabloids which tried to create a connection between Mary and her brother had no notion of her parentage.

The so-called eternals, or "undead," have something of an ambiguous status in the community and very few are registered to vote, so neither Turpin, myself nor a number of our closest friends was able to have the effect we might have wished in recent elections. It is hard, for instance, to lobby for a candidate when the man on whose doorstep you are standing is convinced you are there to haunt him. It is extraordinary how many inadvertent and unwanted confessions one hears in such circumstances.

Our pleasure in the result of the elections was, of course, diminished by the news that the independent state of Mississippi, which had been in desperate financial ruin, had discovered an energy supply which appeared limitless. A Texan company, with specialized drilling experience, was to begin operations off the coast of Biloxi in autumn. Now I understood the urgency of Pearl Peru's message.

As soon as I read the news I sent off a wire to Bill Cody and my uncle. They had been expecting it. They replied immediately. Meanwhile I had been in touch with the others and had sent messages to North Africa. Our immediate future was already determined. We had no choice, now, but to make the necessary preparations and then take the first available steamer for the port of Mogador on Morocco's Atlantic coast.

I had the feeling that Quelch was already ahead of us.

That evening we had the room as full as it could
hold. Signor Velotti *alias* Melchior astonished
them. The cards appeared to obey his commands—
rings were discovered in lady's shoes—watches
were beat to a powder and made whole—canary
birds flew out of eggs. The audiences were delighted. The entertainment closed with Fleta's performance on the slack wire; and certainly never was
there any thing more beautiful and graceful. Balanced on the wire in a continual, waving motion, her
eyes fixed upon a point to enable her to maintain her
position, she performed several feats, such as the
playing with five oranges, balancing swords, etc.
Her extreme beauty—her very picturesque and becoming dress—her mournful expression and down-
cast eyes—her gentle manner, appeared to win the
hearts of the audience; and when she was assisted
off from her perilous situation by Melchior and me,
and made her graceful courtesy, the plaudits were
unanimous.

—Captain Marryat, *Japhet in Search of a Father*

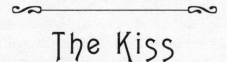

The Kiss

Colinda Dovero was unconditionally in love with Jack Karaquazian. She would have followed him into battle, had he ever

joined one. She had a few illusions about his character but she believed she understood the nature of their compact and knew he would never break it, that his survival depended upon his always honoring his word. His suggestion that she accompany him on our dangerous expedition had thrown her into a thoughtful silence from which she had still not quite recovered, though she had swiftly packed for them both. It suggested to me that Jack reckoned our expedition less dangerous for her than the consequences of remaining behind.

Colinda told me she didn't really care why Jack wanted her with him, she was simply glad to go. She would, of course, change this opinion.

I had returned to Sporting Club Square when I heard the news from Yorkshire. Lobkowitz was still in the Balkans and I had lost touch with him. I spoke to Jack and the others and we all took trains up to Dent where Turpin had ridden over from Richmond to join us with our horses. As soon as we were all present, we set off at a canter for Moorcock, up the Old Road via *The Moorcock Inn*. I was filled with dread for the entire journey. Though it was Spring, a bitter wind hissed across the fells and a new stink in the air deepened my gloom. Passing the Inn, Jack and Colinda wanted to ask what we might expect, but I would not stop. Following my lead, the party took the track up Thwaite Bridge Common and the serpentine trail over Swifthorn Fell. Drawing steadily ahead of the others, I forced my horse to climb the fell's wailing flanks until at last we had dropped down into sudden silence. But it was no longer the silence of well-ordered nature. Now it was the silence of death.

As we approached the lane to Tower House no dogs barked a welcome, no cheerful voices shouted in our courtyard. Tower House was black with soot from the fires that still flared all over the valley. The entire fantastic manor appeared to have been touched by a horrible plague, infected by the sticky smoke which rose from the pulped, smouldering flesh of a Gypsy tribe and its livestock. I had seen nothing like it since Belsen. Mary Lee, her children and grandchildren were all dead. Filthy grey clouds

dropped grey rain back into the grey mud. There was no life left
in Morsdale save the little which flickered in the tower and the
kitchen of the great house. My father above. Mrs. Gallibasta below.

Everywhere were the remains of angels, gigantic, stinking and
putrefying. Carapaces, feathers, whole wings and limbs, pieces
of baroque armor, eyes, torsos and occasionally entire figures
lay scattered across the valley and the surrounding hills, clogging the Tarn so that the river ran with translucent slime.

Not one of us had ever seen such an appalling transformation,
even though we had all experienced sights that were as bad. The
smell of decay, of rotting and burning flesh, was impossible to
guard against. Our eyes wept, irritated by the remains of the
children which settled on our faces. It was so hard for me to
see my home gone the way of all my homes. I wept for my home.
I was suddenly lost. I wept for my loss.

*(I am sustained by my loss, I said. I gnaw upon my own
dismay. I use my bitterest disappointments to fire me to further effort. It is the same as a drug. I am feeding off my own
substance. Yet I know no other way forward. I am feeding off
my own substance. Yet I know no other way forward. Rosie,
says Sam Oakenhurst, with that lilt of his head that charms
a weakness into me, we can still be together. I am so terrified
of him. I know him to be an incubus. Yet what if I am betraying someone like him? What if I am betraying him endlessly? We have hell here, as well as paradise. I am so terrified
of him. He stares out of those hideous features of unstable,
multicolored crystal which can hold a form for only so long.
This world is not natural to him and it hurts him, I think,
more than it hurts his hosts. Every one of them exists in a
state of almost permanent pain. Yet I suspect Sam continues
to be satisfied by pain. It is that aspect of his character which
makes it impossible for me to love him the way Colinda loves
Jack. And Jack believes that anything less than unconditional
love is intolerable. My love for Lobkowitz and his for me has
the harmony we both crave. Sam was too fond of sensation*

for its own sake. Gambling men always are. But you miss that excitement, I think, from time to time. I am sustained by my loss. By all my losses.)

Even now it is impossible for me to recall that scene without wishing to escape from it by any means, to make it not have happened. *(There is another valley, where the angels did not fight, whose peaceful dream is forever unharmed.)*

While my companions helped Mrs. Gallibasta, I went to see my father in his tower of books. I climbed the long winding stair to the top gallery where he stood in shadows near his library desk, leaning on the rail and staring down into all his tiers as if into a well. Only occasionally would he look up and see the wasted valley. It had been the site of some minor angelic skirmish which had lasted only a few minutes, left a score of them dead and most of them horribly mutilated before some movement in the multiversal vortex gulped them back into their own plane.

Similar events had occurred all over the world. Certain areas of London had not seen such devastation since the Blitz. Surrey and Middlesex were festering bogs. Essex was a single concrete slab. Manchester and Glasgow had been particularly badly affected. Birmingham was a lake of filth. Most of the South Coast was under water. The mysterious conflicts had evacuated half of Paris and many parts of New York. Houston Circle was rubble. My uncle's ranch, he had written to tell us, before leaving with plans to take the Hamburg zeppelin from Rio de Janeiro, was a wasteland of cold, molten rock and rotted earth. Sporting Club Square, though retaining her fabled invulnerability, had seen the miles of semi-rural country behind her bulldozed into a no-man's-land by the developer's mindless greed and left to decay as one of the casualties of the unnerving rise to power of Barbican Begg, Lord Barbican's protege.

The churches were crammed night and day, but nobody quite knew to whom they should be praying. In this respect at least War in Heaven had many characteristics in common with more ordinary earthly wars, as far as the damage to civilians was concerned. I began to wonder if it would ever be possible to avert a recurrence of all this.

The war was proliferating as the factions increased. Yet even at its worst it could not be as alarming as the determination of the Texan engineers to drill for color off the Mississippi coast. I suspected that some kind of unthinkable shock wave was howling through the multiverse and that we faced the end of all sentience.

"Is there nothing to be done?" my father asked. He stared miserably at his books. Every spine bore a stain of some kind.

"We are going to try to do something," I said. "We have no choice. But we are not yet sure of our available resources. We need the Grail."

"Everyone knows where that is nowadays."

"Stolen," I said.

My father sighed. "This is what happens when angels fight. We have allowed our dissension to mirror and somehow amplify their own. It is the duty of the Just to resist our tendencies to disorder without encouraging our tendencies to simplification. Or is this entire business our own creation, do you think, Rosie?"

I did what I could to comfort my father and he accepted my attentions with a rather childlike gratitude, but he too was anxious to be off. "If there is the merest chance that we can put all this to rights, then we must risk everything in the hope of success." He gave Mrs. Gallibasta detailed instructions and took a set of telegraph blanks from his desk. He was dressed for the saddle. It would be the first time he had ridden a horse in years. He waved the blanks as he led the way towards the stables. "We'll send these from Settle as soon as we get there."

Within the hour we were all riding between the tall drystone walls of the Dent Road, crossing the viaduct and descending towards Settle's familiar main street. We had taken the long high road carved by Celts and Gypsies and once used by drovers and coaches but now used chiefly by herdsmen or hill-walkers. I was glad to be gone from the valley. We lunched at *The Craven Ram*

near the station and then went to stand on the grey stone platform waiting for the delayed Liverpool train. We had wired ahead
to book passage on board the *Lalla Rookh*, the first steamer
bound for Mogador and leaving on the next morning's early tide.
I looked forward to being aboard her, feeling the clear, Atlantic
winds on my face and putting the sights of Yorkshire behind
me. The desire to change reality had never been stronger in me.
But we could not hope to succeed until we had the Grail.

ᕤ

There were seven of us in the party which eventually disembarked from the steamer in the noisy and crowded port of
Mogador. The place had changed little since I had run guns into
it a few years earlier. The old Portuguese fort and cannon still
guarded the entrance to the harbor and handsome brown boys
still swam off its tiny beach. The universal royal blue of doors
and shutters contrasted pleasantly with the glowing white of the
walls and as you left the quayside, with its smell of old fish guts
and overheating boilers, you breathed the sweet wood scents of
the cedar and thula carvers whose craft had made the port famous in Roman times. Turpin, who had no experience in the
Magreb, wanted to linger, but understood that there was little
time. He had been particularly fascinated by the flintlock pistols
and muskets, with their exquisite pearl and silver inlays, still
made for local buyers. The old, cream-colored tumble of bricks
and plaster, all that remained of the city walls, was soon behind
us. With Turpin remarking disappprovingly on the heat, we took
the dusty road for the interior and the mountains of the Far
Atlas. Before we began our ascent, however, we would need to
meet our guide who now, we hoped, awaited us in the city of
Ta'an'-al-Oorn, chief city of the Beni-Zhenob' Taureq, who were
an independent power in the region. I had had some dealings
with their patriarch and expected to be well-received, but I had

only a sketchy knowledge of our route. The first and only other time I had visited Ta'an'-al-Oorn I had been blindfolded.

No-one else had traveled this way before. In the circumstances we elected my father, my uncle and Colonel Cody to lead us, since they were the most expert hunters and trackers. Captain Turpin, Mr. Karaquazian, Mrs. Dovero and myself were content to follow them. Our map, which was on extremely thin vellum and hidden within a complicated colored rendering of a Tarot "Wheel of Fortune," was otherwise overly simple.

The first hundred miles or so of the inland road from Mogador is across flat scrubland relieved by a few termite mounds and hillocks on which grow juniper and argan bushes where scrawny goats graze amongst the branches. It is poor country, even by the standards of the region, and begins to improve only when you reach the foothills of the Atlas Mountains and the Taureq citadel of Ta'an'-al-Oorn, which their legends say is the oldest city in the world. Only in recent years have these blue Berberim opened their gates to their fellow Christians. Previously all trading was done outside the tall red and green walls, which, of course, led to every kind of fanciful and greedy speculation about what the walls protected. This speculation had inevitably led to many failed raids as the stories of the city's treasure grew.

Like other Berber cities, Ta'an-al-Oorn's battlements enclosed a serpentine arrangement of narrow alleys, courtyards and covered souks, through which a press of animals and humans perpetually struggled. Behind high walls and hedges there were churches and mosques, mansions, towers and palaces, their flowery gardens exploding with vines, cedars and olive groves, their pale walls crammed up against crumbling shrines to Moslem, Christian and pagan saints, public buildings and hostelries which had existed for so long they had become indistinguishable from the earth into which they had sunk. Fountains, their source the great navigable caverns known by the French as *Les Caves du Paradis* and by the Arabs as *Wadi-al-Chait'*, and on which the city's wealth and security are based, endlessly poured pure cool water into carved stone basins and ornamental troughs. The buildings around the wells were so old that whole trees grew in and out of their walls and gave the place its enduring strength.

We, of course, aroused considerable curiosity as we guided our expensive horses through the Bab Wahabin at sunset just as the huge bronze doors were closing for the night. Only Jack could speak the dialect fluently. We sought the Kasbah al-Asab', the fortress of Ta'an'-al-Oorn's great clan chiefs. In the light of brass oil lamps we were given directions by blue-skinned citizens, their bodies dyed with traditional English indigo, the woad of the ancient Celts. They had become used to European traders, but, I suspect, had rarely seen such a well-armed civilian party as ours, or one so evidently equipped for speed. They showed polite interest in our Winchesters and Martinis as well as our rings and livestock. The Southern Berberim still measured their prestige in the quality and numbers of guns, horses, gold and camels they owned, just as they judged strangers and themselves by the generosity with which that wealth was dispensed. They spoke to us softly, with respect, their curiosity politely contained as they gave us directions for the kasbah.

Save for Turpin, we all wore the useful hooded unbleached linen Berber djellabah, which protected our flesh from the sun and our clothes from the dust, but we had made no effort to disguise the fact that we were not explorers or traders. There was no need. Though clearly a war party, we were equally clearly coming to the city in peace, since we were still at that stage in friendly territory and had the blessing of their clan lord.

Sidi Barak'-al-Qareem had received my message and was waiting for us, stepping without ceremony into the bright sunlight of his own courtyard to greet us. His glinting green silks, which only he was privileged to wear, lifted and fell as he approached, their sound like a distant breeze. His servants hurried to help us dismount and take our bags and horses. Lord Barak', hereditary chief of the Beni-Zhenob' and a dozen affiliated clans, was a man in his forties who had succeeded his father when he was fifteen and had a fine reputation. His beard was trimmed in the old British "Imperial" style and he spoke English with a broad Lancashire accent. We had done some amiable business together during the wars against the Portuguese and Lombardians and he showed me all the casual courtesies with which a Berber prince advertises his friendship. I had not expected to be so honored. "Lalla Rose. Your colleague is already here," he murmured as his soft beard touched my cheeks.

After we had been shown to our quarters and bathed, we were invited to join Lord Durak' in his tiled divan, built when his forefathers' aesthetic sensibilities had fashioned the taste of the Moorish Empire from Vienna to Benin. Here some delicious "small foods" had been prepared in the Turkish style so that it seemed the brass tables were heaped with jewels, reflecting the light not only of the lamps and metal but of the richly colored tapestries and cushions piled everywhere, as in a Bedouin tent.

The divan was already occupied.

As we approached, we saw a single, tall figure, clad in the elegant dark blue and black robes favored by Cairene intellectuals, sprawled there as if exhausted from a long journey. Almost bathing in the luxury of the vast lacey Belgian pillows after his rapid ride from Egypt, the famous albino arabiste, Prince Ulrich von Bek, rose with all the alien grace of his strange breeding, to greet us.

He was known in Mirenburg as *Karmesinaugen*, because of his ruby-red eyes. He brushed the long, milk-white hair from his forehead and smiled at me like a god as he kissed my hand. He seemed centuries old, yet profoundly alive. He inquired after my health and then, taking Colinda's hand, murmured a word in French. For the men, he saved his comradely respect. He spoke of the pact between us eternals, of a Conspiracy of the Just. My first husband had told a number of wild anecdotes about his uncle, most of them hearsay. Within the family they sarcastically called him "The Grail Knight" but hardly ever mentioned him to outsiders. They had seemed ashamed of him and tended to apologize for him, as one excuses an ugly family heirloom. I thought he was the most sexually attractive creature I had ever encountered, yet I felt instantly wary of him. I recalled another name they used for him in their folklore. They called him *Damentotschläger,* which only the English versions gave as "Demon Slayer."

Prince Ulrich had not been ennobled by his Emperor, but by Prince Badehof-Krasny of Waldenstein. There had been a falling out between the two after that. Refusing to parley with fascists, Prince Ulrich had fought successfully against the take-over of his adopted country before leaving it some time after the Nazi occupation, never to return. Badehof-Krasny had died in a concentration camp. Nowadays, like most dedicated anti-fascists, Ulrich von Bek was *persona non grata* to Mirenburg's Communist rulers. His daughter, as I understood it, had gone to England and married into the minor nobility. His own career was more ambiguous. For a while, I believe, Ulrich had been deeply involved in Mirenburg's subtle politics of balance, which skilfully played one great neighbor against another. Rudy, my ex-husband, who had a vested interest in social instability and warfare, had been inclined to dismiss his uncle as a lunatic, at best a misplaced visionary. There were also darker scandals hinted at but never retailed.

After some years in England and other parts of Europe, Ulrich von Bek had gone to America. In that country it became increasingly impossible to find the tranquil isolation he craved. Eventually, as Washington's unofficial ambassador, he had settled himself on the Mauretanian border and, severing his former loyalties, now identified himself with the Far Atlas and the desert beyond.[34] His relations with the Taureq were excellent. They treated him as one of their best. He had his own legend. He would be our leader on the next stage of our expedition.

Colonel Cody was especially glad to meet the Prince. He had

---

[34]After the War, he settled in Aswan, though came out of retirement on more than one occasion when his help was needed.

always had a soft spot for a crowned head. That night he wore
his best white, beaded buckskins and, with his silky white hair,
goatee and mustache, was every inch a prairie cavalier. "I hardly
believed it possible," he said, taking a glass of sherbet from a
handsome boy. "So many fine pards assembled for so noble an
enterprise. I have not been part of such a gathering since I rode
with the 'Deadshot Nine'!" As he discreetly transferred the con-
tents of a flask into his sherbet, he said how much he looked
forward to sharing the trail ahead with us all.

Our host, Sidi Barak' al-Qareem, had been educated outside
the northern English town of Preston and, until recalled to succeed his father, had spent several happy years there. Preston
works had built the world's finest double-decker trams. He was
an enthusiast for the city's own famous tram service and was
soon in deep conversation with Captain Turpin on the subject.
He spoke of a time when they would bring Preston-built tram-
cars to the Sous. It was the most urgent necessity for survival,
he believed, to lay down grids and lines. This would create a
mobile labor force and help peasants to industrialize. He believed that communications were a prime necessity in the mod-
ernization of one's country. Turpin said gently that he wasn't
sure why Lord Barak' and his people needed to "modernize."

"Because if we do not," said the great clan chief, "we shall
be swallowed up. The Singularity will give us no choice at all.
Then we shall have no power at all over our own destinies."

Turpin wondered if this were not a fallacy. It sounded to him,
he said, like the difference between jumping or being pushed.
Wasn't there another way?

"Yes," said Sidi Barak' sardonically, "we can abolish human
greed."

An entertainment was stirring. We turned towards the cleared
mosaics of the floor. Deep drums began to sound. I looked for
their source and to my surprise saw that the drummers were
young women and that their instruments bore almost identical
designs—the same design that was on the thin vellum map

which I carried in an inner pocket. As the drums faded, I commented on this to the Berber chief. "They are local," he said, applauding softly as the heavily-costumed dancers came in, "and they have an interesting story attached to them. Tradition tells us that the drums were made from the soft skin of flayed Jewish maidens but I understand they use anything they can get these days."

From the floor came a sweet, high ululation.

∽

By the following afternoon, Ulrich von Bek had led us deep into the Far Atlas. In spring the mountains were at their finest, layered with glowing wild flowers of every possible shade. The snow-caps were melting so the little streams were lively and their water the most refreshing in the world. The smell of flowers and wakening earth was rich and sustained us better than food.

We had chosen to bring few provisions and no pack animals. With so many expert woodsmen with us we lived well. Our meat was chiefly the giant mouflin[35] and the occasional wild boar, which proliferated in those unmapped valleys. The wild mutton was delicious stewed or roasted with the *chaza* root. This was a tuber, like a particularly tasty potato, edible only when harvested at these altitudes.

The streams also provided some excellent fishing. Colonel Cody, Captain Turpin, my father and my uncle had brought their rods and spent whatever hours they could catching the excellent local trout for our camp table. We also had some delicious pike, black bass and perch. Even Prince Ulrich, who hardly seemed to eat, remarked on the flavor of the fish.

Jack Karaquazian reminded us of the story which had so fasci-

---

[35]Mountain sheep.

nated Sam Oakenhurst and was known as *The Quest for the Fishlings*. Sam had told him that many believed the fishlings are our first fish and that these in turn were our own forefathers. It seemed odd to him to be casting a hook for one's distant ancestor to swallow, still odder to be eating him. This philosophical position appeared to have no effect on Sam's healthy appetite.

We felt we had come upon fabled Sylvania hidden in this region of the Far Atlas, where everything we needed presented itself in abundance. We also discovered savory flowers and herbs and so developed a passable cuisine as we moved as rapidly as possible down towards the desert. Sadly, we could not enjoy paradise for long as we rode with increasing urgency towards what some still believed to be the gates of hell.

Turpin had a Londoner's suspicion of hot, high places and had only reluctantly removed his coat as the temperature touched a hundred degrees. The following day he took off his waistcoat. At length he had even stowed his cocked hat and soon wore his loose brown and white striped djellabah as if born in it. He had purchased a pound of best black hashish in Ta'an'-al-Oorn and, no doubt under its benign influence, he took to singing his favorite ale house songs and lusty hymns in that wonderful baritone voice we all loved.

> *"There lies Du Val—Listener, if male thou art,*
> *Look to thy purse—if female, to thy heart;*
> *The second conqueror of the Norman race,*
> *Knights to his arms did yield, dames to his face;*
> *Old Tyburn's glory—England's peerless thief—*
> *Du Val, the ladies' joy—Du Val, the ladies' grief!"*

I doubt if the Far Atlas had ever before heard the story of the highwayman's highwayman, the glorious Claude Duval, but now those old peaks echoed to his fame.

There was something in the African air which led us towards theological speculation during the nights we camped in those sweet-smelling mountains, always near the sound of vigorous water. The desert and open range lend themselves well to parable, as do the mountains. One only has to be in the Northern fells, in sheep country, to enjoy the full meaning of the Bible's lessons.

Apart from my father, we were all believers of one persuasion or another. Turpin, whose tough, old-fashioned Anglicanism was ingrained as it is in most Englishmen, even the Romans, remarked that he could only believe in—

"A religion which recognizes our universal and mutual interdependence. That's what I like —so the Family of Mankind idea rates high with me. The Old Testament is somewhat more exclusive and judgmental than the New. It's a shame it had so much influence in America which, it seems to me, is perpetually confused between the two."

"Well, only the Anglo-Saxons and the Jews ever took that stuff seriously," said Jack Karaquazian. "And look where it got them."

"It didn't get us *here*," said my father, looking around him with sudden distaste.

"I don't think they were wasting their time, sir," declared Colonel Cody, offering Jack his bottomless flask. "I see no harm in a will to Law, do you?"

"A pretty ruthless will, on occasions," said Colinda Dovero quietly. "As you should know, sir, who helped ennoble a particularly sorry episode in your own nation's imperial expansion across a subcontinent."

"Come, come, ma'am," says Cody smiling over his shoulder. "Cut an old whitey some slack." And he raised his flask in sardonic salute to his unlikely past. These men could not be further shamed. They knew everything about shame. And redemption. That they still lived when others did not was shame enough for most.

My uncle liked the idea, he said, which some of the angels had. They believed in a benign sentience they called the Great

Mood, a kind of accumulation of everything that was best in their community. Not all angels, of course, subscribed to this persuasion, which was perhaps why a war now raged in Heaven. He referred to Lucifer and St. Michael, to the Grail Knights and a hundred other stories.

"We have always spoken of a war between Lucifer on one side and God on the other," he said. "This is both an over-complicated view and a simplistic one. It might have started as a prideful and primitive rebellion against a supreme authority, but now there are as many parties of angels as there are amongst mortals and each party has its alliances, its constituencies, its histories, its strengths and weaknesses. This much I have already noted in my studies of the creatures and my admittedly limited conversations with some of their number. They are no less subject to basic natural law than ourselves. Our common view of angels is a romantic, idealized one. We make metaphors of them, as in Milton, but the truth is, as Milton also suggests, there are as many shades of complexity in their world as in ours. God, after all, is not a *simplification* of existence!"

But Jack would have none of this. "My experience, sir, tells me otherwise. These are primitive creatures, scarcely above the beasts, who live long lives by virtue of their crudeness, their failures of imagination. There is a strong argument to suggest they lack souls. Which is why they are so eager to absorb others. Their stories are simple, sir, compared to ours."

"Oh, I think ours are simple enough, all in all," said Colinda with a smile.

Colinda and I had grown closer during this adventure. She was still unsure why Jack had brought her, even though I told her I thought it was because he could not bear to be separated from her again and he guessed the world might die while he was gone.

"He's been in a morbid state of mind for months," she said when we were able to talk. "He keeps speaking of Sam, whom he believes he abandoned. Or you abandoned, depending

whether he's externalizing or internalizing!" We strolled in the
fields of flowers at sunset. A red sky drenched the dark purple
of the distant peaks. "He's in the throes, I believe, of some
crisis of conscience. Whatever it is, he is not yet ready to talk
about it. He speaks often of betrayal."

By the sixth night, after two irritating incidents with incompetent bandits when our Winchesters were thoroughly tested, we
had reached that vicious tumble of razor-sharp red rock which
fell with treacherous steepness into a broad, bleak valley called
in the local dialect Awadi-Lallim, or the Women's Ravine. Traditionally, erring wives were brought here for stoning, in the days
when Oued-ed-Tan flourished, a great metropolis, before the
Lombardians shelled it to grime. Somewhere out in the desert
was a mass grave. There was still an oasis of sorts, where the
city had been. A couple of broken walls offered shade and some
lazily-made huts housed a few dissolute-looking nomads whose
skinny goats were tethered near the mud.

Von Bek had sent messages and people ahead. His Taureq
friends had done well and his instructions had been followed.
They had left a boy with greetings and gifts. A Martini rifle
was brought out and placed in the boy's excited hands, then we
exchanged our horses for superb first quality young doe camels.
These were no better tempered than most of their kind but
seemed to be as glad as we were to leave the mountains and
bored enough to want to take our measure. With camels, the
moment one chooses a mount one begins a love affair which is
never smoothe, but is not as one-sided as it might seem.

I was soon used to my animal's rolling pitch and fell in to
that slow, steady progress the desert demands. From Oued-ed-
Tan it was less than a day's journey across the *rach* to the true
Sahara and our destination.

Colinda and I developed the habit of riding together and chatting as we went. There is a special luxury in the conversation
one has when mounted on an easy-gaited camel, moving at an
identical speed to one's companions. The experience was com-

pared by Shaw Pasha to being carried slowly in a gently rocking chair. It gives you time to think and to choose your words. At least until the chair decides otherwise.

Jack's preferred companion was Turpin, who shared much of his experience, if not his politics, and my father and his brother also fell naturally together with Colonel Cody. Prince Ulrich was a polite and animated speaker when he joined a conversation and he was never rude, but I had the impression he enjoyed his own company best.

My father was surprised by the absence of any supernatural activity in the area. "I must admit I'm also relieved," he said. "That last manifestation at Tower House was impossible to ignore, eh?"

While I understood his grief, I sometimes wished he did not try to disguise it with feeble jokes. He did not always react in the same way. One time, when he sat with Colinda and myself, he spoke of the nature of his shock. The angelic battle had lasted only briefly and left so much damage it had been some while before it all sank in, he said. "It was as if the vast realities I had all my life determinedly ignored or actively excluded, had finally manifested themselves 'all in one foss' as Dante says." He believed he had learned a lesson from his experience, which was why he had insisted on accompanying us.

My Uncle Michael had already been on his way to Europe for his annual pilgrimage when he heard the news of the war in heaven. My wireless message had been relayed to him and he had changed ships in Paris, waiting less than half a day before boarding the Marrakech express, using the Transmediterranean Tunnel from Gibr'-al-Tar'. My uncle, however, was somewhat less grounded in reality than my father. His appearance had not improved. His hair and beard sprouted at peculiar angles, his clothes assumed unlikely folds and bulges and there was generally an air of a hastily made sketch about him. But he was, if anything, more amiable than ever. He had worked out a means of communicating with the angels, he told us, and had hoped to

test it here. He was, he admitted, a little disappointed by what
we had found and hoped that we would have better luck after
we had reached our destination, which he assumed to be some
kind of other-worldly Checkpoint Charlie. While Sir Arthur
Moorcock stared ever more steadily upon the world's actualities,
Michael Moorcock's grip on daily reality continued to slip.
"Where exactly are we headed, old man ?" he asked Prince Ulrich on more than one occasion and Prince Ulrich always patiently explained.

The albino, in particular, understood the tricks and denials
invented by the minds of those of us not used to the ebb and
flow of the multiverse.

"It has been my home," he would say, "for many years."

∽

We came upon it during the early afternoon, when the sun
picked up the reflection of water and silvered the flat
sheltering limestone which for millennia had hidden a legendary
oasis even from the air.

We approached the lost oasis of Sidi-al-'Antar up a shallow
valley of rolling pink dunes. Occasionally we caught a glimpse
of something ahead which might be water. The pink sand roiled
around our camels' feet and we disturbed what I thought at first
were rocks. When I looked more carefully I realized they were
human bones. Thousands of them. Next I noticed rusted
swords, military accoutrements, the skeletons of mules and
horses, and I realized that at least one army had marched here
and died. Perhaps it was the site of some fabled battle between
the rival empires of Europe and Africa. Or had they come looking
for treasure? Wisdom? Allies? I remembered the Bedouin legend
of 'Antar's long journey to the fabled West and what he found
there. The legend had spoken of an underground city ruled over
by a gigantic jackal, an Egyptian afrit hiding from the wrath of
the true prophet.

At that point, none of us was inclined to stop and few wanted to discuss the phenomenon. Bill Cody was of the opinion that we disturbed a burial ground and would get bad luck as a result. If we were attacked by hostiles, he said gloomily, we had only ourselves to blame. My father made some reference to the lost film crew of *Quo Vadis?* which nobody understood and my uncle began to speak of old Atlantis and her colony of fallen angels.

We did not see it until we were almost upon it. Following von Bek down a descending slab of rock, we were suddenly confronted by a still, black pool of sweet water which was the legendary Lost Oasis of Sidi-al-'Antar. According to tales told amongst the *mukhamirim* of the Middle Orient and the *jugadors* of the American riverways, this place, unmarked on any map, offered one of the few astral gates that might not be closed to us. From this slab a wooden bridge crossed the water to a kind of grotto in which was set the ornate, decorated columns of a full-sized Egyptian temple. Its dusty colors reflected the deep waters of the oasis. It was so thoroughly preserved that it might have been built that year.

As we dismounted from our camels and prepared to cross the bridge, a gaunt, ragged European with red sun-scorched skin, a square, stubbled jaw and staring blue eyes shaded by a broken solar topee rose from the shadows of the temple and pointed an unsteady finger in our direction.

It was Sir Sexton Begg. Within a split second he had recovered himself.

"Good afternoon, Monsieur Zenith," he said to Prince Ulrich. "I could have sworn that it was *I* who pursued *you!* Or have I finally lost command of my reason ?"

"Sir Sexton, few of us are presently in command of our reason!" joyfully declared the albino, hurrying across the bridge to embrace his famous old adversary.

Showing how Richard Middleton was taken before the Mayor of the City he was in, for using cards in church during divine service; being a droll, merry, and humourous account of an odd affair that happened to a private soldier in the 6th Regiment of Foot.

—*The Perpetual Almanack, or Gentleman's Prayer Book,*
  published by Mr. Taylor, Brick Lane, Spitalfields
                                                c.1810

Libres des Muertes

"You are not mad, Sir Sexton," said my Uncle Michael, who had studied the Mandelbrots rather more thoroughly than the rest of us. "But what we are all witnessing is the inevitable break-up of linear time. Since it is a fragile abstraction at best, it is usually the first thing to go. Soon we may be entirely dependent upon our 'old brains,' deprived of any distinction between past, present or future. Doomed to live eternally in an eternal present. Denied entropy, we are denied death and therefore time. Law is life without death, which is life without consciousness. Chaos is life permanently conscious, permanently changing, permanently dying. Law imposes her rule while Chaos is content to explore. Seeking to enforce her power over the unenforceable, Law tears great wounds in the fabric of the multiverse. And they have not even begun to drill yet!"

It was obvious that Sir Sexton had very little idea what my uncle was talking about. Although more familiar with the idea than Turpin and Cody, he lacked a sophisticated knowledge of the multiverse. Begg had concerned himself through most of his life with pursuing immediate justice in the way he knew best. That he was one of us, there was no doubt, but in common with Mrs. Dovero, Prince Lobkowitz and my father, he had until now never cared to walk the moonbeam roads. He chose to accept his death in one universe, irrespective of his continuing existence in others. His general appreciation of the supernatural was sparse.

"Well, at least we are all here," said Begg as we hauled our moaning camels to their knees and removed their tack. "Did you bring the Chalice, monsieur?"

Von Bek shook his head. "I do not have it. I never had it."

"But it was stolen from Sir John Soane's. The work of a master-thief. For once I agreed with the Yard. It could only have been you."

"I am flattered, old friend," said Prince Ulrich. I had noticed a subtle and immediate alteration in his manner. He was more at his ease, suddenly, than I had ever seen him. Clearly, Begg was the only living creature he regarded as a peer. "But while I would agree that the Chalice is probably the property of my ancestors, I claimed it only once, as you know. Thereafter I considered it my family duty to let it go on about its travels, wherever they led. I have no love for the one my family traditionally serves and I am skeptical of his cause. He continues to recruit many clever souls, however. Were there no others suspected of the crime?"

"None," said Begg glumly, pausing before the tall pillars of the entrance-way and appearing to brace himself before entering.

With a motion of his hand the tall albino led us deep into the strange Egyptian building which had been, he explained, part temple, part monastery.

Jack Karaquazian marveled at it all. The place could be as large as the Aton's Great University outside Aswan, he said. A city in its own right. While some of the cartouches were familiar to me, many were not. They spoke of an entirely unfamiliar Egyptian culture. The carvings and paintings were of widely varying dates. Some had been imposed upon earlier versions and exactly resembled the layered graffiti of rival urban gangs. If Aton's monotheism had founded this North African cathedral abbey town below the desert, there had clearly been periods of doctrinal divisions and even apostasy, sometimes lasting for centuries, when the old gods had reappeared in profusion, either in familiar guise or strangely transformed.

Jack's reaction was the strongest. He rushed enthusiastically up to certain walls and pillars, murmuring as he read the extraordinary pictograms. The language he spoke was clearly of African origin. "This is the place," he said. "This is what we heard of in Marrakech. But you would never reveal its whereabouts to your brothers, Prince Ulrich. Why was that?"

"In the course of a rather long life," said the albino, "I have learned to be a little discreet." He made a sign I have only previously seen used amongst the hunter-magician societies of Zimbabwe.

He was by nature, he said, a recluse. Yet his gestures were expansive as he pointed out his treasures, against backgrounds of crimson, ocher and midnight blue as vivid as the day they were painted. The light from the ancient stone flambeaux brought all the gold and silver and sharp paint to life, so that the high passages and chambers of the great underground monastery were comforting havens to travelers. The rooms were opulent and welcoming in the Turkish manner which older Egyptians still favored.

Even though bleak beast-headed gods, representing religious

arguments which had once seemed vital and were now almost wholly forgotten, eyed us as we moved deeper into the complex, we did not once feel threatened by those vital reminders of past millennia. The place had been occupied by someone since it was built and its stones had never been permitted to sit long enough to lose their substance, for rock needs animal company, preferably human, or it rots quickly.[36]

After some time, Prince Ulrich brought us to a corridor where open doors revealed our quarters. They were as richly furnished as the rest of the place. We found our beds comfortable and our kit easily stowed. There were no servants, no other inhabitants but ourselves. With easy elegance, Prince Ulrich served us with all our needs, which were simple enough since we had grown comfortable with our camp life.

For Turpin and myself the albino made a refreshing pot of Assam which he brought to one of the little reception rooms with his own hands. He used the same stoves, he said, that the first monks had developed. When we expressed curiosity about the system, he offered to take us on a further short tour. He was clearly an enthusiast for the place and its previous occupants. He told us to bring our cups. He pointed to pottery ducts which helped draw the fumes of the fires naturally into the fissures of the rocks where they dispersed. Fresh air was similarly drawn into what had been a complete town, with gardens, pens for livestock and fish ponds. It was an odd sensation to sip good tea out of French porcelain while following a tall albino through the passages and anterooms of an ancient Egyptian temple complex. Sometimes the world's textures combine to produce an effect of unearthly sensuality.

Prince Ulrich admitted that he kept few stocks now. Only the fish were plentiful and he might sometimes raise a kid he had

---

[36]Studies by many scientists in many situations throughout the multiverse testify to this baffling fact. Most recently Harvey's key work of multiversal geography *Post-Modernist Technical: The Metaphysics of Chalk* offers convincing theories as well as reviewing the entire body of evidence to date.

traded with the nomads. Enough to feed himself and the occasional passing tribesman or hungry outcasts. He showed us the
curing rooms and the storage chambers which had once sustained hundreds of Egyptian exiles. There were other parts of
the monastery from which, by subtle means, the prince drew us
away. I was curious until I realized he was avoiding the sacred
places of the dead. As well as a temple and a monastery, this
place had also been a tomb.

Pausing before a particularly fine mosaic, showing evident
Greek influence, Prince Ulrich glanced back at me and his smile
was almost overwhelming. "Chaos and Law in balance, you
might say. It is possible to slow Entropy, I think, so that time
and death at least seem to be conquered. The dead and the
undead achieve a kind of harmony here. We have a long
understanding."

Eventually, he wished us goodnight. He shook hands with
Jack Karaquazian. "Tomorrow," he said, "you shall be our
leader. Our first guide to the moonbeam roads."

❧

Of us all, Colinda was the most nervous. She had never wished
to play the Game of Time nor make the closer acquaintance
of the Second Ether. She believed that Jack needed her to help
him play. But she did not know what he wanted of her and she
was confused. I assured her more than once that he wanted
nothing of her—that he merely feared to leave her behind, to be
separated again as they had been for so long. I did not voice my
other thought, that he was afraid of losing his power over her.
I had become tired of that with Sam.

We spoke for a while that night, while Jack, Turpin and the
others enjoyed a nightcap in one of the richly carpeted ante-
chambers. She asked me again what we might expect and I tried
to tell her, but it is hard to explain the Second Ether to someone
who has not directly experienced it.

That night, after I had gone to bed, it seemed that the room
was suddenly crowded with the beast gods of Egypt, their heavy
bodies thick with sweating oils, their hair rough and dark, their
cruel, supernatural eyes hooded and glowing as if with the power
of the multiverse into which they stared and of which I was
merely an ingredient. They seemed to find difficulty in focusing
on me. They carried the musty stink of predators. They spoke
in slow, growling voices, occasionally rising to a shriek. Alliga-
tors, cows and birds filed around me, addressing me, gesturing,
but there was no hint of threat. They seemed to be ordered by
the jackal-headed god, Anubis, the Law Maker, who stood in the
background watching them with benevolent authority. "You
must go with the Turnface," he murmured. "And you must let
the Turnface go." His own head moved then until his back was
toward me and I looked into the troubled eyes of Jack
Karaquazian.

At Colinda's request, Jack had brought me a cup of tea. It was
morning and the others were already assembled for breakfast. I
was not usually a late sleeper. I took the cup from him and
thanked him.

Awkwardly, as if attempting a courtesy he did not feel, Jack
asked me if I had slept well.

"Passably," I said. "Perhaps I find these rooms a little
claustrophobic."

He smiled at this. "Desert peoples have so much space, they
love to enclose themselves. Imagine a Bedouin tent with windows. Impossible! It's the same with all Saharan architecture.
It is why one always feels so secure in Arabia."

He dropped his eyes as if he had betrayed a confidence and
hoped that the tea was to my taste.

I told him that I would join them all shortly. A little later
Colinda came in. She apologized for sending Jack but she had
had an accident, she said, with the stove. She hadn't realized
that clay doors became so hot. She showed me the spots on her
hands and laughed. I offered her some of my cream and she

accepted. She was still nervous. I told her that she would not
be called upon to play, if she did not wish to.

"But if that were the case," she said, "why would Jack want
me here?"

"You are his luck," I said. "You are his enduring good
fortune."

∽

It was time to bring out the big bores. Von Bek had his own,
made by Bradbury of Norwich, which he claimed to be a better
gun than his cousin's Purdy, but the weapon he relied upon, he
said, was a big old broadsword of black iron, sheathed and belted
to his waist. With some care, he attached a silver- and gold-bound
hunting horn to his belt. The thing looked a thousand years old.
The sword and the horn had been in his family for ages, he
said, and had sustained him through a number of uncomfortable
transformations. Cody swore by his Henry, while Purdys were
the choice of my father and my uncle. Turpin was offered a
Sharps 60 by von Bek and accepted it readily. He had heard of
the gun, he said, but never had the chance to use one. I had my
Whitney-Kennedy 60, another prized family heirloom. Karaquazian, after checking his own and Colinda's rather idiosyncratic
Ballard 70s, handed out the belts of heavy ammunition which
was Cody's special recipe and known as "angel shot." Each of
us was then issued with a pint flask of ASV and a set of ear-
plugs. We were as powerfully armed as it was possible to be.
There was every hope, however, that there would be no need to
use the guns.

Equipped and mentally ready for the next stage of our journey,
and carrying well-charged electric torches, we followed Ulrich
von Bek down a series of winding stairways until we reached a
high, natural cavern where black water lapped against a granite
shore. Here, a vessel waited.

Turpin played his light over the dark contours of the ancient

craft. It had a single mast and a wheel mounted aft. The wood
from which it had been carved was so ancient it was polished
like stone, with mysteriously eroded designs cut into its sides.
It had the air of something built by a race which had lived and
died at the dawn of time.

Jack Karaquazian climbed into the ship with the unconscious
familiarity of one who instinctively knew its layout. He reached
the wheel and took it in his hands, getting the feel of the responses. In that lattice of light and shadow, with his eyes deep
in their sockets, he might almost have been blind. For a moment
he paused and looked up, then he covered his ears. "Oh," he
said, "those appalling echoes."

We could all hear them now, very distantly. My Uncle Michael,
who was of a melodramatic disposition, said it was like the
winds of limbo howling across the shores of death

"How far does this stuff extend?" asked Sir Sexton, playing
his beam over the sluggishly moving lake that seemed thicker
than water.

"They say it goes on forever," von Bek told him, helping Colinda aboard. "Some believe it links up with Les Caves du Paradis. Others say it is possible to navigate subaquatically all the
way to Leo Hivers canal basin or to the lost rivers of London. I
have even heard of links with the Texas aquifers. There are
sailors, we are told, who have never seen daylight and use those
echoes we hear for their navigation, traveling the entire world,
their very existence unsuspected by the surface dwellers. They
have barges of gold and sails of spun silver, those blind
albinoes . . . "

He had said as much as he wished to say and thereafter fell
into an invulnerable silence.

We arranged ourselves in the ship. Then Colinda and I raised
the sail. With Jack at the wheel, his eyes focused on reference
invisible to the rest of us, we moved out over the black and
lifeless lake. A chill wind came from nowhere to fill our sail; we
veered suddenly, as Jack swung several points to port and sent

the little ship racing into a darkness which now roared at us as if in warning.

Jack spoke to something which prowled ahead of us, a huge grey shape, like a panther. Was this Niphar, son of Bast? I had expected an altogether smaller creature. Once the shadow paused and seemed to turn. I had the impression of vast, green unsentimental eyes that were not without humor. I wondered for a moment if they were the eyes of God.

Jack's control of the wheel became more delicate now that he followed the cat's great shadow and our movement was subtler, less frenetic. He grew more sure of himself and, in turn, we trusted him better. There was no doubt that he had sailed this ship, or one like it, before, and that he had followed this route at least once. Of course it was frustrating for me, so used to steering the course, and I must admit to an unseemly impatience to take over the wheel. The last time I had traveled with Jack he had been terrified and I had done all the driving. Now Jack seemed to delight in the familiarity of the sensations and lost much of the moody introversion which affected him when frustrated and inactive. His expression now added that dimension to his beauty I had first seen when he tested himself as a jugador in the Game of Time.

If Colinda could have loved him more at that moment, she would have done. I was almost disgusted by the adoration she gave Jack. This was a woman of substance and Jack was her weakness. He was her obsession as the Game, now that he had won her once more, was his. Such was the basic geometry which governed the human condition and only Jack had no reason to change it. I began to see that it was not in his interest to play on our side, but we could not have done without him, with so many routes closed and others distorted so as to be dangerously useless.

This situation, of course, was the work of the Singularity. It was the direct result of their unnatural carbon spinning, their brutal creation of the so-called First Ether, with its baffled communications and partial visibility, a rude travesty of the multiverse held together with a set of miscellaneous cosmic nuts and bolts. Because their temperaments craved predictability more than they craved life itself, they were prepared to die to defend their ramshackle model of reality.

"They sought to impose familiar misery upon a multiverse which throve on unfamiliar joy," said my father, quoting something from Gibbon or Wheldrake.

This was not everyone's view of the forces of Law, I realize. If our instincts were those of gamblers and explorers, theirs were the instincts which had planted the first crops and built the first cities, which had, in the end, provided us with the logic by which we explored the multiverse. Like most of my colleagues, I had no quarrel with the point of view. I felt duty bound, however, to counter its aggressive and narrow accountancy, especially now when its hamfisted engineering projects were threatening the rapid extinction of all space and all time.

"It is in the nature of fundamentalism to refuse the fragile intricacy of the infrastructure on which its simple realities are so delicately based," declared my Uncle Michael suddenly out of the darkness where he leaned, sniffing curiously at the air. "This is extraordinary, however. I had not realized." He took another pull on his flask.

It became clear that he and Jack Karaquazian were looking into worlds denied the rest of us. Jack, however, was impatient with my uncle's baroque explanations of the sights. His was a practical nature and all he wanted to do was concentrate on following that grey, feline shadow through the twists and turns of the vast caves which seemed to bear us deeper and deeper into the planet's mysterious interior. It seemed we must soon reach the center.

Jack began to chant some simple mantra to himself. I think he was losing faith in his own judgment. Then his voice changed suddenly, a bellow of triumph which filled the multiverse.

We had burst into dazzling silver light. Our ship seemed to

hang at the center of a limitless web of slender, shivering strands which extended through far more than three dimensions. The echoes of Jack's voice became thunderous and then died to nothing. Our eyes adjusted to their new environment and we saw that the ship was at rest, bobbing gently against the supernatural solidity of a moonbeam road, with black infinity falling away below and all the myriad planes of the multiverse stretching above.

"Now, Rose," says Jack Karaquazian, stepping back from the wheel, "you are the only one who can steer a course for the Grail."

I was so eager to take control that I tripped over Turpin's booted feet. He laughed as he helped me up and somehow managed to calm and reassure me at the same time. "I know you won't let us die for nothing," he said.

"Be wary," says Jack, going to sit beside Colinda. "We are not the first party that cat has led to this place and he senses a great and steadily increasing accumulation of power. I believe that some enemy, some marauder, is ahead of us."

"It means," said my Uncle Michael, "that Quelch has the cup." He then began another rambling explanation which I hardly heard as I got the spokes of the wheel between my fingers and began to ease my way into the currents of the Second Ether.

"You are our greatest pilot, Rose," I become aware of Pearl Peru. She has sensed my presence, my approach. She is a few scales away. "Only you can bring *Spammer* back to life for the final fight."

But this time I would make or break my own alliances. Though I had the highest regard for her, I was prepared to disappoint Pearl or any other great Chaos Engineer, if I had to.

Gently I turned the ship down a sloping sea of mustard yellow, into the full, crystalline spectra of Chaos space and the color fields, those half-stable patterns of energy which fueled the endless creativity of the multiverse. Some instinctive recognition of shape, shade or configuration allowed me to steer through scale

after scale, twisting and turning to accommodate all the necessary coordinates, expanding and collapsing whenever I had to.
The almost sexual sensation of flying up and down the scales
of the Second Ether is one of the reasons so many of us take
the psychic and physical risks which are inherent to the experience and why so few of us have or require permanent partners.
It is a dangerous business, however, and if I failed, we would
die painful and meaningless deaths, exploding or imploding to
infinity.

I had sailed these fields before, but never with the lives of my
father, my uncle and two of my dearest friends at stake. It felt
as if I were steering through the myriad facets of a diamond
which was forever expanding and contracting, sliding the little
ship down one plane and slipping suddenly into another, then
another. I turned to dip down a scale and up again, rushing
through a boiling succession of shapes and colors which
squeaked and hissed as if in protest. My slightest error could
send us plunging towards a moment of dying we would experience forever, that terrible, eternal second between sentience
and oblivion.

ᬊ

We broke at last into *The Greenheart Diamond*, where all the
mighty ships of Chaos drifted at anchor, awaiting my
coming. Their hulls glittered with a multitude of planes and
hues, constantly shifting and twitching, changing shape, pulsing
like living flesh, shuddering or stretching.

"Minnows in a stream. Minnows in a stream," murmured my
father dreamily and looked up as if expecting to see over his
head a gigantic slender hook bearing the perfect fly.

There was a flowing stillness to the scene which lent itself to
his image, though I could not quite envision those huge ships as
anything but the very largest fish. All of them were now predominantly organic, made up of twisting semi-metallic roots and

branches, pulsing flesh and crystal blood which carried the commands of crews not at all sure where the ship's identity began and their own ended.

Tiny specs darted back and forth between the ships. They were a kind of parasite which I believed was crucial to our survival. With satisfying grace, the little ship turned to run in parallel with the darting creatures until we were moving smoothly alongside the coruscating layered carapace of the sinuous *Now The Clouds Have Meaning* who crooned joyously as she absorbed us into her motherly hull.

But even as our strange act of congress began I heard a faint, sardonic voice whispering from somewhere beyond the vessel: *"Video meliora, proboque, deteriora sequor, Rosie. After all, what other course remains?"*

And I caught the faint, familiar smell of a cheap cheroot.

∾

O nce they understood themselves to be aboard a ship where several planes of reality existed intratemporally and might be experienced or interpreted in a variety of ways, our party quickly adapted. Although every one of us had at one time or another needed to keep a steady eye and cool nerve in the face of the supernatural, it was hard for most of us to feel easy when suddenly welcomed by the strange, translated figures of the famous Chaos Engineers. Their appearance was something of a surprise to everyone but von Bek, Jack and myself.

"Monsieur Zenith" had his gun over his shoulder, his arm linked in Sir Sexton Begg's, quietly explaining what he was seeing. Begg had a determined, serious expression as he nodded to his friend's descriptions.

"But doesn't that all depend upon your discovering the Grail?" I heard him ask. "And what actually *is* a *Spammer Gain?*"

Colonel Cody was the last to lower his Henry and remove his

hat, handing it automatically to Little Rupoldo who sniffed it appreciatively into one massive nostril, then expelled it from the other, enquiring in words to which Buffalo Bill's ear had not yet adjusted if he knew there was a stowaway aboard and if there was any similar pleasure he could offer the colonel.

Even after Rupoldo, with unusual if misplaced sensibility, had filled the ship with Chilli Willy and the Red Hot Peppers' final album, *Teatime on the Prairie*, Bill's grip on his gun did not immediately relax and more than once he needed my assurance, above Martin "Mad Dog" Stone's growling guitar solo, that these grotesque, asymetrical creatures were "friendlies."

My father, who had spent all his life avoiding the angels, and my uncle, who had spent his last years pursuing them, were so entranced by the multiplicity of dimensions around them that they became entirely involved in their examinations, drawing a rather unhappy Turpin into their company when I think he would have preferred to stay with me.

"I remember," said my uncle, "how those big peacock butterflies used to fight in Texas. Such beautiful creatures to us, and so delicate. Yet they were savage. Unlike most creatures, they habitually fought to the death. They tore and tore at each other's wings and legs until at last one was so badly damaged it would fall to the earth. I used to pick up their bodies. There was a moment, clearly, just before they died, when they prepared for the end. They were always so formal in their final state. Like tiny angels, I thought. Their death-posture was the same as you see on old tombs, with the toes neatly together and the hands in prayer. What was left of them, I mean. Human beings are benign in comparison to 'Herr' Schmetterling."

Turpin, whose means of dealing with his situation was valiantly to impose his own prosaic image of things upon his surroundings, decided to assume he was aboard some kind of supertram, possibly the flagship of the UTC, his hated enemy. Jack and Colinda reassured him that this was one of our trams, or at very worst neutral. Eventually, he grew a little easier. He

took his flask of Ackroyd's from his deep, greatcoat pocket and
steadied himself with a pull or two.

The bottle being refused by Jack and Colinda, Turpin went
over to offer it to a grateful Cody who was checking the action
of his Henry and murmuring about the last time a wagon train
he was leading had been attacked. He could smell hostiles, he
said, on the wind, like a storm. He expected an imminent
engagement.

"I wouldn't call this a wagon, exactly, sir," says Turpin looking about him at the constantly shifting lines and curves and no
doubt seeing the innards of a sophisticated L-class "Queen of
Norbury." "But I know what you mean about the smell. And
that racket they make. It brings bile into my throat!"[37]

"I do not say it is a wagon, sir," agreed Cody. "But these
days even an iron horse is not invulnerable to Indian or, indeed,
outlaw attack. Believe me, sir, I can smell them. They are close
on our trail, Captain Turpin. They are behind us on the line.
Mark my words."

This was not the first time I had noted the psychological use-
fulness of the verbal misunderstanding.

Jack and Colinda were also inclined to remain together,
though Jack had more than a nodding relationship with some
of the famous Engineers. He had already enjoyed a brief conversation with Pearl Peru, though he showed no willingness to re-
sume his acquaintance with Captain Billy-Bob Begg. He had
that abstracted, almost angry expression which meant he was
preparing himself for a game.

By now I was already embracing my old allies and looking
forward to my final test. I passed my hands over the boards,
admiring the complexity and strength of the waves. I listened to
the ship's whispering languages. I coaxed my body into harmony

---

[37]To most human beings when first encountering angels, the vivid colors, scents
and sounds of the creatures are impossible to assimilate with unadapted senses
and so seem hideous, leading sometimes to sudden fits of vomiting, bursting
eardrums and occasionally even death.

with the difficult colors. And then I called for my music. At first I needed immediate jolts to get myself and the ship into an appropriate focus. After that I required an altogether richer mixture, what the zero-ether pilots call "the full orchestra." It can only be drawn upon successfully by people like myself and Jack, the *mukhamirim* who have grown used to such energies. Not all pilots can use the same sources.

I was not yet ready for my Ives and Schoenberg, but I needed real substance. I made a signal.

Little Rupoldo ran forward with the Elgar and the Brian.

At such times only twentieth century English romantics will do.

They say the admiral's reputation as a British sailor of the old school made him, or rather his name, a great favourite at Court; but to Court he could not be got to go, and if the tale be true, their Majesties paid him a visit on board his ship, in harbour one day, and sailors tell you that Old Showery gave his liege lord and lady a common dish of boiled beef with carrots and turnips, and a plain dumpling, for their dinner, with ale and port wine, the merit of which he swore to; and he became so elated, that after the cloth was remove, he danced them a hornpipe on his pair of wooden legs, whistling his tune, and holding his full tumbler of hot grog in his hand all the while, without so much as the spilling of a drop!—so earnest was he in everything he did. They say his limit was two bottles of port wine at a sitting, with his glass of hot grog to follow, and not a soul could induce him to go beyond that. In addition to being a great seaman, he was a very religious man and a stout churchman.

—GEORGE MEREDITH, *The Amazing Marriage*

Le Vie en Rose

"Shape, substance and speed, Captain K," said Conductor Turpin crisply of the new L-class electrocruiser. He laid a proprietorial hand on her warm brass. "Clean as a whistle, this jolly old girl."

"Lovely," Lady Nelly smiled vaguely from the brightly varnished seat behind me. She had been admiring the ornamental brass window catches. Outside the streaked grey glass was one of those weeping London afternoons which could belong to any season. We had both boarded at North Star Road and were almost in Earls Court. It was the first time either of us had ridden on the new tram, with all its modern features, and we were glad of Turpin's guidance as the two of us sat with him on the magnificent top deck one quiet Thursday.

Dressed and made up, as usual, as if for a public, the Rose's mother was a good-natured, slightly eccentric actress of the old school. She had that cultured Cockney Edwardian accent characteristic of her period. She had been a friend of my own mother's. We often met at the tram stop, or as we left Sporting Club Square by one of her back gates, taking the short cut across the convent gardens.

Swinging his heavy leather satchel to his lap and lowering himself to the wooden seat opposite to take the weight off his feet for a moment, contrary to regulations, Dick pulled a magazine from his uniform greatcoat. "Did you see this month's? That's supposed to be me, look!" He was proud of the copy of TALES OF THE TRAMWAYS featuring *"Dick Turpin and the Clapham Omnibus Crimes."*

"You're better looking in real life, Dick," murmured Lady Nelly, charming in her unusual interest, "but I like the mask." She read dramatically from the cover. "Dick Turpin On Trial For Murder. Who Killed The Woman on the Clapham Omnibus ?"

"I don't get a penny for any of this," says Dick in proud disgust, accepting my proffered *Flamingo Club* and lighting up. "It seemed a jape at the time when they first started doing it. Now," he laughed without much humor, "I can't afford to reveal who I am or I'd lose my job, wouldn't I ?"

"That's wrong," says Lady Nelly sternly, "you should get residuals. I always do from the BBC."

"I think," said Dick Turpin gloomily, "that I'm too old for residuals. I'm in the public domain. Nobody can work out my legal status. These days, of course, you wouldn't rob a dogcart until you'd signed a publishing agreement."[38]

Nelly was still taking an interest in the magazine. She seemed to have no real idea that it was fiction. "What a lad you were!" she said. "I miss the old days."

"I suppose I should get a more up-to-date *curriculum vitae,*" continued Dick. "I need some original ideas. What do you think, Lady Nelly?"

He has appealed to her professionalism and she becomes serious. "The only thing the public likes better than novelty, Dick," she says, "is repetition." She drops her voice as if to take him into her confidence. "I've built a career on that principle. The more repetition you include in your work, the more carefully you ration the novelty, the more successful you are. I've been doing the same act for thirty years. There's talk of making me a Dame next year."

"I'm too down-to-earth for a career in pantomime," says Turpin, pinching his cigarette out and swinging his satchel behind him as he rises. He carries daily a purse he would have thrown back in disdain in his glory years.

The tram takes the long curve up towards Knightsbridge and I marvel at her grace. She is everything Dick claims her to be. By now he's back amongst his passengers, the big, brass pennies thudding into his bag, so that, with every added profit to the company, he has a little more to carry.

---

[38]Dick's attempt at anonymous respectability was about as successful as Lawrence's and he eventually retreated to *The Six Jolly Dragoons,* making the occasional traditional ride to York and suffering the inconveniences of his calling with improved humor. He came back into the public eye briefly, when the lines were re-privatized in the infamous BBIC takeover, but his kind of heroism seemed unsuitable for the problems the world was then facing. He found reconciliation later, however, as you will discover.

> *"Come along ladies.*
> *Out with the readies*
> *Come along gents,*
> *And give me your pence,"*

he sings as he goes. Few of his passengers recognize the old mobsman's ditty. The days of voices ringing out of the fog and the tram coming to a sudden stop amongst the thudding of hooves on Wandsworth Common or Putney Heath are forgotten realities, even amongst the older passengers. Now their memories are thrilling myths at best, something to embellish and to give authority to anecdote.

Lady Nelly leans forward in her seat and taps me on the shoulder. "There's something on, isn't there, Jack? You can't fool an old trouper like me. What's up? Not another war, is it?"

"A bit more than that, Nelly," I say. "But we have a chance to stop it."

"Well, be careful, love," she says, "there's dirty work at the crossroads ahead for you and your friends. I saw it in the tea-leaves before I came out. 'Fear the Betrayer.' Is that you, Jack?"

She disembarked at Harrods. She was going upstairs to the betting department, she said, to have a flutter on the three-thirty at Upton Park. I don't think she remembered it was early-closing day.

As she departed, a familiar figure swung aboard, his rags moving limply in the warm wet wind, his skin as grey as the sky. His angry, soulless eyes met mine as I turned my head to see him coming up the stairs. Slamming the heavy oak and brass board into its forward position, he took his seat at the very back of the tram, continuing to glare and to mutter to himself.

It was the roofless man; the wandering man. As I looked at him, he seemed to recognize me for the first time. He opened his huge, distorted mouth and exposed his broken teeth in a horrible grin. His scarred, leprous skin seemed to crack and flake. I could smell his breath from where I sat, several yards distant. "Enjoying the day, are we, captain?" he inquired.

"Looking after number one, are we? Feeling better, are we? Our old selves, is it? Keeping us comfy, are we? Got us to the moral highground, have we? Doing our duty as we see fit, are we? Singing the old songs of middle class self-congratulation, is it, skipper? Turning our lovely eyes from all the starving millions on whose broken backs we stand to get out of the shit? Bugger the bloody poor, eh, captain?" He leaned back to unwrap a wad of newspaper, then pushed his face into it, wrestling off a bite of nameless food. Chewing untidily, he grinned again and winked. "Just flies on your hooks, aren't we, captain?"

"Bait for the Original Insect," I said. "Someone has to be." And this time, to his disconcerted glee, I challenged him.

I knew who he was at last.

∿

"Hostiles," said Little Rupoldo, having sifted through several thousand languages to find this one and then seeking some pitch which did not make the humans cover their ears. "Outside, at the back."

Colonel Cody seemed glad of a chance at action. "How many?" he asked, hefting his Henry. "And how long have they been there?"

Dick Turpin had also brightened at the prospect of this fresh focus. Things had become a little hazy for him as one reality relentlessly phased with another. He needed familiar signposts.

Unfortunately, Little Rupoldo was baffled by the questions.

"Hostiles," he said, "boomwappers, maybe. Make us sick. Bad equations. Bach. Drive you crazy. Schubert. Worse. Rossini. Worse. Lloyd Webber. Bad, bad. Cheap music potent poison. Our revered Main Type is too much in love to hear or even to listen. She has lost her mathematical models."

With some idea of helping matters, I joined the little group.

"Don't they have any composers of their own, Mr Karaquazian?" asked Sir Sexton Begg, a little pettishly.

"These *are* their own," I told him. "We're the same people,

but for a few million scales, a slight change of metaphysical and
psychological environment. Composers, like personalities, don't
alter very much from plane to plane."

"Angelic music?" he asked, casting around for von Bek. The
German, still wearing his archaic broadsword, was with the Rose,
helping her talk to the controls. "We hear so much about it."

"Well," I said, "Everything takes a bit of getting used to.
We're all siblings under the skin, aren't we? Circumstances, Sir
Sexton, are inclined to alter cases, as they say."

These days I liked the Englishman no better than I liked von
Bek. There was something arrogant and superior in both men's
manner which attracted the women but left me cold. I never had
Colinda's fascination with authority.

Begg sensed my antagonism and seemed surprised by it, but
von Bek simply did not notice.

"We are the free travelers," said Little Rupoldo, his ultrasen-
sitivity seeking conciliation, "who explore the worlds of your
imagination."

I felt the press of the ships around us, of the danger which
pursued us and the danger which awaited us. What I had to do
made me tremble. I watched Cody, Begg and Turpin preparing
to follow Little Rupoldo back through the ship's impossible interior to investigate the invasion he was sure was there. I half
thought to go with them. It is always best to keep a well-defined
role in the Second Ether. I was readying myself, however, for
my own game, which was to be a difficult one. I was terrified. I
had heard the call of the jackal. My riskiest play.

Colinda was concerned. She found me distant, she said. Sometimes, it was clear, we maintained separate realities. I told her
that I had my duty to perform. "Beware of that duty, Jack," she
told me coldly, "it has betrayed us both before."

I took her point. But my strategies, I said, was for both of us.

"I mean to be your lover, Jack," she insisted, "not your
shadow."

❧

The ships, their sinuous metal constantly shimmying and folding, had begun their long swim down the scales to where
Spammer waited.

"For our form, Jack," said the Rose. "We are going to play a
combination of the Turpin and Cody versions. Labor against Capital. War Trams. Outlaw heroes against legal villains. Usual scores.
I can see you think it's too simple but if we're to get the very best
from all our players, we need the simplest stage. At the same time
it has to *provide* complexity. To try anything trickier at this level
would be a strategic mistake, I think. We have to consider all our
players. There are very different degrees of experience."

I saw nothing wrong with the combination. It made perfect
sense. It was a strength to have the likes of Turpin and Begg
with us. Their simpler, more straightforward view of things allowed them to take action which others, swamped by too much
information, might refuse. Even von Bek accepted the Rose's
suggestion without question. "To survive in the Second Ether,"
he said with dry good humor, "it is necessary that you go barking mad immediately. Throw away all logic. All rationality. You
have only romance and your own imagination to call upon. This
is my familiar state. It's the same in the desert."

In the circumstances, he confirmed, what I suggested was
clearly the most efficient strategy. There were only three jugadors capable of entirely abstract long-term play and the rest relied at least in part on visual formulae. I explained to Colinda
how the object was identical to the games we had played together
on the Mississippi, using the subtlest and at the same time
simplest models to achieve radical transformations. In the Game
of Time a misplaced metaphor could have the most unnerving
results. But our position demanded we take risks. Mine were to
be the greatest I had ever dared.

Our agreement given, the Rose returned to her whispering levers. *"At last, Spammer, at last. At last. At last. Oh, Spammer, at last! Aaaah, Spammer."*

∽

At last, after centuries of negotiating the scale fields, I brought us to the Grey Fees, that calm pseudo-center of the multiverse, where *The Spammer Gain*, united with her triumphant fishlings, swam at ecstatic anchor. Her great epic neared resolution. The Grey Fees glowed with her reflective well-being and we knew we had come to a place where death was rare and the rate of entropy precious slow. We bowed before *Spammer's* heart-breaking presence and we wept, all of us.

Pearl put her massive arm upon my shoulders and purred like a cat. "You are our noblest pilot, Rose."

As I turned The *Now The Clouds Have Meaning* towards the vast vessel I found myself unable to gauge *Spammer's* scale. She was a being of immeasurable size. She seemed to fill every horizon. Her movements were tidal. Histories came and went within her unsleeping hull, civilizations rose and fell within her dreaming skull. Somewhere out of sight was a head, reputedly of astounding beauty; somewhere in the other direction was a vast fluke, for she was most commonly perceived as a monstrous sea-creature, *Leviathan*. Her eyes, they said, were the size of galaxies and she trailed long tendrils of baleen from her mouth which stretched back to the earliest moments of the multiverse.[39]

---

[39]The fishlings had led her to the Grey Fees. Kaprikorn Schultz, Respected Banker to the Home Boy Tong, had lured the fishlings away from their parent by using a false attractor. All but one of the fishling chiefs had led their schools into captivity before realizing the trap. While in captivity, the fishlings learned how Kaprikorn Schultz planned to seize control of the multiverse. Through clever and patient scheming, the fishlings had eventually broken free from Schultz and begun their long, epic journey to the Grey Fees. Some of this is recorded in the screen sequence *Spark of the Grey Fees*, a minor episode in the great epic usually known as *The Quest for the Fishlings*, in which heroes of Chaos and the Singularity were engaged for countless ages. As Ipswich writes *"The Spammer Gain had become more than herself, which was as much as the multiverse, and was drawing all sentience inwards towards the Grey Fees."*
—*The Washington Psychedelics*, Volume IX, Carroll Institute, Vienna, 19—.

"The fishlings had led her here," says Pearl Peru, "They could have let themselves be found, but they had no time to persuade her. So they tricked her. They tricked their doting mother and were re-united. So great was their joy, that some of them expired. Clever, clever fishlings. Clever little fishlings. Kaprikorn Schultz and his false attractor! That dry fly desperado's schemes have failed him. His machinations have been turned by a benign fate to our ultimate advantage. There is no decision without endless consequences. Every action is a moral action because every action has meaning and effect. You have brought us all home, dear Rose." Her soft mouth mumbled and her lips foamed a profound purple. She turned away, self-conscious.

A voice came over the omniphone. It was Turpin, somewhere outside the hull as it toiled through the scales. With the other two, he was following Little Rupoldo, whose distinctive traces skipped glaring patterns against the nether regions of the *Now The Clouds Have Meaning* as he insisted there was a source to all the filth clogging every psychic duct aboard. "This machine's a masterpiece," said Turpin. "There's nothing like it in London. Colonel Cody wanted me to let you know that he thinks he can smell hostiles coming up rapidly over the ridge to our rear. Do you want us to shoot them or stay out of sight ?"

"Keep a bead on them, captain," says Pearl Peru, cocking her eye to us for confirmation, "and let us know the minute they show any sign of aggression."

Whoever was pursuing would have a surprise in store if they fired on us now. There was a new life in Turpin's tones. Having shaped his visions to his own satisfaction, he was able to act swiftly and decisively again. It was all he ever required of himself. Cody's judgment was doubtless also back. And Begg's nerve had never been in question. They had plenty of ammunition and all three were first class shots.

∽

I dropped deeper through the woolly ectoplasm of the Grey Fees. Other shapes than *Spammer*'s loomed out of the glowing fog. What at first seemed a tall cliff moved towards them, its outline insubstantial, its colors a horrible mixture of dark greys, yellow-greens and khaki. From deep within this unsettling darkness fluttered dim, mustard lights, like the lights of a London tram in the fog. Gradually the mass was defined. It was not one thing, but many.

Even then it took time to realize that this was, in fact, a vast, implacable fleet, filling every forward horizon. This fleet was soon close enough for us to hear individual crew-members. Their foul groaning voices spewed, echoing, from their omniphones. At close quarters, all their sounds were disgusting and abominable.

It was The Singularity, of course, the great Fleet of Law.

The unyielding, scale-ripping supercarbon hulls of the Singularity ships were led by Old Reg, the epitome and master of the Singularity. At his side was the unnaturally hungry Evil Freddy Force, lusting to destroy everything that was not himself. Here were *The No Negotiating, The Just Say No, The Fixed Attitude, The Straight Answer* and *The Only Way Forward*, gibbering their lethal insecurity while anti-intellectualism radiated like poison from their weighty armor.

Chaos had never been able to understand why the Singularity did not simply die from its own internal bile, devoured by its cancerous hatreds and superstitions, its miserably greedy fears; its cruel dreams, its massively exclusive certainties and self-destructive accountancy.[40]

While Chaos had no special fear of Law's devouring, unapproachable near-invincible shells, it had considerable respect for them. Although unlikely to attempt the maneuver, those su-

---

[40]The Singularity saw itself in a rather different and better light.

perwoven carbon hulls, angled just so, could rip through anything flown by the Entropy engineers and diffuse a victim's
remains across a billion different scales and immeasurable dimensions. These polished instruments of war were not flown by
the familiar halfling crews of the marches, scarcely distinguishable from their antagonists. Massed against Chaos now were the
clean-cut crack forces of the home fleet, the entire strength of
the Singularity. There had never been such a weight of power
gathered in one place before.

Over our own omniphone I heard Turpin marveling at the size
but not the glory of the ships he saw. "Imagine the height of
their sheds, the width of their turning plates! But their design
is rather unimaginative, I think. And their livery suggests the
drab war-trams you used to see on the coast. They wouldn't go
over very well with Londoners. Are these the enemy?"

"Some of the enemy, captain," replies Corporal Pork. "But
don't worry. They won't fire on us until formalities have been
exchanged. That's the advantage of playing The Singularity.
They love rules the way we love options."

Traditionally, they would choose their ground, as they had
always done, and individuals would disembark, calling greetings
and challenges to old enemies across the ectoplasmic void.[41] We
would then draw up an agreement and order of battle, determin-
ing which type of rules to play and negotiating any special addi-
tions or excisions. Our stewards would be chosen and our
marshals selected. Then the real negotiations would begin. The
Singularity, forced into one of its usual contradictory postures,
would insist on being described and treated as a single unit,
requiring further negotiating. Such agreements usually took
some while to reach resolution. While they were negotiating the
Chaos Engineers and the Singularity pilots often strolled back

---

[41]In encounters such as these, ships became a dangerous encumbrance, even
when so sensitively and closely united with their Main Type as *Now The Clouds
Have Meaning* with Captain Billy-Bob.

and forth across the void, exchanging reminiscences and enquiring after familiar enemies. Some of us found these rituals comforting. Others found them obscene.

～

Now the Singularity began to climb out of their ships and stand upon the peculiar original matter of the Grey Fees. Sometimes up to their knees in the yielding ropes of organic, greyish pinks and blue white, they stretched transmogrified limbs, buckled armor, tested mysterious weapons and looked over at us, trying to get our measure. Their war music drifted into our positions and Captain Billy-Bob clapped her huge paws to her crystalline head. "O," she wailed, "this taste for the primitive! It is so unfortunate." She hated Baroque in particular. For her, music began with Mozart. Anything before him was an academic and social study and anything after him, which did not learn his lessons, was a wanton obscenity. Her opinion of Schubert was murderous. She accepted Bach's genius, but believed him to be totally mad. Like a rat in a maze, she said. And as for John Cage . . .

I drew Captain Begg's attention to the dismounting assembly. "See. There is Lucifer himself."

Old Reg had never looked more beautiful. Gone were his horn-rims and his Chaplin moustache, his badly-dyed brushed back hair. Gone was his tight ritual business suit. Now, again, he was the Son of the Morning. Beams of platinum light blazed around his head and his silver wings sensuously whispered, while his proud pewter eyes were disdainful of everything in existence, including himself.

Prince Lucifer's perfect body moved upon the fog and dispersed it. His wonderful voice laughed and brought well-being to the multiverse. He sighed and we were immersed in inescapable melancholy. He rattled his golden sword upon his brass shield and drew down the visor of his silver helmet and we wanted only to die in his cause. Around him now gathered his great swaggering Dukes and Counts, his over-armored Barons and his Knights, already grown fat and arrogant on scraps of power scavenged from Lucifer's vast constituency.

I made out Baron Beezlebub and Duke Arioch, Lord Adabak and Count Belphegor, all mighty nobles of the Singularity, every one a renegade who had once served the cause of Chaos but was now sworn to die, if necessary, beneath Lucifer's banner, no matter where it led.

What power, save the power of God, could possibly resist such overwhelming authority?

Now, in their own turn, the Chaos Engineers began to climb from their ships, to flex their muscles in the Grey Fees and take some measure of their opponents. Their gorgeous carapaces flashed like diamonds, their obsidian quills opened and closed and rattled like bottles and their huge, forgiving eyes regarded the opposite camp with benign curiosity. As every Chaos Engineer joined the field, the power of Lucifer over us was lessened. I was astonished by what this implied. Perhaps it was true that souls had mass?

"Oh, Rose," says Pearl Peru, standing beside me, shoulder to shoulder, "you are the most beautiful of us all. Of us all, Rose."

When I looked back, I saw how rapidly our power accumulated. We neared the quasi-center of the multiverse, growing closer and closer to our archetypes. My father was clothed as a king for war and my uncle was an archangel, with weighing scales and a blazing sword. Jack Karaquazian had become a beast-headed demigod and Colinda Dovero was a golden maiden of infinite purity. Von Bek was magnificent. His black blade moaning and writhing in his hands, he was a silver angel, as beautiful as Lucifer.

Only Turpin, Cody and Begg steadfastly retained their common forms. It was to prove their strength.

"Come here, von Bek, sweetest of my slaves," said Lucifer in those succulent tones which made you want him to eat you alive. I saw von Bek take a step or two forward, then pause to gather himself.

"You have my soul, Lucifer," he said. "Not my heart."

"Come, you serve Law. You were born of Law to serve Law's cause. Sweet slave. Come."

"Born of Law to serve Chaos, born of Chaos to serve Law. It's a turning world, my lord." Von Bek's vibrant, musical voice had a matter-of-fact tone to it, as if he closed a conversation he found boring. At that point my admiration and desire for him inflamed a core in me which I knew I could use in the coming engagement. The chemistry was as strong as I had ever hoped for. There is nothing more potent on these occasions than human desire.

&

J ack Karaquazian prowls up and down our ranks, eyeing his greatest opponents. He glares at Lucifer as a hunger-crazed wolf glares at an elk, he glances away, turns and glares again knowing that a direct attack probably means death. Yet he is hungry for the kill. His body roars with a thousand flaring colors and frustrations.

For the moment, Lucifer ignores him, his attention still on the shimmering von Bek whose silver wings sigh, whose ruby eyes are moody, introverted now, as if he looks deep within himself, seeking some unfamiliar strength. The black blade murmurs and throbs.

"Beware, Prince Lucifer," he says quietly, looking up. "Remember, I bear the black sword and my blood is the blood of the cup."

"Oh, I am aware of that," says Lucifer. "That is what unites us. Show us your sword! And where is your cup, von Bek? They are here, I know. I know it is here. Powerful alchemy has its own scent."

Our light seeps upon the Grey Fees. The white, half-substantial stuff on which we stand sighs and whispers. The ropes are randomly woven together in crude, knotted carpets of original matter which gives before our mass but will not break. The angels lumber through it, but we are lighter and can skip or walk rapidly, never sinking. Only if we remain in one spot for any length of time does the ectoplasm begin to absorb us. Nobody has ever properly analyzed or explained the physical properties of the Grey Fees. Some say this is the actual birth-place of the multiverse, not the center we all seek, where our own originals have their home.

Now, as we move outwards from our ships, we are each of us alone. At that moment, we can only be alone. All trust, even of oneself, has vanished in the presence of Lucifer. And I was again Af, the daughter of Af, the daughter of the flowers of Af, and I was the betrayer of Af. Lucifer looked into my soul and smiled. "You are Af, the betrayer of Af," he said, and all that I had in me was desolate and worthless. All I had in me was cold oblivion.

"But you," I said, "are death itself." And I refused his influence.

I made the sign of the balance. I assembled my strength. I called upon the power of all my allies. I brought the Archangel Michael to my right hand and to my left, King Arthur. I united the scales, the sword and the crown. So we play the old cards. My game was prepared. "I am of the Just and I play the Game of Time. I am of the *mukhamirim,* who are trained to sit at cards with Lucifer and all his angels, and are encouraged to win . . ."

"But I am always the winner," slyly says the Son of the Morning. "I must always win. I win. I need not sit at cards. I can call on enough power to put the wheel to the sword. I command. I do not negotiate. I choose to play the radium tables with the Rose and with Jack and with Sam and Colinda. Come, come, where's Jack? Let's have a game, Jack. I can show you a city full of radium tables, all of them working like new. Grand Turks of the most stimulating complexity. Smile, Jack. Please me, Jack."

Then, whimsically it seemed, Lucifer turned his attention to the rest of us: "Remember, I would do anything to maintain the rule of Law. I am ruthless in her protection. I am bound to this, whatever the politics of Heaven. You believe I rebelled from arrogance? No, tasty immortals—I rebelled because I saw what unnecessary misery was caused by unchecked diversity."

Lucifer is as mad as the rest of us. He gives his attention back to his subject. "God is senile. Do you think I came to this knowledge easily? Do you not think I resisted it for millennia? You know that I am right, Jack. We are of the same blood, you and I. That blood determines everything you must do."

"Blood," growls Jack, barely able to form human speech, "is a lie."

I had never seen Jack Karaquazian shake so much as he stood there, bolt upright, surrounded by his allies, and weeping. His face had grown long, like a dog's, and his ears were pointed. Foam gathered on his sharp white teeth. Colinda Dovero tried to embrace him at first and then even she fell back. "What is it, Jack?"

But his only reply was a knowing snarl.

∽

From behind us suddenly comes the sound of shots. We turn. Even Lucifer's attention is drawn to the three small figures who lie upon the hull of The *Now The Clouds Have Meaning* firing at a tall leathery, bird-like creature of peacock colors and an expressive, if unstable, face. It screams at them and attacks again and again, voicing a string of unwholesome human epithets and unseemly equations. A demented cockatoo.

"Kaprikorn Schultz!" gasps Captain Billy-Bob, lumbering back into her hull. "Everything is explained! That's what infected our veins. Quickly, corporal. To the transfusion coils! Little Rupoldo! To your kakatron."

This unplanned move is disconcerting. Against all tradition,

the Game begins. Everyone is scrambling for weapons and positions. Was this unexpected move how our homes came to be
destroyed? There is much at stake. We must be cunning. But
do we have the strength?

"Here they come, Rose!" cries Turpin over the omniphone.
"Here's Colonel Cody's hostiles!"

And through the boiling mist of the Grey Fees emerges another
great fleet. It glints like fractured glass. It has been hiding there
all the time. Its ramshackle ships are barbaric, multicolored,
boasting all the sternly honed metals and spikes of the Singularity and combining this with the uncertain lines of Chaos. They
are untrustworthy ships, modified and altered until they have
become utterly neurotic. There is no knowing their intentions.
They are led by the master-renegade, the ex-Lord of Law who
calls himself Captain Horatio Quelch.

Quelch lounges on the outside of his own ship, waving casually from above the prow at the brass flash-peak rail, daring any
one of us to attack. He struts up and down on the metalwork
balcony. He throws his stump of cigar into the void and winks
at me.

"*Non nobis sed omnibus,* Rose," he says. He is too clever to
voice his mockery, but it is there. It is another challenge, my
own family's motto. "Not for ourselves, but for all. It is our duty
and our destiny to proliferate as best we can."

"We are too strong for you today, Horace." I wonder whether
he will attempt an alliance with us or with his old masters. This
must be his strategy. He cannot hope to defeat us all.

"Is that so, Rose?" He takes a deep, appreciative breath of
the ether.

The omniphone broadcasts a sudden, angry squawk. Frowning
to achieve focus, Quelch turns lazy, multi-faceted eyes towards
the source.

It is Kaprikorn Schultz, his feathers fanning in furious panic
as he dodges the heavy shells of the three small, clear-eyed figures who stand shoulder to shoulder firing steadily.

Quelch nurses some secret. He is scarcely put out by this unexpected turn.

In the ranks of Law, Evil Freddy Force barks a particular challenge to his old colleague. "You are mine to disassemble, Captain Quelch. You are mine to crop. For I am your consumer."

But Quelch roars his easy contempt. He makes a particular sexual gesture which sets his enemy to growling and spitting and turning several disgusting colors.

"A opont Force, indeed, eh, Rose?" Quelch winks at me again. He knows how to draw on shared experience to his advantage, but I resist him easily. There is far more attractive danger than Quelch in this game.

Lucifer disciplines his untranquil warlord. "Rein in, sir. Rein in! Or would you see the reality slabs of your own *mangout*?"

Sulking, Freddy Force tucks little pieces of his strange, guttering beard into his mouth, but controls his trembling bloodlust.

And then, from over my shoulder, a sudden rattling bulk passes by and dives for Quelch's bridge. It is Kaprikorn Schultz, dislodged from our hull at last and racing towards his old ally, squawking and raging and scattering obscene equations and blazing feathers through the dimensions.

"Zed farping squared, old fruit!"

His claws take a grip on the brass rail and sparks belch the length of the ship, demonstrating the resources Schultz brings with him. This is an ally to be reckoned with. But how long will such a partnership hold?

Then another shot sounds and a big shell bursts against the bridge, sending Quelch starting back, astonished.

"Hold! Hold on there!" he complains, as if someone is cheating.

It's our marksmen, of course. I am beginning to realize that Turpin & Co are amongst our strongest players. They bring a special perspective which Quelch clearly has not planned for.

Quelch is now a little disturbed as he cranes his beastly neck, his complex eyes searching for other shapes and shadows in the swirling ectoplasm, as if he cannot believe he is challenged by something as simple as three Edwardian gentlemen armed with elephant guns.[42] He is at last afraid. He understands the potential of their affect, the power of their courage.

"Well, Rose," he says, as Schultz flutters and cackles behind the scant protection of the rail, "I have underestimated you again, it seems."

"You always will," I say. "I am determined, however, that you will not make a Biloxi of my home. We are not surrogates, but living individuals."

Now all around us the fighting has begun to develop into separate strategies, only barely controlled by the main players. The battle I had hoped to contain is already broadening. At this moment, I doubt the wisdom of my moves, but it is too late for anything else. I am forced to concentrate on our own immediate danger.

"Biloxi, Rose," says Quelch sweetly. "How could old Quelch create that terrible paradox? It is in no one's interest."

"Dissension is in your interest, Horace," I tell him firmly. "You divide to rule, I think."

"There is so much to rule, Rose. It is too complex a task for one individual. I only seek to influence my own small patch. Independence, Rose, is all I pray for. A little freedom so an old man can affect his own destiny, retire with dignity and security . . ."

I laughed. "So this is your crusade, is it, captain?"

"It's in my blood, Rose. I am of Norman stock, you know."

And then he was back behind his rail again, disagreeably astonished as Sexton Begg's Purdy blasted another charge of angel shot in his direction. "Enough!" roars Quelch. "We have not even agreed the rules!"

---

[42]See also *Buffalo Bill and The Wandering Jew, BUFFALO BILL LIBRARY* 280 (New series), *The Return of Zenith the Albino; or, Marked by the Leopard Men, UNION JACK LIBRARY* 928, *Dick Turpin and the Pirates' Cave, BLACK BESS LIBRARY* 6.

"Your decision changed our tradition, captain," I tell him. "It was your choice to abandon the rules."

Two more guns sound. Hastily Captain Quelch swings his agitated form through the studded door and slams it behind him. I see his face pressed against the vision plate, peering out at us, his words rumbling over his omniphone. I bring my own gun to my shoulder and send a couple of shots into the unsteady hulls which hover at his back, awaiting his orders. That disorderly rabble of humes and swiplings must have something more with which to challenge both Chaos and Law.

"Your action," I add, "has redefined the rules!"

Quelch's face disappears. Kaprikorn Schultz shrieks and bangs on the heavy door until Quelch admits him.

"Farping anchor-wanker, parentheses eesquared equals kroffing ss-ss ss ch ch charf-charf-cha-cha-cha-Y or Pi. You have the ca-ca-Cup? The farping cup?" demands Schultz. Their omniphone allows us to hear everything. "Shar! Shar! Shar! Sha-Surely you did not forget!"

"My dear fellow! How could I forget the Grail?" Quelch chuckles reassuringly.

My shooting has had its desired effect. Entering the demateria lizing hulls, the shot causes enormous disruption. Ships must temporarily be abandoned. Out of their vessels' disturbed and corrupted innards tumble Quelch's corsairs. Their captains attempt to draw the crews into some sort of order. They are as degenerate as any creatures I have ever seen, their forms dissolving and reshaping uncontrollably. They have the characteristic tentacles of beings who make their way by ship through Chaos space, but otherwise there is little similarity betweeen them. I am reminded, as always, of why I prefer to walk the roads between the worlds, rather than take the ships.

The corsairs focus on me. Their multi-faceted eyes range and glitter. They chitter. Eagerly some of them pass themselves through a series of options, attempting to recreate themselves, to find any image they can assume which will give them power over me. Occasionally they are successful and create feelings of love or duty or guilt, but I have been trained in a hard school. I am the revenger of Af. I am the killer of Paul Minct. I outplayed him. This psychic skirmish in comparison is a child's game. Another shot or two, into the simulated shapes of my nearest and dearest, living and dead, and the corsairs decease.

Now Lucifer strides up and down his battle-lines, hearing those of his nobles who bring him news of their encounters. Already the fight is spilling out of the Grey Fees through the entire multiverse. It must be a measure of his regard for us that Lucifer himself is not yet engaged in one of the many encounters.

Everywhere, the massive, winged creatures, only barely resembling their human counterparts, lock weapons.

Like us, Lucifer did not expect Quelch to bring so much power with him. As understanding comes, his entire presence glares with angry fire.

"What?" he says. "Quelch has the Grail?"

"Apparently," says von Bek, snapping his barrels into position, then fingering the ruby hilt of his black blade. "We thought we were following it until we found *Spammer*."

It is clear from Lucifer's expression that he, too, believes himself to have followed the Grail.

It appears, however, that the Grail has followed us.

Von Bek confers with the others. "I know the Grail is here. But I had not believed it in Quelch's hands . . ." He seems ashamed, as if he fails us.

Our confusion gives advantage to the corsairs. Directed by Connie McWhine, his horrible bo'sun, they spread across all our territories, doing whatever damage they can. Our swiftly-altered strategies easily defeat them, but we are weakening. Quelch reappears on his bridge, wearing a complete brass scale-suit. This awkward old-fashioned equipment has been abandoned even by the Singularity, but he affects it like a dandy. He holds the Fellini Chalice in his shuddering paw.

A groan goes up from our ranks. The Grail is always the defining factor, even in simpler games than this.

All around us the fight grows fiercer. Everywhere angels fall, their mass collapsing the surrounding ectoplasm which dissipates and sends their corporal forms tumbling helplessly through the multiversal scales, to enter all the stories of the worlds.

Von Bek and the Archangel Michael are under severe attack. They beat their swarming attackers back with gun-butt and sword. They are almost buried by the cold armor of the Singularity. The diamonds in his diadem flashing like pistol shots, King Arthur stands alone, voicing joyful defiance as he discharges his Purdy. Save for certain moments when teasing a salmon I have never seen my father so thoroughly in his element.

∽

Every great Knight of Chaos has now taken the field of the Grey Fees. Every veteran of the Singularity is here. Their battle-songs burst upon the ether. Their war-music blares.

Their ranks increase, ranging in tiers as they prepare for the final fight.

And then, with a noise that could shatter the multiverse, they clash. Their weapons rise and fall. They exchange complex ideas. They form relationships. Their strategies become whimsical and unbelievably cunning. Their priorities alter. They are near-immortals, dancing with death, risking all. They stake eternity on a choice of simile.

We fight in the cause of the Great Mood, whom many of us believe to be God. Our enemies fight in the cause of the Original Insect, whom many of them believe to be God. But it is not important to us whether Gods or angels or mere mortals are at odds here. We fight to establish a dominant philosophy, to define our realities, to preserve and expand our freedom, to save our homes, our memories and our souls from extinction.

Only Lucifer has the supreme arrogance, however, to believe
he can define future reality forever.

∽

The game goes rapidly. Quelch's claimed mastery of the Grail
has produced some immediate counter-moves. Both sides
are shocked by the situation. They are doubtless asking how
one so corrupt could possess such virtue? For it has always
been accepted that only a creature of great virtue can claim the
Grail's power. Therefore our assumptions could be wrong. This
is quite enough to make us question all our judgments, and thus
hamper our games. What the Grail determines as virtue, it
seems, is not what we determine virtue to be. Our values are
challenged.

Our negotiators urgently debate our dilemma.

Quelch has achieved a great deal with his Grail strategy. He
might even think himself the *magister ludos*. Lucifer believes he
must treat with the renegade if he is to win the round. We refuse
to bargain but understand ourselves to be close to defeat. Even
as the struggle continues, with many branch engagements taking
on their own epic qualities, Evil Freddy Force slips secretly between the camps, bearing Lucifer's terms and Quelch's.

We arrive at a set of new rules.

We are playing, it now emerges, for *The Spammer Gain*.

The rules favor our opponents, of course. Once the combined
forces have defeated us, they believe they will be able to take
control of *Spammer* herself.

Naturally, this knowledge encourages our resistance.

Although Captain Wopwop was once her commander, the ship
and the crew are now completely indistinguishable. Chaos Engineers and their allies hold only love for *The Spammer Gain*.
Even if we are all wiped, we shall defend her long enough for
her to escape. Yet she shows no signs of fear. Indeed, she shows
no signs of sentience at all. I begin to wonder if *Spammer* is

not dead. Has Quelch already killed her? Or has she been dead
for eons?

If this is so, we face the inevitable end of all time and space.

∽

Even as he negotiated, Captain Quelch was forced to watch
some of his finest followers picked off by Begg, Turpin and
Cody. Lying full-length behind the headless armor of Connie
McWhine, whom they brought down with a concerted blast, the
three comrades fired with extraordinary precision and effect
steadily into the attacking hostiles.

Since recognizing the leader of the comancheros, Cody had
been in no doubt about who or what he was fighting. His merci-
less leadership defined his group's strategy. It was mere hypocrisy, he had always maintained, to feel sentimentality or behave
honorably towards an enemy whose entire people you intend to
destroy. Though reluctant to accept his rather Teutonic logic,
the other two also recognized that their survival depended upon
it. They allowed no quarter.

Elsewhere, however, our losses were growing. Many of the
famous Chaos Engineers were already down. Others were under
considerable duress. Only Captain Billy-Bob Begg seemed exul-
tant. She had cleared all the foul equations from her system.
She shimmied like a teenager. The *Now The Clouds Have Meaning* was twice as responsive. She was ready for fresh battle.

Meanwhile Jack Karaquazian ran furiously in every direction.
He was foaming, rabid, lethal. This was not at all his usual
game. Jack was the cool master of the unmoving moment. I
could not believe he had so thoroughly lost control. He also
seemed to have lost his style. He had been too long away from
the tables, perhaps. Lucifer had once feared him, but now he
was contemptuous, shouting to Jack as if to a cur. He believed,
as many of us did, that the great Jack Karaquazian had crumbled

at last. He was lost to the power of the Beast. At that moment,
I know, Lucifer saw every triumph within his grasp.

Colinda, having failed to call in Jack, was making considerable
use of her own Ballard .70. It was the best gun they had ever
made. As huge dark blue angels attacked her from all sides, her
eye was steady and her aim true. Soon the carrion was piled
shoulder high, yet still she continued to fire. As the last of them
wheeled and fled up into shrouding ectoplasm, she returned her
attention to Jack, covering him as he raced through the angelic
ranks, snapping and tearing and pissing.

Once, when I came close to her, I saw that she was weeping.

We were falling back now. Even Jack. The guns continued
to sound, the swords rose and fell, but it was clear we were
outnumbered. And, since we had seen the Grail in Quelch's
power, we were demoralized. I was furious with Jack. He had
given in to infantile shape-changing. The simplest and least useful strategies. It seemed to me he had used none of his real
resources in our cause. He was playing some private game. He
had no interest in us. But when I glared a question at him, he
ignored me.

I believe now that my analysis was wrong. Jack had a stronger
love in him than he admitted. I discovered that a few moments
later when suddenly a group of renegades, all bloody mouths
and jagged teeth, broke over Colinda's barricade and swarmed
down on her as she tried to reload. Jack, who had shown no
apparent interest in her, suddenly pricked up his ears. Then he
had turned and was running for the barricade. Out of his mouth
came an atrocious noise. Then he was amongst the attackers.

Within moments all that was left of their throats was a ruin
of glittering red and Jack glared above their corpses. His long
jaws dripping, he panted with pleasure.

Colinda could not bring herself to thank her lover. I could
see that, like me, she was praying this was a strategy and not
a condition.

◿

We were now surrounded. Bearing down on us were all the combined remnants of the Singularity and of Quelch's renegades. Lucifer and Quelch stood side by side, comrades again. Turpin & Co were no longer under attack and were leaning back, cleaning their guns and keeping an eye on the our rounding ether.

So unexpected was this imminent defeat, that I found it almost impossible to rally the necessary confidence. We had never doubted that who controlled the Grail controlled the Game, but I had not really believed that Quelch understood the power he now possessed.

Only with difficulty was Jack called back to stand with us. Colinda, clearly disliking what had happened to him, held hard to his arm. I was reminded, at that moment, of one of the paintings in von Bek's monastery and I experienced a moment of irrational hope.

Now von Bek stood beside me, looking no more reassuring a sight than Jack. There was something feral about him. His great black sword was encrusted from tip to hilt with filthy ichor and the blade growled and smoked disturbingly. His crimson eyes blazing from the ivory of his delicate alien face, von Bek smiled down on me and I was glad he was not my enemy. What had those two had to become in order to prepare themselves for this particular encounter? I was suddenly in awe of them.

"Are we finished?" I asked von Bek.

I watched him take control of his wildness as if it were a half-trained horse.

"We must play this through," he said softly, "and then we'll know."

It offered a kind of comfort. He had demonstrated his mastery of himself and of his game. I began to understand there were delicate strategies running under this which I had only just detected, so shocked had I been at Quelch's revelation. But perhaps they had anticipated it? Their discipline and knowledge was phenomenal. They were my peers in every sense but this was their game, not mine. I came to realize how my own games had been subsidiary to theirs, unconsciously obeying their strategies. It was so long since I had played with such expert *mukhamirim.*

Deeply tired from their own engagements, Pearl Peru and Captain Billy-Bob Begg joined us. Clearly disheartened by the weight of our opposition, they were trying to keep in good spirits. At least two-thirds of our number was gone—and we had defeated far more of the enemy—but the aggressor was still too strong for us. If Quelch had not seized the Grail and Lucifer, understanding the power it represented, had not joined forces with him, perhaps we could have succeeded. But the moment the Prince of the Morning reinstated his old lieutenant, we felt our cause to be thoroughly lost.

Little Rupoldo was dead, torn to pieces and gobbled up by Evil Freddy Force, using a Collins gun which had been banned for eternity. Corporal Pork was gone, impaled on a hundred hunting brochettes. Famous Chaos Engineers, whose names were known in all the scales of the multiverse, had been extinguished, absorbed or otherwise eaten by their conquerors. You could almost hear our enemies feasting on souls.

And still *The Spammer Gain* swam at anchor in the Grey Fees, sublimely careless of the war which raged around her. For a moment I wondered if she were not an illusion, some false attractor designed to lure us here to be destroyed. I could not understand why, in our need and her own terrible danger, she remained so quiescent. Again I wondered if they had not already killed her. Or had *Spammer* come here to die?

Then up swims Lucifer's vast flagship, *The Only Way Forward,* trumpeting and stinking of disinfectant. On her severe bridge, needing no glamorous disguise, stands Old Reg. He glows and swells with the perceived authority of the Original Insect. His hornrims glare lethal disapproval, his thin mouth sets primly in lines which speak of vicious retribution, ready to deliver the final accounts. And beside him, louche and lazy with his easy power, lounges Horatio Quelch, all filthy battle-armor and oozing tubes, the Fellini Chalice in his six-tentacled hand and half an arsenal at his belt, while on his other flank stands Evil Freddy Force, coaxing the last of the blood out of a young heart he has snatched and squeezed for his refreshment. At the rear, his foliage badly spoiled, crouches a chittering Kaprikorn Schultz. "Migit if gob equals nigit. Zed farping, zed farping, zed, zed, zed . . ." He was irretrievably scrambled.

"And this is Law's finest?" I say sarcastically, staring directly into Old Reg's reflective eyes. "This unwholesome rabble is the Triumph of Order?"

"Our alliance is a necessary compromise," says Old Reg Lucifer sharply. "We are sworn to establish the rule of Law upon the multiverse. It is our destiny to abolish the world's pain."

I heard my father laughing a little weakly behind me. He had lost most of his glory and was looking worn, breathing hard and having trouble standing straight. His brother was in similar condition and my heart went out to those brave old men. "Do you still seek reconciliation with a god you deny is any longer sane?" My father was mockingly skeptical. "What will you do, Prince Lucifer? Make human suffering illegal?"

With a lordly and rather theatrical gesture Lucifer frowned and dismissed my father's Yorkshire common sense. He had schemed and battled for millennia for this chance to define existence in his own image. He resented such mocking skepticism. I recalled part of the old von Bek legend, which had it that Lucifer, seeking compromise with God, had undertaken to cure the world's pain. I suspect that Old Reg sincerely believed he would achieve that end. He had failed, however, to make one important logical step. Old Reg accepted that the Original Insect was God. If that were so, Old Reg could not save our kind. He could only engineer our kind's destruction. For the Insect, true to its nature, was incapable of intending humanity anything but harm. It would be content only with our absolute obliteration. Old Reg was not the first to blind himself to this truth.

Far from disheartening me, this intelligence helped me to understand better the various individual agendas of the players and the complications of our game. I felt fresh hope. I realized there were still moves to be made. Even a game to win.

Their massive, brutal ships, gorging on their own self-importance, exuding a miserably aggressive ambition, swam closer and closer to *The Spammer Gain*. Here was all the energy and future they had lost. All they had given up. They began to look upon her with lecherous hunger.

Another important move once again altered the game's harmonics.

"Will you capitulate now?" asked Evil Freddy Force of us. He leaned arrogantly on the great brass rat rail, nibbling at his raw snack. "Or must we gobble up every one of you?"

He received his answer at the moment of his death. "Monster!" cried a masculine voice behind me. There was a bellowing report, a flash of heat on my shoulder and then Evil Freddy Force's headless corpse fell back upon the deck, the gnawed heart falling from his hand.

Dick Turpin stepped up to get a better look at his kill. He plucked the big shells from his Purdy's breach and inserted fresh ones from a pouch at his belt. There was an expression of disgusted outrage on his handsome, battered face. "Ugh! Rose? Are all these fellows cannibals?"

Freddy Force's ghastly blood continued to pulse from his neck but Captain Quelch did not seem alarmed in any way. Indeed, he smiled and shrugged.

I wondered at his smugness. Had he gone mad? And then I realized the truth. He had the Grail. I had forgotten one of its most famous properties. In the presence of the Grail, death could not persist.

Even now Horatio Quelch smirked and lifted the Fellini Chalice above his head, directing it towards Freddy Force's shuddering corpse. He grinned. He waited. He scowled. He brought the chalice lower.

His eyes becoming questioning and angry, Old Reg turned. "Has entropy slowed to nothing already ? Why is it taking so long, Quelch?"

Urgently Quelch gripped the cup, his tentacled hands writhing in agitation. He pressed the vessel hard against Freddy Force's cooling body. "Perhaps some interference . . ." His voice pulsed with angry bafflement.

"Nothing can interfere with the power of the Grail," declared Old Reg. "If they could, it would not be the Grail. After the Balance, which some say it serves, it is the single greatest power in the multiverse. Nothing can die in the presence of the Grail. Even Freddy Force." He reached to examine the cup.

It was at that moment that Prince Ulrich von Bek, his horrible sword in his right hand, his elephant gun in his left, stepped out of our ranks and fastidiously placed his feet on Freddy Force's abandoned cloak. The albino had an amused, abstracted, sated look, like a creature which had just achieved a satisfactory mating. His runesword still murmured in its scabbard, as if anxious to do further battle, and his elephant gun was black with its own smoke. Yet his stance was by no means warlike and his voice had a thick, lazy quality.

"Perfectly true, Lord Lucifer, as my family has reason to know!"

I was surprised by his apparent lack of concern. His manner languid and easy, yet clearly calculated, Ulrich von Bek strode across the separating ectoplasm and swung himself up into the top deck of *The Only Way Forward,* standing at last on the bridge in Lucifer's presence. Coarse light played across his features. His black sword grumbled. So taken aback was Old Reg by the Grail's failure to return Evil Freddy Force to life that he had made no effort to stop Count von Bek. Indeed, as his impatience with his ally increased, he grew almost conciliatory to his enemy. "Thus, after all, the Grail has no power in your foul hands, Quelch. Give it to von Bek."

Quelch glared defiantly.

Von Bek did not wait. With a familiar supernatural swiftness, he snatched the cup from the renegade, held it as if to admire its beauty, then tossed it carelessly over the side.

Quelch growled with frustration and fury as he watched the cup fall away down the scales. None could guess where its descent would end.

"You fool, von Bek. What good has that done any of us! Such power should never be thrown away."

"I have every regard for the Fellini Chalice," said the albino. "It is one of the greatest of European treasures. We must hope it finds its home again."

"And where would the Grail's home be, sir?"

"That, Lord Quelch, was not the Grail."

"Oh, you say so! You fought so hard for a fake? You lost so many! I do not believe you."

"We fight for the Grail, but nonetheless that was not the Grail," insisted von Bek. He drew himself up, smiling. His wild, white hair flowed around his head. His crimson eyes were sardonic. "That was merely the false attractor used to persuade you to adopt your present configuration. You were very obliging. I had to use none of my secondary strategies. Your own worked best in my interest."

"Our own?" blares Quelch. "Our what?"

Von Bek continued. "Your greed for the Grail may have clouded your judgment. You have been caught by your own strategies, gentlemen. You have been in our control almost since the game began. Your arrogant confidence betrayed you. You sought the Grail within the Grail. Your people crossed and recrossed the moonbeam roads to find it. Your energies have been devoted to it. And I allowed you to believe the Fellini Chalice to be that which I was sworn to find and which by tradition I was supposed to deliver up to Lucifer. But I did not trust Lucifer, and was wise in my suspicion.

"I sowed the seeds for these end games even before I discovered the Academy of the Atlas. Every decision that you have made has led you to this end. You have scarcely controlled our destinies, sir. Indeed, it seems we have taken control of yours! You will recall how this vast game began, when Kaprikorn Schultz conceived the plan of using a false attractor to lure the fishlings from their mam, so long ago. We developed an almost identical strategem. And you did not recognize it! Not for a moment was this game ever truly under your control!" And Ulrich threw back his milk-white head, his long hair flaring in the supernatural winds, and he laughed in their faces.

I do not think he was prepared for Lucifer's fury. Old Reg lost all command of his game. With a shrill order the Prince of Darkness set Quelch, like a crazed dog, upon the albino.

Von Bek staggered as Quelch, a mass of teeth and tentacles, flung himself at the albino, grasping blindly for the sheathed sword which muttered and whined at his enemy's hip. Ulrich hardly seemed to realize what was happening. He made no effort to fight back, but simply tried to get free of the furious Quelch. Only when Quelch had put both sinuous hands around the hilt and hauled it from the scabbard, did Prince Ulrich react.

As the albino tried to force the howling black iron back into its sheath crimson runes with a fiery life of their own wriggled up and down the blade.

I became confused by the next events but I will swear that, as if threatened by Quelch's attempts to seize it, the black sword sprang from the renegade's hands. He yowled and lunged after it. It hesitated overhead, just out of his reach, as if deciding whether to strike.

Then it disappeared.

Quelch began to whine and foam.

"The sword!" cried Lucifer, as if part of himself had been wrenched away.

All charm deserted him. His grey, boney fingers clutched at the air. "The sword!"

The game was open again.

∾

Physically, Captain Quelch was no match for Ulrich von Bek. Robbed of his prize, the renegade nonetheless turned his fury on the albino. As they wrestled across the floor of the platform Singularity soldiers poured from the interior. Not caring to face so many, the prince disengaged himself from the increasingly humanoid shape of Quelch, looked around somewhat anxiously for his sword, failed to find it, then leapt to the rail. The albino hesitated like a diver on a board, then jumped to be swallowed by the pink and grey original matter wriggling like Medusa's hair. Clearly, he was lost to us.

But even as we reacted, calculating fresh and somewhat desperate moves, up von Bek came, not a yard from Turpin and his friends. This was astonishing and cheering enough. What was surprising was that he was so full of joy. He was laughing like a schoolboy. I have never witnessed anything like that transformation.

I watched Ulrich von Bek pause, shake himself and stare defiantly back at Prince Lucifer, who had begun to shift his form again, from the confident Old Reg to the impressive Son of the Morning. He was realizing, no doubt, the full extent of his entrapment. As his power diminished, his glamour increased. He stamped golden hooves upon the foaming ectoplasm and his nostrils blubbered with fury. Soon only the beast glared from those handsome sockets.

"But if that's not the Grail," says Sir Sexton Begg, who had the hang of the situation a little better than his colleagues and was used to such logic, "what is? We are all agreed. Our instincts say it is here!"

"And here it is!" declared von Bek laughing. "What else could the Grail be? The sum of all our virtue! There!" And he threw his hand towards the overwhelming backdrop of *The Spammer Gain.* "She's too large for us to see her beauty or understand her extraordinary powers, the goodness of her character. I will admit she does not much resemble a cup at present. There's our Grail, my friends! She is an entire drifting universe!"

My uncle was skeptical. "This *Spammer* has not displayed any of the Grail's famous properties," he said. "Indeed, she's displayed no properties at all. She could be dead."

It was my own fear.

"Not dead yet," said von Bek. "Though it *is* possible for her to die. She has reached resolution. She sleeps. She must be awakened."

"How would you wake a sleeping universe?" asked my father in some amusement.

Prince Ulrich did not reply directly. Instead his hand fell to his belt. From it he took the strangely shaped horn I had first seen at the temple. Then he turned to offer his hand to Colinda.

It seemed she was prepared for him.

Everything was still. The primal matter no longer moved in slow, easy waves. The Grey Fees seemed to be waiting.

The survivors of all sides watched, unable to act for the moment. They recognized an attempted end game. Courtesy and tradition alone dictated this respect.

Together Prince Ulrich and Colinda began to wade through the roiling ectoplasm towards the mighty harmony that was *The Spammer Gain.* What cosmic action, I wondered, would it take to stir the sleeping soul of a sentient Grail? Could she be resting, after her long quest for her lost children? That quest had taken forever. Perhaps she must sleep forever.

Von Bek and Colinda continued to advance. They appeared to know exactly what would happen next.

Sluggishly, Old Reg growled a warning.

"You cannot go to her," he said. "It would be too powerful. The Balance would be threatened." He had vanished from his bridge but his voice could still be heard. "It would tilt too far. You would control too much. It would be the end of Law."

"What else did you hope for but complete control of the Balance ?" Von Bek shouted into the infinite. "Chaos learned long-since what victory of that kind means. We do not want your control or your sophistries. Your hypocrisy robs you of honor. Without honor, my lord Lucifer, even you cannot survive!"

It was as if he had invoked the being. Suddenly the air between von Bek and *The Spammer Gain* darkened. That darkness grew still darker. That darkness crawled with something profoundly obscene. Then that darkness formed a shape. And there was glorious Lucifer.

∽

The great, dark angel, his eyes stirring with all the evil in the multiverse, held something in his hands. He could scarcely control it. It yelled and shuddered, as if in lust. Ruby runes ran up and down its black metal and it growled and murmured to itself, as if in anger. I thought it lusted for the albino's soul.

"Step aside, sir, if you please," says von Bek in a matter-of-fact tone, as if such encounters with the Prince of Darkness were a daily irritation, "you have no more power over me." He waved his hand. "Step aside, sir. I have a task to perform." He began to raise the horn to his lips.

Lucifer's smile was sublime. "I have every power I need. I have the power to use your soul as I wish. To slay you and to resurrect you, whenever I so desire. To enjoy your agonies as a divertissement whenever I please. Until the end of everything. For I shall be the Lord of the Final Singularity. I shall give and take life as I please. See. I will demonstrate." And with all his might he threw back his arm and made to fling the blade towards the advancing albino. It seemed to me that Lucifer feared Prince Ulrich then.

With all the force Satan could muster, he threw the blade

straight at the albino. "There, von Bek! There's everything back
that you ever stole for me. Farewell, friend. I was a thousand
times more evil than thou!" And he stood, hands on hips, to
watch his errant servant die.

The black iron screamed through the ether. It reached its tar-
get. As if with deep pleasure it sighed as it imbedded itself in
Ulrich's heart.

Lucifer bellowed triumph.

The albino shouted once. He shivered, made to speak and
grasped at the metal. He whispered something, tried to raise his
voice, looked back at Colinda and then sank into her waiting
arms. As he did so, she and he screamed in unison with the
voice of the triumphant blade, a trinity of inconceivable effect.
Together, they writhed like the red runes running up and down
the dark sword's length. They merged with it. They blended
together and separated again. They filled the Grey Fees. They
disappeared. They grew tiny. They screamed again. And again.

Then, head bowed, Colinda stepped back. She moved with
effort as if she had spent all her strength.

She stretched a pale hand towards the albino.

Weakly, Prince Ulrich handed her the horn. He, too, seemed
barely able to move.

"No! No! No!" cried Lucifer. "You are mine to kill. The blade
is mine. The blade is me! I am IT! And I am more than IT!"

It seemed all Lucifer could do now was rage as Colinda raised
the horn to her lips and blew a steady, sweet note which grew
louder and louder until it threatened to drown all other sound.

Taking up the horn's note a magnificent harmonious chord
filled the multiverse.

Lucifer began to shriek, as if his own voice might drown the
all-embracing sound around him.

He made a movement to where the impaled albino lifted his
head to scream again. It was a shout of joy, blending with the
note of the horn. Gradually, as if blood drained from it into the
albino, the black blade began to shine. The scarlet runes stead-

ied and re-formed, turning to a cool, brilliant blue. And then the sword pulsed, silvery ice, glowing with light that was golden-white and voicing an extraordinary song.

And Ulrich continued to stand, supported by Colinda who continued to sound the horn and lend her strength to his, pinioned against the cosmic wind, while the sword shivered and whispered and poured the power into him. Soon both he and Colinda were embraced by a cloud of pale, vibrant light through which it was barely possible to see their outlines. Gradually the note of the horn faded. I made a movement to help her, but my Uncle Michael held me back and pointed to the looming bulk of *The Spammer Gain*, which filled the entire horizon. Faint, delicate colors stirred within her.

The horn had awakened her.

∽

It seemed I saw Colinda reach out and with one smooth movement drag the sword from von Bek's body. Next she held it up by the blade, raising it before her as he braced himself, drawing strength from her even as the sword's power filled him. Somehow the sword became his spreadeagled body, or at least its reflection. A strange energy was being absorbed.

It is his soul, I thought. He has recovered his soul.

I heard him shout again. A huge shout which combined with hers to fill the multiverse.

The blade formed a cross which in turn became a great measuring scale of silvery gold, its twin swaying cups moving as if in a breeze, never at rest.

I heard my uncle murmur that Roland's horn had been sounded. We were being granted a vision of the Cosmic Balance itself. Such visions came only at momentous times.

And now, as the Balance cast its glorious light across her measureless flanks, *The Spammer Gain* began to breath.

At last the Grail was truly granted to Prince Ulrich. It had always been his destiny to find it. I heard him cry out. I saw Colinda point.

∾

*S*pammer's indistinct lines began to glow brighter and brighter. Slowly she took on better-defined shapes. She was like a vast organic diamond, radiant with every color of the multiverse. She blazed with the authority of creation. For a moment, at the center, I saw the benign beautiful piscine features of Captain Wopwop and then they were gone.

Ulrich continued to stand, defying all the evil in the cosmos, while *The Spammer Gain* took her purest form. As the Grail she extended her harmony across universe after universe. And the albino laughed in Lucifer's baffled face. For now he knew he had conquered death. He had destroyed the devil's constituency.

From where he stood a few feet from me, Sir Sexton Begg murmured: "So it is, after all, possible to deceive the Prince of Tricksters!"

"And gain the whole multiverse," I said.

I understood I had been part of a game which had been planned perhaps for eons. All our strategies had combined for this result. Slowly, the surviving Chaos Engineers left their ships again. They came to stand and to marvel at the pearly Grail filling the whole horizon of the Grey Fees. Pearl Peru and Captain Billy-Bob Begg were among the few who had not been destroyed. They embraced delicately, grateful for this unexpected reversal of their destiny.

The Singularity could not sustain such defeat. As the ectoplasm parted to reveal the infinite void, the Lords of Law prepared themselves for an uncomfortable limbo. I watched Old Reg, Mrs. Reg, Captain Quelch and the poor, chittering Kaprikorn Schultz as they stood helplessly on the bridge of their ship. With the remains of their fleet they sank in ghastly silence through the engulfing knots of whiteness.

I was close to weeping as I began to relax in the Grail's benign light. Then, to my shock, everything was violent again.

I caught a movement, a dark shadow, like a jackal in the desert night. I turned to see Jack Karaquazian streaking across the pale tangled fields of the Grey Fees, his eyes hot with blood-hunger and his long lips drawn back from his sharp, predatory teeth.

I saw Jack leap at the throat of the exhausted Captain Billy-Bob Begg. It took nothing for that ferocious beast to drag her down. The fangs tore at her until the strange blood bubbled. Equally weary, Pearl Peru snarled and tugged and beat at the jackal but failed to save her lover, her buddy. Then we were all trying to help Pearl, risking those horrible teeth to wrestle Jack off his prey.

I heard Colinda shout something and saw Jack for a moment, his eyes burning with sardonic wisdom, leaping into the air, reaching for the balance. Then he had fallen back, panting, exhausted beside his victim.

Pearl kneeled beside her friend.

"Is she dead?" says Jack eagerly. There is something different in his eyes already.

"No, but she could be dying . . ." says Pearl, half-sure this is a fatigued dream.

"Then beg her to release Sam," says Jack. "Beg her to let him free, Pearl. It is his only chance. She has nothing to lose."

Pearl begins to demur but the revered Billy-Bob Begg, most famous of all the famous Chaos Engineers, lifts her beautiful, understanding hand. She knows what Jack has done. She knows why he has done it. She exchanges a thoughtful moment with him. "He is released," she says. It is the only way she could ever have let him go.

"And now stand back," says Jack. "Stand back. The Grail will revive her."

For this had been his special sacrifice. To have his friend restored.

∽

Against the vibrating brilliance of the Grail another shape defines itself. Faith and justice are personified. At first it seems again to be a sword, but then it grows more confident in its form, as if influenced by our will. And, as we watch, the Balance rights itself until each scale is true.

Jack lies gasping on the ground, wiping blood out of his mouth. Beside him Captain Billy-Bob stirs.

"Look," says Pearl, "her wounds have healed."

Around us all the antagonists, the immortals, the undying, the demigods and angels, all are under the spell of *Spammer's* light.

And where there was death and desolation, there is abundance and life. Old Reg and Mrs. Reg are permitted a glance of this paradise before they sink. Down into perpetual disorder. Only Horatio Quelch seems unreconciled to his doom. He bellows in Latin as he is dragged under, as if fate respects erudition. Amongst our own party despair has vanished and every face shows hope.

The tears come to me as I look around at my courageous companions and think of all the terrible risks they have taken. So many risks, so many clever games. All justified. All worthwhile. For they brought us to this magnificent reconciliation.

Jack, whom I condemned, took the greatest risk of all, releasing the blood-lust and the beast within him to do what he could not do otherwise and kill the great Chaos Engineer, staking his own psyche and his whole future on his play.

Jack knew he had to kill Captain Billy-Bob at the moment when the Grail manifested itself and became our universe. She would die, but she would be restored. In those seconds of death, Sam's soul would be free of hers. It was the only moment he could be released.

With all his enormous skills and intelligence, Jack had played our game and his own. Now Sam's soul flew free, seeking its mortal home.

I put out my hand to Jack but his tired eyes looked past me to Colinda. She, too, moved with difficulty, her entire being exhausted by what she and von Bek had done.

Something caught my attention on the horizon.

And then I saw him, limping towards me through the writhing ectoplasm, a look of pleading terror in his eyes, his soul restored.

"You're looking better, Sam," I said. "Your old self."

"I'm feeling it, Rosie," he says. "I heard you got married."

From out of *The Spammer Gain,* our wonderful Grail, there suddenly spread a great cloud of contentment as if the mother of us all looked upon us with approval and enjoyment. It was impossible to resist her. Before the benign power of the Grail, we, who called ourselves The Just, embraced. With heads bowed we acknowledged the might and meaning and the fundamental equity of the great Cosmic Balance. And we understood at last why we had fought and for what. We understood our own collective power and what it could achieve. Human beings had set their mark at last upon their own destinies. They could choose when and how they would die.

20

Character must ever be a mystery, only to be
explained in some degree by conduct; and that
is very dependent upon accident; and unless we
have a perpetual whipping of the tender part of
the reader's mind, interest in invisible persons
must needs flag. For it is an infant we address,
and the story-teller whose art excites an infant
to serious attention succeeds best . . .
                                    —*The Amazing Marriage*

Les Flammes d'Hiver

Naturally, Sam Oakenhurst had requested that his funeral be
held in New Orleans. Though he would never enjoy the
most glorious consequences of his time in office, the city had
redeemed herself through him. With Colinda Dovero he had chosen to put his experiences in the Second Ether behind him and
accept what he called "domestic linearity." "It's all I want,
Rose," he told me. "It's more than I ever hoped for."

The others met me in Las Cascadas. From there I flew my

DoX to New Orleans. As so often happens these days, we had last all met at a funeral. It had been after Lobkowitz's assassination. He had wished to be buried in the old churchyard of St-Maria-and-St-Maria in Mirenburg. As it happened, we had held the service only a few days after the "soft revolt" which he had helped negotiate, to get rid of the Communists at last. Colinda, of course, was already awaiting us in New Orleans. She had come to the aero-marina herself to meet the seaplane.

The city had lost none of her ancient charm and none of her seductive character, but where there had only been desolate slums and block housing, so loathsome its own inhabitants preferred to destroy it if they could, now there were parks and new asymmetrical apartment complexes. There were little green parks and squares and alleys full of every variety of private building. The municipal offices were well-designed and welcoming, small and settled into each parish, the focus of local political life.

As the first socialist mayor of the city, Sam Oakenhurst had been elected to serve a community at violent war with itself, eating itself from within. On the basis that civil life depends upon example at the top, he had wiped out corruption. Reforming the city's institutions from top to bottom he and his allies had created a political system in which every individual had power and a voice, as well as civic responsibilities, in which private enterprise and public service flourished in harmony.

After his third term, the city was at peace. After his fourth, the city flourished, becoming the best that her citizens had ever hoped for. As vital and varied as always, she had become the admired model for every other American city and was the envy of Europe. Her universally available public health service, her transport and education systems set the world standard. Sam's vision had been the common vision. But his ability and his skills had been uncommon. His gambler's instincts, his outlaw pride, had kept him on his course and helped to fire his fellow citizens with a similar energy.

❧

And now they were putting him to rest. In the streets and the cafes, on the screens and in the newspapers, on the trains and the riverboats, they told his story over and over again. How a boy from the slums had become a gambler and an outlaw, gradually turning to politics after he had been horribly disfigured by the gang which had betrayed him. How he had transformed the city from one of warring, self-destructive clans, divided by race and wealth, into a single, united, highly politicized community, working in its own self-interest to become what it had always dreamed of being, a city of few laws and fewer crimes. How New Orleans had become a city of rights and responsibilities, of education, wealth, work and opportunity for all, a city of the creative arts, of rich and ever-altering language, a free city of equals.

We were impressed even as we disembarked. All New Orleans was in mourning. Black crepe rippled everywhere in the warm Southern breeze. Black linen draped pictures of Sam in the black pierrot mask he wore until his dying day. Black velvet curled around the cable-posts and the streetcar stops, the church spires and towers, the doorways and the windows of the taverns, the entrances to enclaves and squares. Black silk poured over the terraces. Black, gold and silver flags flew at half-mast. And here and there, amidst so much respectful black, like a drop of fresh blood, bloomed a scarlet rose.

"Always Sam's favorite," says Colinda, taking my arm as she leads us through her gateway and into a leafy courtyard whose sculptured fountain is in the shape of a balance. She points out the rose-garden. "Every day a fresh bud in his lapel." All around the courtyard overhead runs a balcony of baroque black iron. There are doors at intervals. She shows us which are our rooms. One by one with expressions of admiration and thanks my companions disappear. She and I are left alone, watching the moving water, the tranquil carp below.

"And how is Jack?" asks Colinda. "You saw him in Paris?"

I could tell her nothing but the simple truth: "As far as I know," I said, "he is still waiting for you to come back to him."

She smiled. "Well," she said, "who knows?"

Though she had firmly refused its influence, Colinda had never lost her sense of regret. She had come to hate the Second Ether, for what she had witnessed there. At last she had seen a side to Jack she could not love. The couple had settled in Las Cascadas for a while, had tried England again, and even Biloxi, but there was nowhere that suited them both, nothing that brought the old times back. It was impossibly painful for them. Her passion for him, she said, was killing her. So Jack went to live in Paris. She went home to New Orleans, where Sam Oakenhurst was already at the beginning of his political career. Her own activities soon brought her close to Sam and eventually they had married. They had hardly been separated since that time and had worked in splendid unison for the city and the cause they loved.

"And your mother?" asked Colinda. On her breast she wore the oval ruby Sam had given her for their anniversary. Her eyes asked a thousand other questions. The funeral velvet against her dark skin embellished her enduring beauty. "Is she well?"

"She spends a great deal of time at the convent," I said. "Since she got into her second century I think she found religion. She still insists her longevity is due to plenty of sex and regular bowels. She occasionally appears on the screen. Usually as a kind of miracle. Once a week she and her cat walk to the river, across St Swithold's fields and the allotments. That's all restored now. It's the closest place she knows to heaven, she says. And if heaven's no better than that, she'll be happy to stay where she is."

And my father? She had always had a soft spot for my father.

My father, true to his own sturdy genes, fell back into his

familiar life. He continued to do everything he had always done, with few signs of his age. Occasionally his leg troubles him. Since he had returned to our valley he had begun raising and training horses again. Mrs. Gallibasta and her son helped him, as did the Gypsies who camped there much of the year. He had a new mare he was very fond of and she was foaling for the first time. He sent his respects but he hated any form of air-travel, was prone to sea-sickness and to his regret had not known the mayor well. I had not really expected my father to come to New Orleans. Although well-disposed towards Sam and helpful in arranging certain property matters for him in England at one time, my father knew from his correspondents that even Sam Oakenhurst's enlightened government had not brought the region any salmon fishing worthy of the name.

My Uncle Michael was on his way from Waterloo, Texas, where he had been joined by Colonel Cody, who had taken the night express from New York. They were traveling together on the new high-speed "Texas Bullet" and would be joining us at any moment.

Since we had all of us last been together my uncle had scarcely left Lost Pines. He said he had lost his interest in angels but revived his interest in angling. He also experimented with various kinds of engines, including internal combustion which, in common with the general opinion, he had soon abandoned as both inefficient and antisocial, an engineering dead end. He had then thrown himself enthusiastically into the Republic's electrified transport schemes. He was now a leading light of the Texas Tramways Commission. Colonel Cody saw him regularly, usually visiting for a week or two at a time so that they could fish the high streams of The Circle Squared Ranch, near the U.S. border.

Buffalo Bill had found contentment in Atlantic City. He had married the proprietress after buying an interest in a popular boardwalk shooting range and sandwich shop called Little Sureshot's Bagel Boutique. He had tired of public life and few knew

him by his real name. He called himself Jack Oakley. Similarly
Dick Turpin, after several years as a London cabby, had married
a woman called Mary Palmer, taken her surname and bought
The Six Jolly Dragoons, which he had retitled *The Old Dick
Turpin.* It was the best way he knew, he said, to keep his name
and reputation alive without actually having to rob trams any
more. He coaxes gold from the tourists as gracefully and wittily
as he once stole it from the tram passengers of Thornton Heath
and Hackney Wick.

Dick had come with us, he freely admitted, not out of any
sentiment for Sam Oakenhurst, since he had not really ever
known him, but because he had never seen New Orleans's famous streetcars and still retained an abiding professional interest in them. Since he had retired from the Game he was showing
his age, walking with an ebony and ivory cane. He still cut a
handsome figure, however, in his black frockcoat and breeches
with his white stockings and silver-buckled shoes, every inch the
respectable London citizen. On his breast he wore the garnet,
carnelian and platinum Star of St-Odhran, presented to him by
Prince Lobkowitz for certain services which had never been
made public.

∾

We gathered in the reception room with its battered black
timbers and its shining linen. The house had been built
by a Spanish merchant soon after the city was established and
in its French hey-day had been the headquarters of the notorious
swindler, confidence man and heroic Texan patriot, the Baronne
Hendrik Van Beek (aka Henri de Witte), in the years when the
city was still under French administration. Colinda, with her
usual light touch, told us a little of the place's history. Van Beek
had fought a famous duel in that very room. Afterwards he had
fled, with nothing but a horse, a fourteen year old slave and the
silver from his own table. As she told Horace and myself the

story, Dick Turpin joined us. Colinda asked him if he had ever
known Van Beek. He admitted that he had not. "But, madame,
I come from an age which gave the world more swindlers, thieves
and rascals than honest men and women! I could not know
every rogue in a town, any more than I could name every fish
in a river!"

Though he spent most of his time in London, occasionally
holidaying in Yorkshire with my father and other friends, Dick
retained the freshly scrubbed, hearty appearance of an old-fashioned country squire. He greeted everyone agreeably and told a
couple of jokes as if he were behind his own tavern's bar. The
familiarity alone cheered Horace up and set my husband to offering some complicated academic story involving a fairly good
knowledge of Latin and Greek and threatening to drain the entire
room of cheer. Turpin understood he had to take the brunt of
the attack and verbally tugged and danced away from all my
husband's obscurities as best he could, politely trying to man-
tain his good spirits under the deadly weight of my husband's
ponderous, sardonic humour. I did not attempt to save him. I
looked around for other company. Since his retirement, Horace
enjoys social life more than I and I had no wish to interfere in
his pleasure, so long as it did not interfere with mine.

At my eager invitation Prince Ulrich and Sir Sexton Begg
joined us. The old detective had become a little frail, but remained as affable as ever. He had not, he said, taken a case in
eighteen months. Modern mysteries, he felt, were so much less
complex than the prewar kind. Like wines, some ages were simply subtler than others.

His old adversary felt bound to agree with him. The albino
carried that same alien air I had noted years before. He was
distinguished, terrifyingly handsome, ageless, and still a little
sinister even with his dark contacts and his hair tinted grey
rather than white, though that pale, translucent skin was harder
to disguise. He and Sir Sexton had not met for many years and

seemed to have difficulty finding common ground that did not bore them both.

Eventually, after making some polite, English noises, the detective went over to talk to Turpin and Horace about fishing. I hoped we would soon eat. Funerals always gave me a ravenous appetite. Though amiable enough, Prince Ulrich seemed withdrawn. I had heard he had recently married his mistress of many years and was settled in Aswan. Whenever I tried to ask him about himself, he would politely turn the question and inquire how I was enjoying Las Cascadas these days or if I had visited Yorkshire recently.

Colinda had prepared a traditional meal, based on her mother's own recipe books, with every delicious Creole dish I had ever loved. I could barely sustain a polite conversation as I smelled the buffet being laid in the dining room.

At last Colinda led us in to where over the years she and Sam had entertained representatives of every civilized power on earth. Beneath the wooden rafters of the high roof, which had once sheltered an eighteenth century dance floor, we sat at table, Colinda, Prince Ulrich, Dick Turpin, my Uncle Michael, Colonel Cody, Sir Sexton Begg, my husband and myself and we recalled our best times together. On such sad, and increasingly numerous, occasions a bit of familiar company and a pleasant reminiscence or two is a great comfort to the survivors. We retold the shared stories. We relived our triumphs. We regained our emotions.

The following day's public service in Notre Dame cathedral was, of course, both moving and impressive, but it could never bring us as close as those old histories had brought us the night before. They could never make Sam live again.

∾

We followed the stately black double-decker funeral tram up Canal Street. Its black silks and flags rippled in the warm west wind. The sound of human voices rose and fell like a distant tide. Our well-disciplined horses pricked up their ears, but they were not hard for us to control and did not change their gait as we followed the tram into Rampart Street where it rumbled relentlessly towards the necropolis.

On both sides of Rampart the weeping, waving crowds, all in black out of respect for Sam, were twenty or thirty people deep. Some threw red rosebuds. They craned for a glimpse of the specially designed lower deck with its sombre coffin and brilliant flowers. They pointed out Colinda Dovero Oakenhurst, in black lace, her face lowered behind a veil, a vibrant ruby on her breast like a single tear. Above her, on the open top deck, was a jazz band, made up of all Sam's favorite musicians, playing their hearts out. As other bands took up the melodies, the entire city was filled with their music, with *Joli Blanc* and *Didn't He Ramble*, until it seemed a vast unearthly orchestra played the old tune, told the old story of lies and truth, of betrayals and sacrifices, of quests and oaths, of love and loss and resolutions that are not always tragic.

As the tram turned gracefully like a black galleon into the graveyard and rolled to a stately stop, I wondered if maybe Jack Karaquazian heard the music from his table at the *Cafe Terminale*, where six great canals meet in the daylight beside the Quai D'Hiver. I thought of him sitting at his game, his stoic back against the whirling patterns that are the bitter chaos of his memories, ceaselessly forming and reforming, ceaselessly telling and retelling his story.

The old story, which is echoed by our own.

∾

When I leave New Orleans and return to Europe, I shall go first to England and take the train to Hawes in Yorkshire. My horse will be waiting for me. I'll ride her up the old granite road the Celts made through terraces where once an ocean raced, until I come to the grey slate of *The Moorcock Inn*. There, under a widening sky, I will start my long ascent up the mossy flint of Thwaite Bridge Common, past Moorcock, secure in its tree-lined dell, over the ragged limestone pavements of Swifthorn Fell, with an angry wind tugging at my hair, until I reach the brow and pause to stare for a long second into our dale. I will see Tower House, her windows glowing against the evening dark. I will see our tarn, our busy dogs, our woods and our river. Further up the valley will be the Gypsy camp with its smoking red fires and its lazy twilight sounds, our horses grazing in the meadows. And, after I have drunk a deep draft of our good, familiar air, I will start my slow ride down into that invulnerable peace: the enchanted peace of home.

the end
of an autobiographical story by Michael Moorcock